FIREDRAKE

FIREDRAKE

ANN EWAN

THISTLEDOWN PRESS

Canadian Cataloguing in Publication Data

Bentley, Tom, 1947 –
Blind man's drum

ISBN 1-894345-41-X
I. Title.
PS8553.E579B54 2002   C813'.6   C2002-910324-X
PR9199.4.B46B54 2002

Cover and book design by Jackie Forrie
Typeset by Thistledown Press Ltd.
Printed and bound in Canada by AGMV Marquis

Thistledown Press Ltd.
633 Main Street
Saskatoon, Saskatchewan
S7H 0J8

Thistledown Press gratefully acknowledges the financial assistance of the Canada Council for the Arts, the Saskatchewan Arts Board, and the Government of Canada through the Book Publishing Industry Development Program for its publishing program.

I'd like to dedicate this book to the many who cared about it along the way. To Janice Dawson who was Briar, my best friend and first audience. To my younger brothers Peter and David Bradstreet, and especially my little sister Jill Harrigan, for whom I wrote the first adventures of Shan, Deakin, and Fletcher. To the writing club at Cemcorp for their encouragement: Tom O'Dell, Bradley Moseley-Williams, and Paul Sahota. To Tina Tsallas, my agent at Great Titles Inc., who believed in the book. And to R.P. MacIntyre, my editor, who believed in Shan and helped me add the final touches to her shadowy world.

Chapter 1

"Stone two three four target, stone two three four target . . . "

The chant was fast and it never varied. On "stone" Shan picked up a stone from the pile at her feet, on "two" she threw it on down the line with one hand and caught the stone thrown to her with the other, on "three" and "four" she repeated these actions, and on "target" she threw the stone in her hand in the general direction of her wooden target. It was supposed to hit the target, but it rarely did. The target, like everything else that was more than an arm's length away, was only a blur to Shan.

Shan hated the stone game with the accumulated hatred of years of playing it, years of misery and humiliation. She had improved tremendously in that time from the seven-year-old who could neither catch nor throw, who missed every catch and cried solidly through every game until her face seemed permanently streaked with tears and red mud. The tears had dried up long since. She never cried now. She played with fierce concentration, eyes screwed tight, teeth clenched, determined not to let down the Cubs on either side of her. She wasted no effort on trying to hit the target. Angry Cubs could get even; targets could not. At one time she had been thrilled to hear the thud that meant one of her stones had hit the target, but now she no longer cared. The game was simply an ordeal to be survived for another day.

It was early spring. The sky was overcast and there was a thin drizzle of rain. Nevertheless, from the slopes of one of the red hills a few adult Wolves were watching. Sometimes one of them would comment audibly on a particularly talented Cub, usually one whose target clanged as the stone flew through the centre, something that had never once happened to Shan. They never said anything about Shan, never commented on a bad throw or a missed catch, for which Shan was silently and deeply grateful to them. All the Cubs were afraid of the Wolves. In their black uniforms they were a threatening shadow of what lay ahead. The Cubs were silent and unemotional but theirs was a trained silence, an enforced silence, and they had their secret hand signals and their moments of unhidden feeling. The adults' silence went deeper. In the ceremony that made them Wolves, so the stories said, their emotions had been stripped away from them. Don't they feel anything? Shan wondered. Will I stop feeling, someday?

Watching the adults, she had lost her concentration, and now one bare foot slipped suddenly in the mud. Shan tried to recover her balance, and the stone she should have caught slipped through her fingers.

"Stone two three four target . . . "

The chant went on, inexorable. The Cub beside Shan threw the next stone to her as she bent to retrieve the one she had dropped. It hit her on the upper arm, hard. She flicked a glance at the Cub and saw him move his head, a quick gesture to show he was silently laughing at her. Angrily, she threw a stone just as the chant reached "target", so that it fell close to the next Cub, who hissed something soft and angry. Then she was back into the demanding rhythm of the game again. Catch-throw. Catch-throw. With great relief, she felt her fingers close on her last stone.

The game was over. The chant died out and Shan could hear the gentle hiss of the rain again. She rubbed her arm, still stinging where the stone had caught it.

"Target practice!" one of the masters shouted.

Shan hated target practice almost as much as the stone game. She sighed as she retrieved her bow from the ground and took the bowstring from inside her tunic. It was damp; the rain was already seeping through her clothes. By tonight everything she was wearing would be soaked.

෪

To the north, on Cardy Plain, there was no rain falling. There had been neither rain nor sunshine on Cardy Plain in a hundred long, grey years. The sky had remained static, fixed in one ugly moment of lowering grey cloud. There was a yellow glare behind it that made the eyes of trav-ellers sore and their tempers short. The Plain had gradually come to resemble the sky above, as the water dried up and the lush grass withered and died until the earth itself was only grey and yellow.

Only Arkanan lived year round on the Plain and in the Maze. They were both the creators and the victims of the sullen sky, and their tempers were always short. They were made worse when the warnings began to come.

"The ashes show every time the same warning!" Varian the seer, the reader of omens, sat in the dust at the entrance to the Maze. "I see in them no other pattern."

She had been staring into the little fire for hours, unmoving, though the last twig had long since fallen into ash. Now she looked up from under the hood of her robe, and realized to her dismay that it was Hinton, not Kron, who had emerged from the Maze.

"Thou seest everywhere warnings," said Hinton. He paced back and forth, scuffing dust onto the dead fire and the pile of tamarack branches. "Thou hast the fears of a child."

"And thou hast the mind of a child." Varian stretched her back and slowly stood up, ready to go back into the Maze. She was not going to stay out here alone with Hinton. "I have made with the ashes a true magic. What magic of late hast thou made, Hinton?"

"I created the Firedrake —" Hinton began, indignantly.

Varian sneered. "Thou? Thou wast one among a great many, a hundred years and more ago! Tarn and Kron gave to the Firedrake life. Thou hast made in many years no magic, and if thou canst make indeed great magic, as is thy boast, then the time is now, for the ashes give repeated warning. The Firedrake is threatened, and with that threat we all — "

"Thou dried-up old woman! How darest thou speak against the Firedrake?" Hinton's anger exploded into magic as usual, though he knew better than to aim it at Varian directly. The pile of tamarack branches erupted into a shower of maggots that fell squirming and wriggling into the dust.

Before Varian had time to respond, Kron came quietly out of the Maze. Like the other two, he wore a hooded black robe and his face was hidden.

"How say this time the ashes, Varian?" he asked.

The maggots disappeared, and Varian shot a scornful look at Hinton as she replied. "The same thing, Kron, always the same. The Firedrake destroyed by our three enemies, a blind woman, a madman, and a wizard."

Hinton gave a harsh, angry laugh. "A blind woman? A madman? How can these be to the Firedrake any threat?"

"The ashes speak not always plainly," said Kron, "but they give this time a clear warning."

"The Firedrake destroyed? Dost thou believe truly this nonsense?"

"I have learned in my long years to be cautious. We must heed what the ashes reveal. The lives of the people are short and their memories are likewise short. Perhaps it has been since the Rebellion too many years. Perhaps it is time to give to them another reminder of our power."

"I could go to Redmetal Town." Hinton now sounded interested, even eager. He came a step closer. "I could choose as an example a Perin family and show the others."

"Perinan?" Kron growled. He pushed back his hood, and his eyes, the only living things in his terrible dead face, blazed out at Hinton. "Dost thou think that I fear Perinan, thou fool? Dost thou think the common people to me, to us, are any threat? If there is any danger it will come from the Kunan Keir."

Hinton flushed. "The Kunan Keir are loyal."

"Of course they are loyal! What choice do they have? But perhaps they grow restless. We must ensure their strength is not turned again against us. Perhaps the Kunan Keir are becoming a danger."

Kron thought for a moment. The other two waited. Kron had been proved right in his decisions many times before.

"Go to Redmetal Town," he said at last to Hinton. "But to the school. Choose one of the masters as an example."

"I shall leave at once." Hinton strode into the darkness of the Maze.

"Hinton!" Kron called after him.

"Yes?"

"Choose the swordmaster. And, Hinton . . ."

"Yes?"

"Give him time to strike at thee."

Hinton's teeth gleamed from under his hood as he turned and grinned.

"But if there is truly a blind woman," said Varian, when he had gone, "she must be Perin."

"Perinan are to us no threat," said Kron, impatiently.

"Perhaps not. But there could not be among the Kunan Keir a blind woman."

"No," Kron agreed, with a cruel smile. "There could not be a blind Wolf."

❧

Practice was suddenly interrupted as one of the masters approached and held up his arms.

"Cubs! The Arkan Hinton wishes to speak. We will assemble in Hall."

This was an unexpected and wonderful reprieve for Shan. She would willingly listen to the Arkan, or anyone else, speak all day if it saved her from any more practising. She joined the others as they walked back toward the school. Most of them walked in twos or threes or little groups, talking, sometimes aloud but more often with hand signals. A few, like Shan, walked alone. Except for the wide variation in age and height they were all alike, lean and muscular, barefoot, dressed in plain brown uniforms with knives at their right hips.

As they approached the school Shan found some Cubs of her own age to go in with, knowing that if she did not find them now she would be lost inside the hall. She followed them in and was disappointed to see that her year was being seated near the back. She sat down cross-legged and stared at the stage. At least the roof did not leak directly over her head, as it had in Hall that morning. If she screwed her eyes up tight, she could make out some movement on the stage and guess at where the Arkan must be standing, but she had no chance, at this distance, of seeing what he looked like. She had never seen an

Arkan up close. Someday, in the Maze, she knew, she would meet them face to face, but she would have liked at least a little glimpse first.

Talking was not allowed in Hall, but plenty of covert communication was still going on. All the masters were seated at the front and there was little risk that they would notice. The girl beside Shan flashed a hand signal to a boy further down the row, and Shan could not resist looking. Meet me, her hands said. Shan could not see the boy's reply, but it must have been, Where? for the girl's next message was, Pool. There was no need for the boy to ask when. Cubs of Shan's year had only one free hour a day. Shan imagined what would happen if she were to flash a message like that to a boy, any boy. Enough to make even a Cub laugh.

"Greetings, Kunan Keir," the Arkan began.

He was flattering the Cubs by speaking as if they were adults, for "Kunan Keir" means, literally, "Dogs of the Pack", and is the Arkan term for Wolf.

"I shall see again later this year some of ye, those who come to the Maze. Others have many years to wait. I am sure ye will be a credit to your packs and to us, the Arkanan, the wizards who care for ye and for this beautiful land of Redmetal . . . "

His voice was cracked and old, but the ancient, formal Arkan tongue gave it dignity and power. Shan was only half-listening as he continued. She was playing a game she sometimes played, watching the Arkan with her wide unfocused eyes to see what he looked like to her. It pleased her that no one else could play the game. The others saw the Arkan as he was. Shan, with her bad eyesight, had no hope of doing that, but she could make him appear as many different things. If she looked at him one way, she could see him as a rat with an enormous head. That dark blur could even be the tail. He was quite amusing as a rat. If she looked at him another way, she could see him as a gigantic grasshopper with blurry black wings. She was so caught up in her game that she almost missed the point of the speech.

Suddenly there was a sharp tension in the air, though the Cubs remained motionless and silent.

"Yes, there is among ye a traitor," the Arkan said, dramatically. "One of your masters, one of your beloved teachers, has turned against us. Ye trusted him to teach ye the best way to serve your homeland. We, the Arkanan, trusted him also.

He has betrayed this trust. We have discovered that he has helped the Perin rebels. He would bring down the Arkanan and have Perinan rule in their place! And I have come here today because we have discovered by our magic this traitor. I have come to expose him. He will be punished!"

There was triumph in his voice, and a thick excitement. He was almost chortling with it. Shan felt repelled by his unconcealed emotion.

"Thou!" he shouted. "Come forward, Wolf!"

Someone stood up from the floor near the front and spoke. Shan recognized his voice at once and knew that it was Ern, the swordmaster. She found it difficult to believe that Ern, so stern and unforgiving, could be a traitor.

"I have not betrayed Arkanan," he said, in the Arkan language, in his flat Wolf voice. "I do not help Perinan. I fought in the Rebellion."

"Thy past is known to us," said the Arkan, "but on whose side didst thou fight, traitor?"

"My pack fought the rebels."

"Yes, and died! All but one. Thou alone of thy pack survived the Rebellion. Thine Alpha survived the Battle of Cardy Plain, but died ten days after. Only thou wast with him." The Arkan's voice rose higher. "Thou killed him!

Thou betrayed thy pack and murdered thine Alpha . . . "

Ern moved, as quickly as only a Wolf can move. Shan could see little of what was happening but she heard his sword leave its scabbard and suddenly the stage was full of motion. The other masters were on their feet, drawing their own swords. It would already have been too late for the Arkan except that, as the Cubs had been taught, Arkanan could not be harmed by any weapon. Shan heard later, from the talk of the other Cubs, that Ern's sword passed right through the hooded figure and left no mark.

"Kill him!" shouted the Arkan.

Someone did. Ern died quietly and Shan, who had suffered much in his lessons and had never liked him, found herself feeling sorry.

"The traitor has been executed," said the Arkan. He was panting a little with excitement. "Cubs, I give to ye as holiday the remainder of this day. Ye may take it in celebration of the death of a traitor."

The stage was suddenly empty, the Arkan gone. Shan almost gasped with surprise, but her training held her silent. Only the very youngest Cubs made a sound.

Even the mystical disappearance of the Arkan was less exciting than the holiday he had given the Cubs. They trickled out of the hall, talking breathlessly, discussing Ern and the Arkan and trying to decide what they would do with the rest of the day.

Shan was the only one who knew immediately what to do with a holiday. She had a secret place of her own to visit. She steeled herself for the familiar ordeal of walking past the other Cubs, who were gathering in front of the school.

"Hey, Squinty!"

"Hey, Ugly!"

Relieved of school discipline, they reverted to their native language, the lilting, questioning Perin tongue, though they spoke it with little emotion and much of the rhythm of it was lost in their flat voices.

"What's your hurry, Ugly?" someone asked her.

"Where are you off to then?"

"Going to meet your boy, are you?"

Shan kept walking, eyes down, face in its usual trained stillness.

"See me, Ugly, can you?"

"See me?"

Three boys of her own year, boys she knew and hated, blocked her way, moving when she moved. Shan did not speak to them. She had never spoken to them. She tried to move past them, futilely, and at last she gave up and stood still, hating in silence.

"See this?"

One of them shoved her, hard. Another stuck out his foot and Shan tumbled into the wet red mud. At times like this she never fought. It would have been futile, despite her training. She knew that the boys had been trained, too, and there were more of them, and besides, their eyes worked properly. She went down without a struggle, and afterward she got up and kept walking as if nothing had happened.

The boys were pleased with themselves. They did not laugh, of course, but Shan was aware of their gestures. When she was out of sight of the boys, under the protecting branches of the first trees in the wood, she wiped her muddy hands on her muddy uniform and began to run.

Running was the one thing Shan was good at. She could outrun most of the girls in the school, and when she ran she felt stronger and more capable than she did at any other time. She loved the way her leg muscles obeyed her smoothly and her bare feet landed solidly and surely on the uneven ground. Running, she felt cleansed. It

FIREDRAKE

was a substitute for the tears she no longer shed.
She knew all the paths through the wood, and
every hiding place, and as she ran she felt as if
she were a real wolf cub, as if she had traded her
ugly and useless girl-body gladly for a lithe, grey,
sure-footed one.

The wood was wet and full of springtime. Even
in the deep places the snow had gone at last, and
Shan saw sudden patches of green-brown,
spotted leaves where soon the dog's-tooth violets
would bloom. Cedar trees dumped water down
her neck as she ducked under their branches, and
the little creek had grown so fat that she had to
take a running jump to get across it. She touched
her familiar landmark trees as she ran past each
of them. She came to the wall that marked the
limits of the school grounds and climbed it with
the ease of long practice, sitting on the top for a
dangerous moment to look back the way she had
come, though all she could see was a dark green
blur of cedars, and then scrambling down into
the same wood on the other side.

Leaving school grounds was against the rules,
and in fact the penalty for breaking that partic-
ular rule was supposed to be death, but Shan had
been doing it almost every day for more than a
month. She did not really believe any of the

masters would kill her if they caught her, and she felt she had no choice but to take the risk. She had searched the school grounds for years for a place to call her own, but every one that she found had sooner or later been discovered by the other Cubs. At last she had dared to climb the wall and find a private and secret place. She returned to it now with a feeling of coming home.

As she entered the tunnel she had made through the bushes and raspberry canes, she felt the branches touching her arms, moving as if they had just been disturbed. Ahead she heard a quick scuffling sound.

Shan was shocked and hurt, and then, uncharacteristically, she was angry, thinking immediately of the other Cubs, of their loud voices and trampling feet polluting her own secret and special hollow tree. But everything had been quiet after that first betraying scurry. Perhaps after all it was only a beast of some kind. If it was, she decided she would kill it. She was not going to let anything lair in her secret place. She drew her knife, breaking another school rule, and crawled carefully into the tunnel.

Chapter 2

As Shan reached the tree's hollow centre, there was a sudden flutter of sound, and a girl's voice cried,

"Don't hurt me! Please!"

The stranger was huddled as far away from Shan as she could get in the small space, crouched against the damp inner trunk of the tree. She looked about the same age as Shan, though she was a little taller. Her terrified eyes were fixed on the knife, which was made of rufer and had a dull red gleam. Shan kept it pointed at her, as she realized slowly that this girl was afraid of her. Afraid! She felt a surge of delight.

"Why shouldn't I then?" she asked, prolonging the wonderful moment. In her flat Wolf voice it did not sound like a question. "In my secret place, aren't you?" She was almost holding her breath, expecting the girl to break into a derisive smile any minute. Surely she must see that Shan was the lowest of the low, no more to be feared than a beetle under a rock.

Incredibly, the girl did not seem to realize this, and, in a voice that shook a little, she said,

"But didn't know. Please, please, believe me. Didn't know. How could I? Please. Go away, shall I? Go away right now and never come back?"

"No," said Shan.

She had never felt such power.

"Who are you?" she demanded. "Where have you come from?"

"From . . . from the farm. Where I live. Didn't mean any harm. Please, please, let me go."

Shan squatted down, still holding the knife.

"What do they call you then?"

"Briar."

"What are you doing here?"

"Hiding. I . . . I heard you coming . . . I was frightened."

"Frightened," repeated Shan, and made a gesture of contempt which only another Cub could have understood. "Should be ashamed to admit it. Sit!"

Briar sat down facing Shan, her eyes still warily on the knife.

"May I . . . may I go?" she whispered.

"When I say." Shan could not remember when she had enjoyed herself so much.

"Please."

"What will you give me then?"

Briar spread her hands.

"Haven't anything, have I?" she said, help-lessly. "But could . . . could tell you a story, maybe. About . . . about . . . "

"What then?"

"About this tree. The ara tree."

"All right," said Shan. She liked to learn things and once, long ago, she had liked to listen to stories. No one told her stories now.

"Let me go, afterward, will you?"

"Perhaps."

Briar took a deep breath and began, speaking quickly as if the beginning were a formula she had often repeated. "Long ago, then, when our land was green, when Arkanan were good wizards and we were all Perinan together — "

"What do you mean?" Shan broke in. All she had been taught cried out against the phrases, but still she would not have stopped the flow of the story except that they were familiar phrases, phrases that she had heard before, had spoken even, before she had come to the school. They were words she had loved and had forgotten.

26

"Arkanan are good wizards now! What else are they? And how do you mean 'we were all Perinan together'?"

"Never said it was true, did I? A story, is all. But know we were all Perinan once, you and I and even Arkanan. A story of those days, this is."

"We never were."

"Want to hear the story, don't you?"

Shan's hand tightened on the knife and Briar, seeing the gesture, gave a little cry of terror and scrambled into a crouch again.

"Don't hurt me! Please! Tell you another story, shall I, a better story . . . ?"

Without warning she began to cry. Shan watched silently, embarrassed for this gangly girl who still cried like a baby. Gradually she began to feel almost protective, the way she sometimes felt toward the little seven-year-old Cubs.

"Won't hurt you." She gave in abruptly. "Was never going to hurt you. Believe me, don't you? Sit and don't cry."

"You were, though . . . you were," Briar sobbed. "When you came in . . . with the knife . . . thought you were . . . "

"Thought you were beast then, didn't I? Lairing in my secret place. Didn't know, did I? Wouldn't hurt you."

"Promise?"

"Promise. Look, put the knife away, haven't I? Promise I won't hurt you."

Briar sat down again. She sniffed and wiped her eyes.

"Why did you have to come here? Was my secret place, this. Come here every afternoon."

"Come here every evening," said Shan, and they looked at each other in silence.

"Break the rules to come here," said Shan. "Climb the wall. Kill me if they caught me, they would."

"Climbed the wall once, too," said Briar, unexpectedly. "My brother dared me. Said Cubs would tear me to pieces if they saw me."

"So we would, if we caught you on the grounds," said Shan, and then, remembering the way Briar's face had crumpled when she started to cry, added quickly, "But won't hurt you now. Promised I wouldn't, didn't I? Was only pretending, before. Playing a game."

"A game!" Briar had been so frightened that anger came easily. "Always a game with Wolves, isn't it? Always do anything they like."

Shan was amazed at this view of her life.

"Wolves, maybe. Not Wolf yet, though, am I? Only Cub. Can't do whatever I like."

"Can, though. Could cut me to pieces and go back over the wall, couldn't you? Who'd know? Who'd care?"

Shan tried to speak, to protest that she had never cut anyone to pieces and never would, but Briar swept on. Her eyes were full of tears again, to Shan's dismay.

"My family would find me and know a Wolf had done it, wouldn't they? Who else kills but Wolves? So wouldn't be able to do anything about it, would they? Always like that, isn't it? Seen it before, haven't I? Wolves doing anything they like. And what they like best is fighting, everyone knows that. And killing. I hate Wolves! Hate them . . . "

Blind with tears, she made a sudden dash for escape which Shan easily blocked.

"Won't hurt you," said Shan again.

Briar went on crying with Shan's arms around her, her sobs shaking them both.

"Hate you!" she cried, choking and sniffing. "Hate all Cubs, all Wolves! Would kill you all if I could!"

"Hate Cubs, too," said Shan. She felt the hate rise in her when she thought of the other Cubs, but it did not touch her voice, which came out clear and cold. "Would kill them, too, if I could. Would kill all Cubs."

Briar twisted away and looked at her, amazed. "Do it, then!"

"Can't," said Shan. "Couldn't hurt you and can't kill Cubs. Trying to make me Wolf, they are, but don't think it's working. Don't think I'll ever be Wolf."

ఞఴ

The gemstones flashed and sparkled in a sudden shaft of sunlight, but the man who held them was past caring about their beauty. His breath came raggedly and his hands trembled as he took the stones from his knapsack. The two men with him were in the same state of exhaustion. They had reached the top of the bank, where the land fell away steeply to the Cardith River below, and there they had at last stopped running and just stood, hands dangling, heads down, gazing wearily at the river.

They wore the plain black uniforms and rufer swords of the Kunan Keir. The man with the gemstones had a sheathed knife on his belt to show that he was an Alpha Wolf, a leader. Of the two men with him, one was tall and dark, the other light-haired with a kind of fire about him,

30

a restless energy that would only be quenched when he slept. There was something tattooed on the back of his left hand, like a snake's head or a lizard's, that seemed to live when his hand moved.

"Never thought . . . we'd make it," he said, panting.

Neither of the other two spoke, but the tall man sat down on the grass as if his legs had at last given way.

"Before sunset," said the light-haired man, and again, with relief, "Never thought we'd make it," and he also sat down on the grass.

Only the Alpha remained on his feet, holding the stones and staring wearily across to the opposite bank of the river.

"Be here any minute, they will," he said. "Know we've come."

The Cardith River marked the boundary between sun and no-sun, between Cardy Plain and the rest of the land. It poured in a noisy torrent down the ravine, tumbled whitely over rocks and smashed into deep churning pools. Grass and red dogwood bushes and pussy willow, already breaking into bud, grew along the edge of it on the side where the Wolves were standing, but on the other side the bank was dead, all stone and gravel. Over there, the sky was permanently grey and nothing grew beneath it. No one lingered on the banks of the Cardith River without purpose, or without fear.

"Shouldn't have come on, should we?" said the light-haired man, softly, to the other man who sat with him in the wet grass. They stared across at Cardy Plain, the deadness of it and the menace. "Should have stayed behind with the rest of the pack."

"Be quiet, Deakin," said the Alpha. "Never know when they'll come."

Even as he spoke, an Arkan — Hinton it was, though the Wolves could not tell one Arkan from another — materialized suddenly on the opposite bank. To the silent Wolf, who was looking directly at the place, it was a strange transition. There was a little flicker of the air, like the shimmer above the grass on hot summer days, and then the air seemed to fold in on itself, to crease, and the Arkan walked out of the crease, black-caped and hooded and solid, or at least as solid as anything could be that was so frail and ancient. The two men on the ground jumped to their feet respectfully.

The Arkan did not speak, but only held out one demanding hand, wrinkled and yellow, in the direction of the Wolves. The Alpha Wolf knew what was expected of him. He held out the shining stones on his palm so that the Arkan could see them, three deep red rubies, two diamonds, a sapphire with a star at its heart. The Arkan's hand made a clawing gesture, beckoning, and in answer the stones began to stir and twitch in the Wolf's hand until they leapt into the air to answer the summons.

But Hinton's magic fell short. A dazzling beam blazed out from the setting sun, turning all the land on the Wolves' side of the river golden under heavy blue-black rain clouds, and it caught the stones in their flight. For a moment they danced and glittered in the beam. Then they plummetted downward and vanished into the river.

The Wolves were seized with terror. They were sure that they would have to pay with their lives for the Arkan's mistake. Their faces did not change, but the Alpha's fingers twitched slightly and the light-haired man clenched one of his fists. Hinton, less restrained, cursed viciously, and in his fury a small brown snake materialized at his feet, hissing and striking at the rocks. His failure had made him furious; that it had been witnessed, doubly so; and he had been made most furious of all by the impassive, incurious faces of the watching Wolves. He cursed them loudly.

"Get those stones!" he growled at them.

"I'll go," said the Alpha, quickly, to his two men.

He unbuckled his swordbelt and dropped it in the grass, and began to half-climb, half-scramble down the steep bank. Hinton raged impatiently above him. At the edge of the torrent the Alpha took off his boots and then paused for a moment, looking upward. To his men he looked small and already far away. There was no word of command from Hinton, but a great taloned bird flew upward from his shoulder and then down into the ravine, shrieking, its wings in tatters. The Alpha ducked as it came straight for his head. Then he plunged into the river.

The current caught him at once and he was helpless, tumbled over and carried headlong. He managed to dive where the stones had gone down, but surfaced empty-handed, some way downstream. He fought the current, trying to reach the bank again. Already he was almost out of sight of his men. He struck his head on a rock and a red stain followed him down the river. The two other

Wolves, certain of their own destruction, waited tensely for the Arkan's word.

But Hinton's anger had abated. The snake coiled itself up and disappeared. Hinton stared down into the river, murmuring something, and after a few seconds the stones flew up to him, sparkling, shedding water in bright droplets. He closed his fist on them. Without looking again at the Wolves, he took a step forward and vanished.

"Murderer!" shouted the light-haired man. He made a sudden movement as if he would jump the river, though it was clearly impossible. "Come back here! Come back and face us! Murderer!"

"Quiet, Deakin," said the other man, urgently. "Hear you, he will."

"Want him to hear me, don't I?" The first man turned on him suddenly. "And why didn't you do anything? Have magic, don't you? Why didn't you prevent it?"

"Don't know how to fight Arkanan, do I? Think I wouldn't have prevented it if I could?"

The light-haired man made a Wolf gesture of disgust and started away down the slope. The other man picked up the discarded swordbelt and knapsack and followed him. There was no emotion to be read in either of their faces.

০৩৪০

In the morning it was cold, a damp, seeping, clinging cold. Shan awoke naked and shivering, crowded together with the other girls under the thin blankets. She jumped up quickly, cold bare feet hitting the cold bare floor, and launched into the readiness drill with which all Cubs began their day.

The drill was a series of exercises, some for strength, some for flexibility, and some for balance. It was also a careful check of the whole body, so that each day Shan knew the location of every bruise, the state of healing of every cut, and exactly how tired she was, how stiff, how hungry; so that she knew, both consciously and on a deeper level, what she could expect from herself that day. Gradually, as she exercised, her shivering stopped, and the small hairs lay down again on the back of her neck.

It was quiet in the girls' barracks, though most of the girls were awake. Talking was not allowed. There were only the slight sounds of movement and breath, and from outside the steady, depressing drumming of rain on the wooden roof. As each girl finished her readiness drill, she dressed and left for Hall.

Shan dressed quickly in her brown shirt and trousers, and pulled her belt around her waist. Her knife was gone. She groped for it in the half-dark under the bed but it was nowhere near her clothes and she knew that someone had taken it again. She began a patient and methodical search of the beds. Gone were the days when she would rush frantically, with growing panic, from place to place, searching and finding nothing. She knew that the knife would be out in plain view, because the other Cubs enjoyed the joke more if they could see it the whole time. This morning it was lying on Holly's pillow, and Shan saw Holly make a gesture of pretend surprise for the benefit of the other girls. How did that get there?

This small humiliation did not bother Shan as much as it usually did, for halfway through her readiness drill she had remembered Briar. No matter what these Cubs thought of her, Briar had thought she was someone to be respected and even feared. And Briar had promised to meet her again that evening. Even if Briar broke that promise, even if she and Shan never met again, Shan had been given a source of powerful daydreams that would last for months. She hardly noticed the rain as she walked the short distance from barracks to Hall.

Talking was not permitted in Hall, either, but until the masters arrived there were numerous silent conversations. The day always began the same way, with the Cubs standing at respectful attention as the masters entered. For the younger Cubs the respect was real, the children still awed by the black uniforms and rufer swords, but the older children held the masters in barely-hidden contempt. After all, they were only teachers and not real warriors. Shan's year was just beginning to realize that.

The Cubs repeated their chant, which began:

"I am Wolf-born, I am young, I am healthy, I am strong . . . "

As usual Shan mouthed the words but did not say them, some innate sense of honesty preventing her. It would have been too much of a lie to have chanted lines like "I am handsome, I am ready," when she so clearly was not, neither handsome nor ready, when she squinted and was ugly and was hopeless at all the games. Being part of the daily chant, even a silent part, made her feel more of an outsider than ever, as if she had somehow stumbled into the wrong life.

The chant was in Arkan, the only language the Cubs were allowed to speak in the masters' presence. They were all fluent in it by the end of their first year of school, but still they all spoke Perin by choice. It was the one thing that was never trained out of them, though the masters told them that it was an inferior tongue and that they, the future Kunan Keir, were fortunate to be able to speak the high, magical language, the language that spells were cast in. They were not taught to cast spells, however, since only wizards could do that, and they found the Arkan language too formal for everyday speech.

After the chant was over and the day's punishments had been given out, the youngest children remained in Hall for morning classes. They had to learn geography and arithmetic, for Kunan Keir were not only warriors but tax-collectors and traders as well. Wolves were the only citizens of the land who were allowed to leave it, so it was Wolves who guarded the borders and only Wolves who crossed them, to trade with Aram to the south or Iluthia to the east.

Shan's year had finished with indoor classes, and this morning they were taken to the pool behind the barracks. Shan was better at swimming than she was at most things, so she was pleased, and she was even more pleased when she realized that they had been brought there not to swim but to repair the dam. For once the Cubs would not be in competition with each other.

The pool had already been swollen with melting snow, and now the rain was filling it further. The creek flowing into it was a tumbling, frothy torrent, reddish-brown with the mud it had collected on its way down, and below the pool the dam was leaking, threatening to fall away altogether and let the creek flow freely. The Cubs worked hard all morning, and by noon the rain had stopped and the dam was solid, a dam that would surely last all summer. Shan enjoyed the morning. As they worked side-by-side in the rain, she felt a rare comradeship with the other Cubs, and when the dam was finished she had an equally rare feeling of accomplishment.

At noon the Cubs were permitted to break their fast, returning to Hall for a meal, which, today, was rye bread and sausages. At this time of year there was no fresh food to be had, even for Wolves, and the supply of winter vegetables was almost exhausted. The Cubs ate as hungrily as if they were real four-footed wolves, and no one got quite enough. For Shan the meal at midday was never as good as the evening one, for it always seemed a little tainted by what was to follow.

The afternoons were spent outside, no matter what the weather, with organized games and practices for all the Cubs. To Shan it seemed that the others were all born fighters, perfect with their fists and knives and blunt practice swords, while she stumbled along, battered, in their wake, always last, always bleeding, always tripping and missing and falling short.

At the beginning of every afternoon they chose teams or partners. No one wanted to be stuck with Shan. She would stand with one or two other unlucky Cubs, quiet and still, doing her best to fade into the landscape, until someone was forced to take her. If she tried to pair up with another unwanted Cub, the master would separate them. "No, Bar, you go with Shan. Help her." The Cub thus chosen would not help Shan. The two of them would set their teeth and endure each other. Shan would not have asked for help from another Cub if she had been dying.

The humiliations in the afternoons were small but constant, some of them caused by her bad eyesight and inability to judge distances, some of them by the other Cubs. Things she dropped were moved, kicked away as if by accident. Stones missed their targets and hit her instead. She bore the bruises with her usual trained patience, but today, while she was thinking of Briar, they seemed to hurt less.

The last practice ended, and Shan's sword was the last to drop on the pile. She flexed her tired arm and trailed the others back to Hall for the evening meal. The Cubs were all soaked through and shivering, and the warm food was so wonderful that Shan wanted to make it last, but instead she bolted it down and ran out into the rain again. She had to know if Briar had kept her promise. She ran all the way to the hollow tree, splashing through the puddles as noisily as she dared and sometimes slipping a little in the mud.

She slowed down as she reached her secret place. If Briar had not come, she did not want to know too soon. She crawled almost reluctantly into the tunnel and kept her head down, not wanting to look up until she was inside the tree.

"Hello," Briar said, timidly, and Shan felt a rush of joy. She almost wanted to laugh. But her voice, when she spoke, was as flat as ever.

"You came," she said.

Chapter 3

S han felt awkward with Briar, almost shy.
"Why did you come back?" she demanded.
"Thought you hated Cubs."

"Never met one before, have I?" Briar was still
as far away from Shan as she could get within the
hollow. "Didn't know they were like you."

"Aren't like me," said Shan.

She urged Briar to tell the story she had begun
the day before, and Briar eventually agreed,
though she eyed Shan warily as she spoke.

"Long ago, then, when the land was green,
when Arkanan were good wizards and we were
all Perinan together . . . "

"Go on," said Shan, when Briar hesitated, and
Briar went on, falling naturally into the formal
language of storytelling.

" . . . there lived a man and a woman who had
no children. And one day when the woman was
cutting firewood she came upon a little brown

baby, lying on a bed of fern among the cedar roots and playing with his toes. At first she thought he was a human baby; then, as she came closer, she thought he was a baby animal; and then she realized that he was neither human nor beast. For he looked human most of the time, but sometimes she would catch a glimpse out of the corner of her eye and know that he was covered with fur, that his teeth were sharp-pointed and his ears were pointed and his face was fierce and wild."

"A Dancer," Shan breathed. She had seen a Dancer once, in early childhood, and had never forgotten a single detail of that moment.

"Yes. But the woman wanted a child very badly, and so she stole the Dancer baby. She named him Cedar. At first her husband was angry, but he saw how happy she was and he gave in. The baby could crawl a little and he soon learned to talk, in human speech which the woman taught him. He would not eat anything but meat, and that he preferred raw."

Briar made a face, which startled Shan.

"After years had passed, the woman found that she was going to have a baby of her own. She gave birth to a girl, and named her Tansy.

"Now human children grow much faster than Dancer children, so that Tansy had learned to walk while Cedar was still crawling, but they were like brother and sister and loved each other dearly. And when Tansy was nine years old, Cedar was beginning to learn to walk, and when she was twelve he could run. He loved to be in the woods, and soon he would not come home at all, but would sleep in the woods all night. Tansy had a secret place that she had shown him, a hollow ara tree like this one, and that was where he slept.

"But each time that the Night of the Dancers came around, his adopted mother tied him in the house, for she was afraid that if he met other Dancers she would never seen him again. At last came the day, fourteen years after Cedar had been adopted as a human child, when she was no longer strong enough to stop him, and he told his sister Tansy that he would go out that night to seek his own kind. Tansy hugged him and wept, and Cedar kissed her on both cheeks and promised her that, if he did not return before, he would return in one year and meet his sister at the ara tree. Then he went away.

"Tansy's parents were so grieved, and wept so long, that Tansy told them of Cedar's promise. When the year was over, they insisted on waiting with her at the ara tree. They waited all night, but Cedar did not come, and Tansy wept bitterly. The next year, she waited alone, but it made no difference. Cedar did not come, and again she wept.

"'Forgotten us, he has,' said her parents. 'Forgotten all about us. Dancer, isn't he, after all?'

"But the next year Tansy waited again, and the next. The Wheel turned and life went on. Tansy married a boy from the other side of the forest. Her parents grew old and died, and Tansy had children of her own. Still she came, always, on the Night of the Dancers, to wait at the ara tree, and she waited all night for her brother, though she no longer wept when he did not come.

"At last Tansy herself was very old and the journey was hard for her, and her children said, 'Don't go this year, Mother.' But she made the journey as always, and at long last her loyalty was rewarded. For a Dancer boy ran toward her through the trees and it was Cedar, exactly as he had been when she saw him last. He stopped at the sight of her and hesitated.

"'Cedar!' she cried. 'It's me, Tansy!' and he knew her then, and they hugged and kissed.

"'Said I'd come back in a year, didn't I?' said Cedar, proudly, and Tansy saw that he had kept his promise after all.

"And that night she danced with the Dancers."

Briar stopped.

"What happened then?" said Shan.

"That's all. That's the end."

"Oh." Shan thought about it. "Waited outside on the Night of the Dancers, did she? Wasn't that awfully dangerous?"

"Wouldn't like to do it myself," Briar agreed.

"Saw a Dancer once, I did," said Shan. "A female one, picking kesterberries."

"Did you?" said Briar, enviously. "What was she like?"

"Long dark hair and big eyes. As frightened of me as I was of her, I think, and I was hardly more than a baby then." Shan could remember the whole encounter vividly. "Was walking through the woods with my family. Been told to stay close, because it was the Day of the Dancers, but my father was going so slowly, holding hands with the boys, Marten just barely able to walk yet, and my mother was slow, too, because was just before my sister was born. Ran on ahead, I did, even though could hear them calling me to come back. Found a kesterberry tree, in a little clearing by the stream, and there was a Dancer. Couldn't hear me over the rushing water, I

47

suppose. Was a little thing, not much bigger than I was, and stretching up to pick berries from the branches. Had her back to me, long dark hair flowing down. Screamed in fear, I did, and she turned and screamed too. Then she was gone, one startled bound across the stream — and I couldn't have jumped it, not there, but she did without hesitating. Like a deer. Ran back to my family and flung myself against my mother. Was crying, I think . . . "

"Crying?"

Shan saw Briar's expression, and quickly returned to the present.

"Wasn't Cub then, was I? Never cry now. Know any more stories, do you?"

"Lots," said Briar. "Could tell you a different story for every tree in the wood."

"Every tree? Show me." Shan led the way out of the hollow.

"Could start with . . . " Briar looked around at the cedars and then pointed downhill. Shan guessed she was pointing to a tamarack that stood almost alone there. "That one."

"Too easy. All know tamarack's magical, don't we?"

"Know stories about it yourself then, do you?"

Shan felt that she might have known stories about the tamarack, once. "No."

"Reads tamarack ashes, my grandmother does. Sometimes can see what's coming. Knows a wonderful story about the tamarack . . . "

That was the beginning of a friendship that lasted all that spring, for Shan was hungry for stories and Briar loved to tell them. After a while, in exchange for the stories, Shan began to teach Briar both armed and unarmed fighting. Though she was the least talented of Cubs, she was nonetheless a far better fighter than Briar was and it gave her great pleasure to teach. She enjoyed the lessons even more than Briar did. Slowly, almost imperceptibly, Shan's own abilities began to improve.

Briar had endless curiosity about the life of a Cub, and Shan was almost as curious about the life of a Perin girl, for she had been at the school since she was seven.

"Who chose you for Cub, then?" Briar asked her.

"Don't know his name, do I? Tall, he was, and dark. Don't know why he chose me. Failed all the tests, I did, except running; couldn't throw the ball straight, couldn't loop the rope around the pebbles. But took me anyway, just grabbed me by the back of the tunic at the last, as the Wolves were leaving, and said, 'This one comes, too.' Screamed, my mother did."

"Course she did. My mother would have been jumping on the Wolves, trying to stop them."

"Would have been stupid to try that," said Shan. "Was holding my sister. And my father had the two little boys, my brothers. Would have lost more children, likely, if they interfered. But screamed, my mother did, and I remember there were tears on her face, and my sister howling in her arms, even though she almost never cried."

"Wonder if your brothers were chosen Cub?" said Briar, but Shan shook her head.

"Waited for them, always, haven't I? Would have heard their names if they'd shown up at the school. Would have looked out for them."

Shan felt sad and uneasy, thinking about her brothers. She changed the subject.

"Told your family about me, ever, have you?"

"Course not. How could I? Think I'm meeting a boy, don't they?"

"And don't mind that?"

"Be of age to get married soon, won't I? Might as well be to a boy of my choosing, that's what they think. Though I know Mother would like for it to be Jason. Probably will be, too."

"Hate boys." Shan was thinking of the Cub boys, louder than the girls and bolder, their taunts harder to ignore, to pretend that she had not heard.

"That doesn't matter, does it? Cubs don't marry. Wolves," and here Briar lowered her voice, as she had heard her mother do, "never have babies."

"So? Don't want babies." But Shan wanted to change the subject. That Wolves had no feelings was something she tried not to think about. She picked a young fern and began to unroll it. The two girls were outside the hollow tree, close enough to dash inside if anyone came near.

"Told my mother once I saw a Cub, this side the wall," said Briar. "To see what she'd say."

Shan looked up. "What did she say, then?"

Briar giggled.

"Said, 'You stay out of its way, girl. Remember even half-grown whelps carry knives and know how to use them.'"

"Tell her you know how to use a knife, too?" said Shan, amused and pleased.

"Course not. How could I?"

Briar hesitated, and then said, "Would like to tell my grandmother about you. Would like you to meet her. All alone she is, all day, except for the children. Blind, she is. Can't see anything at all."

"Would hate me, wouldn't she? Like your mother."

"No, not Grandma. Always talks about how we need Wolves on our side, she does. Always says Wolves and Perinan will have to work together to defeat Arkanan. Says it will be Wolves who defeat Arkanan in the end."

"Why?"

Briar shrugged. "Reads the ashes, she does, and says that's what will be. Be pleased to meet a Wolf Cub who's on our side, won't she? Come with me tomorrow, Shan. Like my grandmother, you will."

"How can she read the ashes if she's blind?" said Shan.

"Have to tell her how they fall, don't I? Come on, Shan," said Briar, grinning. "Never met anyone who sees even less than you do, have you? Say you'll come."

Shan shook her head. "Too dangerous." She stood up and began to pace.

"Not afraid, are you?" Briar trailed after Shan as she circled the clearing. Shan stroked a twig of sumac, still in its velvet spring coat and as soft as fur to the touch.

"Grandma says it's like deer's antlers. Covered with fur in the spring and shedding it in the summer."

"Antlers do that?"

"Told you my grandma knows lots of things."

Shan still did not agree to come, but all the way back to the school she considered it.

She was walking more slowly than usual, and it was just by chance that she noticed a movement on the school wall ahead. She froze. Her heart began to beat uncomfortably fast. Little of the wall was visible through the trees, and at this distance she would not have noticed anything but movement, but now that her attention had been drawn to it she thought she could see a dark mass on the top of the wall. An animal of some kind? Another Cub?

Shan screwed up her eyes but could not make out any details. She walked closer, warily, trying to keep tree trunks between herself and the wall and to make no noise as she drew closer. The thing on the wall did not move again until she was almost upon it, and then it moved its head — that must be its head, she thought — and at last she could identify it. It was a man in a black uniform, a Wolf, sitting on the wall.

Shan withdrew behind the trunk of the tree she had been peering around, and pressed herself against the bark. Had he seen her? She told herself that it was more likely he was facing the other way, watching Cubs on the grounds. But what if he wasn't? What if he had watched her all this time and laughed inside at her stealthy, creeping progress toward the wall, waiting to startle her at the right moment with a word? What if he knew exactly where she was and what she was doing? Would he take her to the masters? Or would he kill her, right here and now, as was surely his right if he found her off school grounds?

One step at a time, quietly, carefully, Shan began to retreat the way she had come. She had to believe the Wolf had not seen her, but all the time her back was hunched against the sudden loud command she expected. It never came. When at last she was out of sight of the wall she began to run, alongside it. She felt weak with relief and slightly sick, but she knew that she had to hurry now if she were to get back to the school before her free hour was over. Brambles tore at her bare arms; sharp stones and unexpected roots bruised her bare feet, and once she stumbled into a marshy place and muddy water splashed all over her.

She came at last, scratched, dirty, and panting, to a place where the wall curved and she could cross without being seen by the Wolf. As she clawed for handholds in the unfamiliar surface, she heard someone walking noisily through the wood on the school side of the wall. Another Wolf? Here? Shan gasped with fear and disbelief, swung her legs over the wall and dropped. She rolled as soon as she hit the ground, and ended up in a small dry hollow under a thorn-bush.

She lay absolutely still, aware of the crash she had made when she landed. The Wolf — she was sure it was a Wolf — had paused for a moment and was now approaching again, not quickly as if he had seen her, but idly, to find out what animal had made so much noise.

Shan lay as flat as she could, with her cheek pressed against the earth, keeping her breathing quick and shallow so it was almost silent. The Wolf came up beside the bush and stood there, probably looking around. All Shan could see of him were his boots, which were brown and made of deerskin. After he had stood there a moment, another, quieter pair of brown boots joined him. Shan could not understand why there were so many Wolves in the wood.

"What was that?" said one.

"Dog?" suggested the other.

That was the extent of their conversation, but they stood there for what seemed like hours to Shan, keeping her pinned down while the sky grew darker and her punishment more certain. She did not want to be caught so close to the wall.

"Coming?" said one at last, and they moved off slowly and noisily, leaving Shan free to squirm from her hiding place and run for the school.

"I fell asleep," she said, in explanation of her lateness, and the next morning she took the expected thrashing without a whimper. Her secret was still safe.

CRASO

Shan soon learned, from the talk of other Cubs, that the Wolves around the school belonged to a pack whose Alpha had been killed. If the rumours were true, he had drowned in the Cardith River. The Cubs' opinion was that he must have been too stupid to be a good Alpha, anyway, since even they knew how dangerous the Cardith River was. What had he tried to do, swim in it? His pack had been left leaderless and were now living at the school while they waited for Redthorn, the commander of Kunan Keir, to assign them a new Alpha, or, more likely, split them up among other packs.

Shan decided, reluctantly, that she had better stay on school grounds while there were so many Wolves around. For the first two days she was miserable, missing Briar, and having nothing to do and nowhere to go in her free hour, but on the third day she decided to go to the range and try to practice. This was an idea that would not have occurred to her a month before, but since she had met Briar she had gained more confidence and she thought that perhaps, if she practised in her free time, she might improve her skills. Someday the Cubs would have to find someone else to laugh at.

The practice range was deserted, as she had hoped it would be. She collected stones and piled them almost within touching distance of one of the targets. When she could hit the target each time from here, she thought, she would move the pile back a little.

It had been a hot day, but now, in the evening, it was pleasantly warm. The practice range in summer was well screened by trees, and the ground under Shan's feet was no longer mud, but red dirt where nothing grew, hard red dirt where thousands of Cub feet had trod down the years. Her first stone thudded against the wood of the target. Her second stone flew through the hole in the target's centre and clanged against the strip of rufer behind the hole, something that had never happened to her before. After a few more throws, she could put her stone through the centre every time. At first she kept wishing the metal did not clang so loudly and she kept turning, expecting Cubs to find her, but after a time she lost herself in the game.

When she had thrown all the stones, she gathered them again, this time placing the pile a bit further back. The target was now a dark blur, but she knew what it looked like. She tried to hold in her mind the size of the target and the hole in the centre, the place where she wanted to put the stones. From here she was not as successful, but she never failed to hit the target; every stone, if it did not clang, at least made a satisfying thud.

She moved the pile back once more before the other Cubs found her.

"Hey, look who's practising."

"Hey, Squinty-eyes, don't you know you're facing the wrong way? Target's over there!"

"Don't need to practise, do you, Ugly? All know how good you are, don't we?"

Shan was disappointed but unsurprised. She had known that they were bound to find her, sooner or later, though she had hoped it would be later. The idea had been doomed from the start. She turned away from the practice range, her eyes on the ground because she did not want to see the gestures of the Cubs, and almost walked straight into a Wolf.

He put out his hand and stopped her and she froze there, keeping her head down so that if there was any fear in her eyes he would not see it. She crouched within herself, terrified, and on the outside she merely stood still and her face remained unchanged.

"This is a practice range," said the Wolf, loudly. He spoke in Arkan, as if he were one of the masters. "Ye will leave it for those who are practising."

The other Cubs disappeared into the trees. Shan would have fled with them, wanted to flee, but the Wolf's hand was still on her shoulder. She could feel herself beginning to tremble.

"Go on then," he said, in Perin this time. "Practise."

He dropped his hand. Shan returned to her pile of stones and groped for one blindly. Equally blindly, she threw it. It crashed into a bush several feet away.

The Wolf said nothing, but squatted down to watch. Shan picked up another stone, reluctantly, willing him to leave. She threw the stone wildly and bent to get another.

"Helps if you look at the target," said the Wolf, quietly.

Would help if you would go away! Shan wanted to scream at him. Leave me alone! But she would never have said anything aloud. She had not even dared to look at him yet.

She looked in the direction of the target this time as she threw the stone, but it made no difference. She could not concentrate. All her energy, all her will, was focused on the effort of not screaming, not running, not crying, not letting her fear and humiliation show on her face.

One by one she threw the stones, finding the strength somewhere. None of them hit the target. Then she turned to look at the Wolf for the first time, just one quick glance to see if he were satisfied, to see if he would let her go. If he would only let her go! She would run straight back to the school, she promised herself, and she would stay there until the whole pack was gone, no matter how many days it took. Better to face a whole schoolful of mocking Cubs than one Wolf.

She took one quick look, and dropped her gaze to the ground again before she even realized what she had seen. Then she looked again, unable to help herself, trying to be certain. Was the Wolf actually smiling at her?

Chapter 4

The Wolf's smile was not, of course, an out-in-the-open, face-lighting smile such as Briar's. It was little more than a lift of one corner of his mouth. But she was close enough to him to be sure it was a smile, far more of a smile than any Cub would ever dare show to another. Shan stared impassively back, fascinated and confused. Was he laughing at her? Was he trying to be friendly? And over those questions, eclipsing them, came the one great fact — this is a Wolf and he's smiling. They do have feelings, Wolves do!

"Try again," he said. "Help you this time, shall I?"

Shan could not remember anyone else ever offering to help her. The Wolf began to gather the stones up again, and after a few confused moments she joined in. Having once looked at him, she found she wanted to keep watching that strangely expressive face. He had fair hair and big eyes, expressive eyes that were always moving, darting from one thing to the next, restless, and gradually she saw that he was the same, restless and never still. On the back of his left hand there was something tattooed, a flattish head, like a snake's, but with large round eyes, and sometimes when he picked up a stone Shan could see that its body went over his wrist and on, up his arm, under the black sleeve of his uniform. She wondered if it were a magic charm of some kind.

"Come then," he said, when they had gathered up all the stones.

Shan was trembling as much as ever, but she was quieter inside and this time she remembered to hold the target in her mind. She concentrated hard, and her first throw thudded against the wood. The Wolf picked up a stone and tossed it through the centre. After a few of these alternating turns, during which Shan concentrated hard and wondered why a Wolf would want to practise anything so simple, it suddenly dawned on her that he wanted her to watch him and learn from him. She began to watch his aim and try to follow his movements.

When they had thrown all the stones, they gathered them into a pile a little further back and did the same thing again. Shan watched the Wolf, who put each stone neatly through the centre of the target, and tried to see what he saw, aim where he aimed, knowing what the target looked like and holding a shadow of it in her mind. She seldom missed, and twice she heard a clang as her stone went through the centre.

The Wolf, probably bored by the whole exercise, began to talk to her.

"Heard what we're doing here, have you?"

Shan was far too much in awe of him to speak, but he went on as if she had.

"Soon hear everything in a place like this, don't you? Got most of it wrong, though. Saying Marsen was stupid and deserved what he got. Isn't true at all, that."

He tossed another stone — he obviously found the game ridiculously easy — and looked down at Shan, and again she could read emotion in his face, though this time it was not amusement.

"Wouldn't have been Alpha if he were stupid, would he? Though I wouldn't say he was always right, nor clever either. Had our differences, Marsen and I. Never could see what was in front of his nose, Marsen couldn't. And stubborn. Never listened to good advice . . . "

Shan, fascinated, missed the target by a foot, but the Wolf did not seem to notice. He tossed another stone automatically, still talking.

"But it was an Arkan killed him, it was, and I'll tell anyone who asks, though there's many Wolves afraid to ask, for fear of the answer they'll get. I'm not afraid of Arkanan. Not afraid of anything, man nor wizard, nor even Firedrake if it comes to that . . . " Even so, he lowered his voice at this point. "An Arkan killed Marsen, and killed him without need. Always served Arkanan well, Marsen did, nor ever said a word against them, and still they killed him. Without reason. I'll never forget that."

He threw his next stone savagely and it clanged hard against the metal.

"Ordered him into the river, for no good reason, and watched him drown. Always their way, isn't it? Never take any risks of their own, do they? Always send Kunan Keir to take their risks for them."

Shan threw the last stone in the pile. She could tell by the sun that her free hour was almost over and that she had to get back to the school, but she did not dare speak and she did not know how to leave. She began to back away. The Wolf stopped talking and regarded her impassively, and suddenly she was afraid, afraid that he had said too much to her, afraid that he might regret his dangerous words and even decide to kill the one witness to them. But he only stood quietly and watched her go. Once she was out of his sight she ran, hurrying back to the safety of the school, her mind humming with the Wolf's dark secrets.

She was exhausted that night, but she would not allow herself to fall into sleep until she had committed to memory, as well as she could, every word that the Wolf had said. Like him, she did not want to forget.

She did not consciously plan, the next day, to go to the practice range, but somehow she ended up there again. She was not surprised to find the Wolf there before her. He had his back to her and as she reached him he threw a knife so that it stuck, quivering, in a tree. Shan watched him as he retrieved the knife and started back with it.

"Stand still," he said, and in the same moment threw the knife toward her. Shan froze. The knife whined past her cheek and buried itself to the hilt in a tree beside her.

"No need to worry," he said. "I don't miss."

Shan turned her head and looked at the knife just beside her head. She did not doubt his words and she even felt pride at the way he had trusted her to obey him, but still it gave her an odd feeling to look at the knife. Would it have bothered him if she had moved and he had killed her? Would it have bothered anyone? Only Briar, who would never know why Shan had stopped coming to meet her. The masters would probably have been glad to be rid of her, she thought with momentary bitterness.

The knife was not made of rufer, like all the other knives she had ever seen. It was not even made of metal. It seemed to have been carved out of a single piece of black stone, polished and honed to a fine edge. The handle, which had strips of leather wound around it to provide a grip, was wider than the blade and ended with a smooth round knob. Shan immediately wanted to touch it, to feel the shiny black polish of its surface. It was one of the most beautiful made-objects she had ever seen.

"Don't touch it," said the Wolf, and his hand closed roughly on hers as he reached her. Shan withdrew quickly, more afraid of contact with the Wolf than she had been of the knife.

"Loses something if you touch it," said the Wolf, more gently, as he pulled the knife out of the tree. "Was made for my hand alone."

"Made it yourself, did you?" said Shan, and that was the first time she had spoken to him. She had forgotten herself, watching him run his fingers lovingly over the beautiful knife.

"No. Not me. Fletch." He did not seem to mind her question. "Got your knife, have you? Good. Knife practice today."

And again he helped her, teaching by example as they threw their knives, and retrieved them, and threw them again. This time Shan did a little better. Again she tried to hold a shadow-target in her mind as she aimed. And again the Wolf talked, randomly and without expecting any response from Shan.

"Wants to separate me from Fletch, Redthorn does, but I won't let him. Won't go without Fletch, not even if they made me Alpha. Like brothers, aren't we? Watch what you're doing with that knife, Cub." This to Shan, one of whose throws had gone dangerously wild.

"Redthorn said to me, 'Never been much good at following orders, have you, Deakin? Going to give you a chance to give some for a change. How would you like to be Second? Second in Moth's pack?' 'Yes,' I said, 'but what about Fletch? We go together or neither one of us . . . '"

Shan was not listening anymore. She had stopped listening after he said "Deakin." Deakin! So that was the name of her Wolf! She had wished she knew his name, last night in the dark, and now he had given it to her unasked, given it to her to be a talisman, a protection in darkness, a charm to be whispered, over and over, in the long cold nights.

"Deakin," she repeated, softly, as they walked together to retrieve their knives.

"Getting tired of this, are you?" He looked down at her, and she saw that he, at least, was getting tired of it. "Not very exciting, is it? Come on, Cub, let's fight. Any better at fighting, are you, than at throwing?"

So they fought, with knives, Deakin touching her in one place and then another, but just a touch, never hurting her. She could not touch him at all, could not even come close. He was too quick for her. He darted in and out, dodging and twisting and striking like a weasel, like a hawk.

It was not at all like the play-fights Shan had with Briar, but neither was it like the painful, humiliating practice-fights with the other Cubs. For Deakin talked to her, encouraged her, told her when to strike, and where, and why, talking all the time and panting only a little, while Shan panted and gasped and stumbled. Once she looked beyond him and saw Cubs, fifteen of them at least, watching silently from among the trees. Something must have shown in her face for Deakin looked, too, and then he bared his teeth at them and growled, as if he were a real timber wolf. The Cubs backed away, uncertain, and began to drift off by ones and twos, as if they had seen enough and had somewhere better to go. Deakin stood staring until they were all out of sight. Then he looked at Shan and he was smiling again, a little quirk at the corner of his mouth. She dropped her gaze, not knowing how to respond.

"Enough," he said. "Better follow them, or be late, you will."

Shan saw that he was right and her hour was almost over, but she stood facing him a moment longer, reluctant to go. She wanted to ask him if he would be there again tomorrow, but the words would not come and at last she turned away.

"Tomorrow, Bright Eyes," he said. "Need to keep practising, you do."

Shan ran back to the school singing inside, feeling as if she could fly. He was coming back tomorrow! And, more precious and more unbelievable still, he had called her "Bright Eyes!" When no one else had ever called her by any nickname but "Pig-eyes" or "Squinty" or "Ugly."

In bed, in the dark, she hugged the memory to her. She would never forget Deakin, she swore then, though years, and miles, and even Arkanan, might come between them. He had called her "Bright Eyes," and in return she would love him forever. If it were ever necessary, she would lay down her life for his. Satisfied with her promise, smiling inside, she slept.

⊂𝕤⊃

Two days after he had called her "Bright Eyes," Deakin let her use his sword. Apparently it was not so treasured a possession as his knife, being only an ordinary rufer sword, and he held it out to her casually, by the blade, and told her to take it and try some moves.

Shan had never held a real sword before, only the blunt and battered practice swords of the Cubs, and she took the hilt of Deakin's sword with a feeling of awe. The Wolf's sword was plain and unadorned, shining red along its deadly length. Shan knew she was almost certainly the first Cub of her year to hold a real sword, and she might even be the only Cub in the school to have done it. She wished the other Cubs could see her now and envy her.

Deakin did not stay with Shan as she practised, but paced restlessly around the edge of the clearing, kicking at stones. A squirrel ran down a treetrunk beside him, and he pinned it to the tree with one savage flick of his knife. Shan jumped. She stopped and looked at Deakin uncertainly, but he made an impatient movement and she continued her practice. Suddenly he strode over to her and snatched the sword from her hand.

"By the Wheel! Like this," he said, and went through the familiar practice moves like lightning, while Shan stood half-shamed, half-awed.

"Could do it like this at seven," he said, "At six, even," which was unlikely because the training of Cubs started at seven. "Any seven-year-old could kill you, Cub. Hopeless, you are. Hopeless."

Shan, agreeing, stood silent.

"Can't see very much at all, can you? Shouldn't be Cub. Won't make it through your initiation. Know that, don't you? Haven't got a hope. Won't live to be Wolf, and it's just as well. Be a danger to your pack, you would."

He sheathed his sword neatly and motioned with his head.

"Go on. Get out of here. Think I haven't anything better to do all day than teach useless little half-blind whelps like you?"

Shan went, stunned and sick at the unexpectedness of it. At the edge of the trees she looked back and he was already gone, striding away in the opposite direction. She squatted down and for the rest of her hour remained miserably where she was, under one of the trees that screened the practice range. She did not know what she had done to make the Wolf so angry, but she was sure she must have done something. Or perhaps he had just been gradually sickened by her clumsiness, her unfitness, her unworthiness. For he was right, she thought. She would die at initiation and never be Wolf. She was a useless little half-blind whelp; she could not deny it.

Most of that night she spent awake in silent mourning for Deakin, who had surely gone out of her life as suddenly as he had come into it. She wished she had not lost the childish comfort of tears. Toward morning her eyes felt wet but no tears would fall. There was only a terrible ache in her throat.

She returned to the practice range next day, driven by an urge to see her Wolf but determined to stay out of his sight. Deakin was there. He was waiting, as he always did, as if nothing had changed. He saw her at once, though she thought she had been silent and had kept hidden as she crept toward him.

"Well?" he said. "Come on, Cub. Going to practise, are you, or just stand around there all day?"

He seemed to have forgotten what he had said the day before. Shan did not trust herself to speak. She came to him obediently and began to gather stones together for the game.

"Hear about the rebels, did you?" he said after a time, abruptly. "Killed two Wolf guards, over at the mine, two nights gone. Hear about that, did you?"

Shan shook her head.

"Knew one of them," said Deakin. "Barton."

He was silent for so long after that that Shan began to wonder if that was why he had been angry the day before.

"Was my sword fight partner in final year of school," Deakin said, when they had thrown all the stones and were picking them up again. "Same height and weight as I was."

Shan hated the thought that she and some other miserable Cub would be paired up together for a whole year. But she realized it would not have been like that for Deakin. She could easily picture Deakin at school, good at everything and surrounded by friends. He would have been one of the boys that the girls talked about in barracks at night, one of those they slipped away to meet in the cedar grove by the pool. He had probably liked school, she thought in wonder, and felt distant from him, alienated.

"Course Wolves got the rebels," Deakin went on. "Five, there were. Two killed then and three later, in the centre of town. Made all the Perinan watch the executions."

Shan's mind flew to Briar, for the first time in days, but Briar lived on a farm rather than in the town of Redmetal itself and had probably not been forced to watch.

"Were you . . . were you there?" she dared to ask Deakin.

"Not in a pack yet, am I? Stuck here in this Cub playground, aren't I? Course I wasn't there. Might have been able to protect Barton if I'd been there. Might have been able to make a difference. If I don't get in a pack soon . . . "

He threw his stone savagely. Shan was afraid he was going to get angry again and, to distract him, dared another question.

"A snake, is that?" She pointed at his tattoo.

He did not seem to mind.

"Salamander," he said. He pushed up the sleeve of his uniform so she could see the whole length of it, the sinuous body and the two tiny pairs of legs, the tail winding up to his elbow. "Protection from fire."

"Magic?" said Shan. "Is it magic, then?" Deakin said, almost sharply, "Only Arkanan have magic," pulled his sleeve down, and went on with the practice. Later that hour, he called Shan "Bright Eyes" again, and she felt truly forgiven.

She practised with Deakin for fifteen days, and, as her abilities improved, so did her relationship with the other Cubs. They all knew that Shan was spending her free time with a Wolf, and it was as if they regarded her as being under Deakin's protection. Instead of getting in her way, they began to draw back from her a little.

On the sixteenth day she went to the practice range as usual, and waited there, hopefully, for most of her free hour. When her time was almost over, she saw the black uniform of a Wolf approaching through the trees and ran joyfully to meet him, stopping abruptly when she realized that this Wolf had dark hair. She had almost run into a stranger.

"Hello, Cub," he said. "Looking for Deakin, are you? Left with Moth's pack this afternoon."

Only then did Shan realize that this was Redthorn, the commander of the whole Kunan Keir, who occasionally visited the school to talk to the older Cubs. She knew him by the long scar that seamed one side of his face, an almost-fatal gift from the Perin Rebellion. She stood with her eyes down and said nothing. For an endless moment he regarded her.

"Expect you'll see him again, someday," he said, and walked away, leaving Shan shaken and alone. She wondered how he had known that she had been meeting Deakin, but she was far too unhappy to worry about it long.

She spent another sleepless night grieving for her Wolf.

Chapter 5

Now that the Wolves were gone, it was safe to visit Briar again and Shan could resume her secret life. As if to prove that everything had returned to normal, the Cub beside Shan hit her with stones twice during the stone game next day, and by the end of the afternoon she had a fierce headache above her eyes. She went to see Briar, but she went slowly, her head pounding, her eyelids heavy from lack of sleep. She knew there was no reason for Briar to be there. Why should she have waited, day after day, for more than a fortnight? She must think Shan had been caught off school grounds, might even think that Shan was dead.

There was someone sitting on the ground by the hollow tree. Shan had made little noise approaching and she was well screened by trees, so she did not think she had been seen, although she could not be sure because, for all she knew, the person might be looking directly at her. She stood where she was, hesitating, wondering if it were Briar or not. Then she gave herself an inward shake and thought, What does it matter? It's some Perin sitting there, isn't it? And any Perin seeing a Cub will run away, that's all. What am I afraid of? She stepped into the open.

"Shan!"

It was Briar. She dropped the stick she had been whittling and sprang to her feet, running forward with her face alight, pausing at the last moment because she was not sure how a Cub would react to being hugged and kissed.

"Shan! You came back! Never thought you would. Thought you were dead, or prisoner at least. Thought you'd been caught."

"Almost was," said Shan, quietly. She did not smile but her eyes were shining.

"How? What happened? How did you get away then? Hungry, are you? I have some cheese, look. I'm so happy to see you!"

This time she did hug Shan, quickly, and then stepped back looking a little embarrassed.

"What happened?" she demanded again.

"Whole pack of Wolves around the school," said Shan. "Almost caught me, getting back in." She sat down where Briar had been, with her back against the tree, and told Briar the story. Briar thrust a piece of cheese into her hand and she ate it while she talked, her headache beginning to ease a little.

"Thought it must be something like that," said Briar, "or worse. Was so afraid it was worse! Came every day hoping you'd be here."

Shan felt guilty at the thought of Briar waiting here every day, faithful and alone, while she had been practising with Deakin and had hardly spared a thought for her friend. She did not tell Briar about Deakin. She did not want Briar to recognize him, to say, perhaps, "But I know that Wolf. Killed my uncle, he did." She did not want Briar to come to her, sometime in the future, and say, "That Wolf of yours killed a whole family in the town." No. If Briar knew of Deakin, Shan did not want to hear about it.

"Going to see my grandmother now?" asked Briar, happily, and this time Shan agreed at once.

She awoke the next day with a vague feeling of uneasiness, nonetheless, though she did not admit to herself that she was afraid of meeting Briar's grandmother. How could she be afraid of a blind old woman?

It was one of those spring days that is almost as hot as summer, a reminder of the sweaty, sticky days to come when running would become an effort and practising almost intolerable. The hot weather brought out the flies for the first time, as yet neither buzzing nor biting, but flying into the Cubs' eyes and their mouths and their hair, so that they tasted flies and breathed them in and felt their soft, unwelcome touches everywhere; so that they shook themselves as they practised as if they were real cubs, puppies.

After a day spent battling flies, Shan was tired and short-tempered and wished she had not agreed to meet Briar's grandmother. But Briar had no way of reading Shan's mood, and she immediately began to lead the way toward her home, chattering excitedly as she ran. Where the forest path permitted the two girls ran side by side, with Briar leading the way where it did not. Shan could outrun Briar easily, despite the other girl's longer legs, but today she hung back and it was Briar who set the pace, urging Shan to hurry.

"Come on, come on! Don't have long, do you?"

The sun had been so unusually hot all day that now, as it fell toward setting, Shan was cold, shivering a little in her thin shirt. She had never been so far from the school before. She noticed patches of violets, bright in the slanting sunlight, and once a clearing full of huge, white search-flowers, nodding on their hairy stalks. Soon she and Briar had left the woods and were running through fields and pasture land. Shan kept her head down, trying to look as inconspicuous and Perinlike as she could. Away from the trees she felt vulnerable and exposed.

When she began to see occasional houses, she felt more vulnerable still, as her childhood memories awoke and tugged at her. Instead of Wolf Cub pretending to be Perin, she suddenly felt as if she were Perin pretending to be Wolf Cub, Perin with only the thinnest layer of capable, unemotional Cub over the top, and that layer was falling away, crumbling, as she returned to the scenes of her childhood.

"Here," said Briar at last, panting, stopping behind a windbreak. "My house."

Shan saw movement and shook her head, unwilling to go further.

"People," she said in protest. She was almost trembling.

"Only children," said Briar, impatiently. "Come on."

"Don't want them to see me though, do I?"

"Why not? Cub, aren't you? What can they do?"

"Tell someone. What if they tell someone?"

"What if they do? Can't very well tell one of your masters, can they? Come on, Shan."

"Can tell other Perinan, though. Most Perinan hate Wolves, don't they? Rebels kill us when they can, don't they?"

"Oh, all right. Wait here."

Briar pushed through the trees and greeted the children, who were pulling weeds in the vegetable garden. She was met with a chorus of "Come and help, Briar!" and "Why aren't you working, then?" and "Your turn, Briar!"

"I will, then," she said. "My turn now. Go on, all of you."

When they were convinced that she really meant it, and that she would explain to their grandmother, the children dispersed noisily and happily. Two of the littlest ones remained, pulling at Briar's hands.

"Come on," she said to Shan, and led the way to the doorway.

Shan followed slowly. She automatically stepped down as she entered the house, onto the smooth dirt floor. As she had expected, it was like stepping back into childhood. The warm smell of soup enfolded her. She looked around her at the wooden table and stools, the raised hearthstone

FIREDRAKE

where a fire burned in spite of the heat, the bowls
and cups and spoons neatly arranged as they had
been in her own home, and memories overwhelmed her; the love in her mother's voice, the
strength of her father's arms around her, the soft
caressing touch of a hand on her hair. For a
moment, against all training, she felt she could
have cried real tears.

The grandmother, preparing the evening meal
so it would be ready when Briar's parents came
home, looked up, cocking her head slightly, and
said, "Briar?"

Briar said, proudly, "Brought a friend. My
friend Shan. Shan, this is my grandmother."

The grandmother's hair, tied back with a piece
of cloth, was almost white, and her face was
creased and wrinkled, but she had a young, strong
voice.

"Hello, Shan. Come from the town, do you?"

"Came from a farm like this one," Shan
managed to say, through her inner tears and
turmoil.

The grandmother sprang forward, finding
Briar by feel and instinct and thrusting her
protectively behind her.

"What do you want here, Wolf?" she
demanded.

"Grandma!" Briar protested. "Shan's my friend."

"Kunan Keir," snapped the grandmother.

"Kunan Keir in training." Shan backed away, feeling like a Cub again. The world had righted itself. "Don't mean you any harm."

"Don't go!" cried Briar. She seized her grandmother's hands. "Grandma, you listen to me. Shan's my friend. My friend a long time. Since winter. Can't help being Cub, can she? Was chosen by Wolves, wasn't she, just like any of us could have been? No one asked her, did they? Had brothers and parents just like me, once, didn't she?" She was almost shouting, her voice shrill and near tears, sounding to Shan like a young child. "Grandma, you better listen! Trusted you. Told Shan she could trust you. If you let me down now, if you make Shan go away, I'll never trust you with any secret of mine again. Never!"

Shan stood silent, amazed as always at Briar's emotional outbursts, unsure whether she pitied Briar for her lack of control or envied her for her outspokenness. Briar's grandmother slowly sat down again.

"Friends, you say?" she said, quietly. "Been friends with this Cub a long time, have you?"

"Since winter," Briar repeated, still passionate and defensive, not sure whether her grandmother had capitulated.

"Well, then. Hello, Shan," said the grandmother, and even smiled a little. "I apologize. Never met a Cub before, have I? Come here, girl. Don't be afraid of me. Let me touch you."

"Not afraid," said Shan, and submitted, warily, to being touched. The grandmother felt Shan's hair and ran her fingers gently over Shan's face as if she could see with her fingertips. Her eyes, unfocused and lost in wrinkles, gazed steadily over Shan's head. She can't see me, thought Shan in wonder, she can't see me at all. I can see more than she can.

"Said we needed Wolves to join us, didn't you, Grandma?" said Briar. "Got us one now, haven't I?"

She pulled a stool over and sat down beside her grandmother. Shan preferred to squat on the floor on the other side of the hearth, facing them through the flames. She listened without interruption or expression as Briar told her grandmother all about their friendship, and then about Shan's life as Shan had told it to her. Shan was necessarily good at reading emotions and she could tell by the end of Briar's story that the grandmother was in sympathy now and would not betray her.

"What would happen if your masters caught you off the grounds, girl?" said the grandmother.

"Haven't yet, have they?" said Shan.

"Beat her, they would," said Briar. "Might even kill her. Caught three Cubs sitting on the wall once, didn't they, Shan? — just sitting on it — and were going to kill them, weren't they, Shan?"

"Not the masters. Wolves, it was, caught those three," Shan corrected her. She remembered how the Wolves had come into the school the following morning and insisted that the penalty for leaving the grounds was death, even while one of the masters was giving the Cubs the usual public beating. Shan had been close enough to one of them on his way up to the stage to have seen his bone-white face and know how close he was to fainting from the fear he would not show.

"But never catch you, will they, Shan?"

Shan was not young enough to believe that. She said nothing.

"Could join Gordin's men, couldn't she?" Briar continued. "Don't you always say we need Wolves to join us?"

Shan knew that Briar used the term "Gordin's men" to refer to the Perinan who had never accepted the fact that the Rebellion was over. At school she had heard a lot of stories about the savagery of these men, and she was glad when the grandmother shook her head emphatically.

"No! Dangerous enough, what she's doing now. Heard of another Cub once, years gone, did what you're doing," said the grandmother to Shan. "Used to come to one of the houses to visit his family, secretly. Wolves caught him and killed him. Do the same to you, they would, girl; don't doubt it. Climbing the wall is one thing, but talking to Perinan, playing with a Perin girl, quite another. Wouldn't listen to any explanations, they wouldn't, if they ever caught you and Briar together. Wouldn't give you a second chance. Nor Briar either."

Shan knew this perfectly well but did not like being reminded of it.

"But you said we needed Wolves," Briar protested.

"And so we do. It is Kunan Keir will defeat Arkanan someday. Not Perinan; not Gordin's men, for all their work and all their courage; but Wolves, trained and vicious and without a scrap of mercy in them anywhere. Turn on Arkanan in the end, they will. Someday they'll see, and perhaps Shan will be the one will bring them to see, that Arkanan are only using them for their own ends, and then things will not be pleasant for Arkanan. How many of them are there, after all? A dozen? Two dozen? Could hardly stand against the whole Kunan Keir, could they?"

"But can't be killed," objected Shan. "Arkanan can't be killed. Could kill all Kunan Keir and not be touched."

"Nonsense, girl! Teach you that, they do, naturally."

"Saw it," said Shan. "Saw Ern attack an Arkan with his sword, and Ern was swordmaster. Did no harm at all."

The grandmother was not convinced. "Was the wrong weapon, then. Or the wrong time. But Arkanan can be killed. They are not so strong as you seem to think. After all, don't live all their lives on Cardy Plain from choice, do they?"

"Don't they?" Shan was fascinated and a little frightened by the grandmother's dangerous talk.

"Course not," said Briar, scornfully.

The grandmother said, "Haven't let you know much about Arkanan at that school of yours, have they? Shall I tell you the truth about them?"

This sounded like a story. Shan hesitated.

"Yes, tell," Briar prompted.

"Long ago, then, when our land was green, it was known as Perinar, the Land of the People. For all the people were called Perinan in those days, even the wizards and the warriors."

The grandmother settled herself more comfortably, and Shan tried to relax as well. She could not help wondering whether Arkanan could overhear.

"Children born wizard could go to the great city of Forix to learn the art of magic. When they had been trained, we named them the Arkanan. Four times a year, at the changing of the seasons, all Arkanan would assemble in Forix to make decisions concerning the land. The rest of the time, most of them remained in their home villages. They were the healers and the settlers of disputes.

"But the land did not remain peaceful, for raiders from Aram began to steal our cattle and enslave our children. There were terrible years of war. The Kunan Keir, the company of Wolves, was created to keep the borders, but they were never strong enough. Families were killed, villages and crops were burned. In the end the Arkanan decided that they had to find a way to defend their people. Somehow they taught themselves a deadly magic, and then they used it to drive the Araman from our land, and so badly defeated them that Aram fears us yet.

"But, because the wizards had used their magic to take life, they had changed. They had learned what deadly power they possessed, and they had learned to enjoy the use of it. They no longer cared about the people of the land. They no longer allowed young wizards to join them. They moved to Cardy Plain and took over the Maze, which was already centuries old. They started a new kind of Kunan Keir, taking children from their parents and teaching them to be loyal to Arkanan and to despise their own people. And then they did an even more terrible thing."

Shan could keep still no longer. "Aren't you afraid they'll hear you?"

Briar looked at her in astonishment, and the grandmother smiled.

"All the way from Cardy Plain? Don't really think their ears are that good, do you?"

"Go on," said Briar. Although she knew the story, she was listening eagerly. "Tell Shan what they did."

"They began to search for the secret to eternal life, so that they could stop the Great Wheel and maintain their power forever. One of them, a wizard named Tarn, had discovered that they would need a magical construct in which to trap a piece of the Wheel, and that they needed to build the construct around a living creature. They chose a salamander, a creature born in fire. They would call their creation the Firedrake.

"Under Cardy Plain, in a vast chamber of stone, they gathered a great pile of bones and a greater pile of isinglass. Using their combined power, they called upon the Wheel of Time, the endlessly spinning Wheel, and by their magic made it briefly visible and present. It was more amazing and awe-inspiring and terrifying than they had imagined, and even Tarn cried out in amazement. Another of them, an Arkan called Kron, pushed Tarn with all his magical strength toward the Wheel. Some of the others joined in, for they were jealous of Tarn's power, and together they forced him into the spokes as they revolved, breaking part of the Wheel, perhaps, as well as Tarn's body, but no one could tell for the flames and the heat. Kron screamed at the other Arkanan to begin to weave the Firedrake, and he flung to the floor the salamander around which the construct would be built.

"Tarn screamed as the fire began to consume him, and as he screamed, and as the Arkanan began to construct their magical creature, the piece of the Wheel stopped turning. Time moved on as it always does and the great Wheel vanished from their sight, but a piece of it remained trapped within their creature. The wizard Tarn remained trapped in that instant. With their joined power the Arkanan called a wind, surrounding Tarn and the salamander, and the wind obeyed them and wove the bones together as they commanded. They constructed a huge skeleton in the shape of the salamander. They covered it with scales made of isinglass, and they used the wind to weave the scales together."

"And Tarn lives still," Briar put in, softly.

"Yes, Tarn lives still, lives in agony, trapped within the Wheel, suspended between life and death. He and the Wheel are the source of the Arkanan's power, and the reason that time goes so slowly on Cardy Plain."

"Would live longer if we lived on Cardy Plain," said Briar.

"Wouldn't live long at all. Wouldn't have anything to eat," said her grandmother. "Nothing grows there. And no one lives there, except Arkanan. For once Arkanan had created the Firedrake, they found they were its prisoners as well as its builders. They could not go too far from it, nor stay away too long, or they would die. And it was the same with the Kunan Keir, once Arkanan stopped training Cubs themselves and left it to Wolves to do it. They need the Firedrake, and at the same time they fear it, and they also both need and fear the Kunan Keir. Even the smallest Cubs, though they may fear Arkanan, do not respect them.

"And now," her voice was quieter, "Arkanan are in real danger. For three Wolves have arisen who may destroy them."

Shan, too uneasy to listen any longer, scrambled to her feet.

"Have to go now."

"Wait! Three Wolves?" said Briar.

"Yes. The ashes identify them as a blind woman, a madman, and a wizard. When these three meet, which they have not yet done, they will have among them the means of destroying the Firedrake. I would guess that Arkanan are trying very hard, now, to find a more permanent form of immortality."

"Couldn't be a blind Wolf," Shan objected, from the doorway.

"Not really blind, no. In fact, probably this Wolf is able to see things that others cannot."

"Shan's eyes — " Briar began, but Shan cut her off. She did not like others to know about her eyes.

"Have to go," she said again, and left the house, almost at a run. Despite the grandmother's assurance that Arkanan could not hear everything that was said about them, she felt lucky to have escaped.

Chapter 6

Beneath Cardy Plain, in its treasure-chamber of precious stones, the Firedrake lived without sleeping. It was secured with a strong gold chain, and it lay among rubies and tigers' eyes, opals and diamonds. Each of its shiny scales was the shape of a teardrop, and through the scales its bones showed clearly. Fragile, shadowy, lovely, woven on the wind, the Firedrake was almost without form. But the piece of the Wheel burned within it, trapped like a flame at its heart, and the scales near its heart were flame-red. Further out they became translucent orange and red-tinged yellow. Only the scales furthest from its heart remained clear as glass, glittering. Its eyes were as yellow as a cat's and as dangerous as a cobra's. Its hot breath was darkness and oblivion.

One by one, in a slow shuffling line, Arkanan came to where the Firedrake waited. They were wrinkled and ancient in the light of the torches they carried, a line of limping, shambling men and women who had lived past their time. Their hoods were pushed back to reveal seamed, puckered faces, white and withered. They did not speak or look at one another, for each was concentrating only on the effort of walking, of reaching the Firedrake one more time. They gasped and coughed. There were twenty of them, each bearing a stone.

The first was Kron. He kept his eyes carefully averted as he approached the Firedrake, and it raised itself up to meet him, its chain rattling against the stone floor. When it stood on its four stumpy legs, from the ground to the top of its head was three men high, and along its body to the slender tip of its tail was twelve men long.

The stone Kron carried was a ruby. He tossed it away from him, past the Firedrake. Eager, with all the avarice of a real dragon, it slewed its body around to pursue the ruby, to examine its newest treasure, and, as it did so, Kron hobbled forward and touched one of its gleaming scales. At the touch, he straightened up and then leaped away from the Firedrake as if he were a boy again. The next Arkan, old and weary, took his place.

The Firedrake did not like the Arkanan, but it knew the moves, had played the game many times before. It knew that each of them would throw it a stone, and then touch its scales, and it suffered the touches for the sake of the bright jewels they brought. Every twenty years or so it liked to vary the game a little, and so, tonight, it let the last stone go past it and did not turn to follow.

The Arkan who had thrown the stone tried to run, but he was still an old, old man and his crippled legs would not obey him. The Firedrake's glittering head swayed back and forth. Its eyes froze him where he stood, and its dark breath came all around him. Closer it came, and closer, and the heat of its body slowly enfolded him. As its breath surrounded him, he forgot all that he had ever known. To the Firedrake, he suddenly became uninteresting. It turned back to its treasures.

The other Arkanan, rejuvenated by the Firedrake's touch, made their way back through the Maze to their own chambers. They walked with springy strides and babbled excitedly to each other as they walked. They did not speak of the one who did not follow. He would die of old age very soon.

Hinton was speaking, as he often did, of preparing the Wolves for war. "We have great warriors and they need to fight. We should have conquered already Iluthia. We would be safer and the Kunan Keir happier. And we would have at last our own source of gemstones." He drew a line with his hand along the wall as he walked and the scene sprang to life where he touched, a line of Wolves visible in the distance, black-uniformed, dangerous, ready to advance on Iluthia.

Leban was insisting that the Arkanan must find another way of achieving immortality. "Now. Now while we are strong. What if Varian is right? We rely too much on the Firedrake. We have been prisoned too long here on the Plain." She flung out her arms for emphasis and lightning flickered about their heads.

Varian was normally the most silent on these journeys, because while she was strong she liked to plan the trips that she would take out into the world, to walk among the trees and to bring back cuttings for her garden in the Maze. But today she was worried about the tamarack ashes and their message of doom. "Listen to me, Kron," she urged him. "The ashes repeatedly warn me. There is a blind woman, and a madman, and a wizard, who can come together and destroy the Firedrake!"

"A wizard," Kron repeated, thoughtfully.

Hinton saw a chance. "How if these three are Iluthians? We know there is in Iluthia much magic, different from ours. Perhaps it is there that this wizard — "

Kron said, "Hinton, we all know well thy desire to attack Iluthia. None of the rest of us has any such desire. Be silent while thy betters speak."

He glared at Hinton, who glared back. Although both their faces were wrinkled and pitted with age, their eyes shone with all the fierce energy of youth. Once more they had tricked the Wheel of Time.

Kron deliberately turned away, speaking again to Varian. "I should like to capture this wizard who comes against us."

"Magic has been forbidden to the common people. He must practise in secret his arts," said Varian. "He will not be easy to find."

"But somewhere, to someone, he must have revealed himself. We shall find him," said Kron. "And a blind woman should be even easier to find. Come."

He strode on and the others followed. The flames of the torches burned green, blue, or crimson as the Arkanan expended their new energy. Illusions flickered into and out of existence along the walls; faces, a cat, a hawk poised to strike. Sparks crackled and danced.

Hinton kept his temper under control with an effort. Yet again he was being treated as an apprentice, the youngest of them and the weakest. Yet again they would not listen to him, and nothing would change. The Wolves would not be sent against Iluthia, and the Arkanan would keep everything the same. They were old men and women, dying. If only he could find Tarn's book of spells, lost in Forix all that long time ago, he could make another construct and this time it would be his alone. He decided it was worth taking another of his trips to Forix to search for it.

"We shall call the Kunan Keir," Kron decided. "We shall repeat the warning against magic and ask them to reveal to us anyone who practises it. Perhaps that will flush out the wizard. And we shall tell them, also, that the lives of all blind women in the land are forfeit. They are to kill them wherever they find them."

"I hope it will be enough," muttered Varian.

FIREDRAKE

They came to a place where the tunnel widened and torches were set into the walls. At Kron's command they formed a circle there. A crow landed on Hinton's shoulder and clacked its beak, but it vanished when Kron gave it a sharp look. Joining their gnarled old hands, the Arkanan began to chant. The chant was not loud, for it was not for ears to hear.

"Kunan Keir . . . Kunan Keir . . . Kunan Keir . . . "

The Call crept outward from the Maze, from Cardy Plain, and spread out over the land, to the Alpha of every pack. Wolves on watch, in woods or in villages, suddenly raised their heads, listening. Wolves riding sleepily toward Iluthia on the loaded carts of rufer came fully awake and looked to the north. Sleeping Wolves were jerked out of dream or nightmare to hear the Call.

 C3ᴇᴏ

Moth was appalled by the order to kill blind women. It was like no order she had ever received. She sat staring out into the darkness after the Call was over, trying to understand why Arkanan would order such a thing.

"What is it?" asked her new Second abruptly, startling her. He would not have heard the Call, but he must have seen her sit up.

"Been ordered to kill blind women," said Moth, flatly.

The Wolf on watch came over when he heard their voices, and she gave him the news as well.

"Blind women? Can't believe it." Her Second made a gesture of disgust. "Not going to do it, are we?"

"Going to do as we're told," said Moth, and lay down again. She had already suspected that her new Second, Deakin, was going to be trouble, and now she was sure of it.

CSSO

It was high summer, and time for the oldest Cubs to leave the school. One morning while Shan was doing her readiness drill, all the Cubs were told to assemble outside.

They lined the path between the school and the gate to the outside world, forming two silent, solemn rows. The Cubs who were leaving walked along the path between them, heads high, not looking to either side. They were leaving the school behind forever. The great iron gate was opened and they walked through it for the second and last time. Some of them would probably die in the initiation tests; all the others, the ones found fit to be Wolves, would make the long journey to the Maze, toward the pain of the final ordeal and then the freedom of adulthood.

Shan's year were all given an extra half-hour of freedom in the long summer evenings.

"Can come for longer now," she told Briar.

"But I can't come at all for a while. Time to bring in the hay. Told you about that, didn't I? Everyone has to bring in the hay. Might start any day now," Briar said, with regret.

Briar had told Shan that high summer was the best time of the Perin year, despite the heat and the hard work. The Alphas and Seconds of all the Wolf packs were gone across Cardy Plain to get their year-orders and their new members, and so the packs, leaderless, and usually unhindered by Arkan orders, spent most of their time sleeping in the long days and drinking ale in the hot nights, allowing almost complete freedom in the town and on the farms. Even the rufer mines closed down. Perin families worked side by side from sunup to sundown to bring in the hay, but at noon they ate and rested briefly, and there was time to listen to a story or two, or to join in a song.

"Could go visit Grandma and the little ones, now you have more time," Briar suggested, "while I'm at the haying."

Shan remembered how it was to visit Briar's house, like returning to childhood. She hesitated.

"Someone might see me. Some Wolf."

"Not with my idea. Going to bring you a tunic like mine. Can change in the wood, here, before you go."

"And leave my uniform here? What if someone finds it?"

"Have to hide it better than that, won't you? Please come, Shan."

Briar brought an extra tunic the next day, but the haying had been going on for several days before Shan wore it. In Perin clothes she felt more Cub than ever, conspicuous and awkward. She was sure that any Wolf would know her immediately for what she was. She kept a careful lookout, all the way to Briar's house.

"Shan!" The grandmother raised her head as Shan stepped down onto the dirt floor.

"How did you know it was me?"

Briar's youngest brother and sister gazed at Shan curiously, the little girl standing and sucking her fingers, the little boy sitting on the floor and cradling something in his arms.

"Hoped you'd come to see me, these past three days. Briar told me you might. Hope you were careful coming, girl."

"Yes," said Shan.

She came closer.

"What is he playing with, the little boy?"

The grandmother smiled.

"Salamander."

With the word, Shan remembered Deakin, suddenly and vividly.

"Salamander," she repeated, looking at the boy's wooden toy.

"Yes. Made it for him. A charm against death."

"Against fire, I thought."

"Comes to the same thing, doesn't it? Aren't we told the end comes in fire? After all, the Wheel of Time is a Wheel of Fire as well. Only salamanders walk through fire unchanged."

"What's his name?"

Shan reached out to the little boy, who made a face at her and drew back.

"Archer. After his uncle. And hers is Willow."

Archer threw his treasure in Shan's direction and she caught and examined it. Archer climbed unsteadily to his feet. Shan noticed that he was watching her expectantly, and tossed the toy gently back toward him.

"Had brothers and sisters when you were growing up, did you?"

"Yes. Two brothers, Dennen and Marten. Marten was just little, couldn't keep up with us." Archer bent over to get the toy, fell down, and climbed laboriously to his feet again, clutching it. "Had a sister, too, I did. Don't know what she was called. Was taken before her naming. Wasn't walking yet, just a baby. Would maybe have been named Lissen."

Archer came staggering over and ran into Shan, thrusting the toy against her leg. The grandmother seemed interested in her story.

"Oldest, were you? Grew up near here, did you?"

"No." Shan had no idea where she had grown up. "Took a long time for them to bring me here. Days. Wasn't usual, I think, for them to bring children so far. Thought they were safe, my parents did, thought their little ones wouldn't be taken. Likely the others weren't."

"What was Dennen like?"

"Serious, was the serious one. Careful, not like me. Always breaking things, I was, and running around exploring. Always just behind me,

Dennen was. Had freckles all over his face. Marten was different, always laughing. Always in a rush. Like this one."

She touched Archer's hair. Briar came dancing in then, still managing to look bright-eyed after a day spent working in the fields, though her face was dirty and pieces of hay were stuck in her clothing.

"Shan! At last! Look so Perin, you do! Wish you could see her, Grandma. Only danger now is they'll grab you and send you to the hayfield," she said, adding, in a deeper voice, "Why aren't you out there doing your share of the work, girl?"

She giggled, and then snatched up Willow and kissed her.

"Willow, this is Shan. Going to be your friend, she is."

Willow looked doubtful, but Archer now seemed to approve of Shan. He threw the toy at her again and waited for her to throw it back. For a few minutes Shan played with Archer while Briar played with Willow. The grandmother finished her preparations for dinner and then joined them.

"Briar tells me you want to learn to read," she said, and Shan agreed eagerly. She had been amazed when she first discovered that Briar could read and write, and she very much wanted to learn the art.

"Come on then, Briar," said the grandmother. "Draw Shan the first sound."

Briar gave Shan a comically disgusted look. She picked up a stick from the kindling pile and traced a symbol on the dirt floor. Shan copied it carefully. Before the end of that hour, she had learned the shapes to represent half the sounds she knew, and the grandmother had promised to teach her the rest.

After that Shan came every day of the haying and on into harvest, when the Perinan exchanged their scythes for short grain sickles and cut oats, barley, and rye. She learned to read and write, and began leaving messages for Briar every time she visited. She lost her fear of being seen, and began to run confidently through the woods and fields around Briar's house.

Then one day, as she emerged from the windbreak by the garden, she found herself in a group of Wolves.

For a moment Shan could not move, could not even breathe. There was no chance that the Wolves had not seen her. She could only pray that they would not recognize her. Steadying her breathing, keeping her head down, she kept walking.

The Wolves did not seem inclined to pay any attention to a small Perin girl. They were standing in a little huddle, trampling some potato plants unnoticed beneath their boots, and two of them were apparently having an argument. Their voices, though still flat, were louder than usual. As Shan drew level with them, one was saying,

"Go in and do it. Won't know anything about it, will she, if you're quick?"

"Not in front of the children," said the other.

"Bring her out here then."

"Do it yourself," said the first, and then Shan was past them.

In a few more steps she had reached the doorway and ducked into the relative safety of the house, drawing a long breath of relief.

Briar and her grandmother were both standing, facing the door, and each of them held one of the small children protectively in her arms. They looked ready to run. Briar cried out in dismay as she saw Shan.

"Shan! Shouldn't have come! Wolves, there are, Wolves! and they'll be back."

"Saw them. Outside the house. But why do you think they'll be back? What's going on?"

"Don't know, do I? Don't know what they want. Sent one of the boys to fetch Father. I'm scared, Shan. Scared. What do they want here?"

"Nothing," said Shan. "Why would they . . . ?"

She saw Briar's face change, and she sprang away from the door. Four Wolves came in, two of them with drawn swords, all of them menacing, black, and silent. The house felt suddenly cramped and small.

Two Wolves went straight to the grandmother and seized her. They removed Willow from her arms fairly gently and put the child down on the floor. Then they began to pull the grandmother toward the door.

Willow began to howl. Shan stood frozen with terror, certain that the Wolves had found her out at last and were going to kill everyone in the house.

"What are you doing?" The grandmother stumbled as she was forced along. "Where are you taking me?"

Briar echoed it.

"Where are you taking her?" she screamed, her voice shrill with panic. She had put down Archer and was trying to reach her grandmother, but the bright rufer swords prevented her.

Shan, slow to realize that the Wolves had not come for her, realized in the same moment that the talk outside the house had been talk of killing. "Not in front of the children," they had said. Arkanan had heard the grandmother's dangerous stories, after all. They had sent Wolves to kill her! Belatedly, as the Wolves left the house, she ran after them. She ducked under the nearest sword and lunged at one of the Wolves holding the grandmother. He dodged her blow easily and knocked her sprawling against the wall of the house.

Shan had learned so well never to wince, never to cry out, that her mouth closed immediately and her face froze into immobility. Then for an instant her panic was all for herself again. They must have seen so many Wolves react to pain in just that way. What if they recognized it? Deliberately, she forced a scream from her throat. She heard an answering scream from Briar and jumped to her feet again.

The two Wolves holding the grandmother were half-pulling, half-dragging her toward the windbreak. The other two, swords still drawn, were preventing Briar from following, but they did not seem to have hurt her. Shan realized that they did not want to hurt anyone but the grand-mother.

She launched herself at the nearest Wolf, landing on his shoulders and bringing the side of her hand down on his neck, but he was moving at the same time, ducking and twisting around in her grasp. He dropped his sword to free his hands and flung Shan away from him. She landed heavily but immediately scrambled for the sword. The Wolf's foot came down, none too gently, on her wrist.

"By the Wheel," he said. "Give it up, brat. Go take a look. All over now."

Shan gasped with pain. She heard Briar sobbing. The Wolf picked up his sword and walked away, rubbing the side of his neck, and Shan saw that he had spoken the truth, that it was all over. The grandmother and the Wolves with her had vanished into the windbreak. By now the grandmother was dead.

Shan lay where she was, panting, her wrist throbbing. Briar crouched beside her and sobbed. After a few minutes it began to rain.

Chapter 7

It rained for five days and nights without stopping. Puddles formed and spread, rivers overflowed, and the trees began to droop under their weight of water. For all the Wolf packs on the move, the steady rain meant no fires, no hot food, no dry clothes, and sleep snatched uncomfortably under wagons or in commandeered Perin huts or under quickly-made shelters of branches. Tempers grew short and Wolves, normally silent, became more silent still; packs straggled, spread out over a quarter-mile as they walked.

Moth's pack, on their way to the southern border, had the added irritant of having Fletcher with them. It was an open secret that Fletcher could make fire. It was also an open secret that Moth's Second, Deakin, had ordered him not to. Discontent and murmurings grew. Fletcher seemed indifferent, as unaffected by the whispered suggestions and complaints as he was by the rain. He trudged along patiently in his soaking wet uniform, dark head bowed, ignoring the comments that followed him and responding to direct suggestions only with a shrug of one thin shoulder. Deakin walked beside him and sometimes directed a hostile glare at the questioner.

Moth finally asked Fletcher herself, approaching him when there was no one else but Deakin within earshot.

"Is it true then?" she asked him. "Can you make fire?"

"Yes," said Fletcher.

"Why haven't you then?"

Before Fletcher could answer, Deakin answered for him,

"Ordered him not to, I did."

"Oh? Ordered him, did you?"

"Too dangerous," said Deakin. "Heard that last Call, didn't you? Isn't safe for him to use magic now."

"No one's going to tell Arkanan."

"Even so."

Moth turned to Fletcher.

"Going to make enemies this way, you are."

"Leave him alone," said Deakin.

"Could order you to," said Moth, still speaking to Fletcher, "but would rather not. Just a small fire. What's the harm? Afraid, are you?"

"No," said Fletcher. "All right. Make one tonight then."

"No, you won't," said Deakin. "Listen, Moth. Arkanan are looking for wizards right now just like they are for blind women, you know that. Looking to kill them. Don't want Fletch making fire, tonight or any other night. Understand?"

"Do I understand?" Moth was getting angry. "Who is Alpha Wolf here?"

She touched the knife at her belt. Only an Alpha was allowed to wear a knife openly, on the right hip, as a sign of authority; an Alpha theoretically had the power of life and death over the pack with that knife, for no Wolf was ever supposed to draw sword on another Wolf.

"Who gives orders in this pack then?" Moth came close to Deakin and stared into his face; she was almost as tall as he was. "I am Alpha. I say Fletcher will make us a fire tonight."

Deakin made a quick gesture of negation with one hand, and Moth's knife flashed, stopping a hair's breadth from his chest.

"Do you want to say something else, Second?"

"Isn't worth all this," said Fletcher, wearily, to Deakin. "Make fire, I will. Arkanan won't know."

Deakin looked at Fletcher out of the corner of his eye.

"Sure of that, are you?"

"Yes."

Deakin dropped slowly to one knee in the wet grass and lowered his eyes as required by the ritual. Moth heard him grind his teeth, but chose to ignore it. She touched the point of the knife to his chest, giving him leave to rise.

"Get up then," she said, and when he did, she added, "Why do you take everything so far, Deakin? Why do you have to keep pushing me?"

She did not expect an answer and Deakin did not give one. After a few moments Moth sighed and left the other two. Deakin picked up a stone and sent it crashing into the bushes.

"Make me crazy, you do, Fletch."

"Wasn't any need for all that, was there?" said Fletcher. "Can make fire tonight quite safely."

"May be safe tonight," said Deakin, savagely. "But what about tomorrow, when they want another one? What about the next night?"

"Can look after myself, Deakin," said Fletcher, quietly.

They walked on in silence. Deakin kicked at the ground. The rain poured noisily down around them.

"Could have taken her, you know," said Deakin, abruptly. "Could have taken her, unarmed and all."

"Course you could have. Both know that, don't we?"

"Should be Alpha of this pack."

Fletcher hesitated, and then said, "Our time's coming, Deakin. Haven't I told you that, over and over? Won't matter, then, whether you're Alpha or not."

Deakin shook his head and was silent. He did not object any more to the fire, though he did not help gather wood either. There were plenty of eager hands for that.

When the pile of wet wood was enormous, Fletcher sat down cross-legged on the ground and simply stared at it. He stared at one spot so intently that his eyes crossed. Wolves who had expected chanting and dramatic gestures, or maybe even flashes of lightning, were disappointed.

Fletcher sat absolutely still, concentrating, and after a while he began to hum, tunelessly, under his breath. A little smoke rose up from the log he was staring at, and then a lick of flame. The log above it caught fire and began to burn, brightly and steadily, as if it were dry. Soon the pile was burning well and everyone was getting warm. They all had hot food that night. The fire was a wondrous thing, burning fiercely through the downpour.

It burned until Fletcher fell asleep.

❧

The Arkanan were at council, at their stone table deep within the Maze. Varian watched a tiny fire, held between her cupped hands, burn on the table in front of her. The flames were blue and green. She fed it a strip of tamarack bark, delicately, watching the fall of the ashes.

"I see a death," she said.

"That much I also foresaw," said Kron. "The way to true immortality demands a sacrifice."

Hinton moved impatiently. "Have we not seen killed by the Wheel over the years many of our own? Yet that has not increased by even one mile the unchanging sky. Nor given us any more freedom, nor any more life."

"Perhaps it is not one of our own that must be sacrificed," said Kron.

"An innocent?" Leban suggested.

This was a new idea, and Kron took it up. "What dost thou say, Varian? How if we were to sacrifice to the Firedrake an innocent? Perhaps a child?"

Varian shook her head without moving her eyes from the flames. "I do not think it is a child that is required."

"Why not try nonetheless?" said Hinton. "We shall feed to the Wheel a child. At worst we shall only fail. And thou mayest gain by it new knowledge, Varian."

Varian had once had children of her own, though that had been long ago. She looked up to protest, but Kron was looking hopefully at Hinton. Resigned, she turned her attention back to the flames.

"Or better," Hinton continued, eying Varian, "let us take each one child. Even if there is but a small chance that children are the answer, we should make the attempt."

Sevrin, who did not often speak in council, protested. "The sacrifice of one child will tell us all we need to know. Why take more?"

"Why not?" said Hinton.

"Because it is a waste! We all know thy love of killing, Hinton, but some of us . . . Some of us do not enjoy it so much."

"If thou dost not wish to come, so be it," said Kron to Sevrin. "I like the plan of Hinton. We shall take each one child."

CRBD

After the grandmother's death, Shan began to vary her routes to Briar's house and made sure she found some hiding places along the way. Briar now had more responsibilities at home, and Shan began to feel as if she had a family of her own. She swept the floor and helped Briar with the cooking. She also looked after the children, carving toys for them from scraps of wood and teaching them songs that she remembered from her own childhood.

Some nights she came back to the school to find that, instead of going straight to bed, her year was to spend some time with one of the masters, Kerin, who was teaching them to read the night sky. They would sit just outside the school where the trees were fewest, in a circle on the damp grass. Kerin, who was not like the other masters, took time to explain the names of stars, and he even told stories about them. He taught the Cubs how to identify the patterns of the stars, and how to find the high fixed star that was the one to follow. When Arkan words failed him during the stories, he would lapse into Perin for a line or two. Shan was amazed at how attentively the other Cubs of her year listened. No hand signals were passed while Kerin talked. The other Cubs seemed as hungry for stories as Shan was herself.

The evenings spent with Kerin were magical. Shan felt a closeness to the rest of the Cubs. The only thing that marred her happiness was that she would never be able to use the knowledge that she was acquiring. For Shan could not see the stars. She could only see a sort of light-haze in the night sky, when the stars were out. She was glad that Kerin never asked any of the Cubs to point to anything.

Gradually the year began to slip toward autumn. The Wolves returned from Cardy Plain, and the barracks began filling up again as some of them brought seven-year-olds to the school, small healthy Perin children who had been chosen for Cub. Some of them cried all night.

Shan, lying awake listening to the stifled sobs, remembered when she had done that herself but could no longer remember what it had felt like. It seemed very long ago. These little ones would all learn soon that tears changed nothing here. Already laughing and screaming had been forbidden to them. Already, awkwardly, they were learning the hand signals, the secret language of Cubs.

One evening, Kerin told the Cubs that the following night was Borean Alari, the Night of the Dancers, and so of course they would not be meeting after dark. Borean Alari was the one night of the year when all humans were glad of a roof and four strong walls between themselves and the forest.

Shan walked quietly and slowly as she went to meet Briar next day, hoping to see a Dancer. She was not afraid of them in daylight. She had not seen one by the time she reached the ara tree, and as she crawled into the hollow, she said, "Briar? Go and see if we can find one of Them, shall we?"

She did not say the word "Dancer," because it was their day, and it would have been dangerous, or at least terribly bad luck.

But Briar was not in the hollow. Shan crawled out again, surprised. She was late today and had expected Briar to be waiting.

She decided to change into her Perin tunic and go to meet her friend. Briar came running toward her before she reached the end of the wood, face flushed and eyes shining.

"Come on, Shan! There's one of Them in our garden! Come and look!"

By the time Shan and Briar reached the windbreak, the news had spread and there were about twenty Perinan, almost all children, watching the garden with avid eyes. The Dancer, unconcerned, was hunkered down in the garden eating a honeycomb with great concentration. Shan had heard before that Dancers could be trapped with sweetness.

The crowd was so still that Shan could distinctly hear the rasp of the Dancer's claws on the honeycomb. She wanted to get close enough to see what a Dancer really looked like, so she left Briar and began to creep forward. She thought the Dancer was aware of her, but not concerned, and she wondered how close it would allow her to get. Suddenly the Dancer's head cocked, and then in a quick scramble it was gone.

Twelve Arkanan had appeared among the children.

Each Arkan grabbed the nearest child. One of these was Archer. Briar, who was close to him, screamed, "No!" and tried to pull him away. A woman hurled herself at another Arkan who was trying to take her child, but she missed the Arkan and fell hard.

Shan's eyes seemed to be working even less than usual. Though one of the Arkanan stood quite close to her, she could see him in two places, rather like the way she saw a shadow-target in front of the target at which she was aiming. Then she realized that Briar was having the same sort of trouble. Her grab at Archer had missed completely.

"No!" she yelled at Briar. "He's not there. To the right . . . ," and she sprinted toward Briar. Briar struck right, touched the Arkan, and then, remembering what Shan had taught her, swung at him with all her weight behind the blow. The Arkan yelled with rage, and Shan heard it even above the screams of the frightened children. He shouted something and made a violent motion as if he pulled something from the air and flung it at Briar. There was a startling flash, a bright flare against Briar's chest. Then the Arkanan and their chosen children disappeared.

Screaming Briar's name, Shan reached her friend as she fell. She was not aware of the tears and panic surrounding her. She could only see Briar. She dropped to her knees and clutched her friend tightly, shaking her, slapping at her face. She rubbed the black burn-mark on Briar's chest, over and over, as if she could rub it out.

Then she saw Briar's eyes and she became quiet again. Briar's eyes were open, but Briar was no longer looking out of them. Briar was gone. Only her body was still here.

Shan held Briar's body, gently now.

"Briar, I am one of the Three," she said, softly. "I am the blind Wolf. I saw where the Arkanan really were. No one else saw that, but I did. Someday I will fight them."

She became aware that there were tears on her cheeks, and she wiped them away. She was not going to let herself cry. She was afraid that, if she did, she would never be able to stop.

She closed Briar's eyes.

"Briar, you are the only friend I ever had. I swear by the Wheel I will never forget you. I swear I will never forget that Arkanan are the enemy."

And then, after a pause, she thought of Briar's grandmother and deliberately added an oath that she knew would be difficult for a Wolf to keep.

"I swear by the Wheel I will never kill Perinan."

Chapter 8

The time came at last when Shan was to become Wolf. She walked through her final days as a Cub in quiet terror. She was terrified of the initiation into adulthood, which she had once been sure she would not survive. Was she fit to be Wolf? She had practised hard since meeting Deakin, and had learned to use the other Cubs as her eyes in some of the exercises, shadowing their movements as she had shadowed Deakin's. But she had no way of knowing if it would be enough. She was even more terrified of the ceremony that came after initiation, the ceremony that would make her a Wolf, for that was when she would become a true warrior, and, if the stories were true, lose her emotions forever. Sometimes she remembered Deakin's emotions and told herself that the stories were lies, but at other times she was afraid that Deakin was different from other Wolves, that he had somehow avoided that part of the ceremony. What if Arkanan took from her all her memories of Briar? What if they forced her to kill Perinan despite her oath? What if she just stopped caring?

One blazingly hot afternoon, Redthorn came to talk to Shan's year about becoming Wolves. He walked into the midst of them at practice, quiet and unassuming. He did not even wear a knife to mark him as Alpha, and for a few moments the practice continued, the Cubs too occupied to pay him any attention. Then one of the masters recognized him and ordered the Cubs to stop.

Shan lowered her sword, with relief, and stood panting for a moment before she realized that Redthorn was standing right beside her. She recognized him at once, dropped her gaze from his scarred face, and took two steps backward.

Redthorn was a legend in the Kunan Keir, the Wolf without a pack, the man who had survived, with no one to cover his back, to become the oldest working Wolf. Even the Cubs knew some of the tales about him. As for the masters, they were standing as silently and respectfully as the Cubs were.

"Wanted to see you," said Redthorn to the Cubs, "before initiation. Have something to say to you all."

Unexpectedly, he spoke in Perin, and, far from objecting, the masters walked quietly away, leaving Redthorn alone with the Cubs.

"Anywhere to get cool around here?" he asked.

He walked away from the practice field toward the trees, and the Cubs closed in behind him and followed.

"Sit down," he said, once they were in the shade. "All look like you could use a rest."

They sat, a little warily, in a circle around him, and Redthorn stood and talked to them. Shan expected a speech like the ones the Arkanan were so fond of, telling the Cubs to be a credit to their packs and to the land, but Redthorn's was not that kind of speech.

"Almost time for your initiation," he said, and Shan's whole body tensed. "Tomorrow morning, if the weather's good. At the Torrent River. Tests of swimming, running, jumping, and climbing. Dangerous tests, but most of you will do fine. Ready to be Wolves now, aren't you? Those who pass go to the Maze, to be seen and accepted by

Arkanan. For the ceremony in which you become Wolves.

"Want to make sure you understand what it means to be Wolf. Isn't like being Cub. Far more dangerous, for one thing."

At this point he smiled, slightly but quite openly, and the smile touched his voice as well. Shan felt the shock that rippled through the assembled Cubs. Unlike her, they had not been aware that a Wolf could smile.

"Arkanan will kill you if you break their laws. Perinan have a rebel army that will kill you whenever and wherever it can. Understand that, do you? Once you leave this school, your lives will be dangerous and will probably be short. Wolves survive only by standing together.

"Being Wolf is a privilege, and it's a privilege you can lose. Break Arkan laws and you die. Break my law and you are marked for life and put out of the country. Don't have any room for Wolves who don't want to be Wolves, or for Wolves who won't cooperate.

"So want to tell you my law: No Wolf to draw sword on another Wolf. No exceptions. Draw sword on another Wolf and you cease to be Wolf yourself, and your Alpha can draw his own sword and mark you and then drive you out of our land.

If you must fight, use your fists. Understand that, all of you?"

Apparently they all did, for no one spoke. Redthorn looked at them for a moment in silence and then said, "Good. Will see you all again soon, after initiation. Until then, may the turn of the Wheel bring you good fortune."

He gave them his little smile again and walked away, leaving the Cubs confused and deeply impressed, and many of the girls already in love with him. For the rest of the day they talked of little else. Shan expected rude comments about her approaching initiation — "Ready to die, are you?" — but no one said anything to her at all.

Now that the time had actually arrived, Shan hoped for rain, but the next morning was bright and cloudless. She awoke early, with a sick feeling in the pit of her stomach, and did her readiness drill with special concentration. Then, with the other boys and girls of her year, she surrendered her knife and left the school for the last time, walking down the path through the grounds, past all the Cubs lined up to watch them go, and through the great gate to the outside world.

The ceremonial walk through the grounds was something that Shan had looked forward to in earlier years. She had thought it would feel wonderful to leave the school behind forever, whatever awaited her beyond the gate. Now she found she was too frightened to enjoy it. She was also incapable of enjoying the summer morning that the Cubs walked through. Every time the road changed direction, or the masters stopped for a moment, she thought that the initiation was about to start, and her chest became tight and her breath ragged with fear.

But the long journey went on, and gradually the hard knot of dread inside her began to unwind. The trembling in her legs was stilled by the walking. She remembered what Redthorn had said, that the initiation would take place at the Torrent River, wherever that was, and she began to hope that the first test would involve swimming.

The Cubs walked steadily south for about two hours, through the gold and green of the fields. At the beginning of the journey they saw haymakers, with their scythes, heading out for a day's work, and once Shan saw a girl chasing a group of sheep, who had wandered onto the road, out of the path of the Cubs. Finally they came to a ford, where stones had been placed to allow wagons to cross. The stones were barely necessary at this time of year. The masters led the Cubs off the road and they all followed the creek eastward. They startled a pair of mallards, who scooted down the bank and flopped into the quiet water, and Shan saw the male's head flash brilliant green against the red earth of the bank.

The track was narrow but had obviously seen recent use. Shan guessed that Wolves were here already. Maybe they even ran the course before the Cubs did. After she had walked for a few minutes in a long line of Cubs, the land dropped away suddenly ahead of them and the track became a rough and treacherous scramble. Shan could hear what must be the Torrent River far below. Then for a few moments she had to concentrate carefully on keeping her footing. An injury now would probably kill her in the tests.

As the Cubs reached the bottom of the gorge, the masters told them to line up along the rocky bank of the river. By screwing up her eyes and staring across the tumbled red water, Shan could make out steep cliffs on the other side.

"This is the Torrent River," one of the masters told them. "Ye can see that it is fast and dangerous. Further down there are rapids, and then a waterfall.

"Ye are to swim the river. When ye reach the other side, ye are to climb one of the ropes. Wait at the top of the cliff until ye are told what to do next."

The other Cubs were suddenly in motion, running for the water, and Shan ran with them as soon as she realized she should. The master must have made a hand gesture. Shan grabbed a quick breath just before she hit the water, and then she headed across the current with strong, regular strokes. The river was pleasantly cool, and for the first few minutes she almost enjoyed herself. All the others had plunged in at the same time, and just ahead of her the water was churning with Cubs.

Then she reached midstream and the current took her.

Shan had never imagined that water could be so strong. Suddenly she was being swept downstream much more quickly than she was gaining the opposite bank, although she was now swimming as hard as she could. After a moment of panic she remembered that she should swim across the current, and she began to strike out for the other bank diagonally.

Gradually she felt her arms tiring. She was a little behind the others and at first that worried her. Then she thought, realistically, what does it matter? Some of the Cubs might swim together, keeping each other silent company, might support one another at need or even search for a missing friend, diving, but no one was going to do that for Shan. No one would miss her. No one would help her. She was, as usual, on her own. There was a bitterness in the thought that made her swim more strongly.

Suddenly the cliffs were there. She raised her head, gasping, and saw a steep rock wall just beside her and a rope hanging down, trailing in the water. It had swept past before she could reach for it. Terrified, she watched it recede. Then she saw a second rope sweeping past, this one occupied. A Cub was climbing, and another clung at the bottom. Shan turned in time to try for the third rope. At the bottom of this rope, one Cub was holding onto another, who was coughing. Shan tried to catch the rope as well, but the girl who was holding her friend kicked out viciously. "Find your own rope, Squinty!"

The next rope was unoccupied, and Shan snatched it and wrapped the dangling end around her hand. For a few minutes she floated there, glad just to rest, and watched as more Cubs arrived.

She knew that the two Cubs on the next rope were called Finch and Leelan, and that they were best friends. Finch had never tried to kick Shan before, and Shan recognized that she was desperate. She began to realize that there might be an advantage in having no friends among the Cubs.

Shan was one of the last Cubs to reach the top of the cliff, not only because she was one of the last to get into the water, but because any other Cub who reached her rope climbed over her. She decided that it was better to wait than to risk being pushed off the rope. She saw Leelan eventually recover from her fit of coughing, or near-drowning, or whatever it was, and begin to precede Finch up the rope, before she began to climb. The bottom of the rope was wet and slippery in her hands, and her sodden clothing wanted to drag her back down. She gripped the rope firmly between her bare feet and inched up the cliff. The cliff was higher than any of the places where the Cubs had practised, and her arms were aching by the time she reached the top. She hoped that there would be no more swimming or climbing tests for a while.

At the top of the cliff, she found herself alone. She looked around quickly, frightened. Surely she hadn't fallen that far behind! Where was she supposed to go next? Then a head emerged as the Cub on the next rope, Burr, dragged himself over the top. After a quick glance around, he looked impatiently at Shan.

"What are you waiting for? Run!"

Shan needed no more urging. Someone that she could not see must be signalling her, and there was only one way to run, away from the cliff. She sprinted across the grass, ignoring the ground underfoot, though once her heel came down hard on a thistle. She kept her gaze fixed ahead, straining to see what she was running toward. She might need every instant of warning that she could get.

The run was slightly uphill, and after a few seconds she was running on dirt instead of grass. She could see movement ahead and she headed for it. She was running so hard that when the trail ended, at a towering grey rock, she almost ran straight into it.

"Better jump," said a Wolf. He was standing against the rock.

Shan did as she was told, without thinking, and launched herself into the air, grabbing, expecting to find a handhold or foothold. Instead, she came down again, scraping herself, but one of her hands had brushed something. She thought it was a rope. She jumped again, as hard and high as she could, and caught the tail of the rope in her hand. It jerked briefly down as her weight took it, and she grabbed it with the other hand as well. She realized that it was being pulled up over the rock, and that she was now being pulled with it. Rather than be further bruised, she pushed against the rock with her feet, half-climbing as the rope dragged her along. She was thankful that she had run fast enough to catch the rope. The rock bulged out away from the cliff and it would have been difficult to clamber up on her own.

At the top, she found that the rope was tied to a tree and several Wolves were pulling on it. Shan scrambled to her feet and one of the Wolves dropped the rope down over the rock again for the next Cub.

"Catch," said another of them, and threw something in Shan's direction. Shan tried to catch but missed, and the object, which she thought was a stone, bounced away down the path. She started to scramble after it.

The Wolf said, "Wait. Look. Trying to find one of these, you are."

Shan was no longer close enough to see what the Wolf was holding up to show her. It was small and brightly coloured, red and blue. A lizard? A cluster of berries?

"Can use a sword to help, if you can earn one," said the Wolf. "Go."

Shan retrieved the stone and ran on quickly, not knowing whether speed still mattered. From the top of the giant rock, the trail was clearly marked. Many feet had run this way through the dirt. After a few minutes she was running straight downhill and there was grass on either side. Because she had been given a rounded stone, she was expecting to have to try to hit a target, and she kept looking for one as she ran. She also looked intently for any spot of colour, either the bright red gleam of rufer that would mean a sword, or the red-and-blue object that she was supposed to find.

Ahead of her, she heard a stream tumbling over stones. The trail reached the bank and turned to follow along beside the water. Shan abruptly came around a bend in the stream to a Wolf who stood with a rufer sword in his hand. She skidded to a stop, her heart hammering. Was she supposed to fight him? Had there been an opportunity to get a sword, and had she missed it?

But the Wolf neither attacked nor spoke, simply stood blocking her path. Shan saw the bright gleam of a pile of red swords behind him. He apparently expected her to know what to do. Looking around desperately, she noticed a vague form across the stream and was fairly sure it was another Wolf standing on the far side. There was something beside him, and, helped by the stone she had been given, Shan thought it might be a wooden target.

She screwed her eyes up tight and flicked them from side to side, trying to determine the target's dimensions. Assuming it looked just like one from the school, half-seeing where the edges were, she could picture the centre. She focused hard, concentrated, and finally threw the stone. There was a satisfying clang as it flew through the centre of the target.

"Good shot." The Wolf tossed her the sword so that it turned in the air and the hilt landed neatly in Shan's palm. She closed her hand on it, grateful to him for the throw, still amazed that she had succeeded in hitting the target.

He motioned her on her way, and bent down and retrieved another sword from the pile behind him.

The trail led upward after that. It was a longer run in the sunshine, and Shan felt her uniform beginning to dry. She could see that her sword was one of the blunt practice swords, probably brought from the school that morning. Although she liked the weight of it in her hand, she was worried about what she might have to do with it.

The stream was left far, far beneath as the trail climbed. Shan could no longer hear it. She thought she must be higher now, even, than the top of the rock.

Then another Wolf stood blocking the path. This one, to her relief, had his sword sheathed. He signalled her to stop. Shan could not see anything ahead except the top of the hill and the blue sky beyond, and she guessed that she was waiting for another Cub to finish the next test, whatever that might be.

After a few moments Burr caught up and waited with her. To her surprise, he flashed her a hand signal. Doing okay? No Cub had ever flashed that kind of question to Shan before, and she was almost too astonished to remember to reply.

The Wolf indicated to Shan that it was her turn. She followed the path up to the top of the hill, and was vaguely aware of the stink of some animal, perhaps a fox. She continued to follow the path, which now descended slightly, until she reached another Wolf. He was standing at the top of a pit that had been cut into the ground. It extended further than Shan could see, and she guessed that she would have to climb, or perhaps jump, down into it.

"Jump," said the Wolf.

Shan could not see how deep the pit was, but she had jumped in practice, with a sword in her hand, many times before. She jumped, hit bottom, and rolled over one shoulder, coming up correctly with the sword ready. She was standing on sand. The stink was overpowering here, and she realized that it was not fox, but weasel. A weasel was trapped down here with her. "Avert," she said, remembering that weasels bring bad luck.

Moving cautiously forward, she saw movement on her right, and then a flash of colour. Red and blue!

Keeping the sword ready, she edged closer. She heard the weasel hiss a warning. Again she saw the blur of colour, and realized it was somehow attached to the weasel. She used the flat of her sword to drive the creature back, trying to trap it against the wall, not wanting to hurt it. Being used, it is, like Arkanan use Wolves, she thought. Doesn't want to be here any more than I do.

The weasel avoided the wall and darted away, but Shan got a close enough look to guess that it was wearing a necklace of red and blue beads. Again she tried to trap it and it squirmed away. This time she grabbed for the necklace and felt sharp pain in her wrist as its teeth grazed her. Not so sorry for it now, she lashed out, trying to hit it with the flat of the blade. For an instant everything was a blur of motion. The weasel hissed and spat, the sword whirled, dirt spattered from the wall. Then she felt the weasel's vicious teeth close on her cheek and cling, and she brought the sword-hilt down hard on its head. She hoped it was still alive, but she did not stop to see. She pulled the necklace off with a quick hard tug, and ran for the other end of the pit, where she was glad to find a wooden ladder against the wall.

She clambered up out of the pit, still holding the sword. She was shaking. She wiped away a trickle of blood that she felt running down her face.

A female Wolf was waiting at the next bend in the trail.

"Well done." Taking the bead necklace and the sword away from Shan, she motioned with her head. "Down there next. Into the tunnel."

Shan wondered how bad her cheek looked. Stupid, she thought, getting my face that close to a weasel. She walked the way the Wolf had indicated, and found herself walking among rocks. Once she had stopped shaking, she cleaned the blood from her face as best she could. She examined her wrist and saw a long red scratch left by the weasel's teeth.

She soon came to a rock wall that would have been a barrier if there had not been a narrow tunnel cut into it. The tunnel provided shade and welcome coolness. Now that Shan's run was over, she was aware that she was sweating inside her soaked uniform.

After a few moments she had left the daylight behind and was feeling her way, with a hand on the walls on either side. The tunnel was smooth and the walk easy. Shan began to wish for a test in the darkness. She would certainly do well in that one! But after only a brief time alone, she could hear Cubs talking softly ahead of her. The tunnel turned and there was daylight ahead.

Shan emerged into the light right behind Leelan and Finch. She found that they were standing on the edge of a chasm. It looked to Shan as if they must have come the wrong way. The tunnel widened here and stopped. Shan could hear the roar of a waterfall far, far below.

"Have to wait," said Finch, softly. Maybe she regretted kicking Shan earlier. "Go one at a time."

Shan did not understand what Finch was saying. To jump down here would not be an initation test; it would be suicide. Finch pointed up and across the chasm. "Wolf there tells you when to go. Jump across, you do."

Shan could not see the Wolf, who must be standing high above them on the opposite bank, but by screwing up her eyes she could just make out the movement of something brown, slowly inching its way up the far wall. That must be another Cub. She had no idea how the Cub had reached the other side of the chasm.

At least she would be able to watch Leelan and Finch go before her, so that she could see how it was done. She waited for what seemed a painfully long time, until the other Cub reached the top, and then she saw another movement where the Wolf must be.

Leelan jumped.

To Shan it was totally surprising. The Wolf must have signalled. Leelan suddenly launched herself into the air, up and across, and Shan realized only when Leelan landed that there was a ledge on the other side, a ledge which the others could see and Shan could not. For an instant Leelan stood upright, and Shan heard Finch let out her breath. Then Leelan's foot slipped and she was gone. She did not even cry out. The stones that fell with her clattered briefly on the rocks below.

Finch did not look down into the chasm. An instant later, presumably when the Wolf signalled, she jumped.

This time Shan watched. She watched as she had never watched anything before. She watched Finch's eyes and exactly where she was looking as she jumped. Inside Shan was shocked and close to panic, but that would have to wait. She had to memorize exactly where that ledge was, or she had no chance at all. While Finch climbed, a slow and careful climb up the steep cliff, Shan stared at the spot where the ledge was. Only once did she shift her eyes, when Finch slipped and there was a sudden noisy shower of pebbles. She jerked her gaze up to Finch and then down again.

It took Finch a long time to finish the climb. Two other Cubs had arrived before it was Shan's turn. As soon as Finch reached the top, Shan took a deep breath to still her trembling, and jumped.

She had remembered where the ledge was, but she had no idea what it looked like, and she landed hard, jarring her whole body. One of her ankles gave way beneath her, and she dropped to one knee. With a rush of surprise and joy, she realized that she was safe.

Her joy faded when she tried to stand. Her left ankle refused to take her weight. Shan gasped again, with shock and pain and terror. Surely she had not come so far through her initiation and done so well, only to fail now! Resolutely, she began to climb. She found a handhold, and then, miraculously, a foothold for her right foot. She dragged herself up and found another handhold. This time her left foot would have to support her, at least briefly. She leaned onto it and almost screamed as it collapsed. Rocks and pebbles skittered down the cliff. Shan pressed herself frantically against the wall and scratched and scrabbled for a hold, scraping her hands and knees. She succeeded in wedging her left foot and most of her left leg tightly into a crack. She clung there and panted, too terrified to shift even one

147

hand from its hold. Sweat ran down her face and stung the cuts on her arms and legs. Her arms began to ache again.

"Keep coming. You can do it." To her amazement, the Wolf above her seemed to want her to succeed. The unexpected encouragement gave Shan a spurt of energy, and again she tried to lean on her left foot, but she was repaid with a fierce jolt of pain. She knew suddenly and surely that she could not make it to the top. With only one good foot, the climb was impossible. She moaned softly, rather to her own surprise, and the Wolf above her said no word of criticism.

She found a slightly higher hold and inched her way toward it. Pain lanced through her as she freed her left ankle, and she felt her fingers slip. Suddenly and clearly she could see herself falling, smashed to death on the rocks below. She moaned again, desperately (and a hundred miles away on the eastern border Fletcher lifted his head and listened) and then again, letting all the fear and despair pour out of her. It seemed to help a little. Gritting her teeth, she forced herself to move, to slide the other hand up over the rock and continue to climb.

Gradually, strangely, she found that the climb became easier. It was as if someone else, someone much bigger and stronger, had added his strength to hers. She felt new energy rushing into her, and she was hardly surprised at all when her groping hands touched the top of the cliff. The climb had become like a dream. In the same dream, she felt a last gentle touch on her mind as the strong presence was withdrawn. Then the Wolf was pushing her away from the cliff edge, and she could sleep.

By night, most of the Cubs were able to walk, though Shan was not the only one limping. They were given a huge feast for supper, with four kinds of meat and five kinds of vegetables, as well as acorn bread, apple bread, and fruits in honey. They ate sitting on the ground, and afterwards some of the masters told them hero-stories of Wolves. Shan found herself sitting behind Burr and she was close enough to see the way his hair, freshly cut like hers, touched the back of his neck. She wished suddenly that she had time to get to know him. But all the Cubs knew they had run out of time. When the boys and girls were separated for sleeping, some of them clung together briefly, and the girl beside Shan gestured to a boy, exchanging last words until he was out of sight.

Chapter 9

The girls were organized for the journey to the Maze into a large pack, whose Alpha and Second were two of the female masters from the school. They would spend the next few days walking and the nights sleeping under the stars, or, when it rained, crowded into Perin houses. The boys left one day before the girls did.

Shan's ankle healed quickly, and she enjoyed most of the walk. Although she was terrified of what lay ahead at the Maze, she was able to forget about it during the journey. She wondered whether she would see Deakin again, once she was Wolf, and how being Wolf would change her feelings about him. She had been thinking of Deakin more often lately, and sometimes having dreams about him.

It was high summer and the girls walked through a green world, bursting with life. Trees and bushes had overflowed and spilled onto the road, and even in the cart-ruts there were weeds and flowers growing. At first they were near Redmetal Town, where they could see the great pits that were the rufer mines, scarring the hill-sides like raw red gashes. They passed men at work with their scythes in the hayfields, and, further on, women and children turning the hay that had been cut the day before. Beyond the fields there was forest, often unbroken for miles at a time, and then they would come to fields again, and more haymakers, and then a village or hamlet, a cluster of houses built around a stream. The road was the main north-south route across the land and was carefully maintained, even when there was nothing to see but forest for mile after mile. After two days, Shan noticed that the dirt underfoot was brown instead of red, and the rivers and streams no longer had the pinkish tinge she was used to. It made the land seem even more exciting.

Sometimes by the middle of the day the heat was intense, and sometimes, near streams or just before rain, the mosquitoes buzzed and bit inces-santly, but nothing could spoil Shan's enjoyment. She saw rabbits, squirrels, deer, and every kind of bird. On the fourth night out, to her lasting delight, all the Cubs got a look at a wolf, the first four-legged one Shan had ever seen. He was standing on a hilltop, sharply outlined against the setting sun. The song of his pack surrounded the Cubs that night, and they took it for a good omen.

The day after they saw the wolf, the presence of Cardy Plain began to make itself felt. They saw no Perin houses all that day, and the vegetation became less and less, interspersed with patches of dirt or bare rock. The trees looked stunted. Rivers were trickles rather than torrents. Even the insect life was less abundant.

Finally there was a small, clear stream which the Cubs were told was the last stream before the Cardith River itself. They spent the night beside it, almost untroubled by mosquitoes, and in the morning they filled their flasks and set out on the last stage of their journey.

Shan had wondered for some time how they were going to cross the Cardith, but it turned out to be a disappointment. This time of year it was not the raging flood that it was in the spring. The masters led the Cubs westward along the top of the bank for several hours, and for the first time they saw the Plain, stretching away from them on the far side of the river, a place of silence and desolation. There was no road here, but the vegetation was sparse and the walk was easy. When the masters stopped, the Cubs could see that there was an island in the middle of the Cardith.

"The first island," said one of the masters. "An easy swim."

This served to take the Cubs' attention away from the Cardith altogether, and some of them exchanged uneasy glances. They knew that the second island was called, in whispers, the Island of Pain. It was where their emotions would be stripped from them and they would become Wolves. Suddenly the pleasant part of the journey seemed to be over. They were too close, now, to enjoy themselves.

One by one they scrambled down the bank and plunged into the river. When Shan's turn came she did not dare to hesitate. The water was icy cold and snatched away her breath, but she had only to swim a few strokes before she was tossed up on the shore of the island. She stood shivering until all the Cubs and the masters had joined her, and then, after one more quick breathless plunge, she scrambled up the beach under the unchanging sky of Cardy Plain.

The journey across Cardy Plain took three days. The Cubs trudged along, hour after hour, with their eyes half-closed against the glare and their bodies sticky in the heat, with nothing to relieve the utter monotony of the journey. The distant mountains, which gave them their direction, never seemed to draw any closer. The Cubs sang continually as they walked, and the masters did not even object when they sang in Perin. Most often they sang an old marching song, with many verses and variations, of which the chorus was:

Cardy Plain, Cardy Plain,
I wasn't born to die
on Cardy Plain (Cardy Plain).
Cardy Plain, Cardy Plain,
I'll live to fight again on Cardy Plain.

In those three long days, Shan learned a new appreciation for simple things. She longed for darkness, or even bright sunlight, anything but endless twilight. She longed to hear birdsong, or cricket-song, or the whispering of leaves. Even a few mosquitoes would have been welcome. Things that she had always taken for granted had now become sweet and unattainable dreams. Shade, for instance. What would she give now for a single tree, for a single moment out of the glare of that horrible sky? Or rain. What would she give, what would any of them give, for fresh sweet drops of water?

They reached the Maze in the end, surviving the journey as hundreds of Cubs before them had survived it. Miserable and exhausted, dusty and bedraggled, they arrived at the entrance to the tunnel. Immediately nine Arkanan, robed and hooded, materialized around them.

As Shan had expected, even the one closest to her looked only like a dark blur, and beside it was another vaguer blur, a shadow that must be where the Arkan really stood. She suspected that the other Cubs saw them clearly, but saw them standing where they were not.

"Greetings, Wolves-to-be," said one of them, and performed the one piece of magic that would have impressed the Cubs at that moment. He gestured at the ground, and a fountain of water bubbled up at their feet.

The Cubs had finished the last of the warm water in their flasks hours before. They flung themselves at the fountain, jostling, pushing, all trying to drink at once and all getting very wet. Shan was the last to drink. She had never tasted anything more wonderful.

"Now," said another of the Arkanan, a woman by her voice. "Ye will follow me. Ye will not talk until we have reached the island."

The other Arkanan began to disappear, one by one this time. Shan thought it was rather like watching bubbles bursting. The girls were roped together by one of the masters, Shan between Ruby and Cress, but it did not seem that the masters were coming with them any further. In silence the girls entered the dark doorway of the Maze.

Shan found herself third, close to the torch the Arkan held. It burned with a steady, slightly greenish glow and did not consume the wood. It was the only light, so that the girls at the rear of the little procession must have been stumbling through darkness.

The Maze was wonderfully cool after the heat of the Plain. The floor was rough and uneven, and there were frequent twists and curves in the passage, as well as other passageways running off it at intervals. At first Shan tried to memorize the turns the Cubs made — first right, third left, and so on — but soon she saw something that made it unnecessary. The markings on the walls, which she had noticed from the first, were writing! Perin writing, which she, alone of all the Cubs, could understand.

She could not often make the writing out, for she had to be within arm's length of the letters to be able to read them, but she could read enough to know that the ancient Perin builders of this place had communicated the way to all Perinan who came after them. By every passageway the words were different, so that anyone not knowing Perin could not decipher them. "Not here," they said, or "Choose another," or "Nothing this way, friend." And then there was "Go this way," and "Take me," and "This tunnel leads to the centre." It was all as clear as daylight, to anyone who could read.

The walk was a long one. Sometimes the Cubs were walking uphill, sometimes down. Shan could not tell if they were walking in circles or on a roughly straight path, whether they were going further underground or remaining on the same level. She had lost all track of time. Surely by now it must be night? She stumbled once, and felt the rope tighten about her waist. Despite their exhaustion and the lack of light, the Cubs were more sure-footed than the Arkan, who often stumbled, and who walked with a noisy shuffle, sometimes muttering under her breath as well. The Cubs walked in habitual silence.

At last they reached a cavern, where the tunnel opened out and the torchlight could not illuminate the ceiling or the wide walls. The Arkan dropped the rope and walked forward alone. Her torch went out with a loud hiss, and now Shan could see more torchlight, far ahead. The first and second girls untied themselves. So did Shan. She walked forward, carefully, in the dark, and found water lapping against her bare feet. Three paces more and it was up to her waist. It was blood-warm, enfolding.

Shan swam slowly and easily because she had no idea how far she must swim. All around her there were girls in the water. She could hear them splashing, and see their heads vaguely whenever they got between her and the distant torchlight.

When her feet touched ground it was unexpected. She walked up onto the underground island, and Arkanan came forward, holding torches. She found that she was in the midst of the other girls, silent, dripping, on a little island of sand.

That was when the magic began. Arkanan, hoods thrown back now to reveal their incredibly, old, wizened — and, to Shan, blurred —

faces, seemed to be competing with each other to impress the Cubs. First one of them made a commanding gesture with one hand and the Cubs found themselves completely dry. Another raised a fire in the midst of them, a fire that blazed up blue and green as well as red and gold, turning the island into a place of wonder, an explosion of colours out of the dark. The Cubs, by the fire, could see each other's grimy faces clearly and the Arkanan, beyond them, vaguely, and then only darkness. Another Arkan gave them food, each Cub finding a full bowl of broth in front of her. Shan thought it must be magical broth, not real, for here were no gardens and no animals, but the broth was thick with vegetables and chunks of meat. "Bat-meat," someone whispered. "Dragon," someone else suggested, to Shan's scorn. She thought it tasted like rabbit.

While the Cubs ate, Arkanan twisted the flames into strange shapes for their amusement. A blue-flame tree grew up out of the fire and sprouted startling green blossoms, which then fluttered down as a rain of green sparks. Flame-birds spread their wings in the heart of the fire and some of them soared out into the darkness. Red flame-snakes wriggled and hissed across the sand to drop, sizzling, into the lake. The Cubs soon learned to avoid these creatures, for they burned, and Shan stopped enjoying the show after a spark landed painfully on her arm. It seemed to her that the Arkanan were deliberately sending their snakes and birds toward the Cubs, enjoying their discomfort. Once she was sure she heard one of them cackle with laughter.

Shan got as close to one of the Arkanan as she dared. She wanted to memorize his appearance so that she would be able to picture it at a distance, later. The height, the breadth, the blurry shape of the hooded robe. She moved her eyes back and forth in an effort to see as much as she could. The double image of the Arkan made her feel a little dizzy.

When everyone had eaten enough, the bowls disappeared into the air they had come out of. The fire went out, and again there was only torchlight.

"Ye must sleep now," said one of the Arkanan. "In the morning, ye will become Wolves."

"Morning" seemed a strange word to use, in that place that would always be in darkness. The Arkanan vanished with their torches, and the dark closed down upon the Cubs. Shan was glad to lie down on the sand and let her weariness overtake her. Some of the other Cubs talked for a time, but one by one they all drifted into sleep. It was warm on the island, and there was no sound all night but the gentle lapping of the waves.

Shan awoke with a sick feeling of dread. For a moment she could not remember where she was, but she remembered immediately that this was a day to be feared. The sand, which had felt so comfortable when she went to sleep, seemed to have become hard and a little colder during the night, and she stood up and began to do her readiness drill. All around her, in the dark, the other girls were doing the same. She could hear the slight sounds of their movements and breathing. There were no masters here to make sure they did it, but today, of all days, they wanted to feel ready. Shan found that her arms were a little stiff from swimming, and there was a hard knot of fear in her stomach.

Before she had finished the drill, she heard splashing. It sounded as if a group of swimmers were approaching the island. She heard them walk up onto the shore. One of the girls spoke, greatly daring since the Cubs had no idea whether they were permitted to speak here. She spoke in Arkan, not Perin, as if she were at school and feared one of the masters might overhear.

"I am Holly. Who are ye?"

Shan expected to hear one of the boys of her year reply, but instead a cold adult voice spoke out of the dark.

"Kneel in the centre of the island."

Shan hurried to obey, moving to where she thought the centre of the island was, surrounded by others doing the same. They crowded together, bumping each other. When they were packed as close together as they could get, they all dropped onto their left knees as they had been taught. No one tried to speak again. Shan was pressed between two other Cubs. She could tell they were boys because they were soaking wet from their swim.

Torches flared to life, and the Arkanan appeared in a circle around them. Now Shan could see the boys on either side of her, their hair plastered down, their clothes stuck to them.

One of the Arkanan said, "Ye kneel at the place between Cub and Wolf, between child and warrior. Ye will not stand on your feet again until ye are Wolves."

The Arkanan then withdrew to the water's edge, and began a muttering sort of chant. They were too far away for Shan to hear what they chanted. Then they began to walk, a slow measured pacing along the edge of the water while they continued to mutter. When they had paced all the way around the island, they drew a little closer to the Cubs.

Still chanting, they moved their hands in a series of gestures and, with a whoosh and a roar, a great red light surged up from the ground where they had paced out the circle. It formed a wall all the way from the sand up to the distant ceiling of the cavern. Shan could feel the heat of it, and she saw the boys' hair and clothing instantly begin to dry. The wall was dazzlingly bright, and it pulsed with red flashes of fury and constant flickers of lightning.

Another of the Arkanan spoke to the Cubs. "With this light, we remove anger! Anger is the enemy of the warrior. Ye will be pure of mind and strive only for the good of our great land."

Then the Arkanan moved away and began another chant, pacing a second circle within the red light of anger. This time Shan could hear some of the muttered words, which were about hunting and killing, the prey and the taker of prey.

Again they moved closer to the Cubs and together moved their hands. With a whoosh and a crackling sound, a blue light sprang into existence within the red light. This wall was cold, sparkling, shining. Shan could no longer see the red light. She could feel the chill of the blue wall.

Another Arkan, a woman, spoke to the Cubs. "With this light, we remove fear! Ye will be perfect warriors, never afraid. Ye will be pure of heart and strive only for the good of our great land."

Again the Arkanan began to circle around the Cubs. They were now close enough that even Shan could see that they were dropping something on the ground as they paced out the circle. She could hear the chant, as well, but it made little sense to her. One of the boys beside her shivered in the chill of the blue light.

This time when the Arkanan moved their hands, a wall of green light sprang up within the wall of fear. It was glowing, pulsing steadily, with flickers and flashes deep in the heart of it. Shan felt neither heat nor cold this time, but a pleasant warmth.

One of the Arkanan said, "With this light, we remove lust! No more need of man for woman, no more need of woman for man, no more desire, no more distraction. Ye will be pure of purpose and strive only for the good of our great land."

The Arkanan faced the Cubs.

"Ye will crawl to the shore. As ye pass through each wall, ye will lose the emotions ye will no longer require. When ye stand again, ye will be Wolves!

"Let the purification begin."

The Arkanan disappeared.

Shan began to crawl, as the others did, toward the green wall. She picked a spot where she could escape from the boys and be almost alone. She realized that she was not as frightened as she had expected. These walls were going to remove lust, then fear, then anger. She was relieved that the Arkanan had not said anything about love, nor anything about removing memories.

Besides, she was certain that Deakin had felt anger. She had seen other Wolves get angry as well. What if, she wondered for the first time, what if this is only a ceremony and not real? What if nothing is going to happen to me at all?

She crawled closer and closer to that pulsing green wall, vaguely aware of Cubs on either side of her doing the same. The green warmth reached out to her, both welcoming and menacing. She thought it must be power that she felt, compelling her, drawing her in.

Hesitating on the edge of the wall, she put a finger and then a hand forward into the green.

It disappeared into the light, but she felt nothing but warmth. Almost unafraid, she took a deep breath, lowered her head, and crawled forward.

Her head shattered. The pain that greeted her was so great that she screamed aloud, all thought of being Cub forgotten. She doubled over, clutching at her head, trying to put it back where it belonged. She vomited into the sand. She lost the world and wandered into dark dreams, unaware. Arkanan and nameless monsters stalked through her dreams, pursuing her, so that she whimpered and cried and struggled to awaken.

She was a little child; she was an adult Wolf; she was murdering Briar's grandmother; she was murdering Briar; Deakin was attacking her with a sword . . . There was a blood-film over everything she dreamed. Then another Wolf walked into her dream. She recognized him as the Wolf who had chosen her for Cub, long ago. He was tall and thin and seemed unhappy, and when he came the blood receded a little. He said, "Move, Shan. Get away from here."

She woke up and crawled forward for a moment, but the pain seized her hard and shook her and she fell into dreams again. The second time the Wolf came, she ran to him and buried her face in his shirt, and he held her.

"Wizard, aren't you?" she asked him.

"Yes," he said, and again, "Move, Shan. Crawl. Get away from here."

She tried to crawl while he was still there, and this time she must have broken out of the green light, for she found herself awake, weak and sick but infinitely better. She lay for a while with her nose and mouth and hair full of sand, aware of other Cubs still moaning and thrashing in the light. She was one of the first through, but one by one the others crawled out of it as well. The warm green light was behind, the cold blue light ahead. It was a long time before Shan sat up and wiped sand out of her face.

All of them were terrified to go on. Losing lust had been the most painful thing any of them had ever felt. Shan thought it might be several hours before anyone touched that blue light, but one of the boys suddenly let out a defiant yell and scrambled straight into it. Others did the same. Realizing there was no escape, Shan screamed, letting out all her terror, and crawled forward as well, head down, eyes screwed shut. At least, after this, she would never feel terror again.

But this time there was no pain. She felt the cold radiance of the wall engulf her, and she could see, when she opened her eyes, nothing but blue. Then she had crawled through and could see the red wall ahead.

Shan wondered why removing fear was painless, if removing lust hurt so much. She was no longer afraid, so presumably it had worked. She crawled into the hot red light without even putting a hand through first.

Again, there was no pain, only a furious blast of heat. Shan also thought she was beginning to feel angry. What were Arkanan playing at? Why had they hurt the Cubs like that? Why was she still angry if this wall was supposed to take her anger away?

She crawled out on the other side, hot, weak, and still a little sick from the green wall. She crawled forward to the water's edge and drank. Around her she could hear other Cubs doing the same, struggling to the water's edge for a drink. When the last Cub emerged from the red wall, all the light disappeared.

Chapter 10

Arkanan did not return for several hours, and the Cubs were left in darkness. Shaken by their ordeal, and unable to communicate with handsignals, they talked more than Shan had ever heard them talk before, reliving the experience and trying to understand it.

"All here, are we?" was the first question. "All alive?"

Someone called the roll, with occasional help from friends in remembering names, and it seemed that everyone was alive. Some were sicker than others, some still barely able to move, but all were there and all conscious. Friends began to seek friends, calling to each other, groping to find each other's hands. Shan sat where she was and felt the others moving around her, often stumbling into her, and asking their soft questions of each other — "Where are you?"

"All right, are you?" "Larian?" "Mint?" — until everyone was found and there was stillness again.

"Was terrible, that," someone said. "Never felt anything like that . . . "

"Dreamed I was drowning."

"Dreamed I was being murdered. Dreamed about you, Mint. Dreamed you were killing me."

"Such dreams, I had. So dark. So much blood."

"And me . . . "

"And me . . . "

For a long time they talked of their dreams, until finally, hesitantly, they began to talk of what it all meant.

"Wolves now, aren't we?"

"Don't feel any different, do you? Only weaker."

"Sicker."

"Didn't hurt, after the green wall, did it?" said one of the girls, hesitantly, and a chorus of voices agreed. It seemed no one had been hurt by the other two walls.

After a time, small groups of friends moved apart to speak more privately. Shan stayed where she was but could hear two of the conversations.

"Never wanted children anyway, did I?" said one girl to another.

"Nor did I."

"Course we didn't. Wolves, aren't we?"

"No choice now, is there?"

A girl was saying to a boy, "Still feel the same about me, do you?"

He said, "All different now, isn't it? Has to be."

"Still try to be together, won't we?"

"Course we will. But . . . you know . . . can't be the same . . . "

Both pairs of friends spoke mostly about the removal of desire and Shan was sure that they, like her, were doubtful that the other two walls had worked. They were not going to say so here, so close to Arkanan.

"Seemed as if that Arkan enjoyed watching, didn't it?" the boy said once.

"Yes. Smiled, didn't he?" said the girl.

"Hate the way they smile, I do."

"Shh. Hear you, they will. How do we know they aren't here right now?"

Shan felt a shiver of fear at the thought, and was quite certain she could still be afraid.

The Cubs spent the rest of that day and the night on the island. Once the Arkanan appeared unexpectedly in their midst, causing Cubs to scatter, but the Arkanan had come only to bring food. They left a fire burning for a few hours.

With nothing else to do, and their ordeal behind them, the Cubs spent most of the rest of the time on the island sleeping.

Eventually they were told to swim back across the lake and follow one of the Arkanan out of the Maze. The journey seemed quicker this time, though Shan was too far away from the torch to see any of the writing on the walls. She knew when they neared the entrance, because she could see the bright daylight of Cardy Plain ahead.

The Arkan said, "Go out of the Maze and wait. Kron comes to speak to ye."

The Cubs emerged blinking into the glare of day. The Plain was unexpectedly crowded near the entrance to the Maze. Wolves had been arriving for hours and were sitting in small scattered groups, some of them eating or drinking. Shan saw some, as she passed close to them, with their boots off and their shirt-sleeves rolled up. She knew these must all be Alphas and Seconds, who had made the long journey across Cardy Plain to get their year-orders and also, in some cases, to get new members for their packs. New Alphas also received from the Arkanan some kind of magical touch that enabled Arkanan to contact them over long distances. Shan had never before seen Wolves look anything but totally confident and self-assured, but here she saw them restless and uneasy, eager to be gone.

One of the Arkanan appeared as soon as all the Cubs were outside. "We will begin," he said.

As the Wolves scrambled to their feet, the other Arkanan appeared one by one, spread out in a half-circle behind Kron. The one who had led the Cubs through the Maze emerged to join the others. The Cubs already knew what they had to do. They got to their feet and formed a line, side by side, facing the Arkanan. Together they walked forward, and together they dropped to one knee on the dusty ground, hands behind their backs, eyes down, chests symbolically open to the knife. The Wolves closed in and stood behind them.

Kron spoke to the Wolves, over the Cubs' heads.

"Greetings all, and welcome. I will give to ye pack by pack your year-orders . . . "

Shan heard little of what was said. From under her eyelashes she watched the Arkan as his dry, cracked voice droned on. Instead of letting her eyes fall out of focus to see what she could make him look like, as she once would have done, she did the exact opposite, picturing the shape that she knew he was, concentrating with all her senses, flicking her eyes back and forth to take in everything she could. She concentrated on the shadow, where she knew he was really standing. She was pleased to find that she felt no awe of the Arkan. She feared him, certainly, but beyond that she felt only revulsion and disgust.

Will destroy the Firedrake someday, she said to herself. Will never willingly serve Arkanan. Will never be a true Wolf. Will never kill Perinan. Will never forget Briar.

When Kron had finished with the year-orders, the Wolves' commander, Redthorn, left the line of Wolves and came to stand beside him. There was a slight lessening of tension among the Cubs. They were pleased to see a familiar face. Redthorn welcomed both the Wolves and the Cubs, and then began the task of assigning each Cub to a pack. At first Shan thought he was doing this at random. He would stop in front of each Cub and stand still for a moment, and then the Alpha and Second of one of the packs would join him there and Redthorn would move on to the next Cub. After a time, as Redthorn came closer, Shan realized, with a shock, that the assignments were not random at all. The commander was deciding on a pack for each Cub and then communicating his wishes, silently, to the Wolves. Or were Arkanan the ones who were communicating Redthorn's wishes? Certainly Arkanan were watching him intently.

Shan, who had liked Redthorn, began to change her mind about him. Was he a wizard? If so, he was obviously working with Arkanan instead of using his power to help the Wolves and the Perinan. Or had Arkanan just given him some kind of limited power because he was commander? Either way, she decided she no longer liked him or trusted him, and when he reached her she stared fixedly at his boots and did not even try to glance at his face.

When Shan's Alpha and Second came to stand in front of her, though, she could not resist looking up at them surreptitiously. Her Second was tall and thin with straight dark hair, a thin face with sharp angles, a dark shadow of stubble on his chin. He looked familiar, but she could not think where she had seen him before. Her Alpha, identified as Alpha by the sheathed knife on his right hip, was shorter than his Second and looked younger, and his hair was blond. It took her only a second to recognize him. When she did, the world seemed to fall away from beneath her. The muscles of her face were too well-trained to move, but she felt her fingers twitch.

Then it was her turn to speak, and she dropped her gaze to the familiar tattoo on the back of his hand, and said, formally, in Arkan, "I am Shan. I ask permission to join your pack."

She wondered if Deakin had recognized her, but he gave no sign of it. He drew his knife, as required by the ritual, and touched the point to her chest. It was an ordinary rufer knife, she saw with disappointment, not the beautiful stone one that "Fletch" had made.

Now he had freed her from her submissive posture and she was officially an adult. But there was something wrong. The knife was not withdrawn. It remained against her chest, making her breathing quick and shallow. Shan looked up under her eyelashes and this time Deakin caught the look. He was watching her, his eyes calm and steady. She could not read his face.

Shan sucked her breath in silently as the knife-point broke the skin. Blood trickled down her brown shirt. The Arkanan crowded closer, watching eagerly. One of them gave a thin dry chuckle of laughter. Shan could hear their harsh, excited breathing all around her.

Going to kill me! she thought, and another glance at Deakin's steady gaze confirmed it. Meet again after all my dreams, Deakin and I, and he kills me, never knowing. Will never see the blue sky again, never see the forest . . . She was not frightened, but she was filled with sadness.

"Deakin," said his Second, quietly.

Deakin flicked a glance at him and then withdrew the knife.

"Granted," he said to Shan, completing the ritual.

She stood up an adult.

The ritual moved on to the next initiate.

"Deakin, I am. This is Fletcher," said Deakin, softly, in Perin.

"Crazy, are you?" said Fletcher. "What were you trying to do?"

"Give them what they wanted. Saw how they all enjoyed it, didn't you?" Deakin was almost smiling, that familiar little quirk at the corner of his mouth. Shan wanted to laugh for joy, seeing his smile.

"Hurt you much, did he?" Fletcher asked her.

"No."

"Take your shirt off."

"Here? Now?"

"Yes. Want to bleed to death, do you? Get another shirt, you will."

Shan took off her shirt obediently, and Fletcher tore it and used it to make a bandage for the wound. Shan looked over his head at Deakin in silent exultation. She was Deakin's now. And hers the only contract that had been sealed in blood.

When at last every Cub had been formally accepted into a pack, Kron made another speech.

"Ye are all now Kunan Keir," he said. "Ye are responsible for the trade in rufer and for the well-being of the Perinan, the common people. Ye are responsible for the defense of our beloved land. Long ago, the first of the Kunan Keir swore an oath, and the oath was . . . "

He paused dramatically.

" . . . I shall attack never anyone who is armed or stronger than I am," Deakin finished for him, under his breath.

He said it to Fletcher, but Shan heard and looked at him, startled. To her amazement, he flashed her the Cub hand sign for laughter.

"The oath was — we shall serve the Arkanan, who have driven back from beyond our borders the invaders," Kron went on. "We shall be no more slaves to the people of Aram or Iluthia.

Keep the oath, Wolves of Redmetal! Our land is in a sea of primitive ignorance a small island of civilization. We protect by our magic and by your bright swords together our land. The future and continued prosperity of Redmetal lies in your hands. Repeat for us, now, your oath of allegiance."

As always, Shan was repelled by his voice, by the open and poisonous emotion in it. She had no intention of pledging her allegiance to these creatures. Mouthing the words, she suddenly realized that Deakin, beside her, was not chanting either. He was not even pretending to chant. Her feelings were a confused mixture of pride and fear for him, so that she drew a long breath of relief when the oath was finished.

"Now," said Kron, "the newest members of the Kunan Keir must be made ready."

A gesture from the assembled Arkanan, and Shan found herself dressed as an adult. She looked around and could no longer distinguish her classmates from the other Wolves. She was awed by the magic. Here on their Plain, there seemed to be nothing Arkanan could not do.

"We shall see again next year here many of ye." Was it Shan's imagination, or did Kron's voice sound weaker, as if the magic had tired him? "Until then, may the turn of the Wheel bring to ye good fortune."

He and the other Arkanan vanished. Instantly Shan and her classmates were dressed as they had been before, but each of them found, in front of him or her, a pile of clothes and a sword.

The Wolves at once began to gather their possessions and drift away from the Maze, moving in a large ragged group. They did not want to stay in that place any longer than necessary.

Shan picked up her new possessions but had no time to examine them, as Deakin and Fletcher were already walking away and she was afraid of losing them in the crowd. She hurried after them. Now that the excitement of the ceremony was over, she was trembling all over and the wound in her chest was beginning to hurt fiercely. She was relieved when Deakin and Fletcher stopped to talk to some friends, giving her a chance to rest and then to get dressed in her new clothes. After that, while she walked, she looked down at herself with delight.

Her uniform was black, with long sleeves now instead of short, and she had boots of soft brown deerskin, which would protect her legs and feet from scratches although not from sharp stones underfoot. There was a leather belt around her waist, with a strap over the right shoulder to take the weight of the sword, which hung in its leather scabbard at her side. She also had a heavy black cloak, which she soon took off and carried. She drew her sword, and could see by the bright glints of red around her that most of her classmates were doing the same thing.

"Same thing every year, isn't it?" she heard Deakin, just ahead of her, saying to one of his friends.

Apparently his friend agreed. "Think I could recite that Arkan speech myself by now," he said.

"Good idea," said Deakin. "Why don't I?" He raised his voice. "Listen to me, Dogs of the Pack!" he shouted in Arkan, and those around him turned to him curiously, ready to be entertained.

"Your land is in a sea of red mud a small island of primitive ignorance. We prevent by our magic and by your bright swords the prosperity of our land. The continued destruction of Redmetal lies in your hands. No, not hands, paws. Repeat for me, now, your oath of allegiance."

To Shan's amazement, someone gave a wolf howl and many others joined in. The howl spread until almost the entire group were howling, releasing the pent-up tension of the day.

Shan, joining in, could hardly believe that she had once thought Wolves unemotional.

Then there was a slight sound from all around her, a concerted intake of breath as the howl died, and a sudden cessation of movement. Shan could not see what the others had seen, but there was a dark blur in the air above them, and a dark shadow with it. She realized that the Arkan was somehow standing in the air. A moment later she heard his voice, tight with fury.

"Will ye mock us on our own Plain? Do ye not know we could here, now, destroy all of ye if we chose?"

There was no response from the Wolves except a slight drawing-together. Their faces were impassive.

Kron's voice came as a low hiss.

"Submit, Wolves!"

They remained motionless. Shan saw the dark shadow move, and sparks flashed around it.

"Submit! On your knees, all of ye!"

This time they knew what he wanted, and for some of them, the Alphas, it was a humiliating thing to ask. One by one, beginning with the Wolves nearest to Kron, slowly, reluctantly, the whole company dropped to one knee and assumed the submissive posture. The faces of most of the Wolves were calm still, but here and there eyes flashed dangerously.

"Now!" said Kron, between his teeth, his voice shaking with fury. "Ye will remain where ye are. Ye will not move. Ye will not speak. Ye will not raise your heads. The first Wolf who moves, dies. Do ye understand?"

They understood. Kron vanished, but no one else moved. Shan felt sick. Her chest hurt savagely with every breath she took, and she could feel herself beginning to sweat. She was sure that she would not be able to remain motionless for many minutes. Desperately searching for distraction, she moved her eyes and was able to watch Fletcher, Deakin's Second, who was kneeling beside her. His face was quiet. He saw her look at him and whispered to her, very low, "Be all right, you will. Hang on."

She recognized him then, not with any shock or surprise but only with a sense of completion. It was as if she had always known him.

"You," she whispered. "Dreamed of you, I did."

"Shh," he breathed. "Not here."

Shan had already been overwhelmed by joy once that day, at her reunion with Deakin. Now a new joy was thrust upon her. It no longer seemed difficult to kneel in the twilight of the

Plain. Fletcher has magic, she said to herself. I have Deakin. We are together. We are the Three. Deakin and Fletcher and Shan, she murmured to herself, feeling the rightness of it, the inevitability. Deakin and Fletcher and Shan.

Suddenly the twilight was split by a horrible screaming. One of the Wolves had moved.

Chapter 11

"The Three have met!"

Varian jumped to her feet in horror, scattering the ashes of her fire. The other Arkanan simply looked at her wearily. They were all sitting or lying in the torchlit cool of the Maze, resting after their exertions.

"Do ye understand nothing that I have said to ye?" Varian demanded. "The ashes tell me that the Three have met. The Three who may destroy the Firedrake!"

Kron appeared in the middle of the chamber. He was trembling violently, partly with exhaustion and partly with rage, for he had just come from his encounter with the Wolves. Varian seized his arm and he pushed her roughly away from him.

"What ails thee, woman?"

"They have met." Varian was still almost shouting. "The blind woman, the madman, and the wizard. They are together now. Probably they plot already our destruction."

Kron cursed her. He slumped down to sit on the cool floor.

"So they have met at our ritual and on our Plain. Thou shouldst have foreseen this."

"At our ritual? Thinkst thou . . . ?" It was a new idea to Varian. "But then they are yet on the Plain. We can destroy them."

"How?" Kron demanded. "We have no way to discover them."

His anger and frustration began to rouse the other Arkanan.

"Yes," one of the others said. "It is clear that the woman is not literally blind."

Kron snarled at him. "So? How dost thou suggest then we find her?"

"I shall find a solution," said Varian. "Soon we shall require no longer the Firedrake. Although the sacrifice of the children failed, it has shown me a way to proceed."

"We could destroy all of them," Hinton suggested. "We know they are here on the Plain."

Kron gave him a long, disgusted look.

"Destroy all of them? Leave all the packs without leaders? Kill an entire year of young Wolves? Thou art a fool. Have I not told thee repeatedly that the Kunan Keir are dangerous? They are many and we are very few. They should hate us not too much. No. The easiest way to find the Three now is to find the wizard."

"Yes! When he uses his magic . . . "

"And eventually he will use it . . . "

"We shall be ready," said Kron. "We shall make of this threat an end. From now on, at all times, one of us will be on guard for any use of magic in the land. The next time this renegade wizard uses his powers," he slapped his palm against the stone wall, "we shall have him."

∞∞∞

Shan was weaker than she had been on the outward journey, and the first full day spent on the Plain seemed endless. Her chest burned with every breath she took, her head ached from the glare of the sun, and her new boots were too big for her and made walking awkward and uncomfortable. She struggled to keep up with Deakin and Fletcher, and to hide her discomfort, and, to her relief, Deakin did not seem to notice anything wrong. He did not question her ability to walk, hour after hour, with the other Wolves. The sweetness of this acceptance was so wonderful, and so rare to Shan, that she was determined to hold onto it as long as possible.

Of course Deakin would find out sooner or later, and probably sooner, how incompetent she was — what was it he had said? "Be a danger to your pack, you would" — and she hated to think of his reaction when he discovered that she had sworn not to kill Perinan. She desperately wanted to live up to Deakin's expectations.

The other Wolves were understandably not so pleased with Deakin, who had been responsible for the death of one of their own the evening before. They refused to talk to him, and Deakin, Fletcher, and Shan found themselves walking alone, near the other Wolves but not among them. Despite this, Deakin himself was in high spirits.

"Want me to apologize?" he asked them at one point. "Put my head in the dust? Hurl myself from the nearest cliff? Offer myself as the main course for dinner? Like that, wouldn't you? Real meat for dinner."

His energy seemed boundless. While Shan and Fletcher trudged along doggedly, hour after hour, heads down and eyes half-shut against the glare, Deakin walked beside them talking of inconsequential things, often dropping behind or hurrying ahead to try to talk to other Wolves and then rejoining his two companions. He put himself in charge of redistributing the clothes of the new Wolves, particularly boots, so that they fit. Shan gladly took off her boots and gave them to Deakin, who presently returned with another pair.

"Don't understand," she said to him. "If Arkanan can make clothes by magic, why don't they all fit perfectly?"

Deakin gave her a long look and she sensed his amusement.

"Think they're magic clothes, do you? Clothes that have never seen needle and thread? Created out of wind and smoke, perhaps, by the will and power of the mighty Arkanan? Called into existence in a flash of summer lightning?"

Shan had to admit that sounded unlikely.

"Aren't they?"

"Course not. Wouldn't want clothes that disappeared when the sun went down, would you? Or that gradually unravelled and drifted away on the wind? First time Arkanan dressed you, when it seemed as if you were all dressed as Wolves, was just illusion. But these clothes you're wearing now were made by Perinan and brought to the Plain by us. For Arkanan to give to you, magically, when the time was right. But what are you waiting for, Shan-Cub? See if these boots fit you any better than the last pair."

Shan dutifully sat down on the ground and pulled on the boots, although the few minutes she had spent barefoot had been the easiest minutes of the day.

"Much better," she said.

"Good. Hard at first, wearing boots, isn't it? Carry them, if you like. Don't mind, do we, Fletch?"

"Suppose I'll have to get used to them," said Shan.

But a few hours later she took the boots off again and carried them. Her head throbbed, the wound in her chest burned like fire, and it was taking all her energy just to keep walking. Fletcher suggested that they stop for the night, and Shan suspected that he had noticed her pain in spite of her efforts to hide it.

"Why?" said Deakin. "Makes no difference where we stop, does it?"

This was true; the whole Plain was so barren and featureless that one place was no better or worse than any other. But other Wolves were also tired. Groups began to settle for the night, taking off their knapsacks and sitting down for a meagre supper.

Shan sat down beside Fletcher, with relief, and had a few more swallows of the water in her flask. She also forced herself to eat a piece of the hard biscuit which was all that was left of her food.

"Got some cheese left, I think," said Deakin. He felt about in his knapsack and produced a chunk of soggy cheese, which he generously broke into three pieces.

"Could use Arkan help now," Shan heard a Wolf saying, nearby. "Could have given us something to eat beside biscuit."

"Arkan stew," said Deakin, softly, as he squatted down beside Shan.

"Roasted Arkan," said Shan, delighted.

"Arkan chops."

"A little tough, wouldn't it be?"

"Probably make us all sick."

The comment about Arkanan had given Shan an idea, and she whispered to Fletcher, "Could make food, couldn't you? By magic?"

She thought she had whispered it very softly, but Deakin heard.

"How does she know?" he demanded, as if Shan were not there.

"Helped her a few days ago, I did," said Fletcher.

"She's the one who . . . ?"

"Yes."

Deakin was apparently satisfied, for he said to Shan, "Can't make real food by magic, Shan-Cub. Might look good, might even taste good, but wouldn't keep you from being hungry. Wouldn't keep you from starving to death."

Shan had finished her piece of cheese, and now she took off her swordbelt and lay down on her new black cloak.

"Anyway, can't do magic here," said Fletcher. "Too near Arkanan. Know it's forbidden, don't you?"

"Yes," said Shan. "What would they . . . ?"

"Who knows?" said Deakin. "Let's not find out."

"Wish you could teach me," said Shan to Fletcher, sleepily.

"Magic?" It was Deakin who answered. "Can't be taught. Either born wizard or you're not. Too late for you, child."

He said more, but Shan must have slept for a few minutes. She awoke to hear Fletcher saying, "Think she's asleep."

Deakin asked, "You asleep already there, Cub?"

"Not Cub anymore," Shan objected, and slept again.

She felt as close to Deakin and Fletcher as if she had known them all her life. She wondered whether the other two felt the same way, and whether they knew about the prophecy, but she found herself reluctant to ask. She thought that Deakin would have one of two possible reactions to hearing the prophecy. Either he would be furious at the reference to himself as a madman, or he would demand that the three of them go back to the Maze immediately and take on the Firedrake. She did not feel at all ready for that.

The next day, deciding to approach the subject gradually, she asked Fletcher about magic while they walked.

"Always thought you could make anything by magic. Now Deakin says you can't make food or clothes. Why not?"

"Cause it's all illusion." Deakin answered the question for Fletcher. "Illusions of anything the wizard chooses, that look real and feel real, but aren't really there and don't last very long."

"Can't you make anything real then? Arkanan make real things, don't they? What about the

Firedrake? That's real, isn't it? What about the fire-snakes I saw in the Maze?"

"Fire's different," said Deakin. "Easy to construct things with fire, for a wizard. And the Firedrake is a construct, too, a made thing. Probably took months to create. Suppose it would be possible for a wizard to construct real food or real clothes, but wouldn't be worth the time and the effort it would take."

"Can you make illusions?" said Shan to Fletcher. "Can you make one to show me? Not here, of course, but — "

"Fletch doesn't do magic for your amusement, Cub," said Deakin, and Shan felt ashamed, but Fletcher said, "See some of my magic someday, you will."

"Does Redthorn have magic, too?" Shan asked. She remembered the commander's strange ability to talk silently to the Wolves. "Is he wizard, too? Why do Arkanan let him do magic, and no one else?"

"Redthorn isn't wizard," said Deakin. "Arkanan have given him some power, so that he can talk to Alphas over long distances, just as they can."

"Can you do that, too?" Shan asked Fletcher.

"Course he can't," Deakin said.

"Redthorn's thoughts are not his own," Fletcher explained, quietly. "Can talk silently to other Wolves, but is also talking silently to Arkanan, and can't do anything about that. Arkanan know everything he knows."

"But you read thoughts," said Shan. "Came to me in dreams. Knew when I needed help, didn't you?"

"Not thoughts. Feelings. When someone is near me, I feel what they feel."

Shan thought about this for some time.

"But wasn't near you, was I? Not at initiation. How did you know? How did you help me?"

Fletcher shrugged.

"Don't know. Some kind of link among the three of us. Can't tell you more than that. Always know when Deakin's in trouble, too, however far away."

Again Shan tasted the sweetness of acceptance, and was silent for a moment to savour it before continuing her questions.

"Were you always wizard?" she asked. "Did you always know?"

Fletcher nodded, and Deakin said, "Used to light fires for his parents before he was ever Cub, didn't you, Fletch? And tell them when it was going to rain. And knew that he was going to be chosen for Kunan Keir. Pretended to be lame, so Wolves wouldn't take him, and might have fooled them, too, but that his sister said, "What's wrong with your leg, Fletch? Hurt it, have you?" So then they knew, you see, and they took Fletch, and his sister as well, though she was only five, and left his parents without children."

"Had a sister as well, I did," said Shan. "Just a baby when I was taken, hadn't been named yet. Talking about the name, we were, trying to decide what she should be called once she could walk. What was she called, your sister?"

"Cloud."

"Where is she now then?"

"Dead," said Fletcher, briefly and calmly.

"Had stronger magic than Fletch did, and less sense," said Deakin. "Was only a small child, after all. Started to make illusions to impress the rest of us at the school. Coloured fish in the stream, rainbows on clear sunny days, things like that. Fletch tried to stop her, didn't you, Fletch? But by the time he realized what she was playing at, it was already too late. Arkanan had heard about it. Came for her. Took her away and killed her."

Shan looked at Fletcher.

"Don't you hate them for that?"

"Hate? No. But should be stopped. Will be stopped, one day."

He said this so definitely that Shan was startled. "You mean you'll stop them?" And when Fletcher only looked at her, she added, excitedly, "No, not just you. You mean us, don't you? Us three."

"Know about that, do you?"

Shan took a deep breath and plunged in. "A blind woman, a madman, and a wizard. Will come together, and will have among them the means of destroying the Firedrake."

Deakin, unpredictable as ever, treated the prophecy with a reaction Shan had not expected: amused indifference.

"Sound like Fletch, you do," he said. "Always talking about how we have a great destiny ahead of us."

"But . . . we do. Have to try to destroy the Firedrake."

"Yes," said Fletcher. "And has to be soon, before Arkanan find some other means of surviving."

"Listen to yourselves! Isn't me who's the madman here, is it? Going to get yourself killed with these silly ideas. Can't fight Arkanan, you know that. Can't kill them."

"*Can* kill them," Shan insisted. "Hard to see, they are, but not for me. Can see where they really are."

"Going to do you a lot of good, that, isn't it? Want to turn around and go back to the Maze then, to destroy the Firedrake? How close do you think you'd get? How many steps — steps, not miles — do you think you'd be allowed to take before Arkanan came to see what you wanted, if you turned around and started back, now, uninvited?"

Shan was silent.

"Have to leave these pretty fantasies behind now you're Wolf, won't you?" said Deakin. "Will be serving Arkanan till the day you die, so might as well get used to it."

"But you hate them too."

"Makes no difference how we feel about them. Still have to listen when they call us, don't we? Still have to obey orders, don't we? What's the good of talking about it?"

He left them abruptly, running as if he would overtake the leaders of that long ragged column of Wolves. He never seemed to be able to maintain a steady pace for long. Shan realized miserably that she still had not told him that she had sworn not to kill Perinan.

"Made him angry, didn't I?" she said.

Fletcher shrugged. "Can't go back to the Maze now, he's right about that. Can't fight Arkanan on their own Plain. Know a hundred Wolves would gladly join us if we could."

"But we'll find a way. You and I and Deakin."

It was not a question and Fletcher did not answer it. Shan walked quietly for a time, and finally asked, "Where's Deakin gone?"

Fletcher pointed. "Not far. Can't you see him?"

"Can't see very well," said Shan. "Don't have good eyes."

She did not mind Fletcher knowing how little she could see, though normally it was her most closely-guarded secret. A moment later she realized that, if he had known the prophecy, he must have known already.

"Chose me for Cub, didn't you, years gone?" She was thinking it out.

"Yes. Wasn't sure it was the right thing to do, but wanted to be able to keep track of you, keep an eye on your training."

"Sent Deakin to help me learn to fight, too, didn't you?"

"Suggested it, yes."

"Hasn't recognized me yet, though, has he?"

"Does it matter?"

Shan thought about it.

"Used to call me Bright Eyes," she said.

"And you want him to call you that again."

Shan decided that it was not really important. She found it peaceful and calming to talk to Fletcher, and was feeling very content. Not since losing Briar had she had anyone to talk to this way. She was sure that she could tell Fletcher anything, and that he would never use any of her words against her.

"Swore to love him forever, I did," she confided, softly.

"Did you?"

"Thought . . . thought they would take that from me, when I became Wolf. Thought they would took away all feelings, all love . . . Doesn't really happen that way, does it?"

"Not love," said Fletcher. "Can't take that away. Only desire. Only need."

"Still need Deakin," said Shan, fiercely.

"Don't talk about it. Understand? Safe enough with me, you are, but other Wolves won't like it. Even Deakin. Might hurt you if you mention it. Anything about what we lost."

Shan was grateful for the warning, as well as for Fletcher's assurance of safety.

"Didn't work, the other spells, though, did they?" she asked, hesitantly. "Didn't take anger away, did they? Didn't take fear away."

"Think they must have worked, once," said Fletcher. "But shouldn't talk about that, not here. Not close to Arkanan."

They walked in companionable silence for a time. Shan could hear Deakin talking to someone over on her left. The Wolves seemed to be more willing to talk to him today, though they were still not being friendly. There was another question that Shan wanted to ask Fletcher, but it was difficult to find the right words.

"Said you feel what people close to you are feeling?" she began, hesitantly.

"Yes." Fletcher did not seem to mind talking about it.

"What did you feel from me, when I was in the Maze? Pain?"

"Not really. Pain isn't that sort of feeling. Fear, mostly. Confusion."

"Like feeling it yourself?"

"More or less."

"Well, how can you . . . be Wolf then? How can you hurt anyone?"

She kept her eyes down as she spoke. If Fletcher's quiet face changed, she did not want to see it. His voice, at any rate, did not change at all. He said, "Isn't easy, being Wolf. For anyone."

When Shan looked up again, Deakin was there.

"Still asking questions, Cub?"

Shan ignored the warning in his eyes. She must trust these two if she were ever going to trust anyone. She would tell them the whole truth, about the oath she had sworn to Briar, and get it over with once and for all.

"Don't think I could ever kill anyone," she began.

"You will," Deakin said, before she could go on. "Don't worry about it, Cub. When the time comes and you have to, you'll do it. Won't have time to think. Training will take over."

"No. Don't think I could even hurt anyone. Not on purpose."

"Talk as if we do it for fun, don't you? What kind of stories have you been hearing at school, Cub? Think we hold contests to see who can kill the most Perinan in a week? Think we practise our knife-throwing on the miners and sharpen our swords on Perin children? Is that what you think?"

"No . . ."

"Isn't like that. Don't have to kill very often, and when we do it's for a reason. You'll see."

"Had . . . had a Perin friend, I did," Shan managed to say at last. "Arkanan killed her. Swore an oath that I would never kill Perinan."

They both stared at her.

"Have to break it now, won't you?" said Deakin. "Wolf, you are now."

"A Perin friend?" said Fletcher. "How?"

"Climbed the wall, I did." Shan spoke softly, not wanting to be overheard. "Every day for a whole year. Met a Perin girl, a little older than me. Used to meet her every day. My first friend, she was. My only friend." She desperately wanted them to understand. "Just like me, she was. No different. Then Arkanan came and took her brother away. Archer. Only a little boy. Tried to rescue him, she did. That was how I . . . I found out. About the prophecy. Could see things others couldn't. Could see that Arkanan aren't where they appear to be. "Swore afterward that I would never kill Perinan."

"Can't keep your oath now," said Deakin, flatly. "Doesn't matter what you were before. You're Wolf now, and you'll do as you're told. Gets easier after a while. Remember the Perin Rebellion, do you?"

Shan shook her head. "Was chosen for Cub that year."

"By the Wheel. Am I as old as all that, then?"

Deakin fell silent. Shan said, hesitantly, "Fought in the Rebellion, did you?"

"Yes. Just out of school, I was then. Just the age you are now. Think I wanted to kill Perinan? Think Fletch wanted to? Had no choice, did we? Would have killed us otherwise, wouldn't they?"

"Don't lie to the girl, Deakin," said Fletcher, unexpectedly. "Couldn't wait for it to start, could you? Couldn't wait to get out and join the fighting."

Deakin seemed surprised, as if he had forgotten that.

"Well . . . yes. But wasn't what I had expected. Wasn't the same. After a while it matters less, Cub, one way or the other, killing or not killing. It comes to matter much less than dying or not dying. Understand that soon, you will."

"No," said Shan, softly because she was afraid. "Will never stop caring. Will never kill Perinan."

"And what if I order you to, when the time comes? What then? Know I'm your Alpha, don't you? Know I can order you to do anything I like, don't you?"

"Yes," Shan whispered.

They had stopped walking. Deakin's eyes were watchful and very bright.

"What if I ordered you to go over there and kill one of the other Wolves? Have to do it, wouldn't you?"

"Leave her alone," said Fletcher.

Deakin ignored him.

"Refuse an order and I can kill you. Know that, too, don't you? What the knife is for, isn't it?" His hand touched the hilt. "Don't want Alphas killing disobedient Wolves on impulse, do we? So have to use a knife. Lots of time to think, while I kill and while you die. Afraid of me now, are you, Cub?"

"Yes," Shan whispered again.

"Good. Always be afraid of me."

He dropped his hand from the knife hilt and walked on. Fletcher followed. After a moment, so did Shan.

Chapter 12

"Became Cub in the year of the Rebellion, did you?" said Deakin, abruptly. His voice was still tight. "A terrible year, that was. A year of treachery and blood. Perinan chose the time when all the Alphas and Seconds, and my year of Cubs, were away on the Plain, and they attacked Wolves everywhere. Killed dozens of Wolves. Half the Cubs at the school were slaughtered; they fought back, you see. Any eight-year-old Cub is a match for an adult Perin; do you deny it? In the end, Perinan tried to overthrow Arkanan themselves. Built bridges across the Cardith. That's why the last battle was fought here, on the Plain.

"Called Wolves from all over the land, Arkanan did, but we were on the Plain already and so we were the first to fight them, the Alphas and Seconds and the Cubs of my year, fighting with Arkanan supporting us, beasts out of nightmare and horrible hissing fire-snakes, and the Firedrake itself, so that we dared not look back at what came behind us. And Perinan had no chance, of course. Had neither the training nor the weapons to stand against us. Broke and ran, they did, in the end, and we chased them as far as the Cardith, where the other Wolves were waiting. Not one Perin who came across the Cardith ever returned."

Shan dared to sneak a glance at Deakin, for the first time since he had threatened her. His eyes had lost their gleam and were wide and unfocused.

"Stacked all the bodies afterward, we did, and fired them. Great stinking piles of corpses, Wolf and Perin both. Stench of the burning was unbelievable. The whole army got sick. Five miles away, we were still gagging on the smoke."

There was a silence. Then Shan felt Deakin's gaze on her, as if he expected her to say something. She had no idea what to say.

"Long ago, that was," said Fletcher, with his usual calm.

"Yes," said Deakin, also calmly. "Long ago. Were children then, you and I. Don't suppose you remember when I first blooded my sword, do you, Fletch? On a farmer swinging at me with a scythe; remember? And remember how I saved your life? Rather forget that, wouldn't you?"

He went on talking about the Rebellion, recalling old friends, bragging a little. Shan was suitably appreciative.

After that day, she did not mention her oath to Briar again, though she was still determined to keep it.

Deakin's energy continued to amaze her. He never seemed to need rest, tolerating it when the others stopped but never suggesting it; standing, or, at most, squatting, while the others sat or slumped on the ground. He seemed to give away more of his food than he ate. He talked constantly, on any and all subjects, and did not seem to require any response; it was as if, in a situation where he was not called upon to fight or hunt or chase, he was forced to expend his restless energy in speech. Shan never found his conversation dull, for it ranged far and wide and he had a gift for vivid description which could bring the past to life, but after a while she found it wearying, exhausting, to try to keep up with Deakin's leaping thoughts.

On the third day out from the Maze, the Wolves reached the Cardith. Deakin ran on ahead, eagerly, and Shan lost sight of him. Most of the Wolves around her stopped on the bank to empty the last of the warm, rancid water in their flasks, a symbolic gesture of release. The water of the Cardith was not fit to drink, but beyond it there would be streams again, and rain. Shan turned her flask upside down and watched the remaining water trickle away into the dust. Then she jumped gladly into the river.

The water was wonderfully cool after the heat of the Plain. This time Shan had no fear of it, and although she was washed some distance downstream by the current she came safely to land. She scrambled up the bank in the midst of a group of Wolves.

It was glorious to be able to look up, free of the relentless glare of the Arkan sky; glorious to see the sky blue again, as it should be. Shan felt she could walk for miles now, could run, even, as far away from Cardy Plain as she could get. She loved the softness of grass underfoot after so long on bare earth, and after a time there began to be small and scattered trees along the track. At last there was a halfhearted attempt at a forest, and as she entered its welcoming shade she could hear running water ahead.

"The first stream," said Deakin, suddenly beside her. "Come on."

The stream was narrow and shallow and full of Wolves, cooling off, washing themselves, splashing. Grass grew thickly on its banks. Deakin, Shan, and Fletcher turned upstream to get a drink, stepping over and around Wolves sprawled in the grass. Above the mud churned up by the waders, they knelt and drank. The water was not cold, but it was fresh and sweet. They walked back downstream along the crowded bank, shed knapsacks, swordbelts, and boots along the way, and splashed into the stream.

Shan waded to the middle and sat down there, letting the water flow over her, with only her head above the surface. She felt clean and cool. When she realized that she was beginning to fall asleep, she stood up, wringing some of the water out of her shirt, and waded back to the bank, where she sat with her feet in the water. After a time Deakin joined her, fully dressed but dripping wet. He was carrying her possessions and Fletcher's as well as his own, and was dragging the knapsacks by the straps. He drew his knife and pointed it at her — playfully, Shan hoped — and then flipped it into the air, caught it, and tossed it to her, hilt first. To her surprise, she caught it. Deakin, of course, had taken for granted that she would.

"Keep it," he said, and tossed her the sheath.

He opened his knapsack and took out the black stone knife that Shan had seen before, the one that Fletcher had made for him.

"Can't wear this on the Plain," he explained. "Don't want Arkanan to see it. Got magic in it, this one has.

"Going on now, are we?" he added, as Fletcher waded out of the stream to join them.

He and Fletcher called out a general farewell and the three of them took to the road again. Before dusk they were in a region of thick forest, where Shan could listen to birdsong and the chit-terings of squirrels. They found a clump of kesterberry bushes near the road and stopped there for a while, kicking aside the vines that tangled around their legs and plunging their hands deep into the thick bushes to find the tiny, sweet kesterberries.

"What's that smell?" said Fletcher, suddenly.

Shan smelled it, too, a rich meaty smell that brought water into her mouth.

"Venison," said Deakin. "Come on, you two."

Around the next bend in the road they found that Deakin was right. One of the Wolves ahead of them had a bow and had brought down a deer. Other Wolves had built a fire in the middle of the road and the deerskin was tied above it, fur side down, to four sticks by the four legs. It was full of water and the meat was stewing in it, creating a wonderful smell that stopped every Wolf that came along. There were more than a dozen of them waiting hungrily by the time the stew was ready.

They ate it on large flat leaves. Shan burned her fingers but did not care.

"Glad we came a little further?" Deakin asked her.

Shan nodded, gravy running down her chin.

After the stew was eaten the Wolves stayed where they were for the evening, grouped around the fire on the road.

"Let's have a story," one of them suggested.

"Yes. Come on, Deakin," said another, to Shan's surprise.

"Haven't heard one of your stories for months, have we?"

"Haven't seen each other for months, have we?" said Deakin. "All right. Let me think of one. Someone else tell one first."

After a bit of "You tell it" and "No, you can do it better," one of the other Wolves began to tell a story, a history, full of battles and glory. Shan listened intently, though she was pleasantly aware, at the same time, of the crackle of the fire, the soft fading of the daylight, and the cool touch of the breeze on her skin. She thought she had never been so happy.

Deakin's story was a long, involved tale which sounded at first like a true history but became wilder and wilder as it went on, until it ended with the hero riding on the back of a dragon and rescuing twelve innocent villagers from an evil bird with a two-mile wingspan. Deakin stood up to tell it, and Shan soon saw why, for he acted out parts of it as he went along. He became the various characters, losing his normal flat tone and changing his voice from character to character, and the lack of expression in his face was compensated for by his gestures and movements. He told the story with his whole body, even drawing his sword when the hero did and fighting— a beautiful shadow-fight in and out of the firelight — when the hero fought, and becoming, near the end, a dragon, crouched evilly, with its head weaving back and forth on its long neck. The Wolves listened and watched with rapt attention.

"No one can tell a story like you, Deakin," said one of them, breaking the long silence that followed Deakin's demonstration of the huge bird's slow death.

Deakin jumped to his feet and bowed gracefully.

"Gets it all out of his head, doesn't he?" said another Wolf.

"Could never think up anything like that, I couldn't."

Some of the Wolves began moving off the road, into the long grass to sleep. Deakin brushed the dirt off his uniform, retrieved his sword, and rejoined Shan and Fletcher.

"Wonderful story," Shan said to him.

"Was, wasn't it?" said Deakin.

Shan undressed and lay down with her cloak wrapped around her. On the Plain she had been reluctant to remove her protective layer of clothing, so that she had even neglected her readiness drill. Now she felt warm and safe. She listened to the little, familiar sounds of the night and watched the soft red glow of the dying fire. She could see Deakin beside her, lying on his back with his hands clasped behind his head, perhaps watching the stars. Shan lay awake for a long time, not wanting the evening to end.

Next day Deakin, Shan, and Fletcher left the road and the other Wolves and struck off at an angle through the woods, walking toward the morning sun.

"But what if the sun goes in?" Shan asked after a while.

"Don't worry about that," said Deakin. "Got our own wizard along, haven't we? Never get lost, do you, Fletch? Rain or snow or Cardy Plain, Fletch knows the way. Anyway, there's not a cloud in sight. Course, you slept so long that it might be dark by the time we — "

Fletcher made a quick gesture of warning and Deakin was silent immediately. Fletcher seemed to be listening to something. Deakin drew his sword quietly from its leather scabbard. He did not seem to require an explanation, but Shan looked from one to the other of them, mystified.

"What is it?" she asked in a whisper.

"Someone's following us," said Fletcher.

"Who?"

"Don't know. Children, perhaps. Watching us right now."

"Don't turn," said Deakin, sharply, just as Shan had been about to.

"Couldn't be . . . couldn't be Perin rebels, could it?" she asked, hesitantly.

"Not likely. Better be ready, though."

Fletcher drew his sword. A moment later, so did Shan. She was beginning to realize that she might be forced to fight Perinan despite her oath. What else could she do it if came to a battle? Stand there and let them kill her? It was difficult to realize that the Perin rebels that she suddenly feared so much were the same people that Briar had called "Gordin's men" and had spoken of with pride.

"Decided to fight, have you, Shan-Cub?" said Deakin. He sounded slightly amused and not in the least worried. "Changed your mind then, have you?"

"Will only fight if I have to," said Shan.

Her heart was racing and she deliberately took long slow breaths to calm herself. If I have to fight, she told herself, then I have to fight well.

They came to a place where the trees grew thickly and close together, hiding them momentarily from any watching eyes. Deakin sheathed his sword again.

"Keep walking," he said, quietly.

He grabbed a branch above his head and swung himself lightly up onto it. Shan and

Fletcher kept walking. Shan gripped her sword tightly and found reassurance in the weight of it. When she heard Deakin drop from the tree she whirled, ready to run back if necessary. She heard a brief scuffle, and then Deakin came over to the more open space where Shan and Fletcher were standing. Shan saw he was holding two frightened boy-children, one in a headlock and the other by the ear.

"Look what was following us."

"Weren't following you! Ow! Let me go!"

The smaller of the two boys protested his innocence loudly and struggled against the painful grip on his ear. Deakin released him suddenly so that he went sprawling, landing heavily on the soft forest floor at Shan's feet.

The other boy seemed too terrified to move or speak. Deakin released him as well, shoving him away and tripping him at the same time so that he landed on the ground beside his friend.

"Why were you following us?"

The smaller boy sat up, panting and covered with dirt, and scrambled away from Shan's sword on his hands and knees.

"No further," said Deakin. "Why were you following us?"

"Weren't following you! Just playing, we were. Just playing! Didn't know you were Wolves, did we?"

"Playing? Almost of age, aren't you? A little old to be playing."

The other boy had not moved, and Shan began to wonder if he were hurt. She nudged him gently with her boot. He gave a gasp of sheer terror and scrambled away from her.

"Thought we were going to try to reach the falls before dark," said Fletcher to Deakin. "Shouldn't we be going on now?"

No response from Deakin, who was watching the boys intently, his eyes very bright. Like a weasel's eyes, thought Shan suddenly. She had once seen a weasel kill a young rabbit.

"Deakin," said Fletcher, forcefully.

"How do we know these boys aren't working for the rebels?" said Deakin, without looking at him. "Have to find out, don't we?"

Fletcher thrust his sword home into its scabbard with a violent movement.

"Not working for the rebels!" screamed the smaller boy. "Not working for anyone. Please, Alpha, let us go. Don't hurt us."

"Where did you get this then?" Deakin walked a few paces back along the path, and Shan could no longer see what he was doing. "Perinan aren't allowed to carry weapons, are they? Where did you get this?"

"Made it, I did," said the boy after a moment.

"Made it, did you? Must have taken you a long time."

There was a long pause, and then a snap as something broke. Shan guessed that Deakin had destroyed the boy's weapon, whatever it was. The boy gave a cry of rage and sprang to his feet as if to rush at Deakin.

"Don't!" said Shan. "Stay where you are!"

She spoke before she knew she was going to speak. Deakin turned on her with a flash of anger. "Stay out of this. Stupid little half-blind brat."

Shan stood silent, shocked. So Deakin did remember her, after all. She could not have been more deeply hurt if he had suddenly turned and knifed her.

"Enough, Deakin," said Fletcher. "Let them go."

Shan saw something startling, a fire that flared in Fletcher's eyes for a moment and made them as dangerous as Deakin's.

"Go on," said Fletcher to the boys. "Get out of here."

The smaller boy grabbed his friend and dragged him to his feet.

"Don't go making any more knives," said Deakin. He returned to where Fletcher and Shan were, looking at Fletcher. His eyes no longer gleamed.

The two boys broke into a run.

"And don't come following us any more," said Deakin.

"All right, Fletch, let's go," he added. "Didn't know you were in such a blazing hurry, did I?"

He was silent for several minutes after that. When he spoke again it was to Shan, abruptly.

"Hungry, are you? Would you like one of the biscuits?"

Shan was hurt and betrayed. She stared at Deakin blankly.

"Because there's one in your hair." Deakin reached over and seemed to pull a biscuit out of Shan's hair. She continued to stare at him. "And one in Fletch's hair as well. Look."

Shan understood that he was offering an apology, the strangest apology she had ever seen.

"How did you do that?" she demanded, with a suspicious glance at Fletcher. "Don't have magic, do you?"

"Course not," said Deakin. "But I'm quick. Very quick. Should have seen me in Carter's Village once. Those people thought I had magic. Remember that, Fletch? Happened when I was Moth's Second . . . "

Shan ate the biscuit and listened to the story. She could not stay angry with Deakin. But would he have killed those boys if Fletcher hadn't been there? she asked herself, and was not sure of the answer.

Chapter 13

By nightfall they had reached the falls Fletcher had mentioned, apparently a well-known landmark, and they made camp near the roaring waters.

"How long till we meet up with the pack?" Shan asked. "Where are they?"

She was dreading the meeting. She hoped fervently that none of Deakin's pack were young enough to remember her from school.

"On the eastern border, near Astin," said Deakin. "Spent last year on border duty."

Shan was relieved. Astin was far to the south and meant at least another week of travelling.

"What about this year?" she asked.

"Same thing," said Deakin. "Been lucky on your first orders, Cub. Real beds to sleep in, good food, plenty of ale."

Shan was not so happy about border duty. She was glad to be assigned so far south, since she

hoped it would be a long time before she would
have to see Cardy Plain again or fulfil her destiny
by fighting Arkanan, but she had been taught
that Iluthia was a constant threat. If the Iluthians
chose this year to attack Redmetal, she would
be in the front lines of the battle.

"What's it like, Iluthia?"

"Not so different from Redmetal," said
Deakin. "Ruled by wizards also. Have an evil
magical queen, they do."

"More freedom than Redmetal, though,"
Fletcher said. "No one has to work in the mines
as well as on his farm. And can travel all they
like, though not into Redmetal, of course,
because Wolves don't let them."

"Been there, have you?" Shan asked, but both
Fletcher and Deakin shook their heads. They had
never travelled into Iluthia.

"Take first watch," Deakin said to her. "Wake
me for the next one."

Both he and Fletcher drew their swords and
put them within easy reach before they settled
for sleep. Shan stood uneasily, holding her own
sword. She had never been on watch before.

"Don't let the fire go out," said Deakin after a
time, startling her.

Hastily she began to tend the fire.

"Can sit, if you like," he added.

Shan sat by the fire and fed it twigs, watching as the shadows of the flames leapt at the black trees and licked at her companions. Fletcher was sleeping closest to her, wrapped in his cloak, with his face turned away from the light and one hand resting on the hilt of the sword that lay beside him. Deakin was further away, but as she looked she caught a gleam from his still-open eyes. She stood up again and faced outward, keeping the watch.

The journey continued in this way for another week. The three Wolves stopped at a village whenever they need to replenish their food supply, and the way that Deakin demanded food reminded Shan forcibly of her promise to Briar. She would never treat Perinan that way, she promised herself.

After the first week there came a day when it rained continually, soaking through their clothes and turning the road to mud under their feet. In the late afternoon they came out of a stretch of woodland and found themselves looking at another village, with cultivated fields and a small cluster of houses. Children were playing in the puddles. A few yards away a man was fixing a broken fence rail.

"Shall we sleep warm tonight?" said Deakin.

He led the way toward the nearest house. The children stopped their game and stood close together, their eyes wary.

"What do you want?" The man who had been fixing the fence spoke up bravely, though he looked frightened. "Haven't done anything wrong. What do you want here?"

"Shelter for the night, old man. This will do." Deakin pointed at the house. "And food. Plenty of it."

Shan thought the man was relieved. He promised to fetch some food right away, and called to his family to get out of the house. A moment later they all scampered out.

That night Shan was warm and dry, though she slept little. She did not think that Deakin slept at all. All through her watch she was aware of him, keeping his own vigil. She stood by the door with her sword ready, and this time Deakin did not suggest that she sit down.

By the third day the rain had settled to a steady, grey drizzle. On the evening of the fourth day, Deakin suggested to Fletcher that he make them a fire.

"Promised you you'd see some of Fletch's magic someday, didn't we?" he said to Shan.

The three of them gathered wet wood into a big haphazard pile, and when they were finished Fletcher sat down and simply stared at it, concentrating on one spot so intently that his eyes crossed. Shan sat down beside him and stared into his face, but there was nothing to see. He was just very still. After a moment, perhaps without knowing he was doing it, he began to hum softly. Shan saw smoke rise from the wood, followed by a little flicker of flame. Soon the fire was burning steadily and strongly.

"There you are. Real magic," said Fletcher.

"How did you . . . ?" Shan began, and broke off with a gasp as the fire suddenly leapt upward.

With a great roar, it reached up to twice its former height, and Shan scrambled away from the suddenly scorching heat.

"Run!" Fletcher shouted.

He grabbed Shan and pulled her with him into the forest. With their eyes unaccustomed to the darkness, they stumbled on the uneven ground and blundered into tree trunks. Behind them the fire had leaped to the lower branches of the nearest trees.

"This way," Deakin shouted. "Upwind. Away from the smoke."

The fire behind them was spreading, lighting up the sky like a red dawn, and soon they could see as clearly as if it were daylight. Their long black shadows raced over the ground ahead of them. Shan smelled the smoke and then tasted it, her mouth open as she panted.

Deakin, ahead of her, glanced back quickly at the fire.

"Fletch, what is it? What happened?"

"Don't stop," said Fletcher. "Arkanan did it. Don't know why or how."

Shan also could not resist a quick backward glance. The fire was gaining on them, and she knew she could run no faster. The flames flung themselves from tree to tree in a great hurtling rush, stripping the leaves and branches from each like some ravenous animal.

There was a huge whooshing roar and a blast of heat, and the flames on their left side swept past them. The three of them angled to the right and kept running. Shan saw that Deakin was yelling something, but his voice was completely submerged in the roar of the fire. The noise was overwhelming. Shan had never heard anything so loud. It battered at her, shook her, so that she longed to press her hands over her ears, but she needed her hands for balance in her headlong flight, as well as to rub continually across her blurred vision. Her eyes burned and stung and filled with water, obscuring further a world that was already distorted by smoke, shimmering in and out of focus. The trees wavered and shifted as she stumbled past them. Above the immense roar and crackle of the fire she suddenly heard something else. Laughter. Loud, inhuman laughter surrounded them like the fire itself.

Shan felt herself weakening, in spite of the panic that drove her on. She was breathing smoke, coughing and staggering. At last she was coughing so violently that she had to stop. She collapsed against a tree, and strong hands pushed her down.

On the ground the air was a little fresher and her coughing subsided, though her body still shook with every breath. She looked up. Deakin was crouched beside her, his face grimy and strained, garishly lit by the monstrous firelight. Fletcher was still on his feet and he seemed to be making magic.

Shan realized after a few seconds that Fletcher was building invisible walls, and she scrambled into a crouch, so as to take up as little room as possible. Fletcher started at the ground each time and worked up, running his hands over the air, chanting words that could not be heard above the fire. Inch by inch he built the walls, while Shan and Deakin crouched at his feet and coughed helplessly, tears from their stinging eyes trickling down their faces. Wherever Fletcher had finished the heat was less intense, the roar less thunderous. He was racked with coughing, too, and by the time he had constructed all four walls he was swaying on his feet. He reached up over his head and began to construct a ceiling for the invisible shelter. The noise was much less until, as he finished, it ended altogether. For the first time his chant was audible.

"Nor smoke nor flame," Shan heard him whisper, in Arkan, the language of wizardry. He sat down on the ground beside her. His face, where it had not been blackened by the fire, was dead white.

"You did it," whispered Shan, in awe, as the flames swept past and over them.

Fletcher muttered a few more words, stretched out on the ground, and fell asleep.

Gradually Shan and Deakin also relaxed, their breathing becoming easier. Shan's eyes stung and her throat felt raw. With Fletcher sleeping diagonally across the floor of the shelter, there was little room left to get comfortable in. She looked across at Deakin in the wavering red light and knew she must look as bad as he did.

Outside, the fury of the fire was receding. Shan watched as the world, soundlessly, shrivelled and blackened and died. She was content for a time just to sit and breathe, to watch passively as the unnatural light faded. To be alive was enough. Apparently Deakin felt the same, for he too was silent.

They were not given much time to enjoy the silence.

Fletcher moaned in his sleep and rolled over, onto his back. An instant later there was a startling flash of bright green lightning, and the carefully-constructed shelter seemed to fly apart, almost audibly, as the noise of the fire swept in, distant now and fading. There was a rush of hot air across Shan's face and a smoke-smell catching again at her throat. At the same time one of the Arkanan appeared, a blurry double figure, standing beside Shan and looking down at Fletcher.

"So. This is the renegade wizard."

The Arkan's voice was harsh and dry, like the crackle of the flames. Deakin and Shan started to their feet together and both of them shouted, voiced some kind of protest. The Arkan did not even glance at them, but raised one withered claw and pointed it at Fletcher's face.

Shan sprang forward to try to stop him, aiming for the shadow where she knew the Arkan stood, though she was not sure what she could do. Deakin was quicker. He drew his stone knife and threw it, in the same swift motion, and, to Shan's amazement, it caught the Arkan just below the breastbone.

The Arkan gave a shrill cry and staggered backward. Then he crumpled to the ground and vanished. The stone knife remained, lying on their little patch of unburned earth.

"What happened?" Shan realized that she was trembling. "What did he want here? What did you do?"

Deakin shook his head; he was as puzzled as she was. He picked up the knife and looked at it. Fletcher slept on.

"Did you kill him?" Shan whispered.

Deakin wiped the knife blade on his shirt, though there was no need. The shirt was filthy and the knife looked clean.

"Couldn't have, could I?" he said. "No. Gone back to the Maze, he has, and the sooner we get away from here the better. Be back with his friends, he will."

He shook Fletcher.

"Come on, Fletch. Come on. Time to wake up now."

Fletcher woke slowly and reluctantly, rubbing his eyes, squinting up at Deakin and Shan and the knife as Deakin explained what had happened. Then he yawned, rolled over, and closed his eyes again.

"Fletch. Have to try and get out of here. Be back, won't he?"

"No. He won't. Hurt him too badly for that, you did. Well done. Now let me sleep."

After Deakin had absorbed this he was jubilant. "Know how to defeat them now! Have to find the others and tell them . . . But how did I do it, Fletch?"

"What did you think the knife was for?" said Fletcher, without opening his eyes.

"But . . . shouldn't we go now? What if more Arkanan come?"

"Know how to fight them now, don't you? But won't be here as soon as this, anyway. Takes a lot of power to send one of them so far from the Plain."

Fletcher went back to sleep. Deakin accepted the necessity of waiting and squatted down beside him.

"Have to tell the others," he said, and looked worriedly out into the darkness, as if he expected his pack to be there. Shan curled up uncomfortably on the ground and followed Fletcher into sleep.

When she awoke it was still dark and Deakin was still on guard, sitting cross-legged with his sword beside him and the stone knife on his lap. Fletcher was awake now, too, and it was his movements that had awakened her. He had raised his head to stare at Deakin, and Deakin was staring out into the darkness as if he was hearing something Shan could not. It took her a moment to realize that Arkanan must be sending out a Call. She waited fearfully, impatiently, for it to be over.

"Let's move," said Deakin, as soon as he could.

The ground was warm underfoot, and the night was very dark.

"Wolves no longer," said Deakin. He kicked angrily at the ground as he walked, and a choking cloud of ash swirled up. Fletcher coughed. "Wolves no longer. To be hunted down and killed."

"By the other Wolves?" said Shan, alarmed, and then, after a moment's thought, "Wouldn't kill us, would they? Wolves don't kill Wolves, do they?"

"Not if we get a chance to explain," said Deakin, and for a time they walked in silence. Fletcher's breathing was uneven. Shan did not dare ask any more questions about the Call, but after a few minutes Deakin spoke again.

"Not Alpha anymore," he said. "Not your Alpha anymore, Cub. Don't have to come with me, do you?" He took for granted that Fletcher would come with him.

"Yes, she does, though," said Fletcher before Shan could reply. "Fated to be together, we are, remember? And where else would she go?"

"What . . . what else did the Call say?" Shan asked, and Deakin repeated the Call for her, word for word but without emotion, as if the Arkanan had delivered it all in a monotone.

"Three who were Wolves have defied Arkan authority. They are Wolves no longer. Their lives are from this moment ended. These three are to be hunted down and killed. They are in the east, in the forest between Pinehollow and the Iluthian border. They must not be allowed to escape. All Wolves in that section of Redmetal are relieved from other duties until the Three are dead. Alphas of all packs in the area are to organize search parties. Find them. Kill them.

"And showed what we look like," he added. "Pictures from the mind of the one who saw us, before I killed him. Us looking all grimy and black from the fire."

Shan caught her breath.

"Where will we go?"

"To find my pack, first. Fast. Tell them they can kill Arkanan. Tell them how Arkanan tried to kill us. And for what?" he added, suddenly. "Why that fire, Fletcher? Why did that Arkan show up?"

Fletcher shook his head.

"Must have learned we three are a threat to them. Don't know how. Believe it now, do you, Deakin? Ready to fight them now, are you?"

"But Wolves will find us first." Shan was sure of it. "Told them where we are, Arkanan did. Don't have a hope of getting out of this forest without being caught."

"Have to keep reminding you we have a wizard with us, don't I?" said Deakin. "Fletch can sense Wolves before they see us."

"Not when he's this tired, he can't," said Fletcher.

"Want to stop, do you?"

"No. Better not. Let's put a few miles between us and the burnt-out area."

Shan felt a little more hopeful. It was true, after all, that Fletcher was a wizard. She thought of the fire and how well he had built that shelter.

"Saved our lives, you did," she said.

"And my own," said Fletcher. "Anyway, you saved mine a few minutes later."

She shook her head. "Deakin did."

"Yes. How, Fletch? Thought Arkanan couldn't be killed. Expected that Arkan to laugh and throw my own knife back at me. Was all ready to jump out of the way."

"Didn't listen to what Shan told you, did you? Arkanan aren't where they seem to be. Didn't you see the knife curve?"

"Yes, thought I'd missed," said Deakin. "Knew it would do that, did you?"

"Made it to destroy Arkanan, if necessary. Didn't know how. Didn't know if it would work, either."

Deakin walked for a few moments in silence. Then he said, "Have to make more now, won't you? One for each of us. Looks like we're going to need them."

The forest was dense, and in the dark their progress was frustratingly slow. Shan stumbled tiredly along behind the other two.

"Going to have to travel like this for a while, we are," said Deakin. "Can't risk the roads, and it's safer to travel by night. Maybe when we get away from here and the search has died down a little, can use the roads after dark."

After a while he said, "Still Wolf, always Wolf, whatever they say. Earned it, fought for it, won't give it up now. Never going to be Perin again."

Chapter 14

In the late afternoon Shan was awakened by a scream. She sprang to her feet and was fumbling for her sword before she realized that it was Deakin who had screamed. Now she had proof that Deakin sometimes slept, for he was deep in a nightmare.

"Father!" he cried in his sleep, his face streaked with sweat, and, to Shan's astonishment, with tears as well.

Fletcher, whose watch it was, knelt beside him and shook him roughly. Deakin woke whimpering, his eyes wide with terror. He rubbed a hand across his face. Then he shook his head to clear it and winced, as if his head hurt. It was a completely un-Wolflike movement.

"What are you staring at, whelp?" he said to Shan, who quickly looked away. "Come on. Almost dark. Might as well start."

"Could rest a little longer first," said Fletcher.

"After that noise? Think no one heard it?"

Fletcher's face went still, inward-looking, for a moment, as it had when he had made the fire.

"No one did," he said.

Deakin ignored him, gathered his possessions, and started walking south. The other two hurried to follow. Shan felt stiff and tense, and wished that she had time to do her readiness drill. For the first time in a long while, she could feel the threat of a headache behind her eyes. She knew all about headaches and was sure that Deakin had a bad one.

They walked in heavy silence. Shan was so used to Deakin's conversation, as a background and a constant comment on what she saw, that she found it strange to be alone with her thoughts. She wondered what Deakin had dreamed. Twice she saw him stumble, though it was not yet dark.

A night which had begun so badly could only get worse.

"Wolves." Fletcher stopped suddenly. "Ahead of us and coming this way."

Deakin motioned eastward and they turned in that direction, hurrying. The sun had set and the colour was gradually running out of the world.

"No good," said Fletcher. "Spread out, they are. Searching for us."

"Well, then?" snapped Deakin. His face looked worn and haggard, the jaw muscles rigid.

"Could easily go back," said Fletcher. "But have to get through them sometime, don't we? May as well be now. Come on. Let's find a place to hide."

They found a solitary oak tree in a small clearing, easy to climb and with plenty of concealing foliage. Fletcher pronounced it ideal.

"Look how far we can see," he said. "Make a few illusions for them now, shall I?"

Shan was the highest, perched comfortably on a thick branch with her back against the trunk. Fletcher was one branch lower but he had wormed his way out along his branch and was lying flat on it. Deakin was the lowest, also lying flat on a branch, with his head cradled on his arms. Shan hoped he would not fall asleep.

Suddenly, with a shock, she saw that the clearing was not empty. There was something big and dark in the long grass a few yards from the oak tree. Shan thought she saw movement.

"Look! Here already, they are!" she whispered urgently.

Fletcher was staring rigidly in the same direction.

"Sure of that, are you, Shan?" he said, without moving.

Shan realized that Fletcher was creating something magical. Screwing up her eyes, she could see there were three dark figures lying in the grass. They must be illusions of the three of them.

"Coming, they are," said Fletcher in a warning whisper.

He went on staring at his creations, and Shan saw them jump up just as a Wolf entered the clearing, walking cautiously with his sword in his hand.

"Here!" shouted the Wolf. "They're here!"

The illusions fled. Other Wolves came running into the clearing. Shan heard the cry taken up and passed from Wolf to Wolf. Fletcher's illusions disappeared into the wood with most of the pack after them.

"Lost them, we have," said Fletcher. "Let's give them time to get well away — "

He broke off with a gasp.

"What is it?" said Shan.

"Coming back!" In his amazement Fletcher stood up, precariously, on the swaying branch. "Look! Coming back, they are. And I'm not controlling them. Not making them anymore, even."

It was almost completely dark. Shan could just make out three running figures, making straight for the oak tree.

"Arkanan controlling them," said Fletcher. He walked back along the branch to the trunk as if he were completely unaware of how high up he was, or that he was in a tree at all. "Should have known it. How they found me the first time, wasn't it? Know when I use magic. Know every time. Know exactly where I am, then, and what I'm doing."

The three figures, the Wolf pack closing in behind them, reached the oak tree and disappeared. Shan and, below her, Deakin, stood up.

"Led them right to us," Fletcher muttered. "Let Arkanan know exactly where we were, I did. Betrayed us."

"By the Wheel!" said Deakin. "Shut up and get ready to fight."

Below them Shan could hear the Wolves deciding what to do.

"Could always set fire to the tree," she heard one of them say.

Deakin heard too.

"No! Want to make it easy for yourselves, don't you?"

He started to climb down. At the sound of his voice, one of the Wolves detached himself from the others and stepped back from the tree, a black silhouette.

"Hello, Deakin."

"Hello, Pike."

Deakin let go of the tree and dropped lightly to the ground, into the silent black ring that was the waiting pack. Shan could no longer see him, but she heard his sword leave its scabbard. The ring of Wolves drew back a little.

Shan remembered Pike vaguely, as one of the Alphas who had been with them on Cardy Plain. She saw Fletcher, below her, start to climb down the tree, and decided that she had better follow.

"Don't want to fight you," said Pike. "Stand still. Will make it clean and quick."

"No Wolf to draw sword on another Wolf," said Deakin. "Know Redthorn's law, don't you?"

"Not Wolf anymore, are you?" said Pike, but he did not draw his sword.

Fletcher, and then Shan, reached the ground. Pike had about a dozen Wolves in his pack. Some of them moved closer now, dark and menacing shadows. Deakin said, savagely, "Think you can take me, do you? Ever seen me fight?"

Fletcher drew his sword and put his back against Deakin's. Shan was not sure what to do. She put her own back against the tree, feeling safer that way, but did not draw her sword.

"Want to know what Arkanan want us dead for? Want to know what you're killing for? Or would you rather not?" Deakin's voice was still savage, un-Wolflike.

"What, then?"

"Hurt one of them. Might have killed him."

There was a chorus of disbelief from the pack.

"With a magic knife. Fletch made it. Reason we have such trouble killing Arkanan is 'cause they're not where they appear to be. Fletch can make knives that can find them."

The pack grew more vocal. They did not believe Deakin, and they did not like this dangerous talk.

"Ridiculous," said Pike. "Couldn't have been dead. And what did you attack an Arkan for?"

"Attacked us first," said Deakin. "Tried to kill us in a fire. And then came and tried to kill Fletch while he slept."

"Trying to kill us because of a prophecy, Arkanan are," said Fletcher, calmly. "Prophecy says there are three Wolves, blind woman, madman, and wizard, who will come together and will have among them the means of destroying the Firedrake. Taking away Arkanan's eternal life.

"I'm wizard. Some of you know that. Why Arkanan were trying to kill us. Deakin is the madman of the prophecy," ("Got that right," Pike muttered,) "and Shan is the blind woman; not actually blind, but not seeing the way we do. Not deceived by Arkan illusions."

"Know how to kill them now," Deakin said. "Don't have to take their orders anymore. Can't you understand that?"

"Know how to destroy the Firedrake then?" Pike asked, and Shan sighed as Fletcher answered, truthfully, "No, not yet."

"Then what are you talking about? What do you expect from us? Heard the orders, didn't you?"

"What are we waiting for?" said another of the pack. "Kill them!"

"Yes, before Arkanan hear us!"

"A chance to win your freedom, this is," said Deakin, loudly, above the confused babble of voices. "Don't want to be Arkan slaves all our lives, do we? Don't know how to defeat them yet, but if you kill us you destroy the only chance we have of finding out."

For a few moments Pike's pack argued loudly and seemed almost ready to come to blows. Gradually Shan realized that Pike was arguing for Deakin's life, and that his Second was backing him up. In the end Pike said, "Alpha, I am, and I say this is what we do!"

"Not sure it's true, what you've said," he said to Deakin, more quietly. "Remember all those stories you make up out of your head. But it's true that Arkanan ordered us to kill all blind women, Shan heard anger touch his voice, "and warned us against wizards. And true that they want you dead. Don't love Arkanan any more than you do. Don't want to kill Wolves on their orders. If we start killing our own, where will it stop?

"So going to put you across the border into Iluthia, and tell Arkanan we killed you."

Some of Pike's pack were clearly terrified by this decision, but they could not argue with their Alpha.

"Lay your swords on the grass, you three," said Pike.

There was a pause, during which Shan hoped fervently that Deakin would obey. Then Fletcher bent down and put his sword on the ground.

Shan did the same. A moment later, so did Deakin.

"And the knife. And where are your knap-sacks?"

Deakin dropped his stone knife.

"Knapsacks are in the grass, to your left," said Fletcher.

Some of the Wolves gathered up the knap-sacks and swords. Pike bent to pick up Deakin's knife.

"Leave it," said Deakin.

"Why? A good knife, this one. Though doesn't look magical . . . "

Deakin lunged forward and kicked the knife out of his hand. It flew over the heads of the other Wolves and landed soundlessly somewhere in the darkness. Instantly there were two swords at Deakin's throat, a third at his back.

"No Wolf to draw sword on another Wolf," said Deakin. His voice was so flat that Shan was sure he was hurt, and after a moment she saw the trickle of blood on his neck.

"Always were quick, weren't you?" said Pike, rubbing his hand. "Think we'd better tie you, just to be safe."

Shan stood passively while one of the Wolves tied her hands behind her back. Pike tied Deakin's hands himself, jerking the knots tight.

They walked for the rest of the night. Pike led the way back to the road, and once there they were able to move quickly despite the darkness. The pack were careful to keep their three captives surrounded. Shan wondered if they, too, had slept all day, for they seemed alert and she did not hear any complaints as they talked among themselves.

Fletcher told Pike everything that had happened — the fire, the sudden appearance of the Arkan, and how Deakin had thrown the knife. He did not hold anything back. Shan had never heard Fletcher talk so much. Pike was fascinated but unconvinced. He did not believe the Arkan had been hurt; he did not believe Wolves had a chance against Arkanan; even if there were a chance, he was not willing to risk everything and try. He wanted Fletcher to show him some magic, but Fletcher explained that Arkanan would know he was still alive, if he used magic, and would probably show up to finish him off. Shan wished that Deakin would speak. Deakin in the right mood, she was sure, could convince anyone of anything. But Deakin remained silent, and eventually Fletcher gave up and lapsed into silence as well.

They walked due east, and by mid-morning had reached the Iluthian border. It was not at all what Shan had expected. As they walked toward one of the guardhouses, Shan realized that the border was a wide swathe of land, carefully cleared of trees and bushes, where even the grass had been cut to give clear vision in all directions. The guardhouse was solidly built of grey stone and some Wolves were on the roof, where presumably they kept watch. Shan heard them talking above her. A group of other Wolves were out on the road, waiting to meet Pike's pack.

"Wait," said Pike, and went forward alone.

He and the other Alpha had a long talk, and finally the other Alpha called his pack together. They all disappeared into the guardhouse, many with curious backward glances.

Deakin, Fletcher, and Shan were taken past the guardhouse and out into the open space of the border. They passed close to an immense pile of wood, and Shan realized that watch-fires would be lit at night.

"Untie them," said Pike.

Shan's hands were freed and she was given a gentle push eastward. Rubbing her sore wrists, she began to walk. Behind her she heard a few isolated voices, Pike's among them, saying good-bye to Deakin and Fletcher, wishing them luck.

Suddenly Fletcher cried out and stumbled, going to his knees in the dirt. Deakin whirled to prevent whatever attack had caused it, but Fletcher gasped, "Magic. My head . . . "

He pressed his hands over his eyes. Deakin grabbed his arm and half-dragged him along, pulling him away from the guardhouses and the watching Wolves, while Shan followed. They left the road as soon as there were trees, and Deakin said, urgently, "Fletch! Should we keep moving?"

"No. Better now. Sleep," said Fletcher.

Deakin let him collapse in a grassy hollow well-screened by poplars and young pines.

"What was that about?" asked Shan.

Deakin had no more idea than she did. "Think Arkanan know we crossed?"

Seeing Fletcher was not going to wake up again, he suggested that Shan sleep, too, while she could. He paced the windbreak, looking often toward the road.

Chapter 15

Shan awoke in the early evening, and found that Deakin had joined Fletcher in sleep. Realizing they had not set a watch, she scrambled quickly to her feet, but all seemed peaceful. She wandered far enough away, keeping a careful lookout, to get a drink from the nearest stream. Then she returned to the other two and began her readiness drill.

The drill took about half an hour to do properly, though Shan could do it in twenty minutes if she hurried. This evening she did it slowly, lingering over it, gradually losing her awareness of the world outside her skin. She started, as always, by standing and stretching, first on her toes with hands above her head, to either side, then down with her legs straight and her palms on the ground, repeating the stretching over and over until she felt her body waking, becoming more supple. She did her balance exercises, standing on one foot and then the other while she went through a series of movements with the rest of her body, slowly at first and finally quickly and jerkily. She did more stretching exercises, forward and backward, and went gracefully through the sword-fight moves as if she were dancing them, with no pauses between. Each movement of the drill flowed into the next. She went to one knee, balanced herself, and stood on her head. She did her strengthening exercises, lifting herself on her arms. She watched how her body moved; she touched, at some point, every part of it; she noticed the many bruises and scratches, some new, and the now-painless scar between her breasts where Deakin's knife had gone. She opened herself to her inner sensations, acknowledging her hunger and finding that, in spite of it, she felt healthy and strong.

Fletcher awoke with a gasp and jumped to his feet, startling the other two. Deakin, who had awakened and decided to follow Shan's example, broke off his readiness drill with a backward roll and ended on his feet.

"What is it?" he demanded. "Still hurting, is it?"

"No. Just . . . had a nightmare, I did."

"What happened to you, back there at the border? Arkanan, was it? Know we've crossed, do they?"

Fletcher shook his head. "Don't know. Don't know what it was. Not Arkanan. Came the other way, came from something in Iluthia."

"Evil wizards in Iluthia," Shan reminded them, uneasily.

"Preventing Arkanan from coming across," Fletcher agreed. "Must have some kind of magical barrier."

"Know you're here then, do they?"

Fletcher shrugged. "If that's how it works. Wish I could remember my nightmare. But think it had more to do with what's behind, back there with Pike, than what's ahead of us."

"Away from the border, then," said Deakin.

He clearly wanted Fletcher to say no, that they could start trying to head back across the border immediately, but instead Fletcher agreed. "Sorry, Deakin. Think we'd better head into Iluthia. Might not be safe to stop here."

They all put on their empty swordbelts, though Deakin said, "Feels a bit unnecessary now, doesn't it? Too bad about that magic knife, Fletch."

"Can make another. Wasn't worth almost getting yourself killed over."

"Wouldn't have killed me. Not Pike." Deakin came close to smiling for a moment. "Wasn't he angry, though? Shamed him in front of his pack, didn't I? Look how tight he tied my hands."

He showed Shan where the rope had bitten into his wrists.

They made their way back to the road and began walking further into Iluthia. The sun was just beginning to set behind them. Though Deakin seemed calm now, Shan was jumpy, afraid that they would encounter some Iluthians.

"What if we're seen?" she asked Deakin.

"Think we're here to trade, won't they? Know Wolves come into Iluthia with rufer. Trade it for gemstones."

Even so, when a herd of cattle wandered across the road in front of them, Shan tensed as she realized she was about to meet her first Iluthian. Sure enough, a small black dog ran busily behind the cattle and there was a man, too, though she only became aware of him when he spoke. She was relieved to see that Deakin, who must have seen him long before, still looked relaxed.

"Welcome," said the Iluthian. "Do you know you're the first Wolves I've ever seen come over the border without a cartload of rufer?" To Shan's surprise she understood his speech, though it was stilted and formal, and some of the vowel-sounds were lengthened. "It's a bit late, but I suppose you'll be stopping at the inn."

"Where's the inn?" said Deakin.

"Just over the hill. You can't miss it."

Shan moved a little closer, trying to get a good look at the Iluthian, but before she succeeded he had moved off with a friendly wave, following his dog.

"Talk like us, they do," she said in wonder.

"More or less," said Deakin. "Go to the inn, shall we, Fletch? Can get a meal there, maybe get some weapons."

Shan had been taught about inns. She knew there were none in Redmetal, since Wolves could stay wherever they liked and Perinan were not permitted to travel.

"But . . . could be Wolves there," she protested.

"Came straight from Cardy Plain, we did, give or take a day or two. No pack's had time to pick up a cartload of rufer and bring it over the border. No Wolves in Iluthia right now but us."

Fletcher started to say something but changed his mind.

"Something wrong, Fletch? Don't think we should go to the inn?"

Fletcher shrugged.

"Didn't have a weapon, did he?" Deakin was still thinking about the Iluthian. "Expected all of them to have weapons, at least near the border. Haven't seen any soldiers at all yet, have we?"

The inn was a large building just over the top of a hill, on the near edge of a village that Shan could see spread out below her. Above the door, a sign swung on a chain. When Shan stood under it and looked up, she could make out a picture of a running black wolf with red eyes and a dripping red mouth. To her delight, there were also letters on the sign. "The Black Wolf," it said, in the language Shan knew as Perin.

They entered the inn and were met with a roar of sound, made up of loud voices, the scrape of benches, and the clatter of mugs and dishes. They were also met with a rich smell of roasting meat that made Shan's mouth water. The conversations faltered and died away briefly as they entered, only to resume moments later. Deakin and Fletcher stood scanning the room, looking for Wolves. Shan received a confused impression of dozens of people in a large, smoky area, all of them talking at once, all using the strange un-rhythmic speech the cow-herder had used.

"What do you want?" One of the Iluthians separated himself from the crowd and came toward the Wolves. He came close enough that Shan could see him, a small nervous man in a leather apron.

"Supper," said Deakin, as he would have said to Perinan.

The Iluthian reacted as Perinan would have reacted. He looked as if he would like to tell Deakin to go away but did not dare.

"Aren't going to hurt you," said Deakin.

"Come . . . come upstairs."

There was a narrow wooden stairway immediately inside the door. The Wolves followed the Iluthian up, Shan coming last. At the top of the stairs, the Iluthian led the way past two closed doors and opened a third.

"Do make yourselves comfortable. Someone will bring the food up in a few minutes."

Deakin closed the door behind him. "Don't like Wolves much here, do they?" he said to Shan. "Suppose he's the innkeeper. Looked as if we terrified him, didn't he? Just like Perinan."

He dragged one of the stools up to the table and sat down. "Didn't have any weapons either, did he? No one did, not that I saw. Not what I was expecting. Thought there'd be soldiers, this close to the border. Don't seem to be ready for war at all, do they?"

Shan explored the room. It had a wooden table, four stools, and two wooden beds with straw mattresses. She dragged a stool up to the table as Deakin had done.

Fletcher remained standing. "Something's wrong. Could sense fear as soon as we walked in. Everyone here is frightened. And angry."

"Why?"

"Don't know, do I? Wish I could remember my dream." Fletcher shook his head impatiently. "Not much good having a wizard who can't remember his dreams, is it?"

"Not much good having a wizard if you aren't going to follow his instincts, either," said Deakin. "Haven't any idea what you're talking about, but if you say leave, we leave. Can we have supper first, do you think? Eat here, make some plans for getting back into Redmetal?"

"Wish I knew what they were afraid of," said Fletcher.

There was a short, tense silence. Deakin pushed back his stool and walked over to the window. Shan joined him. She could hear the sign below creaking slightly as it swung in the breeze.

"Sign on the inn says, 'The Black Wolf'," she said, proud of her ability to read.

"Course it does. Name of the inn, isn't it?" said Deakin, unimpressed. "Named it that 'cause so many Wolves come here, I expect. Could jump from here if we had to," he added, to Fletcher.

There was a knock at the door and a girl of about Shan's age came in with a tray of food. She wore a short grey dress and her long hair was tied back with a piece of red ribbon. Like the man, she seemed nervous, and as soon as she had put the tray down on the table she backed out of the room, keeping her eyes lowered.

Although the people had been a great disappointment to Shan because they looked just like Perinan, the food made up for it. None of the Wolves had ever seen food like this, though Deakin and Fletcher had heard other Wolves talk about it.

There was a whole cold meat pie. There was a dish of beans, cooked long before and kept warm to the point of mushiness. There was a loaf of bread, and two different kinds of cheese, one soft and mild, the other hard, sharp, and crumbly. There were pickled onions and pickled beets, and a big jug of ale.

Shan had never eaten pastry before and she thought the pie was the best thing she had ever tasted. She had never eaten pickles before, either, and the taste of a pickled onion shocked her so much that she spat it out, to Deakin's amusement. After that she ate only pie, beans, and cheese. Deakin and Fletcher ate everything. They did not let the loss of their knives slow them down.

"Been thinking, I have," said Deakin, when the tray was almost empty. "Seems Iluthians aren't allowed to carry weapons, just like Perinan aren't."

Fletcher poured out three mugs of ale, took his own, and settled down on the floor with his back against the wall.

"Need to go find some fighters, if we're to get weapons," Deakin continued, restlessly. "Have swords in Iluthia somewhere, I suppose."

"But won't be able to carry swords, will we?" said Fletcher. "Not once we're back across the border."

Deakin took a gulp of ale and said nothing.

Ann Ewan

"What do you mean?" Shan asked.

"Know we have to go back to the Plain, don't you? Don't think we're going to be able to travel as Wolves all the way across Redmetal, do you? Have to find Perin clothing, we will. Won't be recognized that way. What Wolf ever looks twice at Perinan?"

"Not travelling as Perinan!" said Deakin, with sudden violence.

"What choice do we have?" said Fletcher. "Even at the border. Think we can fight our way back across, do you? Don't forget my head might hurt again. And can't use any magic without letting Arkanan know where we are."

Deakin shook his head. "Has to be another way. Not travelling as Perinan . . . What about you, Cub? Any ideas?"

Shan tried hard to think of something. "Think it would be easier to cross the border at night than during the day," she began, hesitantly, and was encouraged when Deakin nodded. "Have to come up with a story for why we were in Iluthia, we would," Shan continued, "and how we got separated from our pack . . . "

"Not if we wait for a rainy night," said Deakin.

"Oh. Of course. Won't see us at all! Won't be able to light watch-fires in the rain, will they?"

"Don't think it's going to be that simple," said Fletcher.

Both the others looked at him.

"Why not?"

"Arkanan aren't after us just because you killed one of them, nor just because I'm wizard, but because of the prophecy. And if they have some way of knowing about our existence, surely they'll know we haven't been killed. Stands to reason they'd know it right away if we were dead."

"Think they'll still be looking for us, then, do you?" said Deakin. He got up and began to pace the floor restlessly. "But . . . if they know we aren't dead, what are they likely to do to Pike?"

Fletcher went completely still.

"Pike's dead," he said, after a moment.

"What? How do you know?"

"Just remembered part of my dream."

Deakin made a quick, savage movement and his mug smashed to pieces against the opposite wall. Shan jumped. Fletcher did not react at all, but seemed to be lost in dark thought and memory.

"Dead, is he?" said Deakin, the flat calm of his voice deadly after the violent movement. "Make them suffer for that, I will."

He paced back and forth in front of the door.

"Should have let Pike keep my knife, shouldn't I? Might have saved his life."

"Wouldn't have used it even if he'd had it," said Shan. "Didn't believe what you told him, did he?"

"No, but he — " Deakin broke off abruptly and stood still. "Shh. Listen."

"Don't hear anything," said Shan, after a pause.

"Neither do I. Strange, wouldn't you say? Considering the noise they've been making downstairs all evening."

Deakin crossed to the window, glanced out without going close to it, and returned to Shan and Fletcher.

"Fletch?"

He shoved Fletcher with his boot, not gently. Fletcher seemed to return from a far distance, focusing slowly on Deakin.

"Chose a good time to leave us, you did, Fletch. Complete silence from downstairs, and about ten armed men with torches in the innyard."

"Yes," said Fletcher, unsurprised. "Sorry." He ran a hand through his hair. "Uh . . . six or seven people outside the door."

"Good of you to let us know," said Deakin.

The news of Pike's death had thrown him into a savage mood, and Shan could sense the restless energy crackling in the air around him. Deakin was glad to have found an enemy to fight. Shan was not. She felt unprepared and vaguely betrayed, as if she had been tricked into fighting an enemy she did not know for a cause she did not understand. She scrambled to her feet and stood uncertainly.

"Thought they weren't allowed to carry weapons here."

"Didn't say they had swords, did I?" Deakin's eyes were scanning the room, estimating tactical possibilities. "Looked to me like everything else but. Clubs, axes, pitchforks. Thought no one could take you by surprise, Fletch."

"Can't if I'm paying attention," said Fletcher. He was still sitting on the floor. "Anyway, their feelings aren't really hostile."

"Glad to hear it." Deakin picked up one of the shards of pottery from his broken mug and tested the edge with his finger. "Probably come to invite us to their harvest festival . . . Well, Fletch? What kind of fight is it to be? Think you can safely use magic here? Do you want the candles or shall I snuff them? With these odds we might be better off in the dark."

"Not listening to me, are you? Aren't hostile, only very badly frightened. Frightened enough to kill us if we try fighting."

"What do they want then?"

"Why don't we try asking them?"

For a moment their eyes locked, Deakin's angry and restless, Fletcher's calm and inflexible. Then Deakin kicked the door and shouted, "Know you're there, we do. What do you want?"

A young male voice replied.

"You are under arrest. I am Harper of the Queen's Guard, and I am arresting you in the Queen's name."

"Always wanted to meet their Queen," said Fletcher, quietly, coming to stand at Deakin's side. "More powerful than Arkanan, she is."

"Looks like you'll get your chance," said Deakin, and raised his voice again.

"Why? Haven't broken any of your laws. Have you decided to start arresting visitors?"

"This is a land of peace," Harper's voice replied. "You should not have brought your quarrel here. Now that you have, our Queen must decide what is to be done."

"What quarrel? Aren't even armed, are we?"

"Will you agree to come with us peacefully?" Harper asked.

"Why should we?" Deakin shouted back, and angrily jerked open the door.

Fletcher had been right. There were six men outside, crowded into the hallway. They were armed mostly with clubs, though one of them had an axe. In front of them, face to face with Deakin, stood Harper, the only one with a sword. He was a little younger than Deakin, with curly blond hair, and he was wearing what Shan later realized was a uniform — black trousers, white shirt, and a red sash covering the strap of his swordbelt. His scabbard was also red, being made of rufer instead of leather-over-wood like a Wolf scabbard, and it looked bright and conspicuous against his clothes. Shan wondered for an instant why he had the sword in his left hand when the scabbard was also on the left. Then she saw the bandage on his right shoulder and the blood that was slowly seeping through it. His face was white with pain and slick with sweat, and he looked as if he could barely stand, let alone use his sword, but he stared into Deakin's eyes like a warrior, like a Wolf. For a moment Deakin stared back. Then he spread his hands and let the shard of pottery he had been holding fall to the floor.

"Peacefully," he said. "All right, Harper."

They gathered downstairs, Shan sitting between Deakin and Fletcher on one of the long benches. The men coming in from the innyard stacked their weapons by the door as they entered, except for two men who remained on guard. The torches in wall-brackets and the roaring fire, hot against Shan's back, cast wavering shadows across the taut faces of the men sitting opposite her on the other side of the table.

Once the Wolves were sitting down and surrounded, Harper exchanged a few words with the innkeeper and started back toward the stairs.

"Wait!" said Deakin, and made a motion as if to rise, though there were sixteen pairs of angry eyes on him. "Going to give us an explanation, aren't you? Why have you arrested us?"

Harper turned.

"Tell them," he said to the innkeeper, wearily, and continued on, up the stairs.

"There was a man here hunting for you, this afternoon, another Wolf," said the innkeeper to the Wolves. His voice was loud and angry. "'An Alpha with blond hair and a tattoo on his hand,' he said. I'm looking for him and his Second and a Wolf girl.' He said you were escaped criminals, guilty of treason and murder. He wanted me to promise to hold you here for him if you showed up. Well, I couldn't agree to that, could I? So I told him that disputes in Iluthia were settled by the Queen and he'd have to take it up with her, and that if you three showed up you'd be taken to the Queen as well. He didn't like that much. He threatened me. Right here in my own house! He drew his sword and asked me if I valued my life."

There was an angry murmur from the other men.

"He thought I was alone here, but he was wrong about that. Harper and Forest were here on leave from the guard. Harper's my son-in-law; he's married to my daughter Daisy, her who brought your supper tray up, even though she'd been told not to go near you. She's always had a will of her own, my Daisy. She and Harper had come to visit me and to show me my little grand-daughter, and Harper brought his friend Forest with him as well."

Harper was a warrior with a wife and baby! Shan was momentarily distracted. She wished she had taken a closer look at Daisy when she had the chance. When she listened again, the innkeeper's voice had become more agitated.

" — couldn't let him go around threatening innocent people and that he'd better go with them to see the Queen and let her deal with it. They ordered him to put his sword away but he wouldn't. He tried to leave and they blocked the doorway and drew their swords to stop him — just to stop him, you understand, not to hurt him — but he went for them, and he meant killing!" He spoke as if he still had difficulty believing what he had witnessed. "He went for Harper first and got him in the shoulder, and Harper dropped his sword, and then Forest tried to fight and he . . . he . . . the Wolf killed him. It was all over so quick. I hadn't even moved and they . . . they were . . . And the Wolf had gone."

He paused and drew a long breath, pressing the palms of his hands flat against the table. There was a silence.

"So, you see how it is," said the innkeeper, more calmly. "Forest is dead, and for no reason. Will you go with Harper to see the Queen, and allow her to resolve this thing before more evil is done?"

Deakin met Fletcher's eyes briefly over Shan's head.

"Yes," he said.

"Go alone to see your Queen, we will, if you'll trust us," said Fletcher. "Don't want to endanger any more lives, do we? Suddenly seem very dangerous to be around."

"Don't think your Harper is fit to travel anyway," said Deakin.

"I can travel," said Harper, from the stairs.

He came slowly over to the table, and the men opposite Shan made room for him. His shirt was off, his shoulder had been bandaged again, and his good arm was around his wife. He sat down carefully.

"The Queen can heal it," he said, "as soon as I get there."

"Can she?" said Fletcher.

It was so unlike him to speak without a good reason that Shan looked sharply at him and for a moment, to her surprise, saw sadness and longing in his eyes.

"Yes. She just has to touch my shoulder, and when I wake up I'll be able to use it again. And we don't have to go far. The Queen's on a visit to Oakapple."

Fletcher nodded. His face was calm again, familiar, and Shan hoped she had only imagined the expression of sadness. The world seemed much less secure if Fletcher was anything less than serene and whole.

"Do you know this Wolf who's after you?" Harper was asking.

"No," said Deakin. "Thought at first . . . no." He seemed much more willing to talk to Harper than he had been to talk to the innkeeper, as if he considered Harper almost Wolf, not Perinan like the others.

"Long scar down the left side of his face," said Harper. "Dark hair going grey. A little taller than me but not so tall as your Second."

"Redthorn," said Deakin. "But doesn't make sense. Always listens to both sides, Redthorn does. Would never kill unless he was forced to it."

Harper shifted position a little, painfully. "The Queen will sort it out. It's only four days to Oakapple. This is the time of year when half the village goes to Oakapple anyway, to the market."

"Can't travel with half the village," said Fletcher at once. "How many more lives do you want lost because of us? Let us go alone. Want to see your Queen anyway, I do. Think she may be able to help us. Will swear to go straight to Oakapple, if you like. Only let us go alone."

"How can I? Haven't I been told you're guilty of treason and murder? And you're obviously guilty of something; your swords have been taken away, haven't they? I'll tell you what you can swear," said Harper. "You can swear you won't try to escape. In fact, you'd better swear it, or I'll keep you shackled and under guard. I'm responsible for the safety of these people."

Shan hoped he was not going to try to make Deakin and Fletcher kneel and submit to him. She knew they would never do that. Unfortunately, it did seem to be what Harper intended.

"I know how Wolves swear," said Harper. "Has anyone got a knife?"

Someone produced a skinning knife, which Harper took in his good hand. Shan, who was watching Deakin, saw his eyes widen very slightly in surprise and then he was on his feet, looking at something beyond Harper. She and Fletcher came to their feet with him, automatically, and a second later Shan realized that Deakin must have seen the shimmer of the air which heralds the arrival of an Arkan, for someone had just appeared in the centre of the room. It must be the Queen of Iluthia.

Chapter 16

The benches scraped back loudly and everyone in the room, except Harper and the Wolves, dropped to one knee. They did not move as a pack would have done, with unity and grace, but one at a time and awkwardly, some kneeling on the right knee and some on the left. Harper remained on his feet, but after a moment Shan thought the Queen must have looked at him, for he put his heels together and bowed.

Shan was too far away to see what the Queen looked like, but she was relieved to see only one blurred figure, not a double one as she saw with the Arkanan.

"Harper," said the Queen, with a smile in her voice. "And Daisy. Get up, child. All of you, get up. This isn't a formal visit."

When she spoke to the Wolves, her voice became stern.

"I want you three out of Iluthia as soon as possible, taking your evil follower with you. Go on outside now and get a fire started. When I've finished here, I'll come out and hear your story."

Shan trailed her friends out into the deserted innyard. The night was warm, the moon just rising.

"Could walk away," Deakin suggested.

"What use?" said Fletcher. "Must have been her magical barrier I broke coming into Iluthia. Knew we were here, didn't she? Think she couldn't call us back?"

"But why a fire?"

"Magic of some sort," said Fletcher. "Probably to make sure we're telling the truth. Doesn't like Wolves much, but doesn't mean us any harm."

They walked around the inn looking for a log pile. Fletcher seemed excited.

"Has a different kind of magic, she does. Could feel it when she arrived. Doesn't feel like what Arkanan do at all. Why they've never tried to take Iluthia, probably. Don't know how to fight her."

"Sure she's going to let us go back?" asked Deakin.

"Don't know, but could give us powerful help if she chose. Want to talk with her, I do."

"Course you do," said Deakin. "Never met another wizard before, have you? Not sure I trust her."

Fletcher stopped walking abruptly.

"Listen to me, Deakin. Ruled this land twenty years, she has, and kept it peaceful all that time. And can heal. Can still heal. Understand what that means, do you?"

"Yes. All right," said Deakin.

"What does it mean?" asked Shan.

Fletcher did not reply. Deakin made a gesture that Shan had no difficulty in interpreting as, Shut up or you'll regret it. Mystified, she said no more.

They found firewood stacked behind the inn and laid a fire in the innyard, piling more wood beside it. Fletcher had to light it magically, as Deakin's tinderbox had been lost along with all their other possessions, and he made it a small, low fire, with the smoke going, strangely, straight up. Shan sat down beside him. Deakin paced the yard and speculated aloud as to what Redthorn thought he was doing.

When at last the Queen emerged from the inn, Shan and Fletcher stood up and Deakin joined them, all of them standing close together, defensively. Shan got her first real look at the

Queen. She was as tall as most men and she walked straight-backed, her head high. Her hair, thick and dark, gleamed red where the firelight caught it. Her dress was long and pale, belted with a chain of a light-coloured metal that Shan had never seen, but that she guessed from the stories must be gold. Her dark travelling cloak was fastened with a brooch of the same metal on one shoulder, and she had another chain around her neck.

"Harper has told me his story," she said. "Now I will hear yours."

She sat down close to the fire, her dress spread out around her. Shan saw that her face was drawn and haggard.

"Healed his shoulder, did you?" said Fletcher, and Shan understood the cause of the Queen's exhaustion.

"Yes," she said. "He's sleeping now."

She looked up, into Fletcher's grave eyes, and her own eyes widened.

"I didn't expect you," she said, wonderingly. "Who are you?"

"Fletcher."

He sat down, gracefully, cross-legged, on the other side of the fire so that they faced each other through the smoke. Shan and Deakin remained standing, outsiders now, observers.

"Fletcher?" The Queen seemed intrigued. "What kind of name is that for a wizard?"

"Only one I've got."

"A wizard with a name in the common tongue? You'll be telling me next you don't speak the True Language."

"Arkan? All speak Arkan, we do."

"Show me."

"I am speaking now in Arkan, the high language of wizardry," said Fletcher in Arkan.

The Queen frowned. At her request, Fletcher repeated the sentence more slowly.

"I see," she said. "It sounds a little like the True Language, but it has changed so much that I'm surprised to learn that it has any power at all. Has your land lost so much of the old knowledge, then? What can you do, wizard, maker of arrows, with your half-forgotten pieces of language?"

She did not speak unkindly, and Fletcher did not seem to resent either the question or the reference to his name.

"Make illusions," he said. "Make fire." He thought for a moment. "Sense where other people are and what their intentions are. Sense emotions. Sometimes get glimpses of the future or the past."

The Queen waited a moment, as if she expected him to say more.

"That's all?"

Fletcher nodded. The Queen looked at him thoughtfully.

"You must be very unhappy," she said.

"No," said Fletcher.

"Why?" demanded Deakin at the same time.

"Because he has enough power to share the pain of others and not enough to relieve it. Enough power to see evil coming and not enough to prevent it." The Queen looked up at Shan and Deakin as if seeing them for the first time. "And how do they call you two?"

They gave her their names. The Queen asked them to sit down, one on each side, so that the four of them made a square around the fire. Shan could see Fletcher and the Queen clearly, one on each side of her, but Deakin only vaguely, through the smoke.

"So only the wizard has been given a name in the common tongue," said the Queen. "That seems a little unfair, doesn't it? I see you know what your name means, at least," she added, to

Deakin, who shook his head. "You don't? Why the tattoo, then? Where did you get it?"

"Another Wolf did it for me, years gone. Protection from fire, isn't it?"

"There must have been another reason."

Deakin hesitated, but the Queen continued to gaze at him and at last he said, "Was my father's name for me. Salamander."

"Because it is your name," said the Queen. "'Deak' is the True Language word for 'fire' and so 'deakin' means, literally, 'fire-born', but it is also the word used for the salamander. I wonder how your father knew that. Was he an educated man?"

"Was Perin, my father, and stupid as all Perinan are," said Deakin, flatly.

The Queen raised her delicate eyebrows. There was a long pause.

"What does my name mean, then?" asked Shan, at last.

"Your name means 'shadow.'"

Shan was pleased. She thought of her eyes and how she could see shadows where the Arkanan were. The Queen looked at Fletcher again.

"Now that we all know each other," she said, with a trace of irony, "I want to know what you're doing here and why you're being hunted."

Fletcher told her, truthfully and undramatically. After a time the smoke began to twist itself into shapes to illustrate his story. Shan was not sure that he was making the shapes on purpose, for he did not seem to be concentrating on the fire at all and was, in fact, staring through the smoke into the Queen's eyes. It was as if his power was drawing on hers. Shan watched, in the smoke, as Pike stood under the tree, as Deakin kicked the knife out of his hand, as her own hands were tied behind her back. She also watched, with horror, as Redthorn, under control of the Arkanan, murdered Pike and the other Alpha who had permitted them to cross the border. That was a part of the story she had not known. She was not sure that Fletcher had known it, either, before he began to speak.

The fire had grown uncomfortably hot and Shan wanted to draw away from it, but she found it took tremendous effort to move. She was held, transfixed, by the play of the smoke, and the heat was so intense that she began to pant for breath. Opposite her, she saw Deakin drag a hand across his forehead. Fletcher and the Queen did not seem to notice the heat.

"We'll go back to Redmetal as soon as we can," Fletcher concluded, and the smoke-picture resolved into three small figures, walking away.

"To destroy your fellow wizards?"

"Isn't like that," said Fletcher. "Don't consider me a fellow wizard, do they? Don't allow any other wizards. Have been the only wizards for centuries. Want to live forever."

"And you think that's wrong?"

"Not to want it, perhaps. But to control the whole land the way they do, that's wrong. To oppress the Perinan and to train the Kunan Keir in violence, that's wrong. All of it just to keep the rufer trade going, so they can get enough precious stones to give to their Firedrake. Allows them to touch it then, it does, and they live a little longer."

Again there were images in the smoke and Shan watched, fascinated, as Arkanan brought stones to the Firedrake, arriving bent and old and departing full of youthful energy.

"So they have captured a piece of the Wheel of Life and prisoned it in this dragon?" said the Queen, and the smoke formed a wheel, spinning upward into the night sky. "Do you know how?"

"Through a wizard called Tarn," said Fletcher.

"Tarn? The great healer?"

"Knew him, did you?"

The Queen smiled slightly. "I'm not as old as your ruling wizards. I've only heard of Tarn. He was one of the greatest healers who ever lived. He could even bring the dead back to life, they say, and that might explain why your wizards trapped him. He was useful to them because he had power over the Wheel. He had two apprentices, Varian and Sevrin, and Varian had a gift for reading the future. But I suppose they're all long since dead, the ones who were good wizards. How many wizards remain now, do you know?"

"About twenty, I think."

"Twenty. And with centuries behind them. How are you proposing to destroy them?"

"Won't have to if I can get to the Firedrake. Need it to go on living, don't they?"

"Supposing you could get to it, how do you propose to destroy the Firedrake?"

"With a spell of unmaking."

"You know one?"

"Used to practise making real things, constructs, when I was Cub," said Fletcher. "Used to unmake them afterward."

"The Firedrake has been made a long time," the Queen warned.

"Yes."

"You think you are strong enough to unmake it?"

"Have to be, won't I?"

"And what then?" said the Queen. "What if you succeed? Who rules the land then? You?"

Deakin cut in unexpectedly. "Are you suggesting Iluthia should?"

Shan tensed. Fletcher and the Queen both seemed startled, as if they had forgotten Deakin was there.

"I thought you were asking for my help," said the Queen, still to Fletcher.

"Don't need that kind of help," said Deakin.

"Very well. I wasn't offering it. My responsibility is to Iluthia. What you do in Perinar is up to you. Your land is so unhappy now that I doubt if anything you can do will make it worse, and you may succeed in making it better. The three of you are a strange mixture. One who can use magic, one who is unbound, one," her eyes rested briefly on Shan, "who can see. Perhaps you'll turn out to be exactly what the land of Perinar needs."

She made a leisurely gesture and the fire seemed to become hotter, more intense.

"I point out that you may be glad of my help to get back across the border. You, at least, wizard, may find it difficult because of the barrier. I will let you return only if I am sure that you have told me the truth. Will you give me permission to look into your minds, all three of you?"

Fletcher agreed. Shan, still staring into the smoke, opened her mouth to agree also, but found that she could not speak. With a great effort, she dragged her gaze away from the fire. Instead she looked at Fletcher, who was still staring at the Queen, and his face was well worth looking at. For several minutes she watched as expressions chased each other across it, none of them overt but all of them there: anger in the momentarily-narrowed eyes, grief in the quick drawing-down of the eyebrows, joy sometimes softening the corners of his mouth. At last he looked away and drew a long breath.

"Shan?" the Queen asked.

Shan gazed into the Queen's eyes and began to remember, with extraordinary vividness, the events of her life, all the way back to the happy days of her early childhood.

The Queen seemed to be fascinated by Shan's friendship with Briar, and dwelt longer on those memories than on any others. She was also interested in the initiation. The rest of the memories flickered by quickly and Shan found herself abruptly released again, flung back disoriented into the quiet night. She blinked hard and swallowed.

"Deakin?" asked the Queen.

"No," said Deakin.

He scrambled to his feet, quickly but without his usual grace, and began to back away from the fire.

"Stay out of my mind."

"All right," said the Queen. "Of course I will, if you feel like that. Come back and sit down."

"No," said Deakin. "Had enough of this."

He turned and strode away toward the village. Fletcher and Shan stood up, uncertainly.

"Sit down," said the Queen, sharply, to Fletcher. "We haven't much time. You three must leave Iluthia tomorrow."

Fletcher looked at Shan and sat down again, slowly. Shan, who had understood the look, followed Deakin. As she went she heard the Queen say to Fletcher, "He's dangerous. You know that, don't you? He's been in one battle too many, that one."

Chapter 17

Shan trotted after Deakin, glad to be away from the oppressive heat of the fire, and caught up with him halfway down the hill to the village, on the moonlit, empty road.

"What do you want, brat?" He whirled to face her.

Shan had not expected this.

"Nothing. Just thought . . . thought you might not want to be alone."

"Course I want to be alone. What I left for, wasn't it?" He advanced on her and Shan backed away. "Don't want anyone prying into my mind and don't want anyone following me about, either. Understand?"

Shan had backed into a tree and could back no further. Deakin rested his hands on the trunk, imprisoning her between them, and stared down at her.

"Don't want anything from you, Cub. Not now and not ever. Understand that? Can't give me anything I want, can you? Went through the ceremony just like I did, didn't you? So why don't you stop trying? Now get out of here."

Shan did not understand what she had done to make him angry this time, but she saw with surprise that he was trembling and her fear of him dissolved.

"What's wrong?" she said, impulsively, and reached out toward him.

Deakin knocked her hand aside. For a moment she was sure he would hit her, and her muscles tensed in fearful anticipation. Then he slammed his fist into the tree instead and strode away down the hill. Miserably, Shan watched him go.

She followed Deakin through the sleeping village, hoping fervently that he would not turn and see her, but not wanting to abandon him while something — what? — was wrong with him. Dangerous, the Queen had said; been in one battle too many. Shan did not believe it. Anyway, hadn't Fletcher been in as many battles as Deakin had? She walked quietly in his footsteps, afraid that he would break into a run and leave her behind, but instead his steps became slower and slower. He walked only as far as the river that bounded the village on the west, a rushing black torrent spanned by a stone bridge. For a time he stood on the bridge looking into the water, and Shan crept close. Then he came back to the village side and sat down.

Shan would have liked to walk over quietly and sit down beside him, but she could not bring herself to risk it. She went as close as she dared and stood with her back against a tree, hidden in its shadow. She heard Deakin moving around for a while, and then he was still so long that she was sure he must have fallen asleep. He was incapable, otherwise, of such stillness.

What if Redthorn were to come creeping along right now and attack him while he slept? Shan thought. She would have to protect him. She pictured Redthorn creeping through the trees, his hands still stained with the lifeblood of Pike and the other Alpha, his face hard and merciless, his sword drawn. She remembered past daydreams, while she was still at the school, in which she had saved Deakin from just that sort of peril. Although she could still remember the dreams, they no longer gave her the same special feeling. Took that from me, they did, she thought with a sense of loss.

She was jerked out of her thoughts by a sudden
sound from the direction of the road, a sound so
familiar and yet, in this place, so terrible, that she
froze instantly. All her muscles locked in fear. She
had heard, unmistakably, the sound of a Wolf
sword being drawn.

Redthorn came quietly through the trees and
paused within arm's length of Shan, looking at
Deakin. Shan was absolutely still; she did not
even dare to breathe. Redthorn was one of the
best fighters in the Kunan Keir, possibly better
even than Deakin was, she thought in terror. She
was half his size and unarmed, and she knew in
that moment, all fantasies forgotten, how badly
she wanted to live. She was keenly aware of small
things; the rough bark against her back, the
music of the river, the smells of night air and
distant woodsmoke and windfall apples, all
suddenly sweet and precious. She could not will
herself to move, to jeopardize all that.

Redthorn raised his sword and started toward
Deakin, and Shan unfroze at last. She lunged
desperately for Redthorn's legs.

Driven by terror, she moved as fast as she had
ever moved in her life, but, even so, it was barely
fast enough. Redthorn whirled and she felt his
sword slash across her back. It parted her shirt

and scraped a line of fire from one side to the other as she dove under it. She grabbed his legs and threw him off balance, coming up into a crouch as he went down, ready to spring for the sword arm as she had been taught. Deakin was there before her, wrenching Redthorn's arm backward with brutal efficiency. Redthorn gave a single, choked-off scream as his shoulder was dislocated. Then Deakin was standing over him and his own sword was pricking at his throat.

Shan felt slightly sick. She pressed her hands together hard to control their sudden trembling.

"Why are you hunting us?" Deakin demanded.

He was panting a little but his voice was calm. The anger had passed. Redthorn glared up at him with open hatred and did not speak.

"Why did you kill the Queen's Guard? Why did you kill Pike? Did Arkanan force you? Are they controlling you?"

Incredibly, Redthorn tried to attack. The point of the sword drew blood as he struggled against it.

"What's wrong with you?" Deakin put a foot on Redthorn's chest and forced him down. "Trying to kill yourself, are you?"

Redthorn continued to struggle. It looked as if he would cut his own throat if not released. Deakin lifted the sword and stepped back.

"Get out of here then," he said. "Can't do much harm now, can you?"

"Kill you, I will." Redthorn leapt to his feet.

"With your left hand and no sword? Give it up, Redthorn. Don't know what's wrong with you but don't wan — "

Redthorn charged him, futilely. Deakin, trying not to hurt him, forced him backward and finally knocked him into the river with the flat of the blade. He disappeared under the dark water and the current carried him rapidly out of sight.

Deakin looked at Shan, stretched, and rubbed the back of his neck.

"Went to sleep sitting up, didn't I? Not very comfortable. Not very safe either, was it? Course I knew you were there. Let's have a look at your back, Shan-Cub." He took her by the shoulders and turned her gently around.

"Hardly touched me," said Shan, and added, proudly, "My first real wound, that is."

"Can't call it a wound. Just a scratch," said Deakin. "Made a mess of your shirt, though."

He picked up the sword and wiped it clean on the grass.

"Probably saved my life, didn't you?"

Shan thought there was no "probably" about it. Deakin lifted the sword to her in a kind of salute and then handed it to her with a bow, hilt first. He also gave her the half-smile that was the only reward she really wanted.

Shan was so happy she was almost dancing.

"Didn't think I was that good, did you?" she said. "Didn't think I was fast enough to get under Redthorn's sword with nothing more than a scratch, did you? Surprised, aren't you?"

Deakin admitted to being surprised. Shan swung the sword up, feinted at him, then whirled away and charged invisible enemies on the bridge. She fought her way up onto the middle of the span, slashing and parrying as if she were facing two armed adversaries at once. She killed one of them with a final thrust and then pursued the other down over the bridge, before returning triumphant to Deakin.

"Jumped into the water, did he?" said Deakin. "Would have helped you if I'd had a sword."

"Didn't need any help," said Shan. "Need to practise more, though," she added, for she had felt her arm tiring a little.

"Make a warrior of you yet, we will. Feel good now, don't you? Fighting does that, when you win."

"Going back now, are we?" Shan asked, hopefully.

"If you like. Not that they will have missed us."

They walked together, companionably, back through the village, Shan still carrying Redthorn's sword and occasionally skipping for a couple of steps.

While Deakin was in this mood, Shan could ask him anything. "Doesn't seem very dangerous, Iluthia, does it?" she asked. "Not what we expected. Think we can trust the Queen?"

Deakin shrugged. "Fletch thinks so, doesn't he?"

"Why? Because she could still heal, he said. What was he talking about?"

"Can still heal because she's never taken a human life."

Shan's happiness fell away abruptly. She stared at Deakin's face.

"Then Fletcher can't."

"No."

"Shouldn't have taken him for Wolf," said Shan, angrily.

"No use being angry about it now," said Deakin. "All long past now. Could heal when he was Cub, though he kept it secret. Used to be the one who bandaged wounds and helped set broken bones and took cups of water to sick or injured Cubs . . . "

"Didn't the others make fun of him?" asked Shan, fascinated.

"Course not. Wouldn't have dared. Was my best friend, wasn't he?"

Shan acknowledged the advantage of being Deakin's best friend.

"Always recovered overnight, those Cubs did," Deakin continued. "Didn't know Fletch was responsible until we were nine. Then a Cub in his senior year was stabbed and almost killed in a practice fight. Knew he wasn't going to survive the night. But he did, of course. His wound healed overnight, and next day Fletch was so tired he could hardly stand. Spent the whole day trying to keep him awake and covering for him when he fell asleep. Knew for certain then, I did. Never said anything to Fletch about it, then or for years afterward. But I knew. And he knew I knew. Started making little illusions for me, once in a while, when no one else was looking. Healed a broken arm for me when I was twelve."

He stopped. Shan said, softly, "Must have been terrible for him to lose that power."

"Yes. Especially to lose it in the Battle of Cardy Plain, just when it would have been the most use."

"Did he know it was going to happen?"

"Thought he might lose all his magic, altogether, the first time he was forced to kill. Think he almost hoped he would. But didn't happen that way. Just the power to heal."

"Isn't there some way he can get it back?"

"No. And don't ever mention it to him, understand?"

"Course I won't."

"Look at that," said Deakin, suddenly.

Shan screwed up her eyes and looked where Deakin pointed. She could make out the fire on the hillside, but only as a vague blur of light.

"What is it?"

"Coloured sparks," said Deakin. "Even better than smoke pictures. Wonder what they're doing up there. Come on. Have to tell them what a hero you are, don't we?"

They started up the hill. Before they reached the top, Shan, too, could see the sparks flying up from the fire. They were brilliant blue and occasionally she saw a startling green one amongst them.

The fire itself had changed, she saw when they reached it, and her curiosity drew her close enough to see. It looked as if Fletcher and the Queen had piled stones in the centre of the fire, and the stones were glowing from within like huge, misshapen jewels. Something else lay glowing in the heart of the fire as well, a fire-snake, perhaps, but coiled and still. Fletcher and the Queen were sitting close together, on the same side of the fire, and both were chanting, in different languages but with the same rhythm.

Fletcher glanced quickly at Shan and Deakin, saw the sword in Shan's hand and stood up, still chanting but at the same time turning his right wrist inward in the Cub hand signal for "hurt" or "wounded." Shan and Deakin shook their heads to reassure him. As his gaze had left the fire the flames had flickered and died a little, and now the Queen stirred slightly and looked up at him in protest. Fletcher sat down beside her again, with his gaze still on his friends.

"Don't have time for us now, do they?" said Shan, disappointed.

"Get you a drink, shall we?" said Deakin. "Something you'll enjoy more than ale."

First he explained to Fletcher what had happened, signalling "high" and then "Alpha" to signify Redthorn, and miming on Shan what he had done to Redthorn's shoulder. Fletcher nodded his understanding and returned his attention to the fire.

Deakin and Shan watched for a few moments longer. They saw the Queen put her hand into the flames and draw out the glowing snake, which shone with a strong blue light as she lifted it. Fletcher bent his head and the Queen placed the circle around his neck. It did not seem to be hot. For a moment it shone against his skin, and then the blue light ran out of it and Shan could not see it anymore. Fletcher and the Queen continued to chant.

"Come on," said Deakin. "Could be hours yet."

They went into the inn. The main room was deserted and dimly lit by moonlight, the fire and the torches out.

"Like some cider, would you, Cub?" said Deakin.

"Wolf."

Deakin went behind the bar and poured ale for himself and cider for Shan. They sat down at one of the tables and drank.

"Tired, are you?" Deakin asked her.

"Not much. Slept all day, didn't we?" But as soon as she had spoken Shan realized that she was tired nevertheless. "Maybe a little."

"Can go to bed when you like. Want another drink?"

Shan shook her head. Deakin went over to the tap and helped himself to more ale. He also found a knife and brought it back to the table.

"What do you think is wrong with Redthorn?" Shan asked.

"Something Arkanan did to him, probably. Doesn't seem to be responsible for what he's doing."

"Still separated his shoulder though, didn't you?"

Deakin looked at her in surprise. "What did you expect? Would have killed me, wouldn't he?"

"What is the first rule of battle?" he added, switching to Arkan as if Shan were back in school.

"That there are no second chances," she answered in the same language.

"Right. Generous of me to let him live, I thought," said Deakin.

After a moment, he said, "Should have tried to bring him back here, shouldn't I? Maybe the

Queen could have helped him. Too late for that now."

"Wouldn't have come with you. Even at swordpoint." Shan yawned widely.

"No. Would have had to knock him out and carry him, wouldn't I?" Deakin seemed to find the thought amusing. "Why don't you go to bed, Cub? Wolf," he corrected himself, immediately. "Small but very brave Wolf."

"Not really Wolves any more, though, are we?" said Shan, as she stood up.

"Course we are. Not going to listen to what Arkanan say, are you?"

"Suppose not. Good night then, Alpha."

"Good night, Shan-Wolf."

Shan turned, almost smiling, but her Alpha was no longer looking at her. He was busy carving a salamander into the top of the table.

Chapter 18

When Shan awoke it was almost noon. The room looked grubby and uninviting in full daylight, and there were fresh flea bites on her legs, which she scratched at absently for a few minutes before she got up. Fletcher was asleep on the floor beside the bed, curled up small and breathing peacefully. He was fully dressed, even to his swordbelt and boots. There was no sign of Deakin.

Shan stood up and stretched, a slight soreness across her back reminding her that she was a real warrior now. First wound, she thought. First battle. But of course it hadn't really been either of those things. Don't get to feeling too confident, Shadow Eyes, she told herself with an inward smile. She did her readiness drill slowly and carefully.

Just outside the door of the room someone had placed a bowl of water, a sharp, short-bladed knife for shaving, and a small pile of Perin clothing. Shan sorted through the pile and found a dress. It had probably once been red, but now it was a patchy and faded pink, and it fell almost to her feet when she put it on. She closed the door quietly behind her and went in search of Deakin.

The inn was completely silent and deserted. Shan walked out into the yard and found Deakin, all alone and still dressed as a Wolf, sharpening a sword. Another sword lay beside him. He barely glanced at her.

"Where is everyone?" Shan asked.

He jerked his head toward the village. "Burying Forest."

"Oh," said Shan. "What about the Queen?"

"With them."

Shan walked into his line of sight so that he would have to notice the dress.

"Like it?" She twirled around.

"Trying to be a woman, are you?" His voice was cold. "Take it off."

"But Perin women — "

"Not going to travel as Perinan! Told you that!"

"Not as Perinan? But . . . " Shan remembered what Fletcher had said, about how hard it would be to travel as Wolves all the way across the land, hunted. She thought for a way to convince Deakin, and suddenly found inspiration.

"Travel as Arkanan, shall we?"

"What?"

"Too dangerous to travel as Wolves, and you don't want to travel as Perinan, so let's travel as Arkanan."

"Can't do that."

"Why not? Can get black robes somewhere, can't we?" Shan persisted. "Wear hoods up like Arkanan do, so no one can see who we are."

Deakin obviously hated the idea. "What if Arkanan see us?"

"Not likely, though, is it? Much safer than travelling as Wolves, isn't it? Wolves always talk to Wolves, you know that. Will ask why we're travelling without our pack. Will call us to share food with them. Will want our stories. But not like that with Arkanan, is it? Won't want anything to do with us. Will run away when they see us coming."

"Can't travel as Arkanan," said Deakin, but Shan hoped she had at least made him start thinking about how dangerous it would be to travel as Wolves.

She turned to go back inside, but then noticed there were three stone knives lying on the ground by the door. She squatted down to examine them.

These knives were not black but made of common stone, red-brown and mottled. Like Deakin's black knife had been, they were completely smooth and glossy, each of them honed to a fine point. Someone had wound strips of leather around the handles to provide a grip. It took Shan a moment to realize that the knives had been made from the stones she had seen in the fire the night before.

"How did they do it?" she asked in wonder.

Deakin shrugged. Shan picked up one of the knives and touched the edge carefully. It was sharp. She put the knife down and picked up the one beside it, tracing the pattern on it with one finger. The stone was cool and smooth to the touch.

"Have this one, can I?" she asked as she stood up.

"What difference?"

"The pattern. All different, they are. Like this one best."

"Take it, then."

"Don't have a sheath for it, though, do I? Or even a knapsack."

"Sheath and knapsack both. Decided to be generous to us, the Queen did. Saw the things on the table, didn't you? All for us."

Shan had not noticed anything on her way through, but she was not going to say so. She pushed open the heavy inn door and went back inside to examine the pile she found on one of the tables. There were three leather knapsacks, looking almost new. Two knife-sheathes for Shan's and Fletcher's knives. An axe with a sheath of its own. Water flasks. Cups, bowls, and spoons of polished wood, which Shan touched with pleasure. Short rufer knives with bone handles. Two tinderboxes, both old and rusty, but complete with firelighters and already full of shredded bark. Three woollen cloaks. Linen for bandages. Cords for bowstrings. Goose feathers. Rope.

She did not have much time to look, for Deakin followed her in and said, "Told you to go up and change. Can't travel as Perin woman. Hair's too short. Have to put a tunic on and be a child, you will."

Shan saw that she had won the argument. They were going to travel as Perinan.

Upstairs, Shan met Fletcher coming out of the room. He had shaved and without his beard she thought he looked much younger and more vulnerable. She wondered what he thought she looked like in a dress, but he did not comment.

"Was good to us, the Queen," she said. "Gave us lots of travelling gear."

"Need it, we will," he said. "Don't want to go near any villages in Redmetal if we can help it, and we're ten days from Cardy Plain. But yes, was good to us, she was. Promised to lift the magical barrier for us to get across, as well, tonight."

"Tried to get bows and arrows, did you?" said Shan.

Fletcher nodded. "None in the village. Said we had to have goose feathers, at least."

"What about swords?"

"Got two now, Forest's and Redthorn's. Forest's had a scabbard, and Harper gave us his for Redthorn's. Leaves you unarmed. Seemed to want it that way, the Queen did."

Shan was secretly relieved. She heard Deakin coming up the stairs behind her.

"About time you got up," he said to Fletcher. "Try on Perin clothes, shall we?"

Shan found herself a plain brown tunic such as Perin children wear, and put it on to make sure it was not too small.

"Leave it," said Deakin, as she was about to take it off again. "Wear your uniform over it."

"Suppose that means us as well, does it?" said Fletcher. The men had to wear more than simple tunics.

"Sorry, Fletch. Don't know what kind of trouble we're going to run into at the border, do we? May have to become Perinan in a hurry. And might have to fight. All those beautiful new possessions in our beautiful new knapsacks won't do us any good if we have to drop them to fight, will they? At least this way we keep our Perin clothes."

"As long as you don't expect me to run very fast," said Fletcher.

When they were all dressed, they went back downstairs to pack for the journey. Everything they could not afford to lose went into Shan's knapsack, so hers was by far the heaviest.

"Share it out properly once we're over the border," said Deakin.

The burial ceremony had ended, and the inn was full of men, women, and even a few children, eating and drinking. The Queen seemed to have left, but Shan saw Harper, conspicuous in his bright uniform. He appeared to have fully recovered from his wound.

"Are you off now?" asked the innkeeper. He was trying to keep the relief out of his voice but to the Wolves it was obvious. "No, no, you don't owe me anything. Our Queen was more than generous on your behalf."

Harper came over as Shan was sliding her knife-sheath onto her belt.

"Are you leaving already?"

"Going to walk north for a few hours," said Deakin. "Don't want to cross the border anywhere near where we crossed before."

Harper trailed them out to the innyard.

"I could come with you as far as the border," he suggested. "I know the roads."

"Better not," said Deakin. "Don't know if Redthorn might come back, do we? And you're the only one here knows how to fight."

"Good luck to you then," said Harper. "Deakin. Fletcher. Shan."

He put his heels together and gave them one of his formal bows. They inclined their heads in return, and Deakin said, "May the turn of the Wheel bring you good fortune."

Banks of cloud were building up in the sky, and the three travellers walked alternately in sunshine and in shadow. Deakin and Fletcher's rufer scabbards were dazzlingly bright when the sun caught them, looking lurid and unnatural against the plain black uniforms. Shan thought, with momentary sadness, that this might be the last time she would see them dressed as Wolves.

"May rain before night, if fortune's with us," said Deakin.

They stopped briefly at the bridge, and Deakin showed Fletcher where he had been sitting the night before, where Shan had been standing — he knew the exact place — and where he had knocked Redthorn into the river.

"Think he drowned?" said Shan, looking down into the swift, dark water.

"No," said Fletcher.

Deakin said, "Not Redthorn."

On the other side of the bridge the road forked and they turned northward. Shan was glad that she had only a tunic to wear under her uniform, for the day was warm and her knapsack was heavy. Still, it was good to be wearing a knapsack again. The new knife in its leather sheath in front of her right hip felt comfortable and familiar, as if she had returned to being Cub. Deakin began practising with his, throwing it at a tree along the road ahead and then retrieving it when he got there, so that conversation became difficult.

Fletcher, still excited by his visit with the Queen, talked occasionally about Iluthia. "Have wizards in all the big towns, they do," he said. "Can tell they're wizards when they're babies. Could tell I was wizard, just by looking at me, couldn't she?"

"Take the babies for training, do they?" said Shan.

"Don't have a school, not really. Other wizards teach the young ones. Doesn't take much teaching, she says, just encouragement. Have different kinds of wizards, too. Some are good farmers, she says. Can tell exactly when to plant and when to harvest."

Shan was amused by the idea of wizards as farmers. It was true that the harvest looked rich and plentiful. Most of the land was under cultivation, and most of it was fenced off from the road, giving the landscape an order and pattern that Shan had never seen in Redmetal. From the top of a hill, looking down, she was reminded of the paths that the young Cubs had sometimes made in the snow. Iluthia seemed not quite real, a land built by children. Sunlight and cloud-shadows chased each other across its face, lightening and darkening the neat blocks of land.

Most of the people on the road hurried by and avoided them, perhaps because of Deakin's target practice. Shan watched them and wondered what they thought of Wolves, and what they thought of that jealously-guarded border so close to their homes. Iluthia seemed a very peaceful place.

After a while Deakin said, "What's that?"

He pointed at Fletcher's neck and Shan saw a glint of gold.

"The Queen's chain. A chain of unmaking, it is now," said Fletcher. "Wove the spell into it last night. Any magical construct that it touches will fall apart, separating into pieces of whatever it was made from. Touch this chain to the Firedrake and you destroy it. Understand?"

Shan and Deakin nodded. Shan said, "Can I hold it?"

Fletcher slipped the chain off over his head and gave it to her. Shan rubbed the tiny links gently between her fingers and found that the metal felt warmer than rufer and somehow softer.

"Beautiful, this is," she said.

When she tried to give it back to Fletcher, he suggested that Deakin take it.

"Why?" said Deakin, and then, "What did you see?"

"Nothing. The Queen saw our future, I think, but wouldn't tell me. Only . . . didn't want me to make the knives. Told her they were the only weapons we had found against Arkanan, but she said it was dangerous to make weapons by magic. Said that someday they might require a blood-price from their maker. But don't worry, Deakin. Made you a knife before, didn't I? And nothing came of it."

Deakin did not look as if he found this reassuring. Neither did Shan. She looked down at her knife uneasily, as if it might attack her.

Deakin put the gold chain over his head and tucked it down inside his shirt.

"Wouldn't help me make the knives," Fletcher went on. "And afterward she took them from me and put a spell into them. Can only be used once, these knives. The first time they draw blood, and that includes whatever Arkanan have left in their veins, they'll fall into dust. Said she hoped that would encourage us to save them until we reached the Maze instead of killing Perinan on the way. Doesn't have a very high opinion of Kunan Keir."

"Why did you let her?" said Deakin.

"Didn't have much choice, did I? Sorry, Deakin. Knew you wouldn't like it, but what could I do?"

"Knew we couldn't trust her," Deakin said. "Doesn't she realize what we have to do? Cross the border without being seen. Travel across Redmetal for two weeks with every Wolf in the land looking to kill us. Cross Cardy Plain without Arkanan knowing. Find our way through the Maze. Walk up to the Firedrake and touch it with this little chain that I'm wearing around my neck. And she wants us to do it unarmed."

The bleak recitation of what they were trying to do terrified Shan, though Deakin was completely matter-of-fact about it. He kept on talking about the stone knives, worrying around a problem the way he always did. To Shan the day had become perilous. Suddenly the border seemed to loom ahead of them and she could think of nothing else.

As if in sympathy with her mood, slow, heavy drops of rain began to fall.

"Good," said Deakin. "Come on, clouds. Keep it up."

The clouds obeyed his wish, drawing in steadily until the sky was grey. Gradually the rain soaked through Shan's clothes, soaked her hair, ran trickling down her back and over her face. She did not mind being wet. It was a small price to pay for greater safety at the border.

They turned westward well before dark, when they found an area that was thickly wooded, and moved carefully, keeping out of sight, until Deakin caught a glimpse of one of the guard-houses through the trees. They were a long way east of it, but still Deakin ordered them down and they crawled the rest of the way on their bellies over the wet ground, cautiously, wary of the guards on the roof. Shan was glad she had no sword to worry about. All three of them were breathing hard and almost unrecognizable with mud by the time they had a clear view of the border.

As at the other guardhouse, the grass had been cut short. Shan assumed that there were guard-houses on either side, but she could not see either of them from here. Nor could she see anything moving.

"Staying out of the rain, they are," said Deakin. "Though still got guards on the roof."

He talked restlessly. "Looks like they're growing vegetables. Keep the grass very short, here, don't they? Must spend hours cutting it. One of those targets needs fixing, look at it.

What are those sticks there for, do you think, Fletch?"

"Been playing Markers," said Fletcher.

"So they have. Can see the markings on the grass, too," said Deakin.

Markers was a Perin team game. It had not been taught at the school, but some of the Cubs had played it in their free time. Shan knew it involved a lot of running, passing sticks from hand to hand, and trying to break through the opposing team's lines.

She gazed across to the dark blur of the trees on the other side.

"Are we all going to run together?" she asked.

"Yes," said Deakin. "Have patrols, they will, come dark, but no watch-fires. Not in this weather. And Fletch can tell when the patrols are coming. Can tell when it's safe to run. Then we run straight across. No stopping for anything, Cub, you understand?"

Shan looked at his mud-streaked face through the bracken between them.

"But what if we get separated?"

"Can't separate us. Fletch always knows where you and I are, remember? Don't worry about it. Just keep going till you reach the trees. Haven't got a sword, so if it comes to fighting the only thing you could do out there is get yourself killed. So keep running."

"All right," said Shan, uneasily.

Then they had to be quiet, for one of the Wolves was coming toward them. He squatted down by a pile of wood, and Shan heard the rasp of a firelighter as he tried to start one of the watch-fires. For a long time he worked at it, with the darkness closing in. Twice Shan saw curls of flame, but the driving rain extinguished them almost immediately. Finally the Wolf stood up, said a few nasty words in a perfectly calm voice, and walked away.

A few minutes later, though it was not yet full dark, two Wolves came walking along the border. Shan realized it must be a patrol.

"Watching for us, aren't they?" she whispered, once those Wolves were gone.

"Whole pack, looks like." Deakin had not expected this. "Heard what happened to Pike, I suppose."

A little later he added, reassuringly, "No reason for them to expect us to cross here, is there? Wet and miserable, they are, and bored as well. Probably keeping their heads down."

Shan hoped he was right.

One of the sentries was so small and slight that she was sure it must be a girl of her own year, but she could not tell who it was. She wished fervently for full darkness, for the long wait to be over. She was beginning to shiver in her wet clothes, and all her muscles were tense. Whenever she relaxed them they tensed again, gradually, while she was unaware. A flicker of lightning across the sky made her jump violently.

"Lightning. All we need," Deakin muttered.

Shan wished she could get up and pace about. She could feel herself becoming more frightened with every dragging minute. At last it was so dark that she could no longer see the movements of the patrols, and then it was so dark that she could not see Deakin, beside her, in his black uniform — only, faintly, the oval of his face and the gleam of his hair — and at long, long last she heard him whisper, "Ready to run, are you?"

Shan stood up, quietly, and stretched the stiffness and some of the trembling out of her muscles. She heard Deakin move around to her other side to place her between himself and Fletcher. The three of them took hands. Then Fletcher whispered, "Go!" and they ran.

Chapter 19

The rain attacked them viciously as they left the shelter of the trees, driving down straight and hard onto their heads. Their boots slipped on the wet grass. Shan knew that the other two could have crossed more quickly without her, and she ran as hard as she could. The darkness hid holes and ruts, and twice she almost fell, but the others kept her on her feet.

Fletcher stopped abruptly, almost pulling her over backward. Deakin felt the tug on his hand and stopped as well. A patrol passed in front of them as they stood frozen, trying to breathe quietly. Then they ran on, sure-footed, invisible, part of the darkness.

They almost made it. They were nearing the trees when another flash of distant lighting lit the sky, and there was a shout from the guardhouse and, simultaneously, a shout from one of the sentries. Deakin muttered a curse. He and

Fletcher dropped Shan's hands and she heard the harsh rasp of metal on metal as they drew their swords, still running, and the sound of other running feet as the nearest pair of Wolves tried to intercept them. Someone yelled out, "Get them, Wolves, or we all end up like Farion!"

Deakin swung round as the footsteps reached them, and his sword found a target. Shan heard a gasp of surprise, or possibly pain, and a woman's voice shouted, "This way! Here! Over here!"

Shan hesitated. She heard Deakin's sword clang against another, and then he stepped back into her, almost knocking her down, and she heard the soft thud of something hitting the ground. His knapsack. She picked it up by the straps.

"Run!" Fletcher seized her hand and dragged her with him.

They ran a few steps northward and then west again, Fletcher knowing where the Wolves were. "Run!" he said again, and dropped her hand. Shan heard his sword hit someone else's, so close behind her that she ducked instinctively. She obeyed him and ran on into the darkness. She expected any minute to run into a Wolf, or, worse, into a sword raised to stop her.

The whole night seemed to be full of shouting, and running feet, and occasionally the sound of sword swinging against sword, telling the rest of the pack where the enemy was. Shan tripped over something and crashed sprawling into thick bushes, and knew that she had reached the forest. Clinging to the trunk of a tree, panting, she stood up slowly.

The treacherous lightning flickered around the sky again and showed her, for an instant, the whole strip of land, full of running black figures converging on the fighters. The pack were trying to surround Deakin, who had nearly reached the trees. Fletcher was fighting a single Wolf only yards away from Shan, and two others were running toward him. As the darkness closed down again, she heard a scream from that place, a scream that died off into a horrible moaning. Fletcher, she thought, and her breath stopped. Down. Wounded. Dying. Her nails bit into her palms.

An instant later someone stumbled into the forest only a few feet away and she could hear his harsh breathing. The moaning in front of her went on. So did the shouting.

"Here! Over here!"

"Len? Where are you, Len?"

"On my way."

"This way! Come on!"

"Where's the other one?"

"Don't let him get to the trees!"

Shan whispered, "Fletcher?" into the dark.

Her companion was temporarily too busy breathing to reply, but at last he whispered back.

"All right, are you?"

"Yes. Are you?"

"Yes. Shh."

The fighting seemed to have stopped. Just when Shan thought she could not bear the moaning for another second, that stopped, too. Wolves came and went, noisily, shouting to each other.

"Where's Deakin?" Shan whispered.

Fletcher came to her silently, despite the darkness, and whispered directly into her ear.

"A little to the north of us. Staying quiet, I hope."

Shan heard a Wolf approaching, his boots squelching on the wet grass.

"Blackbird?" he called. He sounded young. "Blackbird?"

He did not call again. It was much quieter now. A group of Wolves were talking urgently, too far away for Shan to hear what was being said.

A woman was also calling Blackbird's name, further off.

"Here," said the young male voice, unexpectedly close to Shan and Fletcher. The voice was loud and had a tremor in it. "Here he is. Stepped right on him, I did."

"Dead?" said the woman.

Shan heard her footsteps approaching. There was a silence. Then the woman's voice said, "Well? What are you waiting for? Help me get him inside before he wakes."

At the same time there were more quick footsteps and a new voice, male, authoritative. Alpha, Shan thought.

"Found him, have you?"

"Yes," said the woman. "Badly hurt. Got across, did they?"

"All three of them."

"Arkanan will kill us," said the boy. "Like Farion and Pike."

If my voice was going to shake like that, Shan thought, I'd have the sense to keep quiet.

"No," said the Alpha. "Got three wounded to show we tried to stop them."

Shan heard small scuffling sounds and a grunt, and guessed that they were lifting the injured Wolf. Then there was a silence so long that she strained to see what was happening, squinting futilely into rain and darkness. It was broken by more approaching footsteps, quick and light.

"Garen?" A young girl's voice, presumably the sentry Shan had seen earlier. "Are you there? Garen?"

"Here," said the Alpha.

"Got Cricket inside, we did, and think she's going to be all right . . . " She broke off. "Who's that? Blackbird? Is he . . . "

"Dead," said the Alpha, quietly. "Just died."

Shan turned her head aside. She did not want to hear any more. Fletcher took her hand, and she thought that he had sensed her emotion and was trying to give comfort. It took her a full minute to realize that it had been Fletcher who had killed that Wolf out there, and then she jerked her hand out of his abruptly. Even through the rain she thought she could smell blood on him. Her nose wrinkled like an animal's and she backed away, putting the tree trunk between them.

Gradually she admitted to herself that if Fletcher had not fought she would probably be dead by now. Or taken prisoner, which would certainly come to the same thing. Didn't mean to kill anyone, did he? she said to herself. Only wanted to get to the trees and couldn't see, in the dark, to disarm anyone, could only swing wildly and hope. She realized slowly that Fletcher might have taken her hand not to give comfort, but to receive it.

She groped for his hand again, but he had felt that wave of revulsion and had moved away, and in the next flash of lightning she saw him standing, erect and remote, facing the border.

As soon as there were no Wolves close by, the two of them walked deeper into the forest.

"Wait here," said Fletcher, impassively. "Going to get Deakin."

Shan stood where he left her, still holding Deakin's knapsack by one strap, weighted down by her sodden clothes and feeling miserable and tired.

Deakin arrived noisily, exhilarated, as Shan had been after the encounter with Redthorn, because he had survived. In the lightning, which was more frequent now, Shan could see that he had taken off his shirt and tied it around his right shoulder.

"Hurt, are you?" she said.

"Not really. Bandage it for me, will you, Fletch? Had to tie it with my teeth. Is that my knapsack you're dragging through the mud, Cub? Good. Only lost Fletch's, then."

Fletcher managed to find linen in Deakin's knapsack and made a proper bandage in spite of the rain and the darkness.

"Only bandaged it because it kept bleeding," said Deakin. "Isn't deep. Some Wolf I never even saw took a chunk out of my shoulder just as I reached the trees. Lucky I'm not any shorter, isn't it?"

Deakin wanted to talk about the fighting he had just done. Neither of the other two had any inclination to talk at all, and Shan did not even think she could bear to listen. Fletcher seemed to feel the same way, for twice he told Deakin to shut up. The first time Deakin ignored him, and the second time he asked Fletcher who he thought he was talking to. There was nothing left of the easy camaraderie that had existed among the three of them a few hours before. Shan was almost glad when the storm broke directly over-head and put an end to all further conversation.

Hours of struggling through wet undergrowth, stumbling into hollows full of water, and scratching their hands and faces on brambles and thorns, had their effect even on Deakin at last. By the small hours of the morning, when the rain had subsided to a monotonous drizzle, he was talking only sporadically and had sobered up enough to admit that fighting with other Wolves could not really be called fun. The three travellers found a path and followed it until a house loomed up out of the darkness in front of them. It was half-fallen, but it was much the driest place they had found, and they stumbled thankfully inside.

"Should be safe enough now," said Deakin. "Build a fire, shall we?"

A moment before, Shan had wanted nothing more than to collapse on the dirt floor and sleep, but the idea of a fire was immediately attractive. Not only would she be able to get really dry, but, more important still, she would be able to see. She felt as if she had been stumbling through darkness for days, rather than hours.

"All right," she said.

"Give me the axe, then."

Shan removed her knapsack carefully, since the straps had been cutting into her shoulders painfully for most of the night, and found the axe. Deakin went out into the rain again. Fletcher and Shan stripped off their sodden clothes, and Shan squatted down against the wall, jerking awake when Deakin returned with the wood. She helped him lay the fire, and managed to light it on her third attempt. It smoked a great deal, but, as a large portion of the roof was gone, this did not matter. Shan found it wonderful to be able to see.

Fletcher was already asleep, curled up against one wall with his back to the room. Shan and Deakin spread out all the wet Perin clothes and as much of their uniforms as they could find space for near the fire. The contents of their knapsacks had stayed relatively dry, although Deakin's tinderbox had come open in his and showered everything with bark. Deakin divided their possessions more evenly and said that he and Fletcher would carry the two knapsacks next day.

Shan thought she had never seen Deakin quite so restless as he was that morning. He paced about, talking, rearranging the clothes, once going out to cut more firewood. She was amazed that Fletcher could sleep through so much activity.

"Aren't you going to go to sleep?" she asked at last, hopefully. She had found a dry spot to lie down in.

Deakin made an impatient gesture. "Can't sleep. Can't ever sleep after I fight."

"Why not?" said Shan, reasonably, looking at Fletcher.

"'Cause I'll have dreams. Nightmares. You've seen."

Shan leaned up on one elbow and looked at him, mystified.

"Thought you liked fighting."

"Better than anything. Wolf, aren't I?"

"So am I, but don't like fighting," said Shan, but Deakin ignored her.

"What we're trained for, isn't it?" he said, pacing again, making impatient jabs at the air with his knife and then tossing it from hand to hand, sending it arcing high in the firelight. "What we're best at. And I'm the best of all of us. Can't ever touch me. Tonight, that was nothing. Barely a scratch, and in the dark, besides. Blind luck. No one's as good as I am, Shan-Cub. Know that, do you?"

He dropped into a crouch beside her, the movement so sudden that Shan flinched away.

"No. Yes," she said. She had almost been asleep.

"No one's ever going to get me. No one," said Deakin, softly.

Shan realized that he was not really talking to her. She put her head down again and stopped listening. For a few minutes more she was aware of Deakin beside her, and then she slept.

Fletcher woke the other two well before noon. Deakin grabbed for his sword at Fletcher's touch, but Fletcher had taken the precaution of putting his foot on the blade first. Shan did not awaken so violently, but she, too, felt tense and nervous. None of them had slept long enough.

"Safe enough here, we are," said Fletcher. "Can't sense anyone else nearby. But should be moving on anyway. Wolves from the border might come tracking."

"Did magic, did you?" said Shan, worried. "Won't Arkanan know?"

"Sensing isn't magic. Just have to be quiet and feel it."

"Even so." Deakin was worried, too. "How sure are you of that?"

Fletcher shrugged.

Shan dressed in her tunic, which was grey-brown and had short sleeves. It fell to about mid-thigh when she had belted it. She took the strap off her swordbelt to wear it as an ordinary belt. Deakin and Fletcher had red-brown tunics with longer sleeves, as well as loose brown trousers, which they had worn uncomfortably under their uniforms the day before. All three of them put on their boots, which were practical and did not identify them as Wolves, although it was a little odd for a Perin child to be anything but barefoot in the summer. Dressed, they were strangers to each other.

"Going to travel by daylight, are we?" said Shan.

"Why not? No Wolves within miles of here. No towns, no mines, almost no Perinan."

They ate in silence. When Deakin had finished he buckled on his swordbelt, sword and all, over his tunic.

"No one to see us, is there?" he said, in answer to Fletcher's unspoken question.

"Never want to wear a sword again," said Fletcher.

"Did anyone ask what you wanted?" Deakin picked up Fletcher's sword and belt and dumped them on Fletcher's lap with a weary gesture, then began to pack the three uniforms into the knapsacks. "Put it on, Fletch."

"Killed a Wolf last night, I did," said Fletcher.

"So did I, probably. At least one. Would have killed us, wouldn't they? And got no right to keep us out of our own land."

"Think the Queen was right, though," said Fletcher. "Can't help the people of Redmetal by killing them. Have to make this journey not as Wolves, but as three of the people."

"Put it on," said Deakin, without turning round.

"Don't think we're going to need — "

Deakin reached him in one bound, jerked him to his feet, and pinned him roughly against the wall. Shan stood up, uncertainly.

"Haven't got much patience today, Fletcher." Deakin's voice was still flat, but that was the first time Shan had heard him use Fletcher's full name. "Gave you an order twice and that ought to be enough for anyone. Now put on the cursed swordbelt and let's get moving."

Shan held her breath, afraid that Fletcher would point out to Deakin that he was no longer Alpha, and afraid that, if he did, the two of them were going to have a real fight. But when Deakin released him, Fletcher picked up the swordbelt without another word.

The rain had stopped, although the sky was grey and close. In daylight Shan could see that the house they had spent the night in did not stand alone. There had once been a village here, with cleared land around it, and for several miles there were traces of a cart track.

They kept walking roughly northeast, guided by Fletcher's sense of direction, avoiding swampland when they could. They travelled through dark stands of cedar and hemlock where their feet were almost silent. They pushed their way through brambles and clumps of sumac in the open places. Shan saw deer and rabbits, squirrels and groundhogs, two sleeping porcupines and innumerable birds. At least there seemed to be no danger of starvation.

A few hours into the journey, a weasel crossed their path and all three of them said "avert" almost in unison, to turn the bad luck aside. After that, though they did not look at each other, Shan felt that they were become friends again. They found apple trees on a hillside, and munched sour apples as they walked.

Thinking about bad luck reminded Shan of something she had forgotten until then.

"Almost Borean Alari, isn't it?" she asked, abruptly.

She had switched to Arkan, instead of saying "Night of the Dancers," because she did not want to mention the Dancers by name when their Night was approaching.

"Three days away," said Deakin.

"But what are we going to do that night? Isn't safe to sleep outside, is it?"

"Probably not. But possible," said Deakin. Neither he nor Fletcher seemed worried. "Knew four Wolves who did it once, on a dare, and no harm came to any of them. And Fletch has done it, too, haven't you, Fletch?"

"Twice," said Fletcher, "though not for fun."

"Why, then?" asked Shan.

Fletcher shrugged.

"Because I was wizard and had no one to learn from and thought I might be able to learn something from, you know, Them."

"And did you?"

"Not really. Aren't concerned with us, with our world. Just chance that our worlds draw together on that one night of the year, so that they can see us and we can see them, and then draw gradually apart again. Can't share much with us. Play tricks, sometimes. Sometimes give gifts."

"But aren't — They — terribly dangerous?" said Shan. "Don't They sometimes kill travellers?"

"Might have killed Gale," said Deakin.

"No," said Fletcher. "Was his own foolishness killed Gale."

"Who was Gale?"

"Was in Marsen's pack with us," Deakin explained. "Went out on Borean Alari, very drunk, with his sword and a rope, saying he was going to the forest to capture one of Them. In Redmetal Town, we were that year."

"Didn't your Alpha stop him?" said Shan.

"Think Marsen was glad enough to be rid of him," said Deakin, with a flash of amusement in his tone. "Anyway, Gale never came back. Perin miners found him dead in one of the tunnels next day. Fell down a ventilation shaft and broke his neck. Hardly surprising, given how drunk he was. But we never found his sword. Or the rope."

"Don't worry about Borean Alari," said Fletcher to Shan. "Promise you we'll be quite safe, even outdoors."

Fletcher sensed no other human beings anywhere, all that day. At night they camped by a stream, and Deakin took the first watch. After it he awakened both the others, Shan to take the middle watch and Fletcher to concentrate for a moment and see if anyone were near them before returning to sleep again. Fletcher was to take the final watch, because first light was the most likely time for an attack.

Shan hated middle watch. She sat by the fire and sang softly to herself in an effort to keep awake. Her watch was short, because Deakin began to scream and cry in his sleep, calling for his father as if he were a child again. After he had awakened himself and Fletcher twice, he said that Shan might as well go back to sleep and let him stay on guard.

☙❧

Varian appeared in the middle of her garden in the Maze, laden with cuttings, plants, and even a terrified rabbit that she had hypnotized with her touch. She released the skirts of her robe and let all the new life spill out onto the grass and moss. The rabbit disappeared behind a jumble of rocks by the waterfall. Varian bent down to retrieve a thornbush. She should find a home for it as quickly as possible if she wanted it to survive here.

In a swirl of black robe, Kron appeared in front of her. "Varian, I am happy to see thou hast again time to waste on thy garden. Thou hast solved no doubt for us the riddle of immortality. I await eagerly thine answer."

In the soft white light of the cavern his gaunt face was impatient. Varian could feel his power and was suddenly aware of how magically exhausted she was at this moment. Unlike her, Kron had magic to spare. She stumbled through a reply, the thornbush sagging unnoticed in her hands, its roots dripping dirt onto the grass.

"I have been working constantly on the problem. I find sometimes a journey can concentrate my mind . . . "

"I have been working constantly also. I have been studying the Firedrake. I have been thinking. Perhaps if we were to prison another wizard, one as like to Tarn as possible, the power of the Firedrake might be increased. Thou and Sevrin were apprentices of Tarn, were ye not?"

Varian was not seriously afraid of Kron, for she knew he needed her talents, but she suspected the threat to Sevrin was real. He had not been useful to Kron for a long time. She sought quickly for a distraction.

"Thou hast thought well, as always. Perhaps if we work together, we can reach a solution. Sit and eat with me." She plucked a ripe pear and tossed it to him, but Kron was not in the mood for eating. It smashed on the moss, splattering some nearby leaves.

Kron paced back and forth across the lush green floor of the garden. "Rememberest thou,

Varian, when we sacrificed the children? Rememberest thou how the Firedrake was to them no barrier, as to us it is? It had no power to prevent them from reaching the Wheel. They passed through it."

Varian did not like to think of the children, but she made an effort now. "Yes, and were consumed then by the Wheel. They grew old and died, helping us not at all."

"I have been wondering why it is that the Firedrake did not prevent them reaching the Wheel, as it prevents us. Why, Varian? Tarn reached the Wheel, and with his power protected himself, but we cannot. Dost thou understand this?"

Varian nodded. "I have been following the same thoughts. I believe that what Tarn had in common with the children was that he had never taken life."

"What? What sayest thou, old woman?" Kron in his pacing had been trampling some of the new cuttings and now he stood still with his feet in lily leaves. "He had killed like the rest of us."

"He pretended," said Varian. "Few of ye knew. Tarn was the greatest healer who ever lived, and he feared greatly the loss of that power."

"Tarn had never killed?" She saw that Kron was reaching the same conclusion she had already reached.

"No. Like the children, he was able to touch the Wheel. With his magic, he was able to protect himself. It might be that if we found another like Tarn, a healer, we could use him in the same way. But Kron, believe me, I have thought long of this. We have no one. I have taken life, Sevrin has taken life, long ago in the war. This Wolf we seek has likely also killed. There are no healers left."

Kron's wrinkled face broke into a smile. He almost pranced on the lilies. "Thou art wrong. If we need healers, we can find them."

"What dost thou mean?"

"Varian, thou canst not feel all that I feel. Magic is used even yet in the land. There are places still where people see the future and have power flow through their hands. They are untrained but the power is there."

"Then we have the answer!" Varian's face was alight. "We shall find these Perin wizards. We shall teach them magic, whether or not they want to learn it. We shall teach them to protect themselves. Then we shall give them to the Wheel, and they will achieve true immortality.

Long ago, as thou mayest remember, we thought it would be that simple for all of us."

"But — "

"I know how we can do what remains," said Varian. "We can forge a link between the healer and one of us, and one of us can take his body. And that body, having passed through the Wheel, will remain forever unchanged. Think of it!"

They stared at each other, bright-eyed, triumphant.

"To leave the Plain and live in the sunlight!" said Varian.

"To be young again, with a strong new body!" said Kron.

"And if this works," he continued, thinking it out, "we shall need never again to renew our youth. If a body can be found for each of us, we shall need no longer the Firedrake."

"We must tell the others." Varian's energy was renewed. "Where are they?"

Kron sent out a quick thought. "They are all in the Maze, excepting only Hinton, who is afar off."

"No doubt he is in Forix, searching yet again for Tarn's lost book," said Varian, dryly.

Kron cackled with laughter. "The young are so restless, are they not? But no, he is not so far as that. Let us astonish him with the wisdom of his elders."

They walked through the Maze to the Council chamber and Kron called the Arkanan to join them there. Hinton came last, on a wave of anger and protest. "I had him! I was keeping guard as ye asked, ready to detect the renegade wizard if he used his powers! And I felt just now magic, just as ye summoned me and blasted it out of existence! Why did ye think I went so far from the Maze? Yet again ye have stood in my way, prevented— "

"Thou hast found a wizard?" Kron said, eagerly.

"I doubt it is the one we seek. He was east of Cardy Plain, not west. I sensed him only briefly. Whether I can find him again now thou hast interrupted — "

"We shall try together," said Kron. "We want all the wizards we can find. If thou hast found one, it may be that thou wilt be the first to walk in the sun. Listen. Varian and I have wonderful news."

Chapter 20

Deakin must have slept at last, for he was still sleeping peacefully when Shan awoke. She could not see Fletcher, but she heard the axe and knew where he was. She had a drink of water and did her readiness drill.

"Make arrows, can you?" Fletcher asked her, quietly, when she had finished.

"Can try," said Shan.

He had cut two good pieces of hickory for bows, and Shan felt half-ashamed and half-relieved that he was not going to make a bow for her. She knew that she could not see well enough to hunt. Fletcher walked a little way downstream and cut a pile of willow sticks for the arrows, and the two of them sat down by the fire to work.

"Using your stone knife, are you?" said Shan, in surprise.

"Don't you know magic knives never need sharpening? Just don't cut yourself, all right?" said

Fletcher, and Shan was not sure that he was joking. She was very careful.

Fletcher measured the potential bows with his eyes and showed her how long to make the arrows to fit them, and Shan spent the rest of the morning carving. Fletcher made two plain and sturdy bows, thick in the centre and thin at the ends, with nocks for the bowstrings. Shan made a pile of arrows, straightening them as well as she could with her knife and then smoothing them with a rough stone. They worked in silence, but Shan enjoyed the morning and felt quietly content.

When Deakin awakened he did not seem inclined to talk either. He did his readiness drill, and then sat down beside Shan and picked up her arrows one by one, doing a little repair work when they were not perfectly straight. One of them he considered beyond repair, and he snapped it in half and threw the pieces on the fire without comment. As he finished each arrow he hardened the point in the fire and then fletched it, using linen threads to attach the feathers. The three of them worked together until there were no goose feathers left.

The day was well advanced by the time they set out again, and they covered few miles in what remained of it. Deakin and Fletcher walked with their bows strung and shot at anything that moved, mostly for practice, so that they spent some time standing still to shoot and a great deal more time retrieving arrows.

"Could make more," Shan suggested once, after Deakin had spent several minutes searching a thicket and finally emerged with a broken arrow.

"Need the feathers," he said. "Won't find any others as good as these. Want a turn, do you, Cub?"

Shan took the bow, not because she wanted it, but because she suspected that the cut on Deakin's shoulder was becoming painful. She was hopeless at shooting. Sometimes she could not even see the target that Deakin pointed at, and even when it was close enough for her to see she could rarely hit it. Trees were the only thing she could sometimes hit, because it was impossible to overshoot them, and even with trees she often missed. She also had trouble seeing where her arrows landed, and usually Deakin had to retrieve them. After he had twice been forced to climb trees to do this, he took the bow away from her.

"Never be a hunter," he said. "Have to teach you to set traps, won't we?"

Both he and Fletcher shot rabbits during the course of the afternoon, so that when they stopped for the night there was rabbit stew for supper. Shan was hungry and thought the meal was wonderful, though it seemed to take an unreasonably long time to cook. They used apples to flavour the gravy, and the last of their bread to soak it up with.

"Why doesn't anyone live around here?" Shan asked, as the world faded into soft darkness. "If I were Perin, I'd build my house in a place like this. No Wolves to interfere."

Deakin shrugged. "Perinan like to be with other Perinan."

"Why aren't there any villages here, then?"

"There are. Small ones. Not worth bothering about. More danger from Perin rebels, here, than from Wolves. Nothing much north of here until we reach Forix."

"Forix?" Shan's heart jumped. She remembered what Briar had told her of the legendary city of the wizards. "Near Forix, are we?"

"About a week south of it."

"What's it like?"

"Never been there," said Deakin. "Why? What do you know about it?"

"Used to be the capital, didn't it?" said Shan, and, looking into the fire, she repeated Briar's story-formula softly. "Long ago, when our land was green, and Arkanan were good wizards, and we were all Perinan together."

She had wondered if Deakin might object to this, but instead he said, "Didn't know you told stories, Cub. Go on, then."

So Shan continued, formally.

"In those days the land was called Perinar, because it had not yet become known for its red metal. Rufer was mined for the people's needs, but there was no trade in it. Aram to the south and Iluthia to the east kept trying to push into our land, so the Kunan Keir, the company of Wolves, was created to keep the borders, and also to prevent raiders from Aram from stealing our cattle and taking our children as slaves. Wolves fought with shields as well as swords, then, and the packs lived mainly off the land, patrolling up and down the borders, and might spend years without . . . without . . . "

Shan had forgotten what they had done without.

"Eating toasted cheese?" suggested Deakin.

"Washing?" suggested Fletcher.

" . . . without sleeping under a roof," Shan finished, ignoring these suggestions. "The Kunan Keir were greatly loved and respected by all the people. Anyone who wanted to join could go to the school when he came of age. There were no Cubs in those days. The land was ruled by the Arkanan, the wizards, who met four times a year in Forix. Children born wizard would usually go to Forix when they got old enough, to learn from the wizards there and to practise their art. A few stayed there, but most returned to their home villages, so that there were wizards in many places. They were the healers, and the settlers of disputes, and the people went to them for advice. A wizard would often know where he or she was needed, and would go there without being told. But Forix, being the city of the wizards, was the most beautiful city in the whole land and was full of marvels.

"Suppose it's not like that now?" she said, lapsing into ordinary speech.

Deakin shook his head.

"Ruins now. And some of the water around Forix is still poisonous."

"Poisonous?" Shan was surprised. "Why?"

"Fletch knows that part of the story, don't you, Fletch?"

"Not for certain," said Fletcher. "No one does, except Arkanan themselves. But know more than most, I do, because I've seen pieces of it."

His voice was so soft that Shan had to be completely still, and forget all else, in order to hear him.

"There was war first, real war, against Aram. The Araman forced the Kunan Keir back all the way to the town of Redmetal, burning villages and destroying the land. Wizards who had once been able to defend their towns found that the Araman no longer feared their illusionary armies. They had learned that the illusions could do them no permanent harm. Eventually one of the wizards, a man called Kron, discovered a way to throw fire, to destroy the enemy by magic. The wizards were able then to destroy the Araman army, and they pursued the Araman back into their own country, killing and destroying, wounding the land as our land had been wounded. Very few Araman survived to return home, and there were no more wars after that.

"But, because the wizards had taken life, they found that they had lost their powers of healing. Perhaps they saw no purpose, then, in returning to their home villages. Perhaps they were hurt by what they had done, so that they began to look inward instead of outward. Or perhaps it was that they had learned what deadly power they possessed, and had learned to enjoy the use of it. Don't know. Haven't ever used magic to kill, or even to hurt, so don't know what it did to them.

"But they no longer ruled the land for the good of the people. They stayed in Forix and never went outside it, and they no longer allowed other wizards to join them. The city of Forix grew richer and more powerful, and while others went hungry, food and wealth poured into Forix.

"People began to question. Eventually a group of young wizards challenged Arkanan, and there was a magical battle, which lasted three days and three nights and levelled half of Forix, killing many of its people. Arkanan won the battle, and after it they turned what was left of the city into a stronghold, surrounding it with pitfalls and enchantments. In the middle of the city they created a lake, and then they poisoned the sources of all other water in the region, so that for three days march around Forix there was no water safe to drink.

"When the young wizards did not return, the handful of wizards who were left, and the Kunan Keir, and a great many other people as well, marched against Arkanan. But the water was poisoned, and of all those who started for Forix, only about half lived to reach it. And they were sick and weak, easy prey for Arkanan. Some may even have tried to retreat, but they had no water to drink on the return journey. None of them got inside the walls of Forix, and none of them ever returned home."

Shan thought sadly of all those long-ago Wolves. Were they like us? she wondered. Did they look like us, dress like us? Were they allowed to cry or did they have to keep their feelings hidden? Did they all die in silence?

"That was when Arkanan moved to Cardy Plain," Fletcher said. "Forix was no longer habitable. The Plain was not barren then, of course. But Arkanan started working on the secret to eternal life, to maintain their power forever."

"How many wizards were there then?" Shan asked.

"Lots. Dozens."

"Well, why aren't there lots more now, then? Why aren't there so many wizards being born?"

"There are," said Fletcher. "But have to practise in secret now, don't they? Have no one to teach them and no one to help them, and, worst of all, no way of learning Arkan unless they happen to be chosen for Cub. Can't cast spells if they don't know the language. But didn't you tell us that Briar's grandmother had a gift for reading the future? And many villages have their healer, even now.

"One of the things that frightens me," he added, almost in a whisper, "is that Arkanan are trying to find me by my magic. How many wizards have they found, since they began searching for me? How many wizards have already given their lives for mine?"

Deakin stood up, as if he had come to a decision.

"Sword, Fletch," he said, and held out his hand for it.

Fletcher handed over his sword without comment. Deakin struck it against a rock until the blade sang aloud and snapped. Then he did the same thing with his own sword. No one said anything. Deakin returned quietly to the fire and sat down beside Shan, poking at the embers with a stick.

In daylight Shan might have been pleased that Deakin had destroyed the swords, but in the darkness their fire seemed like a tiny spark in the forest and the three of them small and defenseless. She could have wished for better weapons than wooden arrows, or knives that could only be used once. That night, alone on watch, she huddled close to the fire and strained her ears for any unnatural sound, keeping her fingers closed around the hilt of her knife.

Before the end of her watch, the moon emerged from behind clouds and flooded the world with a soft, friendly light. Shan relaxed a little. She heard a single wolf howl somewhere to the north, and then the rest of its pack joined in, their voices weaving in and out of each other's in random, complicated harmonies. My wild brothers and sisters, thought Shan, and was sorry when their song ended. It had made the night less lonely.

Her watch ended at last. She awakened Fletcher and watched his face go still and the light fade out of his eyes as he checked for the presence of other minds around him. Shan waited, but his gaze did not return to her. Slowly he stood up.

"What is it?" Shan whispered.

She saw Deakin lift his head.

"Redthorn, I think," said Fletcher.

He left her and walked quietly into the forest, on the southwest side of the clearing. Shan and Deakin both followed. Fletcher did not turn, though he must have been aware of them. He led the way, quietly but without caution, and the three of them walked in silence for about ten minutes. Shan was mystified. Redthorn was probably no physical threat to them now, but he had only to catch a glimpse of them to let Arkanan know exactly where they were. Why were they walking toward him? Shouldn't they be running in the opposite direction?

Fletcher stopped.

"Stay here," he said to the other two, and went on alone. Fletcher could move almost soundlessly when he chose, and not even a rustle marked his passage as he disappeared among the trees. Whether this ability were a magical one, or whether he simply had very good night vision, Shan did not know.

She whispered to Deakin, "What's he doing?"

"How should I know?" said Deakin. "Not wizard, am I?"

They waited tensely. Fletcher returned a few minutes later and signalled them to come with him. They followed him to a place where the trees thinned out, a rocky hillside that they had crossed that afternoon.

Redthorn lay face down in the open, with his left arm flung out as if he had tried to break his fall. Shan thought at first that he was dead.

"Asleep," said Fletcher, softly. "Exhausted."

Redthorn had found help somewhere, probably at the border, for his right shoulder was tightly bound and he was wearing a sword again. His head was turned a little to the left and the long scar showed, startling against the pallor of his face. He looked frail and old. No one would have guessed that he had once been commander of the Kunan Keir.

"Look at him," said Deakin. "No food, no supplies, no bow. What was he planning to live on?"

The use of the past tense hit Shan like a blow in the stomach. She looked at Deakin quickly, her lips parted to object or question, but Deakin motioned her to silence. He squatted down beside Redthorn and put his hand on the hilt of Redthorn's sword. No response. His eyes flicked a question at Fletcher.

"Would take a lot to wake him now," said Fletcher.

Deakin drew the sword from its scabbard, very slowly and cautiously. When it was done he stood up with the sword in his hand and stared down at Redthorn.

"Know we should kill him, don't you?" he said. "Didn't take him long to track us this far, did it?"

Neither of the others spoke, but Shan felt the knot in her stomach dissolve. She knew Deakin well enough to know that if he were going to kill Redthorn he would have done it by now, without hesitation and certainly without discussion.

"Should cripple him, at least," said Deakin, "so he can't follow us any further."

He made no move to do it. He began to scratch in the dirt with the point of the sword.

"Doesn't look like he's going to get much further anyway. What's wrong with him?" he demanded of Fletcher.

"Isn't eating. Hasn't slept for a long time," said Fletcher. "Isn't doing anything but hunting us."

Shan saw that the drawing in the dirt was a salamander, crude but recognizable. Deakin was here. When he had finished it, Deakin drove the sword into the ground a few inches from Redthorn's face. Deakin was here and could have killed you.

"Shouldn't we take the sword away from him?" Shan suggested.

"Why? At least with a sword he looks Wolf. Might be able to get food from Perinan, if he sees any Perinan."

Deakin turned away.

"Come on. Let's get some miles between us and him before dawn."

Chapter 21

For the next two days they walked almost constantly. Deakin pushed them hard. He seemed to be angry, perhaps at himself for not being able to kill Redthorn and remove the threat, perhaps at Redthorn for arousing his compassion. Occasionally he would mention something savagely practical that he should have done to prevent Redthorn from following them any further.

On the third day, which would end with the Night of the Dancers, his mood had changed, and in fact he spent part of the day singing as he walked. Shan joined in, once she had picked up the tune.

"Have a pretty voice, you do," said Deakin. "Sing something for me."

Shan had always loved singing, and once she got over her self-consciousness she enjoyed singing for Deakin, who kept silent and listened for a whole half hour. After Shan had sung all the songs she knew, he taught her more, including all fifty-one verses of the Song of Lin. Lin had lived among the wolves, and some said that was the reason the army were called the Kunan Keir.

"Lucky thing it was wolves," said Deakin. "Could have been raccoons."

"Squirrels," said Shan, amused.

"Skunks."

Because it was the Night of the Dancers, Fletcher suggested that they should make camp in the early evening, well before dark. The two men took their bows and went off in search of supper. Shan built a fireplace and collected armloads of wood. On one expedition, she found a fallen tree and chopped away at it until she had some good logs. The ring of the axe was the only sound in the stillness, and she suddenly realized that the forest had been still all day, although she had been too busy singing to notice. It was as if the forest were waiting for something. As she carried the logs back to the camp, she thought she heard a laugh, but when she froze and listened, the whole forest was silent.

She started a fire and waited, uneasily, for Deakin and Fletcher to return. If she had known where to start, she would have gone in search of them. She was suddenly sure that they would not find anything to hunt, and, although she had not eaten all day, she no longer wanted them to try. There was no more laughter, though she waited for it tensely. Instead, a few minutes later, there was a scream.

The scream was real; there was nothing vague or illusory about it, and before it had ended Shan had drawn her knife and was running along the bank of the stream. Ahead of her, a child began to wail.

There were two children, she saw when she got close enough. They were small Perin boys, no more than five or six years old. Shan sheathed her knife, not wanting to frighten them any more than they were frightened already. One of them was running about on the grass, wailing. The other, who seemed too terrified to make a sound, had fallen from the top of the bank and was clinging to a tree, just above the water. His eyes were huge and his face pale. Shan was amused by all this exaggerated panic. The water was probably no higher than the boy's waist.

She took off her boots and waded out into the stream. The boy weighed almost nothing and she scooped him up easily. She was tempted to duck him, just to show him that a little water would do him no harm, but he screamed and clung to her so pathetically that she relented and set him on the bank beside his friend. The two boys hugged each other, and Shan scrambled up beside them. Only then did she realize that they were not human children.

She took a step backward, more in surprise than in fear, and watched as they began to talk to each other. Their speech was a series of "churrs" and chitterings, rather like a squirrel's, shrill and expressive and totally unlike human speech. They jumped about as they talked, unable to stay still for an instant in their joy at being reunited.

Looked at directly, they were very like the Perin children Shan had taken them for. They were dark-haired and brown-skinned, dressed in ragged brown clothes. Their eyes were black, as deep and lustrous as water by night, and their teeth were unexpectedly bright and slightly pointed. All this Shan could see when she looked straight at them. But if she happened to catch a glimpse of them out of the corner of her eye, as she had while climbing up the bank, they did not look human at all. Then they seemed to be covered with short brown fur, and she could see pricked ears and sharply-pointed, wild little faces. As soon as she looked at them directly, they became human again.

This was disconcerting. Not sure how to react, Shan sat down and put on her boots. The children seemed to remember her then and ran to her, laughing and chattering, taking her hands in their own little hands, or paws, and pulling her to her feet. They obviously wanted her to go somewhere with them, and Shan, intrigued, allowed them to lead her further into the forest.

The three of them travelled quickly, the boys running, pulling at Shan's hands. Once there was a clear whistle from somewhere ahead, a little tune of six notes, and Shan's escorts answered with four notes which completed the tune. This happened again a few minutes later, and Shan wondered if it were a password. She began to catch glimpses of other Dancers among the trees, all hurrying in the same direction. Then she could hear voices ahead, a great many of them, chattering away in their strange animal language.

She was led up a steep and wooded hill and onto a wide plain of rock, scrub grass, and low bushes, where the wind blew cold and strong. By now there were Dancers all around. The sun had gone down, but there was still some light left in

the western sky and against it Shan could see the
sinuous silhouettes of the gathered Dancers,
hundreds of them. Her escorts led her through
them, though not quickly, for all the Dancers
were fascinated by Shan and flocked around her.
She felt their soft paws on her face, her clothes,
and her hair, while the boys apparently
explained, interminably, why they had brought
her here. Few of the Dancers were any taller than
Shan was. They seemed to find her amusing, and
she had never seen so many laughing faces, nor
so many sharp white teeth. On the edges of her
vision they were terrifying. They were like giant
weasels, she thought, and wondered if that was
why weasels were considered unlucky. She turned
her head and swivelled her eyes constantly, trying
to keep them all looking human.

The Dancers, in turn, were as wary of Shan as
she was of them. If she moved suddenly or
reached toward them, they would all spring away
and then return, laughing, as if to show that they
had not really been frightened at all. Shan was
offered food, some of the Dancers trying, with
their quick, eager movements, to thrust it into
her mouth, but she turned her head aside and
would not eat. She had heard many tales that
warned against magic food, and although she was

hungry she had no wish to be turned into an animal, or sleep for a hundred years, or forget her friends forever.

By the time she reached the centre of that strange gathering, the light of the sun had died and been replaced by cold moonlight, and Shan had a large crowd of excited followers. In the centre she saw a group of musicians, with pipes and drums and stringed instruments. Behind them she caught a glimpse of another kind of animal, bigger, and with great leathery wings.

He was the tallest Dancer she had seen, and, now that she looked at him directly, his furled wings had become a tattered brown cloak which hung down behind him. Because none of the others were winged, and because they had made room for him and fallen into silence, Shan was sure he must be their Alpha. She was not afraid of him, perhaps because something in his face reminded her strongly of Fletcher, but she felt an unaccustomed awe and wondered if she ought to kneel. No, not just Alpha; must be their King, she decided as he came closer.

Then her eyes met his.

She felt a downward rush, a sudden fall into darkness as the world slipped away from her. When she found herself again she was on her knees, though she did not remember kneeling, and she felt confused and a little frightened. Then she looked up into the King's face again and her fear left her. He was talking to the two boys, but his gaze remained on Shan and she felt she could have knelt at his feet forever. She had forgotten about Deakin and Fletcher. She had forgotten who she was. All need to think or question had left her, for a little time, and she was relaxed and deeply at peace.

Behind her the music began, at first only a high, joyous piping in which the same ten notes she had heard before were often repeated, the pipers weaving in and out of each other's melodies. The soft beat of the drums came in beneath them, and finally the low-pitched, insistent throb of the strings. The King smiled at Shan, a gentle smile except that his teeth were so pointed, and then the two boys took her hands and pulled her with them, into the dance.

The rest of the night whirled past Shan like a dream. She spun from Dancer to Dancer, from human to animal and back again, from moonlight to shadow, surrounded always by their laughter and their great goodwill, held by their strong hands, leaping and running and turning in wild celebration of the Night. Sometimes she sat in the grass while Dancers crowded around to compete for the honour of feeding her, offering smooth slices of some strange and delicious meat, or bowls of sweet, sticky liquid. She had forgotten her fears as well as everything else.

Once one of the boys — she could not tell them apart — knelt in front of her and whistled again their little ten-note tune, indicating that he wanted Shan to repeat it. She was eating the Dancers' food contentedly, in a dreamy haze, and he had to take her head between his hands and frown fiercely into her face before, much amused, she tried to whistle the tune back to him. She had never learned to whistle well, and the Dancers chortled with delighted laughter. The boy only smiled, with a quick flash of white teeth, and urged her to try again. He was so insistent that Shan obeyed, not only then but many times throughout the night, and the tune became a part of her as she became a part of the dance.

The dance ended for Shan with the first stain of dawn, although for the Dancers it only seemed to move somewhere else. They whirled away into the forest, following their King, and for a while Shan pursued them, not wanting the dance to end. They outdistanced her and she stumbled to a halt, confused and suddenly exhausted. She stretched out on the ground and fell immediately into sleep.

When she awoke it took her a little time to remember who she was and how she had come there. She lay quietly, staring up through apple tree branches at a dazzling sky, ignoring the excited voices around her, and gradually her self came back to her. She remembered the wonders of the night, the joy she had felt, the wild beauty of the dance and its Dancers. Then she remembered how she had rescued the boy, and at long last she came back to a slow realization of who she was and a slow remembrance of her life. She sat up, not at all frightened to find herself surrounded by strangers. They were saying ridiculously obvious things like, "Waking up, she is," so she knew they must be Perinan. She brushed grass out of her hair and looked around her.

There were perhaps fifteen Perinan gathered under the apple trees, all children except for one ancient, toothless woman. From what they said, Shan knew that someone had gone off to fetch the adults from wherever they were working. Two of the oldest boys, who were about twelve years old, had bows and arrows, and the bows were drawn and the arrows pointed at Shan. The sight of those arrows brought her back to the real world.

"How did you come here?" demanded the old woman. "Who are you?"

Most of the children had never seen a stranger in their lives, Shan realized, and she was an object of suspicion on two other counts as well. She had no knapsack or supplies, and she was armed.

"Shan." She stood up slowly. "Just a traveller. Don't mean any harm."

"Wolf, are you?" said the woman, at once.

It had shown not only in Shan's flat voice, but in her stance and expression as well. She decided the truth was best.

"Used to be Wolf. Not any more."

"Draw your knife slowly and drop it on the ground," said the woman, and Shan did as she was told. "What do you mean, 'Used to be Wolf'? Ran away, did you?"

"No. Killed an Arkan, my Alpha did."

To Shan's dismay, the children did not know what "Arkan" meant, while the old woman firmly maintained that all the wizards had died years before.

"But who do you think rules the land, then?" Shan asked.

"Wolves, of course. All know that."

Shan felt a touch of fear. "No. Arkanan rule. Tell Wolves what to do."

"Haven't I told you that all Wolves are liars?" said the woman to the children, complacently.

"Maybe she's a Wolf spy," one of them suggested. "Dressed like that to fool us."

"Why would Wolves want to spy on us?" said the woman. "Anyway, look at her. Only half-grown."

But the children liked the idea that Shan was a spy. Several of them began to talk at once. Shan tried again to explain who she was, but no one was paying the slightest attention to her now except the two boys with the bows, who had clearly been trained, for hunting, to stand with their bows drawn for long periods of time, and were still guarding her valiantly.

"What's going on here?" From behind the children, an adult voice cut sharply through the babble. Shan thought she knew that voice. The children fell silent.

"Why? Who are you?" said the old woman.

"Gordin's men," the newcomer replied, curtly. "Looking for a runaway girl, we are, and sounds as if you've found her for us."

It was Deakin, but he spoke as if he were Perin. Fletcher was with him, behind and a little to one side like a personal guard.

"Said she used to be Wolf," said the woman to Deakin, uncertainly.

"Used to be Cub," said Deakin. "Escaped from the school." He and Fletcher had almost reached Shan now. The two boys lowered their bows and stared at the men with awe. "Caught her, Wolves did, and left her for dead, but she survived. Been this way ever since." He picked up Shan's knife from the ground and handed it to her, still talking. "Her mind's gone. Doesn't know where she is, half the time, or what she's doing. Wanders off on her own like this."

He had been looking at Shan, who was glad that her face would not show her amusement. Now he looked directly at the old woman.

"But very good at killing Wolves, she is," he said, and grinned suddenly, showing his teeth.

The children looked uneasy, and two of them actually took a step backward. Shan saw disgust in the woman's face.

"Get out of here and take the poor girl with you," she said.

"Come on," said Deakin, and Shan was only too glad to obey, especially as she could hear the adult population of the hamlet approaching.

"Where are you going?" asked one boy as Deakin passed him. He blushed a little at his own daring.

"Don't ask where he's going," said another boy. "Can't tell you that, can he?" and the first boy blushed even redder.

The woman called the children back to her.

"Going to join you one day, I am," said the second boy, quickly.

He started back, turned, and shouted after Deakin, "My name's Victor!"

The three travellers were out of his sight now, but they heard him and Deakin muttered, "Wants to kill Wolves, does he? Hope the brat gets chosen for Cub."

Shan thought that there might not be any more Cubs chosen soon, if Arkanan were defeated, but she did not remind Deakin of this. The three of them walked quickly and in silence until they had left the hamlet far behind. Then Deakin unexpectedly stopped and took Shan by the shoulders, gazing into her face. Before she could ask what he wanted, he gave her a hard shake and released her.

"What were you playing at last night, wandering off alone like that?"

Shan stumbled into explanations, but Fletcher interrupted. He sounded amused.

"Had Deakin worried, you did. Kept telling him you were all right. Although there was a moment . . . " He became serious again. "Met him, didn't you?"

"Who?" asked Deakin, but Shan knew.

"Their King," she said. "Yes."

"Is that what you call him?" said Fletcher.

"Isn't that what he is?"

"If you like."

"Have you seen him?" asked Shan, and, when Fletcher shook his head, she said, "Looks like you. A little."

"Does he?" said Fletcher, strangely unsurprised.

Their eyes met and Shan saw the likeness again, the faint echo, in Fletcher's eyes, of the power that shone from the King of the Dancers.

"What are you two talking about?" asked Deakin.

They started walking again, and Shan explained how she had heard the boy scream and had gone to help him.

"Would it have killed him? The water?" she interrupted herself to ask.

"Would have made him mortal," said Fletcher. "One of us."

Shan went on to tell the rest of her story. The other two listened with such fascination that she enjoyed herself. Fletcher, she thought, was impressed and even a little envious when he learned how Shan had spent the Night of the Dancers.

"Not many humans have joined that dance," he said.

"What about the tune the boy taught me?" Shan asked.

She had not thought about it at the time, but now she wondered if the boy had meant it as a gift, a safe-conduct through his strange world.

"Owes you a life, he does," said Fletcher, "and means to repay it if he can. Probably wants you to whistle that tune if you ever need his help."

Now Deakin was impressed as well. "Even if it isn't their Night? Shan wouldn't be able to see him, would she?"

"Perhaps not. But he'd answer all the same, and help her if he could. Think you'd have to be in the forest, though," he said to Shan.

Shan was thrilled to hear that she had such a powerful ally. It was like something out of Briar's tales. She finished her story, explaining how she had awakened to find herself surrounded.

"Do you know those people had never heard of Arkanan?" she said.

Deakin was not so surprised by this as Shan had been.

"So? A long way from Cardy Plain, aren't they? And a long way from Redmetal Town, as well. No one takes their children for Cub. Heard of Gordin's men, though, hadn't they? Did it well, didn't I?"

"Yes. Sounded exactly like Perin, you did," said Shan.

Deakin remembered something and turned on her suddenly.

"Just how blind are you, anyway? Not only did you fall asleep alone and unguarded, but you chose an apple orchard to do it in. In apple season. Would have served you right if we'd left you there."

"Yes, Alpha," said Shan, solemnly, and saw the corner of Deakin's mouth twitch.

Chapter 22

For a few more days they travelled north, undisturbed. Several times Fletcher sensed people close by, and twice they turned aside to walk around a farm or hamlet, but they saw no other human beings.

On the sixth morning, Shan stepped on something unpleasantly soft in the underbrush and found, to her dismay, that it was the body of a weasel. She did not tell the other two, but by noon it was obvious to all of them that their luck had turned.

"Had a dream, I did," said Fletcher, softly, while they were walking. "Dreamed of a healer. An old man. Found by Arkanan, while they were looking for me. Captured and taken to the Plain."

When he stopped and did not go on, Deakin asked, "Dead?"

Fletcher nodded. After a moment, he said, "Teaching him magic, Arkanan were."

"Teaching him magic? Why?"

"Not sure. But didn't succeed in whatever it was. He knew ... knew what they wanted. Deliberately provoked one of them into killing him. Chose to die rather than do ... whatever it was."

Fletcher said nothing more, and Deakin was also silent for some time after that.

The sky was cloudless, a deep clear blue, and sometimes there was a lone hawk patrolling it. The three travellers found themselves almost at once in low, swampy country. It stretched as far as they could see ahead of them and to both sides, with bright green vegetation, few trees, and rich black earth, the all-too-familiar signs of soft and treacherous ground.

There was no way to avoid it, and they did not waste breath complaining about it. Their progress was slow, as some of the time they had to wade rather than walk. The mud dragged at their boots, and the stink of swamp water gradually pervaded everything they wore. The ground was cruelly unpredictable, so that Shan could not tell whether her next step would be onto relatively firm mud or into stinking black slime that oozed over the tops of her boots.

It was exhausting work. Even Deakin seemed tired, though for a while he managed to talk and often he took Shan's hand and helped her when she floundered. His help was given so casually that she did not resent it. Twice they found solid ground and rested briefly, squatting down and drinking water from their flasks.

For a long time the landscape did not change, and Shan was not sure they were making any progress at all, but the smell kept getting worse and she noticed that the vegetation had become less. Abruptly Fletcher pointed to the northeast, and said, "Forix."

Shan straightened up for a moment and squinted, to try to catch a glimpse of the mythical city, but it was too far away for her to see and she soon lost interest as she struggled onward. The sun was directly overhead when she looked up again, and this time she could see a fuzzy line of hills. The swamp was not, after all, endless, and there was higher ground ahead, which the other two must have been able to see a long time before.

Fletcher stopped suddenly and raised his head. "Being watched, we are."

There was nowhere to hide.

"Where from? Should we turn back?" said Deakin, and Shan almost cried out in protest, thinking of the slow and horrible miles behind them.

"Forix," said Fletcher. "Can feel hate."

"Redthorn?" said Deakin. "How could it be Redthorn? Saw the condition he was in, didn't you? Couldn't have kept up with us all this time. Couldn't have passed us . . . "

His voice trailed off.

"Think it might be Redthorn?" Deakin asked again.

"Yes," said Fletcher.

The three travellers were facing each other, standing deep in mud. Their faces were still. Deakin drew his knife and the other two did the same.

"How long for Arkanan to get here, if Redthorn has seen us?" asked Deakin.

"Maybe seconds. Maybe a few minutes."

"Not the place I would have chosen to fight in. Come on."

Deakin started to move again, more quickly, and the other two squelched after him. Shan's fear gave her new strength. She would have liked to continue, to try to get out of the swamp, but

Deakin stopped as soon as he found firmer ground.

"Backs together," he said, and the three of them took up positions facing outward, with their stone knives ready and their shoulders almost touching.

Shan felt a little better on the ground that Deakin had chosen, where the mud was only just over her ankles, but it was much more difficult to stand still than it would have been to keep moving. She could feel her body shake with the rapid pounding of her heart.

When about five minutes had passed, Deakin said, almost as if he were disappointed, "Would have come by now, wouldn't they?"

"Probably," said Fletcher. "But still being watched, we are. And hated."

They were all used to waiting. Fifteen minutes more they waited, standing relaxed but with knives ready. Shan felt her head beginning to ache in time with the thud of her heartbeats. Finally Deakin said, "Let's at least try to get out of this stinking swamp."

They kept their knives in their hands as they walked.

"Think it could be someone else? Not Redthorn?" Deakin asked Fletcher after a few minutes.

Fletcher shrugged. "Could be that Arkanan are not in touch with Redthorn right now. Or could be that it's not Redthorn. Which means someone else wants us dead, as well. Got any enemies, Deakin?"

"Lots," said Deakin, and then, stating the obvious difficulty, "but none that could recognize me at this distance."

"If it isn't Redthorn," said Fletcher, "then it's someone who knows there are three of us."

Something in his voice made Shan ask, curiously, "Does it hurt you? To feel it?"

"No. Just feels . . . disturbing. Distracting. Waves of hate coming at us."

"Be away from it soon, we will," said Deakin.

They had almost reached the end of the swamp, and even Shan could see Forix now. It had been built on the highest hill in the region, and it looked to her like a pile of stones, black, white, and granite-red, against the blue sky.

Shan was desperately tired. Her exhaustion was due partly to the hard slogging through the swamp and partly to the tension of waiting for Arkanan, but she thought there was more to it as well. Not only the mud was dragging her down. She almost imagined she could feel what Fletcher felt, the hatred pouring down on them from Forix. She no longer had any desire to see the city, and was relieved that they would pass some distance west of it. It seemed ominous to her now, brooding, and all the land beneath it seemed blighted and unhealthy.

Gradually the ground became firmer and the trees more frequent, and at last the travellers found themselves in cedar forest. They could no longer see Forix, and, Fletcher reported, the watcher could no longer see them. Shan sheathed her knife and cleaned some of the mud from her legs, and, as the smell of the swamp receded behind them, so did her fears.

The exhaustion that she felt had affected the other two as well, and they did not walk much further that day. They found a small, clear creek, washed themselves clean of black mud, and then decided to make camp nearby, although it was not yet dark. They could not get out of the region of Forix before nightfall, and at least in the forest they were not directly overlooked by it. The two men went hunting and Shan, as usual, was left to cut wood and lay the fire. She was singing quietly to herself when a sudden memory of the swamp intruded. For a moment she had smelled swamp water.

She carried the firewood back to the camp and then decided to investigate. If there were another swamp around here, she would prefer to know exactly where it was. Perhaps they should move their camp. She walked westward and easily found the smell again, a slightly sweet, unpleasant taint of decay hanging in the air. As she followed it the smell became stronger and more disturbing, until it was far worse than the swamp had been. She had walked about a quarter-mile, mainly uphill, before she found its source.

At her feet the hillside fell away abruptly, and there was a sharp drop to what she assumed was a river below. She could not see the river through the mist that coiled and swirled above it. Long tendrils of mist groped upward toward her and with them came the smell, rotting, choking, drifting dangerously in the wet air. Shan did not need Fletcher to tell her the river was poisonous. Like Forix, it seemed to have a malevolent, brooding intelligence of its own. The tendrils of mist were unpleasantly like long white fingers, wrapping themselves around her feet as if the river were hungry for a human victim. She began to back slowly away.

There was metal, sudden and cold, against her throat.

"Hello, Wolf," said a harsh male voice beside her.

Shan did not move. For a moment she could not speak, either. Then she said, flatly, "Hello."

A strong brown hand reached around and pulled her knife from its sheath. Keeping his own knife at her throat, the man turned Shan to face him, and she could see that there were three other men with him. To her relief, they were dressed in Perin clothes.

"Who are you?" their leader demanded. He was older than Deakin and Fletcher, and his eyes were never still. "Why are you dressed as Perin? Talk fast, before your friends get here."

Shan's momentary relief deserted her. These men were clearly fighters, and their leader was wearing a Wolf swordbelt, complete with sword. There was only one way he could have acquired it.

"How did you know I was Wolf?" she asked.

The man's face tightened and she felt the prick of the knife point.

"No questions. Talk, Wolf."

It was difficult to speak. Her mouth was dry and she wanted to swallow. It was also difficult to think, with that misty ravine gaping just behind and the smell of decay sickening her. Shan told briefly but as clearly as she could what had happened on the night of the forest fire and some of what had happened since. Her hopes died as she spoke, for she could see that the man with the knife and the restless eyes did not believe a word. Gradually he began to smile, giving Shan an uninspiring view of his rotten teeth.

"Interesting tale," he said, as soon as she had finished. "Had it ready, did you? or were you making it up as you went along?"

"All true," said Shan.

She thought that the other three men were half-convinced, and she was sure, from glances they had exchanged, that they were afraid of magic, but their leader had no doubts at all.

"All Wolves are liars," he said. "Spies, aren't you? Sent to discover our headquarters. Watched you all morning, I did. Knew who you were as soon as I saw you."

Shan felt cold terror as she realized whose mind had been the source of the hatred Fletcher had sensed.

"Why didn't they send more Wolves, that's what I'd like to know," the man rasped. "Not sure yet, are they? Suspect we're in Forix but don't know it. So they sent you three. Know who I am, do you?"

She guessed an instant before he told her.

"Gordin. That's right. Heard about your Alpha's clever little game, we did. Can't have Wolves pretending to be Perinan, can we? Would have had to go looking for you if you hadn't saved us the trouble by coming here. Had to find you, didn't we? Had to find out what you want, and what you know about us. And then kill you."

He continued to smile. Shan felt him draw the blade gently across her throat, not breaking the skin. She was terrified, frozen. His mocking eyes held her pinned like a panicked animal. She was no longer consciously controlling her emotions, though habit kept her face still. She had none of the calm acceptance of death that she had felt at initiation when she thought she might die by Deakin's hand. This time she was screaming inside, protesting her youth, her innocence, her unreadiness. A terrible wave of sickness passed over her at the touch of the blade and left her weak.

"Scared, Wolf?" said Gordin, and smiled more widely. "Didn't think Wolves got scared. Look at her," he said to the others. "Just turned white as milk."

"Well? Little more than a child, is she?" said a big, bearded man, and Shan heard the faint disgust in his voice. "Why don't you save it for the men?"

"Don't matter how young she is, Cat, she's still Wolf."

There was a low whistle from somewhere nearby, and Gordin's three men disappeared into the trees.

"Must be your friends coming," said Gordin to Shan, and then he shouted out, "Hey! Wolves! Got your little girlfriend here, I have, and she's half-dead from fright already. Want me to finish the job? Otherwise drop your weapons where you are and come forward without them. Quickly. Now, or I kill the girl."

Shan felt a little better when Deakin and Fletcher emerged from the trees. She said at once, "All right, I am."

"So far," said Gordin.

Fletcher was in the lead, and he did not struggle or protest when the man called Cat grabbed him from behind and pushed a knife against his throat. Deakin made a quick movement but thought better of it when Cat said, convincingly, "I'll kill him."

"Let it go," said Fletcher to Deakin, softly. "Didn't I tell you . . . " and stopped when Cat jerked the knife.

There were six of Gordin's men altogether. They forced Deakin and Fletcher to stand against trees. Gordin motioned to one of the other men to hold Shan, and, to her relief, this man dragged her away from the edge of the cliff and made her stand beside Deakin.

"Know you, I do," said Gordin to Deakin. "Going to be more fun than I thought."

He was looking at the tattoo. He pushed Deakin's sleeve up so that he could see the whole of it. Then he looked at Deakin's face and gave another slow, cruel smile.

"Pretended to be Perin, didn't you? For that alone I'd have killed you. But there's more to it than that, isn't there? One of the ones we've heard about before, you are. Like to hurt people, don't you? Shall we see how you like it yourself, Alpha?"

He said "Alpha" as if it were a curse word and at the same time he lashed out without warning. The flat of his hand cracked against Deakin's cheek, and Deakin's head hit the tree. Deakin blinked but did not otherwise react.

Gordin, clearly infuriated at this lack of response, raised his hand to strike again.

"No," said Fletcher, quietly and firmly. "All on the same side, we are now."

"Who asked you?" Gordin demanded, turning on him furiously, and for a moment it seemed he would hit Fletcher as well, but then his eyes met Fletcher's and his hand dropped. Briefly he looked uncertain. Then he turned back to Deakin and jerked the gold chain.

"What's this?"

"Magic," said Fletcher. "For destroying the Firedrake."

"This?"

Gordin stared at him incredulously and gave a short laugh. He dragged the chain off over Deakin's head and tossed it to one of his men. The man jumped backward with an audible intake of breath, as if the chain might burn him, and let it fall on the ground.

"Pick it up!" Gordin glared around at his men. "Don't be silly. Do you really believe this man's a wizard? Look at him! Don't see him using any spells to free himself, do you?"

"Because Arkanan are looking for us," said Fletcher. "And if I use magic, they'll know where we are. Don't force me to use it."

Most of the men were now clearly terrified. Even Cat, who had his knife at Fletcher's throat, no longer looked confident.

"Aren't Wolves any more, we three." This time Fletcher held Cat's eyes as he spoke. "If we destroy the Firedrake, there won't be any more Wolves. Don't fight us. Help us."

"Gordin, listen to him," said Cat, unexpectedly. He lowered the knife, and for a moment his eyes locked with Gordin's. Gordin made a gesture of frustration and defeat.

"Don't . . . have any quarrel with you," he said to Fletcher. "You can go. And the girl too. But this one . . . " He looked at Deakin, and again he began to smile, slowly, savagely. "This one pays for his crimes. Now."

One of the men still had a knife to Deakin's throat. Gordin raised his own knife with deliberate slowness. He was watching Deakin's face, for signs of fear perhaps, but Shan, who knew better than to look at a Wolf's face at such a time, looked down and saw that Deakin's knees were slightly bent and his weight as far forward as he had been able to shift it unnoticed. He was not going to die without a fight.

She looked frantically at Fletcher, but he was too far away for her to see his expression. Next instant, with a roar, the tree behind Gordin burst spectacularly into flame.

Gordin gave a yelp of surprise as he whirled around, and two of his men fled into the woods. The others began to back away.

"Did you . . . are you . . . ?" Gordin stared at Fletcher. He raised his knife again, as if by reflex. The fire in the tree went out and there was sudden silence.

"Put the knife away," said Fletcher. "Will be your hand next time."

Gordin swallowed.

"Let's go," Fletcher said, urgently, to Shan and Deakin, and immediately began walking.

Shan trotted after him. Deakin hesitated, eyeing Gordin.

"Deakin?" Fletcher turned. "Arkanan will . . . "

One of them stepped into existence out of the air in front of him. Only one, and he looked incredibly ancient and frail. His face under the black hood was as seamed and puckered as a withered apple, his body fragile as a corn husk, so that, after the first shock of his appearance, Shan found it difficult to fear him. It must be time for Arkanan to touch the Firedrake, to have their failing life renewed, she thought. Fletcher took one involuntary step backward and then stood his ground, face to face with the Arkan and only a few feet away.

"What dost thou want?" he demanded. "Why hast thou come? Thou hast now no power. Return to thy Maze or we will kill thee."

The Arkan began to chuckle, a dry rasping sound.

"I have come for thee, wizard. I have even now enough power to do what I have come to do. And who art thou to speak of power? Thou hast not even enough power to see the peril in which thou standst. Now, wizard. Prepare to die."

His face was alight with triumph as he raised his trembling arms. Both Shan and Fletcher leapt toward him, to prevent whatever spell he intended, but Deakin was quicker. He pulled his stone knife from his boot and threw it, in one swift, controlled motion.

The Arkan, before it reached him, did what he had come to do. He simply disappeared. And the knife, with all Deakin's strength behind it, sliced through the air toward Fletcher.

Chapter 23

Strangely, it was Deakin who cried out. Fletcher made no sound at all. He staggered back against a tree with one hand pressed hard against his chest, and bright blood welled between his fingers. The knife had vanished, as the Queen had said it would.

"Fletcher," Shan whispered.

Her eyes met Deakin's and she saw her own shock reflected there.

"Was that an Arkan?" said someone else, also in a whisper. Gordin. All his men had fled. "Never though — "

He broke off as Deakin lunged at him. Deakin's eyes were no longer shocked; they were mad. They glittered with a hard, dangerous light, and when Gordin saw it he tried to run, though he was armed and Deakin was not. Deakin caught him at the edge of the cliff. Gordin had no time to draw his sword, but he lashed out with the knife. Deakin stopped the blade with his upraised arm and struck it aside as if it were a blade of grass instead of metal, apparently not noticing it at all though his arm was suddenly a sheet of blood from wrist to elbow. He could have sent Gordin over the cliff then, and saved himself, but it seemed that his only thought was to kill Gordin with his bare hands. Perhaps he did not even know the cliff was there. They went over together, Deakin's hands locked on Gordin's neck, and Shan heard two splashes and then silence.

Both she and Fletcher started for the edge of the cliff, automatically, but Fletcher's legs buckled and he dropped forward onto his knees. His collapse forced Shan into deliberate motion for the first time since the Arkan had appeared. She dropped beside him and helped him to pull off his belt and blood-stained tunic, and to make the tunic into a rough bandage. She was terrified to see how much blood there was.

"Going to get bandages," she said. "Put your hands here. Hold it tight. Be right back, I will."

"What about Deakin?" said Fletcher.

"Lie down," said Shan. "Don't talk."

She sprinted to the camp and back, dumped the contents of one of the knapsacks to find linen, and bandaged the wound. She worked mechanically, trying not to think, trying not to notice the blood that was soon all over her. Fletcher's eyes were closed but both hands were pressed tightly against his chest, as ordered, and she forced them away with difficulty. At long last she sat back on her heels and let herself look at his face.

"Be all right now, you will," she said, a little unsteadily. "How do you feel?"

Fletcher opened his eyes.

"Thirsty."

His voice was much weaker than it had been. Shan got one of the flasks and gave him a long drink. She also picked up the gold chain from the ground and put it around her own neck for safe-keeping.

"What about Deakin?" Fletcher said again. "In trouble, he is. Hurt . . . "

"All right. All right. Find him, I will." Shan left him the flask and stood up. "But only if you promise you'll be here when I come back. Promise me! Promise me, Fletcher, or can't leave you. Promise me you won't . . . won't . . . "

"Won't die," said Fletcher, in a whisper, his eyes fixed on hers. "Promise you that. Now go."

Shan obeyed. She scrambled down the side of the cliff into the source of that noxious smell, into the cold groping fingers of the mist. She held onto roots and bushes while her boots skidded on sand and loose stone. As she descended, the world became smaller and colder, stinking. She shivered at the touch of the coiling tendrils of mist on her face. Then the earth gave way beneath her and she slid the rest of the way, ripping her skin painfully and snagging her tunic on brambles and thorns. She managed to save herself from rolling into the river only by a last-second grab at a thornbush.

The river was wide and fast. Mist crawled and writhed across its surface, completely obscuring the further bank. There was no sign of Deakin or Gordin. Shan began to trot downstream, moving quickly despite the uneven ground and the nauseating smell. She was not sure how far she should go; every minute away from Fletcher tore at her. Nevertheless it was true that Deakin might need her, too. The hope that kept her going, the hope that she clung to desperately, was that she might meet Deakin returning, Deakin alive and well and able to take charge. That hope drove her on, half-running, until she reached the end of all hope. The end of the river.

She stumbled to a halt at the foot of a high cliff wall, even steeper than the place where she had scrambled down, and turned around, bewildered. The mist lifted briefly as if to give her a clear view, and she saw that the river widened further here, into a black swirling lake surrounded by cliffs, and went no further. In the centre of the lake the deadly water sucked everything down into itself. Shan had never seen a whirlpool before, but she recognized the danger and stared at it in misery. If Deakin and Gordin had come this far, then they had vanished into the malevolent black heart of the river.

The mist closed down on her again, and suddenly she could no longer bear the soft cold touches on her skin.

"Get away from me!" She brushed at it ineffectually. "Get away! Get away! Leave me alone! What have you done with Deakin?"

She raised her head and sent his name echoing round the cliffs.

"Deakiiiin!" She was shocked at how young and shrill her voice was.

"Deakiiiin!" Once she had started screaming it was difficult to stop. "Come back! Come back! Deakin! Come back now! Now!"

There was no response. She fled back the way she had come, stumbling, panting, choking on the reek of decay. Her throat ached from screaming. She was filled with a black terror that Fletcher might die before she could get back to him. And I'll be all alone, she thought. All alone. All alone. Her feet pounded it out in a rhythm of despair, and sometimes she moaned aloud as she ran. She reached the place where she had descended and flung herself recklessly at that impossible climb; she crawled and scrabbled and fought her way up out of the mist, away from the reek of the river, to the top of the cliff where the air now seemed clean and sweet. By the time she reached it, she was sobbing for breath, her whole body heaving. She dropped to her knees beside Fletcher.

For a moment she thought she was too late. His eyes were closed and his face was starkly white.

"No," she whispered. She bent over him and put her ear to his mouth, and after a moment she heard the faint intake of breath. His chest barely moved.

Shan knelt there, watching with tense antic- ipation for every breath, as if her own life required it. After a time she tried, gently, to awaken Fletcher, but he was past awakening. She also tried to give him another drink of water, but his teeth were locked. She could think of nothing more to do for him. Soon, she knew, there would be no next breath. Only magic could save him now.

Magic? Suddenly she remembered the Dancers. The boy owes you a life, Fletcher had said, and will repay it if he can. Shan had to swallow some water from the flask before she could whistle.

When she had whistled their little tune five times, both the Dancer boys appeared in front of her. They looked tired and dishevelled, but concern flashed into their wild little faces at once as they saw that Shan was covered with dried blood.

"No," she said, and stood up, wearily, to show them that she was unhurt. "Not me. Fletcher. See? Help him. Please help him."

The Dancers could not understand the words, but they understood the meaning and were angry. One of them poured out a long string of furious chitterings while he pointed repeatedly at Shan.

"Don't want you to help me," she insisted, shaking her head. "Help him instead. Please."

They turned their backs as if to leave and Shan ran after them, desperate.

"Have to help him! Don't you understand? Deakin went into the river, and the river's poison, and he could be . . . could be dead already and there's just Fletcher and I, and if he . . . if he . . . dies," to her own amazement she began to cry, "What will I do? Where will I go? Please . . . please . . . "

The words dissolved in sobs and the tears, unexpected and unasked-for, spilled down her cheeks and trickled salty into her mouth. Fascinated, the Dancers lingered. They touched Shan's face and let the tears run over their fingers. They held them up and watched them shimmer in the last of the daylight. They licked at them with long animal tongues. Shan's tears seemed to make them regard her with a new respect, even with awe, and at last they consented to come over and look at Fletcher.

As soon as they did, they seemed to recognize him. They talked excitedly to each other and then explained to Shan, with gestures and many shrugs, that they were not sure they could help him but they would do their best.

Shan swallowed tears and nodded.

She and the two boys picked up Fletcher between them, the two boys taking one of his legs each and Shan holding his shoulders, and began to walk through the darkening forest. Shan soon realized that they were walking in the direction of Forix, detouring around the end of the river and continuing eastward, uphill, but she did not much care where they went. Her tears had dried and she felt hollow, empty. Once she almost stumbled against an upright stone in a field and realized that their path led across a graveyard. This grave had an image, a child carved in stone. It was not something she wanted to see.

By the time she realized that they were going to enter Forix, they were already passing under a wide stone archway. Shan heard voices and knew that people must be up there, on the wall. Guards, she supposed. They seemed not to have noticed her, as if they could not see her while she travelled with the Dancers.

Once they had entered the city, Shan found herself on a long wide street covered with stones. They were set so close together that it was impossible to walk between them, and at first this seemed, in her present state, to be an obstacle past bearing. But the boys did not hesitate, and Shan found that she could walk easily on the stone surface. The street was smooth and almost pleasant to walk on, certainly no more difficult than walking in the forest.

Large stone buildings flanked the gate and overhung the street, blocking out some of the remaining sunlight. Shan saw more buildings beyond them, and more beyond that. The boys seemed uneasy to have left the forest, and chittered softly to each other as they walked. They turned away from the wide street onto a slightly narrower one, also covered with stones underfoot. In a minute or two Shan could no longer see the city wall and was not sure where she was. The semi-dark was full of unknown shapes, and there seemed to be many different streets. The boys still carried Fletcher easily, but Shan's arms were beginning to tire.

Shan and the boys made their way around and over piles of rotted wood as well as occasional chunks of stone. Once they had to walk around a kind of stone pedestal with an animal, perhaps a dragon, carved on top. Grass grew at the edges of the streets and between the stones, and trees grew at crazy angles, some of them jutting through pieces of buildings, some of them growing in the streets themselves. No one had used carts in Forix, it seemed, for a long time.

At last the boys led the way into one of the towering buildings, and Shan found herself in a cavernous hall. The boys walked straight through it, toward a light that burned further in. Shan saw no people in the big room, but she passed a pig in a wooden pen and two chickens.

There were no people in the inner room, either, but there were six beds. A rush-light was burning on a wooden table. Shan and the Dancers put Fletcher on one of the beds, and then the Dancers took one last long look at Shan and vanished. Shan leaned back against the wall. She could see that the bandage was soaked with blood and she told herself that she had to change it, but somehow her feet would not move. She was so desperately tired.

She must have slept, briefly, on her feet, and she jerked awake as a grey-haired woman entered the room. The woman was carrying a bucket. She stopped in the doorway when she saw Shan and Fletcher. Her eyes flickered quickly over Shan but lingered on Fletcher. She dropped the bucket without spilling its contents, sprang to a cupboard, and took out a small carved wooden vessel. It looked very old. She returned to the bed, cradled Fletcher's head in her arms, and poured something from the vessel into his mouth. She had to force it past his clenched teeth.

"What is that?" said Shan. "What are you doing?"

The woman looked startled. "You're Wolf!"

Before Shan could react, Fletcher gave the first sign of life he had shown, catching his breath in a kind of sob. A great black crow took flight from the pillow and flapped soundlessly around the room for an instant before it disappeared.

"Did he do that?" Shan looked around in terror, afraid Arkanan would sense it.

"Must have done. Dreaming aloud." The woman had still not taken her eyes off Fletcher's face.

"But he can't. Mustn't! Arkanan will come."

"What do you mean? Wizard, isn't he? Can't stop him dreaming, girl."

The woman continued to work, unwrapping the wound and staunching it with the cold water from her bucket before carefully bandaging it again.

"Knew I'd need cold water," she said. She seemed excited, happy even. "But didn't expect this. A wizard! In my house!"

Shan was silent, confused. Again Fletcher dreamed, and this time it was a battle that he

400

dreamed. The room was momentarily full of struggling, desperate men and women, of weapons that clashed in unnatural silence and blood that spurted as people fell. Shan decided she had better be ready for Arkanan to arrive. She kept her fingers on the hilt of her knife and watched in silence as the woman worked.

"Who are you?" she asked, finally.

"Raven. Healer to Gordin's men. Come to fight them, did you?"

Shan did not answer, and the woman did not need to ask again. Fletcher's dreams continued, and in the most frequent of them, he dreamed of how he was wounded, the same few seconds over and over — the terrible old Arkan facing him and laughing before he disappeared, the shock of the knife, Deakin screaming without sound.

All night, all the next day, and all the night following, Shan did not dare to sleep for more than a few minutes at a time. She leant against the wall at the foot of the bed, watching Fletcher's tortured face, watching the illusions flicker around him. Raven worked hard to keep him alive. She boiled witch-hazel leaves to make compresses for the wound. She boiled willow leaves to make a tea to reduce the fever. She gave him warm milk, and warm ale with honey in it.

Shan watched quietly, but several times she had to struggle against crying, as if she were a seven-year-old again, and her throat ached constantly with unshed tears.

Finally, the following morning, Fletcher looked at Shan and whispered a word. "Deakin."

Shan went to him and knelt by the bed. "Gone," she said. "Remember?"

"No."

"Went over the cliff into the river. Deakin's gone, Fletcher."

"No."

"No?" Shan stared into his anguished eyes. "Where is he then?"

"Down the river. Floated. In a cave."

"Where?" said Shan, but he had gone from her again into the private, fevered world of his own pain. Shan turned and looked at Raven.

"The poisoned river. After the whirlpool, where does it go?"

"Goes underground. Drains into the swamp, eventually. Why, girl?"

"Have to follow it. Have to go after Deakin."

"Don't be ridiculous!" said Raven, sharply. "Be going to your own death, you would, beyond a doubt. Deadly poison, that river is, and in the whirlpool you'd swallow enough of it to kill you, even if by some miracle you didn't drown."

"Have to go after Deakin," Shan repeated.

"But if he's still alive then he must be trapped somewhere. Can't you see that? What use is there in getting yourself trapped with him?"

Shan watched Fletcher's face.

"Wouldn't have told me to go if it was hopeless, would he?" she said, simply.

"But he's feverish, isn't he? Delirious. Probably didn't know what he was saying . . . "

Shan knew that Fletcher had been, for that brief time, conscious and aware. She ignored Raven's words, and instead asked the one question for which she needed an answer. "Will he live?"

"Still too soon to say, girl. Can only promise I'll do all I can for him."

Shan nodded. Still on her knees, she stroked Fletcher's damp hair back from his forehead. Then she stood up, went to her knapsack, and took out a coil of rope. She wound it around and around her waist.

She decided to leave her knife with Raven against the remote chance of Arkanan arriving, but she did not expect Arkanan to come after all this time or she would never have left

Fletcher's side. No, she thought, they could not detect Fletcher's unconscious illusions.

"Better keep my knife." She drew it abruptly and handed it to Raven, who looked startled. "Can kill Arkanan with it."

She walked out into the morning.

Chapter 24

Four white stone pillars in front of the door supported a little roof, lower than the real roof but jutting out so that people could stand in front of the door in the rain and not get wet. Shan touched one of the smooth stone pillars, wondering if it had been made by magic.

She had no idea which way to go, but Raven had followed her outside and now pointed.

"That way. The gate."

She stood and watched Shan out of sight.

Shan could see a little more of the city in daylight. She had a vague impression of tall, towering buildings with smaller ones in their shadows, some of stone and some of wood, some partially fallen into the road. Once she saw a glint of red metal and guessed that a watcher had shifted position among the tall spires and jumbled rocks. She was sure that Gordin's men must have been able to see her the moment she left Raven's house, and she wasted none of her failing energy on concealment.

She passed under the archway and out of the city without being stopped by the watchers on the wall. Wearily, she backtracked along the Dancers' route, so that instead of going directly to the river she reached the cliff where Fletcher had been wounded. She was recalled to where she was, forcibly, when she came upon the two bows, lying in the forest where Deakin and Fletcher had dropped them. They had been left strung and the bowstrings would be useless now. Shan had to fight back tears before, furious with herself, she could look around for Fletcher's knife. She found it stuck into the base of a tree, tested the edge, and sheathed it. Had Fletcher known, she wondered, that Deakin had hidden his knife in his boot? Probably. In some things even Deakin was predictable.

Just be all right, she said to him, silently, and I'll forgive you everything. Just be all right.

She felt so weak already that it took an effort to force herself to climb down into the mist and the stink. She breathed through her mouth and tried not to think about being sick. The mist seemed to recognize her and flung itself upon her joyously, as someone long-awaited, and again she was forced to endure its soft, cold, too-intimate touches on her face and her bare arms and legs.

At the edge of the lake she pulled off her boots and stood barefoot on the stones, shivering a little, to summon up her remaining strength and her faltering courage before she jumped. The water was deep and fast but warmer than she had expected, warmer than the air, and she was reminded of the lake she had swum in the Maze. She felt the tug of the current at once and let it take her.

The whirlpool was hard against the cliff, and the first wide circle took Shan right up to the cliff wall, where she looked for caves or openings and found none. Even if she had, she suspected that the current was already too strong to fight. She tried to keep her mouth shut, to snatch breath only when she could be sure it would be the foul air she would breathe and not the tainted, deadly water. Another circle around and another, tighter and faster, drawing her in. The chances to breathe were less frequent now, and once as she gasped a splash of water slapped her face and leapt into her mouth. She gagged, spat, and lost the precious gulp of air. Soon she was breathing whenever she could, taking in water and air together. The current dragged her inexorably inward and downward. She saw, suddenly and clearly, that she had no chance, that the whirlpool was too deep and she could not survive that long dizzying descent on one breath, could not — and then there was no more air, only the walls of black water that spun and shifted around her. She was as helpless, as weightless, as a fallen leaf. Dizzy and already breathless, she spiralled from circle to circle to ever-smaller circle, sucked down into the victorious grinning mouth of the river. The need for air overwhelmed all else and she began to fight, struggling without effect, reaching for a spinning surface that receded moment by moment though she strained upward with every muscle. There was no hope, no cave, no tunnel, no escape. She was betrayed and doomed. Her heart thudded in her ears, lights flared in her eyes, and suddenly, as consciousness faded, some trick of the current flung her free of the whirlpool and sent her, in a rush of tumbled water, headfirst into darkness.

She awoke to violent pain and was immediately sick. After she had retched up more water than she thought she could possibly have swallowed, the pain in her head and stomach receded enough for her to notice her surroundings. She was huddled on a stone shelf where the river had thrown her, with water washing over her but the main part of the river flowing, turbulent and fast, just a few inches below. When she rolled over, away from the water's edge, she saw that she was in an immense cave, with the daylight coming through a hole in the roof, far above her. Several yards away, near the wall where the light could not reach, she saw a dark shape that might be a man.

Shan sat up, too quickly, and gasped as the poisonous water clawed at her insides. She became sure of what she had seen.

"Deakin!"

Despite everything it was very nearly a cry of joy. She got to her feet, closed her teeth against the pain, and staggered across to him. He was lying face down beside a spring of clean water which bubbled up through the floor of the cave. He was shivering as violently as Shan was, and the deep knife-cut on his forearm was badly infected. Shan winced inside when she saw it. She turned him gently onto his side.

To her dismay, his eyes stared at her and saw nothing. His face was flushed with fever and fragile with hunger and exhaustion, the bones clear beneath the drawn skin.

"Deakin. Deakin, what's wrong? Look at me. Look. It's Shan."

She shook him and he seemed to become aware of her for the first time. His eyes rolled, disconcertingly, and then found a slow focus on her face. He looked at her dully and without recognition.

"Deakin? Don't you know me?"

She sat down beside him on the stone floor and talked to him while she unwound the wet rope from her waist.

"Going to get you out of here," she said. "Going to be all right now, Deakin. Going to take you to Fletcher. Hear me, Deakin? Fletcher's alive."

To all her efforts there was no response. Deakin's eyes had slipped out of focus again. Shan, as she wondered tiredly what to do next, did something totally unexpected. Curled up around the pain in her stomach, with Deakin keeping a strange, futile, blank-eyed watch, she fell suddenly into sleep. It was her first real sleep since Fletcher had been wounded.

CRBSO

Arkanan were strong again. They had just come from the Firedrake, and now as they sat in council their eyes glowed as brightly as the coloured flames of their torches. They argued in firm, impassioned voices.

"It was a splendid plan!" Hinton was almost crowing. "Such a simple plan, to work so splendidly."

"It was a stupid plan. Have I not told thee to consult with thine elders before leaving the Plain?" Kron reminded him. "Thou art fortunate that thou still livest. In thy weakened state, thou couldst easily have been killed."

"Not that any would miss thee," said Leban, and some of the others snickered.

Hinton pounded his fists down on the table, which broke into a thousand tiny pieces, clattering away onto the stone floor.

"But it worked! Can none of ye see what I have done! I have delivered to ye the renegade wizard, and ye need now do nothing more but send Kunan Keir to kill him. Ye dried-up old sticks, I have ended the threat!"

Some of the Arkanan stood up angrily, shouting insults in return. Varian continued to stare into the green-and-blue flames of her little fire, now apparently suspended in the air. "It was a great victory," she said, softly. "Now is the time to celebrate, not to argue amongst ourselves."

No one was listening to her. It was Kron who eventually got them seated again, roaring at Hinton to restore the table.

"Ye are all so eager for his death!" said Kron. "Consider how young and strong he is, and how useful he could be to us. He has not yet discovered a tenth of his power. He could be another Tarn. If we could capture and control him . . . "

"No!" Hinton objected, back on his feet at once. "We tried already thy way! Pantan was sent to take captive the wizard, and as a result Pantan was killed. Thy plan failed, Kron. Mine succeeded. Now there is no need for any of us to endanger himself further. The Wolves can kill for us the renegade wizard."

Kron stood up as well. Red light flowed around him. "Thy plan? Having one of the Three kill another? Dost thou call that a plan? I call it a desperate attempt to redeem thyself, after thou so stupidly killed the old healer! Thou destroyed thine own chance at immortality, Hinton, and none of us has forgotten that."

"There are other healers . . . "

"Yes, and next time we shall keep thee far from them! If I have my way, thou shalt never get another opportunity!" The light around Kron flickered dangerously.

"If thou hast thy way, thou distorted piece of worn-out flesh, everything will go on as always it has until we are all dead! I was the one who found the healer . . . "

"Thou arrogant insulting toad!" The light flashing around Kron coalesced as he raised a hand, and a lick of red flame shot straight at Hinton's face. Hinton gasped. He raised his own hand and the flame vanished, but not before it had come close enough to singe his eyebrows and make his face drip with sweat. He slumped briefly, but then red light began to flicker around him as well.

Kron said coldly, "I remind thee, Hinton, that thou art the youngest of us all and hast the least experience. I for one would have been able to hold my temper. Whatever names the healer had called me, I would not have killed him."

"Hinton is an arrogant insulting toad," Leban agreed, "but, Kron, he speaks here a truth. We do not need another Tarn. Let the Wolves dispose of the renegade wizard."

The light around Kron grew stronger again. His voice was tight with anger. "Do ye all feel as Hinton does? Do none of ye agree with me in seeing a use for this wizard?"

"I agree," said Sevrin, unexpectedly. "I want no more killing. Let us bring the wizard to us here."

"So only thou agreest?" Kron was furious now. "And what wouldst thou suggest that we do with him?"

Varian said, "Sevrin . . ."

"Perhaps we could learn from him!" Sevrin jumped to his feet. "There has been too much killing and too much dying! Hinton is right when he says we need change. It is time we brought in a new wizard. It is time we sought wizards, not to take their bodies, but to find new knowledge. As Hinton said — "

"I said we needed change, not more wizards to share eternity! There are too many of us already!" Hinton protested.

"I agree," said Kron.

For a moment Kron and Hinton looked at each other's angry faces, and then they both reached out, as if they would join hands. A red flame leapt up between them and knocked Sevrin hard against the stone wall of the chamber. Sevrin did not fight back, and none of the other Arkanan moved to help him. For a few moments the flame flickered over Sevrin's body, while he jerked like a puppet against the wall.

"I have . . . reconsidered what I said," said Hinton to Kron, panting a little. He was still maintaining his part of the magic. "Sevrin has . . . made me realize . . . thou mayest be right. We should take the wizard while he yet lives."

"Good." Kron moved his hand very slightly and the flame widened, shifting toward Hinton while it still held Sevrin in its grasp. Hinton sucked in his breath; his face twisted with the effort of keeping the flame from touching him. After a moment Kron closed his hand and his part of the flame vanished. Hinton, now breathing in harsh gasps, followed his example. He slumped to the floor. Sevrin's dead body slipped down beside him.

"We know that the renegade wizard is in Forix." Kron resumed his place. "The miserable commander of the Kunan Keir" — a small image of Redthorn appeared on the table in front of him — "is at present within a day's journey of Forix. We shall order him to remain where he is, and we shall send out a Call, ordering all Wolves within five days of Forix to report to their commander. In five days time, when all are assembled, we shall send them to seek out and kill two of the Three. We shall tell them to leave alive the wizard, the wounded one. Through their commander we can issue our orders, and through his eyes we shall see all that occurs."

"The Three will hear the Call also," Leban pointed out. "One of them is Alpha, is he not? He will hear, and he will know our intentions."

"Yes. We cannot prevent that. If he and the woman choose to flee, they may be able to escape us. Then we will perhaps have to kill the wizard."

"They will not flee without him," said Leban. "Sometimes the unthinking loyalty of Wolves one to another can be very useful. But how if they manage to take him with them?"

"How say the ashes, Varian?" asked Kron. "Is it likely they will take him?"

Varian was stunned and sick at Sevrin's death. She gazed at Kron and then down at her little fire. The Arkanan waited.

"He cannot travel now," said Varian, with an effort. "His life lies in the balance. The ashes fall this way and he lives. They fall that way and he dies."

"Let us send the Call," said Kron, and Hinton hobbled over to take his place in the circle.

It was midmorning when all Alphas within five day's journey of the small and insignificant village of Snowdown were ordered to report to their commander there. They were given no further orders. Those on their way out of the country were not even told what to do with the ore-carts and the oxen. All over the land, Wolves looked at each other in excited speculation. Was it war? Some of them knew what had happened to Redthorn, and far more of them had heard rumours, so there was uneasiness as well as excitement among those ordered to report to him.

But the Alpha whom the Call most affected was completely unaware of it. Deakin had forgotten who he was, and he heard the Call without interest or comprehension. He did not remember a time when the agony in his arm had not filled all his inner world, just as he did not remember a time when the outer world had consisted of more than stone walls and a cold refreshing trickle of water. The Call meant nothing to him at all.

Chapter 25

Shan slept for twenty-four hours. She awoke only once, in darkness, feverish and sick, and curled her body against Deakin's so that she could feel their hearts beating together, his breath on her hair. Then she slept again, long hours of oblivion and healing.

When she awakened for a second time, it was in the cave's dim daylight. She was weak and a little shaky, but the pain and the fever were gone. She pushed the hair out of her eyes and sat up.

Deakin's eyes were open, and she wondered uneasily if he had kept vigil all night. What was he seeing with that wide, blank stare of his? Better not to know. It was not, she thought, a vision that she would want to share.

"Going to get out of here today, we are," she said.

She had a drink and began to explore. The river that had carried her there flowed turbulently the length of the cave, and she followed it. Suddenly, among the sticks and animal bones that littered the cave floor, she noticed a strange object and picked it up. It looked like two pieces of leather, sewn together, and between them were thin strips of animal hide covered with writing. On the front piece of leather was a single word.

"Tarn! Deakin, look! Talked about Tarn, Fletcher did, remember?"

Shan ran excitedly back to Deakin, who paid her no attention.

"Must be a book! Have to give this to Fletcher, won't we? Let him learn all kinds of new magic!"

She had not forgotten how to read Perin, and, although the words were in Arkan, the letters were the same. Shan slowly began to read the book aloud, but to her disappointment it did not appear to be a list of spells. There were ten pages, and every one of them was completely covered with tiny, careful handwriting. There were no titles and no pictures. It did not seem, after all, to be a very useful book. Shan put it inside her tunic, and once more turned her attention to finding a way out.

The river, after flowing the length of the cave, disappeared beneath a wall of solid rock. There was no way of knowing when it next emerged into the air. Shan was not inclined to trust her life and Deakin's to the chance that it might do so soon, especially since she was sickened by the thought of plunging into that poisonous water again. She was not sure that she could have done it even if there were no other way of escape. And there might be another way, that distant hole in the roof.

Shan circled and squinted upward, trying to choose the best wall for the two of them to climb. With her rope and Fletcher's knife, she thought they might make it. She squatted down beside Deakin and tied knots in the rope at regular intervals. When she was finished, she shook Deakin gently until he looked at her.

"Deakin. Going to get out of here now, we are. Going to see Fletcher. Come on."

He did not respond, but when Shan took his good arm and pulled, he stood up and let her lead him to the place she had chosen for their starting point. He held his wounded right arm tightly against his body, and Shan was suddenly assailed with terrible doubts as to his ability to climb a rope.

"Didn't you tell me once that all great warriors could use either hand equally well?" she muttered, reassuring herself rather than talking to Deakin. "Going to see whether you're a great warrior or not now, aren't we?"

She tied the rope to the knife to weight it, made a loop, and threw it up and over a spur of rock that jutted out from the wall above her head.

"First shot," she said, proudly. "And weren't even watching, were you?"

She tightened the loop and swung on the rope. The spur of rock held.

"Now, Deakin. Think you can climb up there?"

There was, as she had expected and feared, no response. Shan reached up and gripped his shoulders hard.

"Deakin. Look at me!" He did. "Have to come with me. Have to climb the rope."

For several minutes she pleaded with him, with no effect. She put his hand on the rope and he held it, but he would make no attempt to climb it. Shan began to despair.

"What's the matter with you?" she shouted at him, miserably. "Do you want to die here? Climb the cursed rope!"

He blinked, and for a moment there was comprehension in his eyes. Then he reached for the rope with his good hand, wound it around his hand, and pulled his feet up onto the first knot. Shan watched amazed, not sure whether she wanted to laugh with relief or burst into tears. Isn't Cub training wonderful? she thought, confusedly. We may go mad, we may kill our best friends, but, by the Wheel! We never forget how to obey orders.

The climb took them more than two hours, mainly because Deakin was terribly weak and had to do everything one-handed. If they had not had the magic knife, it would have been impossible. Sometimes they even had to use the knife as a spike, but it held their weight and did not slip once.

Since Deakin had only one hand to hold on with, it was Shan who had to throw the rope, sometimes many times before she hooked what she was aiming at. She was concentrating too hard to be afraid of falling, taking responsibility for Deakin's movements as well as her own. As the climb progressed he seemed better, forced by circumstances to concentrate on something outside himself, and soon he was no longer blindly obeying orders and Shan could see his eyes measure distances, calculate chances. But he was weakening, and several times she thought he was on the verge of fainting and ordered him, frantically, to stay where he was and rest. She told him over and over again that they were going to see Fletcher, that everything was going to be all right.

The long climb came to an end at last, and Shan pulled herself out through the hole and collapsed on the grass beside Deakin. For a while neither of them moved, and then Shan forced herself to her feet. Even from here she could see the ruins of Forix, giving her the direction to Raven's house.

"Come on."

Deakin stood, weary but still obedient. There were dark smudges under his eyes and lines of pain around them, but it seemed to Shan that unlike Fletcher, who had aged noticeably over the last few days, Deakin had grown younger. It was a small child who looked at her out of those eyes, hurt and confused but still waiting, passively and trustingly, for her guidance.

Shan took his left hand in hers and found it was hot, though he kept shivering. She began to lead him through the forest. She tugged him after her into the first stream they came to, for Raven was not going to welcome them into her house reeking of river-water, and besides, Shan herself could not bear the smell anymore. She ducked her head into the stream, and got Deakin to do the same.

"Come on," she said again. She shook water from her hair. "Almost there. Going to see Fletcher, we are, and then you can rest."

"Going to see Fletcher," Deakin repeated.

Shan's initial delight faded as she saw that his expression was still childlike.

"That's right. Remember Fletcher, do you?"

Deakin only looked at her in silence.

The two of them were not alone in the forest that afternoon. Before they had gone far, they were seen by a group of children, who followed them at a distance, and Shan realized that there must be a village close by. No doubt it was near the spring where Raven had gone for cold water. The children seemed curious but did not approach. Three of them scampered ahead when Shan and Deakin neared the city, one of them shouting a greeting to someone up on the wall. This time, passing under the archway in daylight, Shan saw that the wall was made of blocks of grey and brown stone.

Shan walked hand in hand with Deakin, dripping wet, along the stone-paved streets of the city. She did not think she could have found her way to Raven's house without help, so she was glad that the three children had come. They looked as if they intended to run right into Raven's house, but a tall man with a bow blocked their way. Shan wondered if she would have to fight him to get to Fletcher. She readied herself, but he moved aside for her without speaking. She guessed that one of Gordin's men had been assigned to keep an eye on Raven and her strange visitors.

Shan led Deakin through to the inner room and was relieved to find Fletcher and Raven still there. She gave Deakin a gentle push, and he went forward to the bed and gazed down at Fletcher.

The miracle Shan had hoped for did not happen. Deakin showed no sign of recognition. But Fletcher whispered, "Deakin," apparently in his sleep, and then his eyes opened and for a moment there was welcome in them, even joy, before the pain clouded them again.

"Is he any better?" Shan asked of Raven.

"No worse, anyway. Slept well today, without dreams. Brought me another one to look after now, have you?" Raven examined Deakin's arm without touching it. "Where did you find him?"

"In a cave. Behind the whirlpool. Climbed out, we did."

"Amazing." A touch of awe was in Raven's voice. "You're amazing, girl. Didn't the water make you sick?"

"Yes," said Shan.

Raven shook her head and seemed to be at a loss for words.

"Is there anything to eat?" Shan asked.

"Made some soup, I did, in case . . . Get out of those wet clothes and I'll heat it up."

Shan and Deakin stripped, obediently, and wrapped themselves in blankets, sitting on the bed next to Fletcher's to eat. Shan put Tarn's book under the bed, for safety. When Deakin had finished eating, he leaned back and closed his eyes.

"Can't sleep yet," said Raven. "Have to look after that arm of yours first."

"Can't it wait till tomorrow?" Shan asked, quickly. She was afraid of what Deakin might do if Raven hurt him.

Raven frowned. "Waited too long already. Come on. What's your name? Deakin? Come on, Deakin, wake up. Better have a drink. Can't spare you any corn-liquor, I'm afraid, but there's plenty of ale."

Deakin looked at Shan, as if for orders, and then took the ale Raven offered.

"Hold his arm."

Raven opened Deakin's wound with one quick slash of a knife. Shan held his arm steady, and at the same time she watched his eyes closely for any sign of that fatal glittering. She was ready at any moment to get between Deakin and Raven, but Deakin's only reaction to the pain was that his eyes filled up with tears and some of them trickled down his cheeks. Raven cleaned the wound, which took a long time, while Shan held Deakin's arm and talked to him, constantly, reassuringly. When Raven had finished, she poured liquor into the freshly-opened cut to keep it clean. Deakin cried out — he seemed to have completely forgotten that he was Wolf — and Fletcher startled both Shan and Raven by saying, urgently and clearly, "Deakin. What's wrong?"

"Fletcher?" said Shan, but he was asleep again, if he had ever been awake at all.

Raven bandaged Deakin's arm and Shan wiped his tears away, and he went peacefully to sleep. His head slipped down onto Shan's shoulder, and then, when she shifted position, onto her lap. If Raven thought that these two Wolves were behaving strangely, she did not remark on it, accepting Deakin's tears and Shan's solicitude as incuriously as she had accepted Fletcher's presence in her house.

"Sure you're all right, girl?" was all she asked.

"Yes," said Shan, softly. "Thank you. Been very good to us, you have."

"Oh . . . well," said Raven. "He's wizard, isn't he? What else could I do?"

She finished her work around the house and settled down to sleep herself. Shan remained wakeful on Deakin's bed much of the night, watching Deakin's face and, sometimes, Fletcher's illusions. As if to make up for his good sleep during the day, Fletcher was very restless, turning his head from side to side, and moaning, and sometimes muttering unintelligible words.

Toward dawn Shan dozed at last, jerking awake an hour later with a feeling that something was wrong. It took her an instant to realize what it was. Fletcher had not moved in a long time.

She pushed Deakin away and stood up in sudden fear. Fletcher was lying completely still, the first flush of dawn staining his haggard face with soft pink light, and for a moment she was afraid to touch him. Then she took courage and reached out; felt his breath on her hand; touched his forehead and found it cool. The fever had broken at last.

Shan gazed at Fletcher's face for a long time, while the hard lump in her stomach dissolved and melted away. She looked at Deakin, still sleeping peacefully, and one last time she felt tears prick her eyes. This time she let them fall.

When Raven awakened she seemed to know at once, before she even looked at Fletcher, what had happened. She seized Shan and hugged her hard, and Shan, to her own surprise, hugged back. Turning Perin, I am, she thought in amusement. Crying and now hugging. Be laughing next, I will.

Both Fletcher and Deakin slept all morning, while Raven and Shan worked quietly together. Shan felt a song welling up inside her, though she did not sing it. Happiness had returned, tentatively, and she was aware of it as she had never been before. She was also aware of the fragility of it, of how easily it could be shattered, perhaps forever. She felt that she must move carefully, or her happiness would break like an egg and there would be nothing left inside her.

This inner fragility made her a little wary of Deakin when he awakened, for she felt a harsh word from him might destroy her, but he was still the same child he had been the day before. He said "Good morning" in response to Raven's greeting, but did not answer when she asked him how he felt. His arm was clearly very painful and he seemed perfectly content to lie still, wrapped in a blanket, watching the others or dozing, relaxing in a way the old Deakin could never have done.

In the early afternoon, Fletcher opened his eyes at last.

"Welcome back," said Raven, and Shan pulled Deakin off his bed to stand beside her.

"Shan," said Fletcher, in quiet acknowledgment. "Deakin. Who are you?" he asked Raven.

"Raven."

"Of course. All those dreams of crows."

"What do you mean?" Raven seemed frightened. "Never told you my name was Raven. Wasn't my fault you dreamed of crows."

"Two wizards together . . . Thoughts get tangled." Fletcher blinked sleepily. "Shan? Could I have a drink?"

Shan was proud that it was her he had turned to. She brought him a cup of water, but he had fallen asleep again.

"Be all right now, won't he?" she said to Raven.

Raven smiled absently, and Shan knew she was still considering what Fletcher had said. She was wondering if she were a wizard. Now that Fletcher had pointed it out, Shan was not particularly surprised, but she was envious.

Fletcher woke again before supper. Raven gave him ale-and-honey to drink and he said, unexpectedly, "What is this stuff? Trying to poison me, are you?"

Raven smiled widely. Shan came close to smiling as well.

"Like some soup, would you?" said Raven.

"May I?" asked Shan, and Raven looked at her and said, "Think you've earned the right, girl."

So Shan sat on the bed and held Fletcher and fed him a little soup, one slow mouthful at a time, and began to tell him everything that had happened since he was wounded. He fell asleep before the end of the story.

The next afternoon Shan told the story again, this time to a fascinated audience, consisting not only of Fletcher, Deakin, and Raven, but also of a group of children who crept inside the house to listen. Raven said that she never turned the village children away from her house. But it was Fletcher that Shan watched as she spoke. As always, she felt that he understood more than she said.

"Saved my life, you did," he said, after she reached the part about the Dancers.

"No, not me. Was Them, and then Raven . . . "

"Was you," he said, and looked at Shan so long and hard that she felt her face flush. Then he said, "Grew up, didn't you? Not Cub anymore," and Shan was pleased.

She continued the story, telling how Fletcher had told her where Deakin was and how she had gone into the whirlpool after him. Deakin, who had been listening with rapt attention and an un-Wolflike frown on his face, suddenly interrupted her description of the cave.

"Remember that place, I do. But not the before. Don't remember any of the before." His eyes on Shan's were almost the old Deakin's eyes, and she held her breath. "Should remember, shouldn't I? Should remember . . . Gordin . . . Gordin . . . "

"Found his body in the swamp, they did," said one of the children, unexpectedly.

Deakin turned sharply. "Are you saying I killed him? Are you saying that?"

The child stared at him with her mouth open, and Shan jumped off the bed to get between Deakin and the children. The child squealed, "Was the river killed him. Drowned, he did."

Deakin had apparently lost interest. He began drawing patterns on the dirt floor. Shan resumed the story, telling about the climb out of the cave.

"Found a book in the cave, I did," she said, suddenly. She had forgotten it until then. "Tarn's book. Told us about Tarn, didn't you, Fletcher? Must have lost it in Forix, long ago."

She pulled it out from under the bed. Fletcher was so excited that he tried to sit up.

"Tarn wrote it? How do you know?"

"Says so, doesn't it?"

Fletcher looked at Shan with a kind of wonder. At last he said, slowly, "Shan? Are you telling me you can read?"

"Yes," said Shan, proudly.

"May be part of the reason you're one of us," said Fletcher. He settled back on the bed. "Start reading, then."

Shan opened the book. It started straight away, with no introduction. Shan read:

"Thou who seekest control of the weather and the winds, the sum . . . sum-moning of storms is not to be lightly att-empted. Master first the pre . . . pre-ven-tion of storms. If the balance is to be main-tained, then thou mayest not summon a storm that is more than twenty miles distant, nor send further than that distance a storm. Thou mayest recognize by the distant seeing a storm, and thou shouldst in-fluence only those storms not magically created . . . "

She very soon regretted having found the book. She found it slow and difficult reading, and Fletcher would not let her stop until she had read it all. The children soon grew bored and wandered off, but Fletcher was fascinated and occasionally interrupted with excited comments.

"Will be able to travel like Arkanan can!" he exclaimed once.

Shan, who had just read a section of the book explaining that all places were really one place, and had not understood a line of it, looked at him in astonishment.

"Will you?" she said, doubtfully.

Another part of the book was about the removal of fear, anger, and lust, for the creation of perfect warriors.

Fletcher said, "Made the spell that took desire away, did he? Has a lot to answer for, Tarn does."

"But sounds like he was still working on it, doesn't it?" said Shan, who found this part of the book a little easier to understand. "Wasn't sure any of it would work. Doesn't sound like he ever got a chance to try it."

"Got most of it wrong, didn't he?" said Fletcher.

A few lines later, Shan came to the word "reversal" and Fletcher almost sat up again. "Reversal? Understand what's he's saying, do you? Can reverse what was done to us, to all Wolves!"

Shan read that part eagerly.

"Going to do it, are you?"

"Not now. Would take days of practice, even if I were strong." But Shan could tell Fletcher was planning to work on it.

Fletcher made Shan read the book to him all the next morning, and repeated it back to her until he had it by heart. He was so much better by that afternoon that Shan felt she could leave him for a few hours. It was the time of year for laying in supplies, and she thought that she and Deakin might be able to help the villagers with their preparations for winter.

"Where's the village?" she asked Raven.

"Just outside the city," said Raven. "Walk up along the creek."

Leaving Deakin for the moment, Shan stepped outside, and immediately found herself facing a man with a bow, not the same one as last time. She realized he had been guarding the house.

"Guarding against us, are you?" Shan was amused. "Isn't any need. Going to try to help the villagers, I am, that's all. Can cut firewood, or . . ."

"Was waiting for you," he said. "Shan, your name is? Your brother, I am. Marten."

Shan froze. She felt herself beginning to shake.

"Heard your name in the village, I did, and wanted to come talk to you, see if it was you. Remember me, don't you? Remember you well, I do, remember you being taken for Wolf."

He looked nervous, not sure of her reaction. He put the bow down on the ground.

"Look just like our mother used to, you do."

Shan found her voice. "Dead, is she? Don't want to know, don't want to hear. Lived without you all, all this time. Don't have families, Wolves don't."

Marten gave a wry smile. "Not exactly encouraged for Gordin's men, either."

When he smiled, Shan was startled. She saw an echo of the small active boy he had once been. He continued, hastily, "Fine, she is, mother's fine. Got old, but she's fine." His smile had widened and his eyes were very bright now, as if he might cry. "And father's fine. And Dennen, too. And Lissen."

"Lissen." Shan kept her voice flat. "Named her Lissen, did you, like we talked about?"

"You remember!" Marten sprang forward as if he would wrap his arms around her, and Shan backed away quickly. He stopped.

"Yes, named her Lissen. Looked a lot like you, growing up. Still lives with mother and father, she does, not married yet. Dennen's married. Got two little ones, a boy and a girl."

"Makes me an aunt, that does." Finding that she was unable to stop shaking, Shan sat carefully down on the ground.

"Yes. Got a nephew and a niece, you have."

"And you? Married, are you?"

"Not me. Told you, joined Gordin's men instead. A fighter now, like you."

"Could teach you a few things," said Shan.

"Always could," he agreed. "Always used to, remember? Wish you could . . . could come with me and see them all. A bit of a journey, it is, but . . . haven't been home in a long time, have you?"

"Home," Shan repeated, feeling the strangeness of the word. She looked up at him, her tall brother, grown up. "Why weren't you taken for Wolf? Why wasn't Dennen?"

Marten gave a snort of laughter. "Dennen! Never could throw a ball straight, Dennen couldn't. Me, I was just lucky, I guess."

He sat down beside her on the ground, and began telling her about Dennen and Dennen's children. The girl, he said, was called Shan. They stayed there, talking, until it got dark. Shan let Marten give her a hug before she went back inside.

Shan asked Marten to take her to the village the next day, but he suggested that he show her the marvels of Forix, first. They walked together through the streets, Shan occasionally darting little glances at her brother, still finding it hard to believe he was here. She was beginning to enjoy the city. The stones underfoot, which she had at first thought of simply as potential obstacles, she found beautiful now that she had time

438

to examine them. They had been laid flat in the mud, arranged by someone as if laying a wall, and over the years they had been pushed down and worn smooth. They were all different colours and shapes, and Shan loved the roundness of them, the feel of them under her feet. In some places they were laid closer together than in others, as if they had been added at different times, like the buildings.

Marten took her first to see what he called the castle in the air. He said it was the greatest marvel left in Forix.

The castle was built of a warm yellow-brown brick. It had slender and graceful tall towers, one on each side and another in the middle. Shan had to stand right underneath it and look up before she could be truly amazed. Gazing up from underneath, she saw only fuzzy cloud. She backed up slightly to see what she could of the shape of the castle.

Marten grinned, watching her.

"Does anyone go there?" asked Shan at last.

"Can't get there, can we? Maybe your Fletcher could get there, could he?"

"Think he can fly?" Shan was doubtful.

Next Marten took her up a narrow stairway to the top of the city wall, and she found it was wide enough on top for the two of them to walk comfortably abreast, with waist-high walls on either side of them so that Shan felt in no danger of falling.

"Maintain the wall, we do," said Marten, with pride. "Got some skill with stone."

He pointed at landmarks in the surrounding countryside, including the village and the quarry, but Shan saw mostly the dark blur of the forest. She did better when he pointed out things in the city, especially because some of the buildings were higher than the wall, and she could make out the shapes of them where he pointed. Many of them he said were broken, the tops fallen, but to Shan they were all amazing.

They walked through the stone-covered streets and in and out of the houses. Most of these buildings had been houses, Marten said, and it was hard to imagine how crowded it would have been with so many families living here. He showed her some buildings that he said had once been shops. One of them was a smithy, open to the street, where a smith had worked right in the city itself. There were still hooks attached to the wall and they speculated he might have been an armourer and displayed his weapons there.

At the corners of the streets there were pedestals, each carved into the shape of a different animal, and stone basins under them that had held water, when the water in Forix was safe to drink. Marten showed Shan fountains where water would have been flung into the air in beautiful patterns. He showed her short stone pillars called light posts, where he said the wizards had lit the city streets with coloured flames at night. "Would have liked to see that," he added, wistfully.

"Fletcher can make coloured lights," said Shan. "Show you someday, he will."

Later that day, Marten took Shan to the village and introduced her to the villagers as his sister. They gladly put her to work making preparations for winter. Marten returned to his duties in town, but when Shan returned at night, he climbed down from the wall and gave her escort to Raven's house.

So it was that Shan and Deakin were out gathering acorns, and Fletcher was home alone with Raven, when the Wolves arrived.

Chapter 26

S han and Deakin were in a small clearing under an oak when Deakin asked in his unWolflike voice, "Who's that?"

Shan raised her head unhurriedly, and found that two Wolves were facing her across the clearing.

Her stomach twisted. She moved to stand beside Deakin. The Wolves were only a few years older than she was, and neither of them seemed to have recognized him.

"Who's that?" he said again.

"What is he?" said the female Wolf, without taking her eyes off Shan. "Simple?"

"Yes." Shan lowered her own eyes respectfully, wondering why the Wolves kept staring at her. "Be quiet, D . . . Don't talk."

"What are you doing?" demanded the female Wolf, who was a year or two older than her male companion and seemed to do the talking for both of them.

"Gathering acorns," said Shan. "For the pigs. For winter."

She knew it must be perfectly obvious what she was doing, and she was becoming more frightened by the minute. Where there were two Wolves, there was almost certainly a whole pack within call.

"Where did you get that knife?"

So that was it. Shan had completely forgotten that Perinan were not allowed weapons.

"My . . . my father made it," she said, at random. "For skinning."

Her fear was not feigned, and she let it show. The female Wolf came over to her and held out her hand for the knife.

"Give it here. Your father with the rebels, is he?"

"No. No, isn't anything like — "

The Wolf hit her, hard enough to knock her down. Shan saw the blow coming and did not avoid it, not wanting to arouse suspicion. As she fell the Wolf kicked her in the side, hard, and just as the kick landed Shan saw Deakin explode into motion. She had no breath with which to shout a warning. Deakin seized the Wolf's head in both hands and twisted it downward, brought his knee up into her back, and broke her neck. She was dead before her companion realized what was happening.

"Deakin!" Shan screamed.

The other Wolf drew his sword as Deakin reached him, but the force of Deakin's charge sent them both to the ground. They rolled apart and came up into the same kind of crouch automatically and simultaneously, as if they were comrades, old friends who had often fought at each other's sides. The boy slashed at Deakin's head and only just missed.

Shan bent down quickly and drew the dead Wolf's sword. She tossed it to Deakin so that it turned in the air and Deakin caught the hilt in his right hand. He switched it to his left immediately.

The boy was handicapped by his lack of size and experience, Deakin by his half-healed wound, but both of them meant killing and the fight was short and savage. The boy drew first blood, high on Deakin's left arm, and Deakin wounded him in almost exactly the same place a moment later. Surprised, the boy faltered, and Deakin opened a deep gash across his ribs with a continuation of the same stroke. The boy clenched his teeth and fought on, but after that he weakened quickly, from pain and loss of blood. Deakin drew blood twice more before the boy went down.

Shan, who had watched the fight in dismay, launched herself at Deakin at the same moment and seized his arm before he could give the final stroke. They struggled silently for possession of the sword, and then Deakin wrenched it away from Shan and turned on her with it.

"No!" she shouted. "Not with a sword! My Alpha, you are, remember?"

He hesitated, sword raised.

"Can't kill me that way," said Shan, more softly, watching his eyes. The hard shine was fading out of them. "Have to use a knife, Deakin, remember? My Alpha, you are."

He lowered the sword and gazed at it as if he had never seen a sword before. He looked from the wounded boy, who had fainted, to the dead girl.

"Shan? Shan, did I . . . ?"

"Never mind now." Shan knelt beside the boy and tore up his shirt to bind the worst of his injuries, working quickly because she expected the rest of his pack to come along at any moment. She took his sword.

"Come on," she said to Deakin. "Let's go. Have to warn Fletcher there are Wolves here."

"Fletcher," said Deakin, and then, "Killed him, too, didn't I."

It was not a question. Shan stared at him, and then seized his hand and pulled him with her. He held onto the sword, though he had not cleaned it and he let the point drag on the ground behind him as he walked.

"No. Didn't kill him. See him in a few minutes, you will, if Wolves don't catch us first."

Deakin followed her, but he said, slowly, "Killed him, I did. Swore no one was ever going to hurt me or mine. And then did it myself, didn't I? Killed him myself."

"No," said Shan again. "Didn't kill him."

"Swore it when I was six years old, I did."

Shan continued to lead him quickly through the forest.

"Swore no one was ever going to hurt me or mine. Swore it when I was six years old. And no one ever did, did they? No one till I did it myself."

There was another silence.

"All the sheep died, didn't they?" said Deakin, and at that Shan turned around and stared at him in dismay.

"What sheep? Deakin . . . "

"And my mother died," said Deakin, still speaking slowly and apparently to himself. "And my little sister died, and it was so cold that people could walk all the way across the lake on the ice, and there was nothing left to eat. So my father said we would find us a better place to live. Carried me on his shoulders, he did, when I got tired. Said, 'Hang on tight, Salamander, we're off to a better place.'"

After a moment he repeated it, softly.

"Hang on, Salamander, we're off to a better place."

They had almost reached the city now, and Shan had seen no more Wolves.

"Wanted to go to Iluthia," Deakin continued. He was speaking more like an adult now, though his voice was still openly emotional. "Don't think he even knew the border was guarded."

"*Wolves* killed your father?" Again Shan turned and stared at him.

"Couldn't protect us, could he? Let my mother die, let my sister die. Said he'd take me to a better place, but couldn't do that, either, could he?" Deakin was definitely looking at Shan now. "Shot him with arrows, Wolves did. Was weak, my father, like all Perinan are. Couldn't fight them. Didn't know how. Couldn't protect me.

447

Deserved what he got, that was what Wolves said. Deserved what he got."

"Deakin, he didn't — "

"Watched them kill him, didn't I? Let them kill him. Wolves helped me, didn't they? Told me I'd be one of them. Told me no one would be able to hurt me or mine, ever again. Agreed to make me a Wolf, didn't they? Took me for Cub. Passed me from pack to pack, all the way to the school at Redmetal Town. Gave me lots of food, the packs did, and warm clothes to wear, and promised me I'd be Wolf. Wolf! So no one . . . no one would ever . . . "

He drew a long, shuddering breath.

"Fletcher's alive," said Shan. "Alive. Come on. Show you, I will."

This time he heard her. He wiped tears away with the palm of his hand and Shan saw the hope dawning in his face. She no longer needed to pull him along. Half-running, side by side, they ran under the archway and into the city. Using the stones underfoot, Shan found her own way to Raven's house.

Deakin stood in the doorway of the bedroom and gazed at Fletcher, with his eyes full of love and guilt and pain. Fletcher, who was sitting up in bed, gazed back. Neither of them spoke.

Perhaps there was no need. After a moment Shan saw all the emotion vanish from Deakin's face, cleanly and completely, so that he looked more Wolf than she had ever seen him. Even his eyes were cold.

"Met two Wolves, we did," he said. "Killed them."

"One of them," Shan corrected. "Think the boy will live."

"Looking for us, aren't they?" Deakin ignored Shan. "How many are there, Fletch? How far away?"

"Three or four packs," said Fletcher, to Shan's dismay. "Redthorn is with them. Spread out right now, they are. Searching for us."

"How long before some of them get here?"

"Take them a while to find this place, it will," said Shan. "City is guarded by Gordin's men, as well." She thought worriedly of Marten.

"Good. As long as they come one or two at a time . . . " Deakin was pacing the room and playing absently with the sword, all his restless energy returned. "Can talk to them, maybe . . . Can you fight?" he asked Raven, abruptly.

Raven, who had never seen Deakin-as-Alpha before, simply stared at him.

"No," Fletcher answered for her. "But can do a little magic, if necessary. Was going to get her to heal me, Deakin. Think she can do it now."

Deakin nodded. "Go ahead. No, wait . . . Both have to sleep after that, won't you?"

"Not necessarily. Can wake us," said Fletcher. "In fact, better wake us. Arkanan will know where we are, once Raven does magic. But be able to hide somewhere in the city, we will, once I can walk. Better than waiting here."

"All right."

Fletcher and Raven had clearly talked of this healing before. Raven seemed nervous and excited. She knelt by the bed and placed her hands gently on Fletcher's chest. Her eyes closed. Fletcher's remained open, watching her.

Shan would have liked to watch also, but she knew that Redthorn's Wolves might arrive at any moment. She and Deakin stood guard at the door to the house. Behind them in the bedroom, they could hear Fletcher softly encouraging Raven, helping her to use a talent she must have possessed all her life.

"Feel the magic. Let it come. Let it come through you. Through your mind, into your hands, through your hands, let the magic run.

Start saying the words now, Raven. Say the words. Let the magic come . . . "

And Raven's voice, chanting in bad Arkan, rose gradually and drowned out Fletcher's soft words. When the magic came, both Shan and Deakin felt it. They turned together. Shan saw a light emanating from the inner room. The magic was compelling, beckoning. She wanted to run toward it and thrust her hands into the light. But she stood still, and the light faded.

Shan and Deakin released held breath and turned back quickly to their neglected watch.

"Think we're too late," said Deakin, softly.

Shan saw movement at the end of the street. "What is it?"

"A pack. Searching in and out of the houses."

Shan caught her breath. She had thought that Gordin's men would at least delay the Wolves.

Deakin called back into the bedroom for Fletcher and Raven to wake up, and said to Shan, "Stay here. Yell if they're coming in." He walked away across the big room and Shan guessed that he was looking for another way out.

He was back sooner than she had hoped. "Wolves out the back as well," he said, in answer to Shan's unspoken question.

Shan slipped the chain of unmaking off over her head.

"Should take this back," she told Deakin, softly.

Perhaps because it seemed unlikely, now, that they would ever reach the Firedrake, she wanted the chain back in its accustomed place. Deakin ducked his head and let her put it around his neck.

Fletcher and Raven came through from the bedroom and joined them in the doorway. Shan was glad to see Fletcher on his feet. He looked tired and weak but no longer in pain.

"Can you start a fire like you did with Gordin?" Deakin asked without turning.

"All right," said Fletcher.

"Try to talk to them first, I will."

"Won't work," said Fletcher. "Redthorn is with them."

No one spoke after that. There seemed little doubt that they were caught at last, for, even if Raven's magic had passed unnoticed, and the Wolves had simply tracked them from the woods, Arkanan would know where they were as soon as Redthorn did. Shan was glad that she and Deakin had succeeded in reaching Fletcher first.

It seemed important that the three of them be together.

Shan could not see the Wolves clearly, but she knew when they spotted her little group because one of them yelled an alarm, probably to another pack further away. She did not hear them draw and thought they must have been walking through the city with swords ready in their hands.

"Don't want to fight you," said Deakin.

He kept hold of his sword but he kept the point down, and Shan, who still had a sword as well, followed his example. Deakin greeted three of the Wolves by name.

"Bay. Birch. Tanon. How's the leg?"

The man he had addressed hesitated, and one of the others said, sharply, "Don't talk to him."

"Know me, don't you?" said Deakin. "Know you can't do this. Why should we be loyal to Arkanan? Or even to Redthorn, whose mind is being controlled by them? Not really commander any more, is he? Didn't he always tell us Wolves don't kill Wolves?"

The only Alpha in the group said, flatly, "Drop your swords. Will make it as quick and painless as we can."

Another group of Wolves had reached them now. Deakin and Shan, side by side in the doorway, found themselves facing a line of red swordpoints and backed up, into the house, Deakin still protesting.

"Know me, don't you? Can't kill us."

"Stop!" said Fletcher, suddenly and loudly. "Don't you know I'm wizard? Some of you know, at least. Can kill you all if I choose."

There was some hesitation, but not much. Redthorn did not hesitate at all. Shan could see him in the lead and she could see that none of the others wanted to stand too close to him. She held her sword ready, wondering if Fletcher were going to have to use magic to hurt someone, at last, and whether he would find that he could not do it. Then bowstrings twanged and, before she had time to register the sound, Redthorn had crumpled to the ground with four arrows in him.

"Stand still, all of you!" a voice shouted. "Or every Wolf here dies!"

The Wolves froze. Gordin's men, with arrows nocked and bows drawn, were concealed on the roofs and among the ruins, and now many of them revealed their locations with triumphant yells. They had waited a long time for a chance like this one. Three of them, including the one called Cat, who seemed to be in charge, emerged from hiding and began to collect the Wolves' weapons.

"Come out of there," said Cat, and Shan, Deakin, Fletcher, and Raven left the house and walked through the captured Wolves toward him. One of Gordin's men jumped down behind them, having apparently been hiding on the little roof above Raven's door. Now that all the Wolves had been disarmed, more of Gordin's men began to move noisily out of concealment and some of them began to pick up swords. Marten came close to Shan, protectively.

"So it was true, what you told us," said Cat to Shan, ignoring his men. "Wolves want you dead. But what about . . . "

But there were more powerful players in this game, and, once Redthorn had fallen, it was inevitable that Arkanan would come. Even as Cat spoke, six of them shimmered into existence on the stone street beside Redthorn.

Chapter 27

If Deakin, Shan, and Fletcher had still been in the doorway they would have died at once. The Arkanan had their fireballs ready, and they immediately launched them at Raven's house. Deakin's shout "Down!" came an instant too late. Nearly half the Wolves and several of Gordin's men fell in that first attack. Some of them struggled to their feet again, or tried to, and one of them blundered in a circle, burning and screaming.

Deakin and Raven charged the Arkanan as soon as the fireballs had been released. Raven yelled as she ran. Deakin ran silently, pulling out his sword.

The other Wolves had expected the Arkanan to be on their side. Confused and betrayed, they were slow to react, but some of Gordin's men changed their aim quickly and retaliated. They had not been conditioned, as the Wolves had, to believe that Arkanan could not be killed.

Deakin and Raven reached the Arkanan, and Shan saw the first swing of Deakin's sword go wild. "Left! Deakin, no, left!" She had to scream to make herself heard above the screams of the wounded and the chanting of the Arkanan. The Arkan that Raven had attacked seized her with both hands, yelled something incomprehensible, and disappeared, taking Raven with him.

"Can't kill them," said Marten, beside Shan. The arrows had done nothing but anger the Arkanan, several of whom had begun to chant, to prepare more fireballs.

"Yes, you can! Look!"

Before she had a chance to think, Shan stepped out in front of him, drew her stone knife, and threw it. It would probably have missed, but the Arkan it was aimed at was taking no chances. He vanished as the knife left Shan's hand.

She had no time to savour this small victory. Suddenly she was looking straight into the eyes of an Arkan. He thrust his hand up and outward, and Shan saw a fire blaze to life. She flinched away, but instead of flying toward her, the fireball flared up into the Arkan's face, burning him. He gave a yell of pain and anger, pulled his cloak around himself, and disappeared. Amazed, unable to believe she was still alive, Shan heard Fletcher yell, "See that, did you?"

He sounded incredulous and very un-Wolflike. A few seconds later, another fireball disintegrated in the same way, burning only the Arkan who had created it. He vanished as well, and so did the Arkan whom Deakin was distracting. Deakin whirled and attacked another. The last of the Arkanan disappeared together, one of them shooting a final fireball at Deakin's head. Deakin dropped and rolled, and again the fireball exploded in the air, harming no one.

When Shan looked at Fletcher, she saw that the lines of pain in his face had returned.

"Didn't know I could do that, did you? Was a wonderful book you found for me, Shan."

He raised his voice to speak to the crowd.

"Need bandages and blankets, quick as you can get them. And a fire. And sorrel, for the burns . . ."

His voice trailed off, his eyes closed, and he slid slowly to the ground. Deakin ran to him, made sure he was only sleeping, and then tried to take charge.

"Heard what he said, did you? Get bandages. Get blankets."

No one obeyed him. Gordin's men and the Wolves who could still walk separated into two groups, eyeing each other nervously.

Bodies lay sprawled haphazardly in the street. Shan saw a man stagger to his feet and collapse again; half his face was gone. She saw a pile of Wolves, horribly burned. Someone deep in the pile was moaning. Shan wanted to help, but she found that her legs were shaking so that she could not walk.

Deakin started back toward the carnage. The Wolves and the rebels stayed where they were.

"Tell them to give us our weapons back," said one of the Wolves, flatly.

Deakin stopped. He and Cat looked at each other for a long moment.

"All fighting a common enemy, we are," said Deakin.

"Perhaps," said Cat.

Though Marten agreed, some of the other men disagreed loudly, and there was a brief, heated discussion. Shan realized that they were calling Cat "Gordin." He was their new commander, then. Sickened by the sounds of dying men, she became sicker as she listened to the argument. Cat urged his men to return the Wolves' weapons, saying, "What harm? Can't even walk, most of them," but his men insisted that the Wolves were their prisoners.

Shan remembered that there were bandages in Raven's house, and by the time she had walked carefully through the crowd to fetch them her legs were steadier, though her hands shook uncontrollably and she had to fight down sickness. Dead men stared up at her with open eyes; wounded men sobbed and screamed. Two of the Wolves, beyond saving, were given merciful deaths by members of their own packs. Shan thought wretchedly that Raven, with her magic, could have saved them. She wondered what horrible thing was being done to Raven now.

Redthorn was one of the worst hurt, with numerous arrow wounds. Shan stopped the bleeding and bound the wounds, but he remained deeply unconscious. Perhaps it would be kinder to kill him, she thought, but he had no pack, and no one wanted to take the responsibility for killing their commander.

Another Wolf pack arrived about half an hour later. Cat — or Gordin — had failed to convince his men to cooperate with Deakin. Some of them had collected firewood from Raven's house and built a fire, and a few had gone to gather healing plants, but most of them were still here, wearing the Wolves' swords and keeping the Wolves surrounded.

"What are you doing with those swords?" The newcomers did not wait for an explanation, but pulled their own swords out as they spoke. Both Deakin and Cat tried to explain.

"Aster," Deakin seemed to know all the Alphas by name, "listen to me — "

"Ordered to kill you, weren't we?" Aster's sword was ready. "Who are these men? What's going on? Joined the Perin rebels, have you?"

"Tried to kill us, Arkanan did. And not just us. Look at Fox over there. Arkanan did that. Go on, look."

Aster and her pack stared at the injured Wolves.

"But Perinan wearing swords? Who are they?"

"My men," said Cat. "I'm Gordin."

Most of the pack turned, glad to react to something that they understood, and if Aster had not shouted, "No! Don't kill him!" it would have been too late for Cat. As it was, the Wolves left him disarmed and groaning on the ground.

"Tell your men to give the swords back," ordered Aster.

"Doesn't matter," said Deakin, surprising Shan. "No good against Arkanan anyway, are they? And don't need them against these men. Should all be fighting on the same side now."

"Give them back!" said Aster. "Arkanan or no Arkanan, still Wolves, aren't we?"

Then the rebels seemed to realize belatedly that Gordin was down, and they charged.

"No!" shouted Deakin. "Shouldn't be fighting each other! Fletch! *Fletch!* Stop them!"

Shan sprinted across to Fletcher and dragged him unwillingly out of sleep.

"Shan? What . . . ?"

"Stop them fighting!"

Fletcher blinked, licked his lips, and then seemed to realize what was happening. Gordin's men were no match for Wolves in a swordfight, and, even with Deakin trying to intervene, the fight was very nearly over.

With Shan's help, Fletcher got to his feet and stared at the chaotic scene. His eyes slid slowly out of focus. A fire sprang up in the midst of the fighters, on the stones, blazing blue and green and purple. The crowd drew back from it and fell into silence, awed.

Most of the Wolves had disarmed their opponents without damaging them much, but the man whom Aster's Second had been fighting was lying curled in a gradually-widening pool of blood.

"Bearclaw's been killed!" shouted one of Gordin's men. He looked as if he wanted to go on fighting, and the Wolf beside him looked ready, too, though he was silent, watching Fletcher warily.

"Enough!" said Fletcher, and his eyes blazed as suddenly as the fire had done. "Haven't you all had enough fighting? Want you to surrender your weapons. All of you. Now. Deakin, take care of it."

Deakin began gathering up all the weapons, not only swords but also bows and knives. He made a large pile of them in one of the houses. For the moment, everyone was enough in awe of Fletcher to give in.

"Have to leave," said Fletcher to Shan, urgently. "Be back, they will, and stronger."

When he let go of Shan, his knees gave way, and Shan helped him to lie down.

"Stay here, tonight, shall we?" she suggested, helplessly.

It was beginning to get dark, but no one seemed inclined to leave the fire. Wolves and Gordin's men settled on opposite sides, and each group set a double watch, so that there would always be four of them on guard. Shan thought that they were more concerned with watching each other than with watching for Arkanan, and she wondered if she should try to stay awake as well. She was not sure that she would be able to sleep, anyway, after the horrors she had seen.

Then she awoke, cold, with stars burning overhead. Fletcher was sitting up. On the other side of her, Deakin still slept peacefully.

"What is it?" she whispered.

"Redthorn," Fletcher whispered back. "Awake."

He got up, stepped carefully over and around the sleepers, and spoke quietly to one of the Wolves on watch before going to Redthorn. Shan followed. Redthorn had been left near the fire, where it was warmest. His eyes were open and bright with fever, and he snarled at Shan and Fletcher like a wounded animal.

Fletcher squatted beside him and put a hand on his forehead. Redthorn reacted violently, writhing and thrashing about, his eyes blazing hatred. Then he became still, and at the same moment Shan saw Fletcher's face contract in pain and understood that he had opened his mind to the feelings of those around him. She was frightened. There were so many wounded here.

Fletcher took his hand away and sat down cross-legged, without shifting his gaze from Redthorn's face. Redthorn's eyes were closed and he seemed to be asleep, his breathing even and deep, but Fletcher's breathing was now ragged and painful and there was sweat on his forehead. His eyes remained steady, however, and to Shan it looked as if he were far beyond pain, in another place altogether. She sat down beside him and put her arm around him, to lend him what strength she could, though she did not think he was aware of her. They sat like that for a long time. Shan was nearly asleep when at last Redthorn stirred.

"Fletcher?" he whispered.

Shan caught her breath.

"Fletcher? Is you, isn't it?"

"Yes," said Fletcher, softly.

"What happened?" Redthorn tried to sit up and gasped as the pain prevented him.

"Been shot, you have. Going to be all right now. Sleep, Commander."

"Who shot me?" said Redthorn, his voice slurred with exhaustion. "Where are we? Who are we fighting?"

"Sleep, Commander," said Fletcher again, and this time Redthorn closed his eyes.

"Doesn't want to kill us anymore." Shan gazed at Fletcher in wonder. "Healed him, didn't you? Healed his mind."

Fletcher looked at her and she saw that his eyes were shining. "Was a kind of healing, wasn't it? Fought Arkanan and won, I did. Never felt so strong!"

He managed to get to his feet, with help from Shan, but stumbled after two steps and landed hard, sprawled on the street.

"Never thought I could do it," he whispered, happily, and slept.

The weather turned colder overnight, and Shan woke early, shivering. She helped some of the others move the wounded into Raven's house, for warmth. One more Wolf had died.

Fletcher showed no signs of waking, and the others moved quietly around him. So far, the uneasy alliance between Wolves and Gordin's men was holding. Some of the Wolves went out of the city to bury their dead, and Gordin's men stayed out of their way while they did it.

Another Wolf pack arrived in the city mid-morning. Seeing Wolves without swords, they pulled their own swords out as they approached.

Their cloaks billowed out behind them in the cold wind.

"What's going on?" the Alpha demanded of Deakin and Aster.

His pack watched Deakin carefully. They also watched the other, unarmed, Wolves, who might have switched sides or been magicked. They ignored the Perinan. They did not regard unarmed Perinan as a threat.

Gordin's men, outnumbered, unarmed, and ignored, were angry and some of them were beginning to panic. Being Perinan, they said whatever came into their heads.

"Better watch themselves. Don't know who we are, do they?"

"Where's Fletcher?"

"Got us to surrender our weapons, didn't he? So Wolves could kill us!"

"Trusted him, didn't we?"

"Should have known better than to trust Wolves, shouldn't we?"

Shan wondered if she should run and wake Fletcher again.

"Yes, what's going on, Deakin?" Another voice cut suddenly through the babble, and Redthorn came slowly over to join the group. Shan was amazed to see him on his feet. He was trembling visibly, and she could feel the heat coming off his body as he passed her. "Don't you think you owe us all an explanation?"

Turning to the other Wolves, he said, sharply, "Sheathe your swords. Don't see any threat here, do you?"

"Will tell you everything," said Deakin. "Sit down."

Redthorn motioned to the Wolves to obey. He managed to stay on his feet until all the Wolves, and all Gordin's men, were seated. Then he sat down as well.

Deakin related the whole story, speaking flatly at first but gradually becoming more expressive as he was caught up in the storytelling. Gordin's men commented from time to time, but the Wolves were silent. Redthorn turned so much paler when he heard what he had done that Shan thought he was going to faint.

When the story was over, the Wolves remained silent, waiting for Redthorn, as their commander, to speak first. For a moment he seemed unable to speak at all, and when he did his voice was hoarse.

"Want to come with you, to the Plain." He swallowed, and went on, speaking to the other Wolves now, "Deakin's right. Don't have to serve

Arkanan anymore. Aren't any match for all Kunan Keir together, are they?"

"Ordering us to come with you, are you?" Aster asked him.

Redthorn shook his head. "Not ordering anyone. Just saying what I'm going to do."

No one pointed out that he could barely walk.

"If you go," said Aster, "we'll go with you."

"So will I," said Cat, unexpectedly. "Been fighting the wrong enemy all these years, haven't we?"

Several of his men protested, some of them jumping to their feet.

"They're Wolves! Seen what Wolves do, haven't we?"

"Not going to join Wolves now!"

Marten said, "I'm going as well," and looked across at Shan.

"You can come with me, then," said Cat.

"Here comes the wizard," someone muttered, and everyone fell silent.

Fletcher came across to the group, more of whom stood up as he approached.

"Wants to come with us, Redthorn does," Deakin told him.

Fletcher shook his head. "Not taking any of you with me. Haven't you lost enough already?

Only Shan and Deakin. And have to go now. Too dangerous to the rest of you, being here."

"Can't go by yourself," Redthorn objected.

"Want to go with you," said Marten at the same time.

"Can't take any of you with me," said Fletcher. "Don't want any more lives lost."

"But taking Deakin and Shan, aren't you? Might as well — "

"Not because I want to," said Fletcher, almost angrily. "Think I'd let them come if there were any alternative? But has to be us three. None of us has a chance alone."

Both Shan and Deakin objected to this way of looking at things, speaking quickly and almost in unison.

"Think we'd let you go alone?"

"Think you could stop me?" said Fletcher, sharply, and for a moment his eyes flashed like Arkan eyes.

There was a complete silence and an almost imperceptible drawing-away from Fletcher, who had dropped his gaze at once.

"Didn't mean that. But too many have died already."

When no one spoke, he looked around the circle of eyes again. "Commander," he said to

Redthorn, "take the Wolves and go to the school at Redmetal Town. Can do more good there than you can here."

Redthorn was clearly reluctant to agree, but he was equally reluctant to argue with Fletcher.

"Has to be you," said Fletcher. "Even masters at the school take orders from you, don't they?"

"But what do I tell the Cubs? That all their training's been for nothing?"

"Still going to need an army, even with Arkanan gone," said Fletcher. "But tell them the truth. Tell them our story. Tell them we're all Perinan together. And then open the gates, Redthorn. Let the little ones run home to their families, if they want to."

Wolf eyes met Wolf eyes, though all their faces were still.

"Will be something to see, won't it?" said Redthorn.

Shan thought of the seven-year-olds, unbelieving, running out of those great iron gates, free again to laugh and to cry. Would the eight-year-olds follow, after a while? The nine-year-olds? Would the whole school go in the end? She envied those children so much that for a moment she hated them. Why hadn't Redthorn come when she was seven?

Well before noon, she hugged Marten goodbye and walked under the archway out of the city, following Deakin and Fletcher north, into the winter wind.

Chapter 28

Shan was relieved to be moving again, relieved to be away from the pain of the wounded, and vaguely guilty about the relief. She knew that sometime in the future, if she had a future, she would have to think about what she had seen. For the moment, if Fletcher were right and Arkanan would come again soon, she had no time to give in to dark dreams. Besides, if she survived, she would return to Forix, and Marten would take her home.

The wind was cold on her face. Its voice rose to a howl as it rushed along the road toward her, chilling her cheeks and whipping her breath away. It bent the grasses flat. The sky remained blue, but the wind was a bitter, winter wind.

"Saved us all yesterday, you did," Deakin said, after a time, to Fletcher. "Learned to smash fireballs now, haven't you?"

It seemed to be an effort for even Deakin to talk.

Fletcher roused from some inner darkness. "Yes. Weren't ready for that, were they?"

"Can you make fireballs now as well?"

"No!"

There was another silence. The wind made speech difficult. The road climbed a long hill, and they saved their breath for climbing.

"But might be able to do something else," said Fletcher. "Might be able to find a way to travel to the Maze instantly, the way Arkanan do it."

"Instantly?" Shan felt more hopeful. "Take us with you, can you?"

"Can try. Better try, I think. Will be back, Arkanan will, as soon as they can."

"Think you can take us all the way to the Firedrake?" Shan was not looking forward to being back inside the Maze.

"Don't know where it is, do I? Can't go to a place I've never seen. Have to be able to picture it."

"Need time to practise, too," he added.

As they reached the crest of the hill, the road turned east, and for a time they walked along the ridge. The wind whipped their hair across their faces and snatched at the bows on the men's backs.

"Storm coming," said Deakin, as if he would welcome it.

At last the road turned north again, winding down the hill and into a more sheltered valley. Sheep dotted the further slope. A plank bridge crossed a stream at the bottom, and, as they reached it, Fletcher stopped.

"Make camp now, shall we? Think we've come far enough. Won't be a danger to the others, now."

"Hours of daylight left." Deakin was reluctant to stop moving, and Shan felt the same way.

"Told you, need to practise. Want to get us to the Maze before Arkanan return. Be more powerful, they will, now they have Raven."

Fletcher led the others along the stream until he found a place where others, perhaps Wolves, had camped before. He swung the knapsack off his back and sat down cross-legged in the grass.

Deakin and Shan watched for a time, to see if anything would happen, but nothing did. Fletcher hummed under his breath.

"Cut some wood, shall we?" said Deakin at last. "Going to be another cold night."

The trees in the valley were sparse, and it took Shan and Deakin a long time to cut enough wood to last through the night. Once Fletcher stirred, blinked, and looked at them both.

"Any good?" said Deakin. "Think you can do it?"

"Don't know yet, do I?"

"Well . . . when will you know?"

"Don't know that yet, either."

Fletcher's eyes lost their focus again. Deakin wandered restlessly around the camp, fingering his bow. He would have liked to hunt, Shan thought, but he could not leave Fletcher vulnerable and unguarded. Shan was awed by Fletcher's patience. All afternoon he sat quietly, apparently doing nothing. He did not seem to feel the cold. He did not become either bored or discouraged.

"Taking a long time, isn't it?" said Deakin, next time Fletcher looked at him.

"Have to learn to see the world in a whole new way," said Fletcher. "But you're right, Deakin. Can't take much longer."

Deakin was beginning to lay out the preparations for an early and meagre supper, when suddenly Fletcher was no longer there. Shan's eyes widened as she noticed; Deakin whirled.

"Where did he go?"

For one terrified instant, Shan thought, To the Maze! Alone! and as her gaze met Deakin's she saw that he had been seized with the same terror. Then Fletcher's quiet voice said, "Not far," and he came walking back toward them.

"Where were you?" For a moment Shan felt an un-Wolflike impulse to run to Fletcher and hug him.

He pointed.

"Over there, by that pine. Didn't dare go far. Arkanan must have felt it when I travelled that way. Though I doubt it matters now."

Even so, Shan took out her stone knife and put it by her hand, and Fletcher gave his stone knife to Deakin. They did not intend to be caught unprepared.

"What was it like?" Deakin asked Fletcher.

"Easy. Easier than lighting fires, once I started."

"But didn't go far, did you? Think you can go all the way to the Maze?"

"Don't think distance matters. All the same place, isn't it?"

"Distance matters to Arkanan," said Deakin.

"Only because they're travelling away from the source of their power. Should all have been dead long since, remember. Return to the Plain quickly enough, don't they?"

"What's the source of your power?" asked Shan, curiously, and Fletcher in answer made a gesture that included all the world around him, the bright blue sky, the soft grass, even Deakin and Shan.

"Does that mean you can go anywhere quickly?"

Fletcher shook his head. "Not used to it yet. Takes me a while to prepare. But eventually, yes, I probably can."

"Think you can take us with you?"

"Can try right now, if you'd like," said Fletcher. "Though will probably take some time. Not very good at getting started yet."

He sat down between Deakin and Shan, and suggested that the three of them hold hands. They all sat cross-legged, knowing this was the easiest position to maintain for long periods of time without moving.

"Where are we going?" asked Shan.

"Same place. That flat space by the pine."

"Should we try to picture it, too?"

Fletcher considered. "No. Try not to think of anything. Would probably be easiest if you were asleep. Maybe can try later when you're asleep, if I can't do it now. Just close your eyes and let yourself drift."

Shan closed her eyes obediently, clung to Fletcher's hand, and tried to let her mind drift. Gradually, the comfortable way she was sitting, the subdued moan of the wind around the valley, and the privacy behind her closed eyelids, began to put her to sleep. She relaxed, almost dozing.

Then Fletcher's hand tightened painfully on hers, and another voice spoke.

"I have waited a long time for this," it said in Arkan.

Shan's eyes flew open in shock. Raven was standing facing them. She was dressed in a torn and bloodied tunic, and she was smiling a broad, unfamiliar smile.

"Raven?" Deakin said.

Fletcher said, "No. Not Raven."

"I am Kron." Standing in sunlight, openly, with the sunlight full on his/her face, the Arkan enjoyed an instant of triumph. Then the Wolves jumped to their feet. Kron snarled and his hands flew in a series of complicated gestures. A fireball glowed into existence between his palms.

As he launched it, Deakin gave Shan a hard shove that knocked her off balance and sent her sprawling to the ground. He and Fletcher dove the other way and went down together. Shan heard the fireball hit, a crack like the lash of a whip, but felt no heat. Before she could scramble to her feet, someone smashed her across the face and she realized that the other Arkanan had arrived.

Half-stunned, she was dragged to her feet by wizened Arkan hands. A female Arkan held her with surprising strength, one arm around her neck and the other hand twined in her hair, and grinned down at her triumphantly. Shan wanted to close her eyes, but she was not going to give her captor the satisfaction of seeing her wince. Instead she yanked her head to the side, ignoring the painful pull on her hair, and looked at her companions.

With hopeless grief she saw that Deakin had been hit by the fireball. He was lying face down, hands outflung. The back of his tunic was scorched black and Shan could smell charred flesh. Two Arkanan were dragging Fletcher out from beneath him. A burn mark slashed across Fletcher's face, and his eyes were dazed.

Deakin rolled over and tried unsuccessfully to sit up. The effort forced a small sound of pain through his clenched teeth. One of the Arkanan kicked him brutally in the side.

"Enough," said Kron. "Let me finish it."

But as Deakin felt the kick, Shan saw his eyes change. They were hard and bright and not sane. He grabbed the foot and threw the Arkan off balance. As the Arkan crashed heavily to the ground, Deakin struggled to his feet and launched himself at Kron.

The woman holding Shan made an unsuccessful grab for Deakin. Shan wrenched herself free, leaving a chunk of her hair behind, and drew her stone knife. She jabbed it sideways into the woman's stomach, and saw the woman stagger, gasp, and disappear. At the same time Kron began to scream, a high wail of terror and anguish.

"No-o-o-!"

Now that Kron occupied a human body, it seemed that Deakin could find him. He had reached the Arkan just as he had been about to release a fireball, and had clamped his hands over Raven's smaller ones to prevent it. Kron could neither break free, nor contain the power he had called into himself, and he screamed and struggled as he felt his long life coming to an end. Just as Shan looked, the power consumed him. There was a tremendous explosion, with a searing burst of light and a thunderclap so terrifying that she cried out against it, her cry unheard even by her own ears. She found herself flat on the ground, blind and deaf, disoriented and terrified. Burned into her memory was an image of Kron, disintegrating, flying apart, and of Deakin being flung violently across the clearing.

Then a hand clutched hers in a grip of iron. She fought and struggled, but could not break free. The world flickered and faded and twisted sideways, as if it were being sucked into a whirlpool. She felt a sudden tug, like being jerked over the edge of a cliff. The world became completely dark. And silent.

"What? Where . . . ?"

"At the Maze, we are," said Fletcher's voice.

The air seemed to close in around Shan, oppressively, and she could smell the stone of the walls. She had not known, until then, that stone had a smell. For Shan it was associated with pain, and was a sudden, wrenching reminder of her earlier experience in the Maze. Terror seized her. Fletcher must have sensed it, for she felt his fingers tighten briefly on hers before he released her hand.

"Brought a branch with me. Going to make us a light."

For a moment Shan clung to him, and then he pushed her gently away. She heard him tear a piece of cloth from his tunic, and then she heard the familiar, somehow reassuring, rasp of a fire-lighter. After a time she saw light, increasing steadily as the cloth burned. Then she could see Fletcher's face, intent as he concentrated on the thick branch he held, and then she could see the wall behind him and finally the tunnel, narrow, stretching away into darkness.

"Need to find a proper torch, we do," said Fletcher. "Don't want to light anything magically. Don't want Arkanan to know where we are."

"But how will we find the way?" said Shan.

"Hope I can sense the Firedrake. Must be very strongly magical. Got the chain, have you?"

Shan's eyes widened in dismay, and Fletcher must have read the answer in her face. Neither of them spoke. There was nothing to say.

The chain of unmaking was around Deakin's neck.

Chapter 29

Fletcher led the way and Shan followed, wishing she still had her stone knife to clutch. Ahead of Fletcher she could see only darkness. With every step he took, she could see a little of the tunnel ahead, and with every step she expected Arkanan to come visible, standing menacing, waiting. She startled at every rock, at every unexpected corner. She was acutely aware that neither she nor Fletcher had any weapon.

At the first choice of ways, Fletcher stopped. Shan came up into the circle of light. Her voice shook a little.

"What . . . what's wrong?"

"Not sure of the way. Not close enough to the Firedrake, yet, to be able to feel it."

"Still going to the Firedrake, are we, then?" Even as she said it, Shan realized there was no other choice.

"Have to unmake it myself, I will, like I meant to in the beginning."

Fletcher peered down one fork of the tunnel.

"Might be able to find the way," said Shan, hesitantly. "Can read the letters on the walls."

"Letters? Where? Show me."

Shan took the makeshift torch and walked a few steps down one of the tunnels.

"Says 'goes nowhere,'" she reported.

"What about the other one?"

Shan tried the other tunnel, holding the torch high to read the writing.

"Says 'come this way.'"

"Come on then."

Shan tried to give the torch back, but Fletcher gave her a gentle shove. "Go on ahead. Need you to read the writing."

Shan took the lead, reluctantly. She kept swivelling her head from side to side and thrusting the light into every dark corner. She did not know what she would do if Arkanan were to attack again.

"Shan." Fletcher stopped her with a hand on her arm, and waited until she turned and looked at him. "No Arkanan near here. Would know, wouldn't I?"

"But . . . could suddenly appear, couldn't they? Must be looking for us."

"Maybe. Maybe not." The burn-mark across Fletcher's cheek stood out lividly. "May not care. May not consider us a threat to them, now, with one of us gone."

Shan stared at him.

"You mean Deakin . . . Deakin . . . "

"Saw the explosion, didn't you?" Fletcher kept his hand on her arm. "Shan, even if . . . if he survived that . . . well, have to make very sure, won't they? Can't risk leaving him alive."

When Shan simply kept staring, Fletcher gave her a little push onward. She walked. She led the way along another corridor, into another cavern. Then grief tore through her between one step and the next, so that she doubled over with sobs wrenching at her, momentarily unable to go on. Fletcher stopped and waited. He did not speak or reach out, but when she could see again he was watching her. His eyes were as they always were, grave and calm, and there was comfort in that. Shan did not think she could have borne it if Fletcher had cried.

"But . . . but . . . without Deakin . . . can we do anything?"

"Don't know. Always thought it would be all three of us, in the Maze. Now . . . " Fletcher faltered, then went on calmly. "Gave us this chance, Deakin did. When he pushed me down . . . whispered to me that he would give us the chance to reach the Maze. Have to do what he wanted us to."

Shan walked more steadily after that. Her eyelids felt swollen and her head was beginning to ache. She held the flaming branch high and stopped at every fork in the tunnel to read the writing. The branch burned smokily, and she wondered uneasily how long it would last.

"Think this writing will lead us to the Firedrake?" she asked.

"Probably leads to the centre of the Maze," said Fletcher.

Shan soon realized that they were following the same route she had taken with the Cubs. Whether it was that the Cubs had walked more slowly, or that her sense of time had been different then, they reached the lake long before she expected it. The corridor widened and became a vast cavern, and the torchlight shimmered on water. Before they reached it, Shan found a corridor with the writing, "Follow me." They would not have to swim.

"Wait." Fletcher stopped before they entered the corridor.

"What is it?"

"Arkanan. Up ahead."

"With the Firedrake?" Shan asked, hopefully.

Fletcher shook his head. "Closer." He shrugged. "Have to go on. What else can we do?"

"But . . . if you can sense them . . . Must be able to sense you as well."

"Only if they're paying attention."

They moved slowly and quietly. Soon Shan could hear Arkan voices, raised in anger, and she understood why Arkanan had not sensed Fletcher. They were arguing, perhaps even fighting among themselves. She saw a faint light ahead. She stopped and pointed, and Fletcher indicated that she should put out the torch. They moved on cautiously, in semi-darkness.

Fletcher touched Shan's arm and she jumped. He pointed up, and Shan saw that they were walking under a row of unlit torches. As they passed each one, Fletcher reached up and removed it carefully from its bracket. He gave two of the torches to Shan, who felt better with a stout stick in each hand.

The torchlight was pouring from a rounded stone doorway. Fletcher gestured Shan to stand where she was while he crept closer. He pressed himself against the stone and peered carefully into the light. Then he motioned to her to join him, and to run across when he gave the signal. Shan waited tensely. It sounded as if all the Arkanan were in that room together, and they did not sound victorious, or even happy.

Fletcher motioned with his head, and Shan dashed across the doorway. Fletcher joined her an instant later. Arkanan made no outcry, and they continued on their way quickly, undetected. When they thought they were far enough away to risk the sound of the firelighter, Fletcher lit one of the new torches.

"What were they doing?" Shan whispered.

"Arguing. You heard. Seem to be trying to decide who's to lead them, now that Kron's gone."

"Did that, at least, Deakin did," said Shan.

"Got us here, Deakin did," said Fletcher.

The tunnel sloped upward, and eventually opened into a small cave. Again Shan saw light ahead, streaming from an arched stone doorway. This time she thought it was not torchlight, but daylight. Dismayed, she pointed. "Led us the wrong way, have I?"

Fletcher shook his head. "Not daylight."

"Arkanan then?" Shan asked in a barely-audible whisper.

Fletcher nodded. "Just one."

They went forward warily, one to each side of the archway. Fletcher's eyes were half-closed, and Shan thought he was trying to prepare magic, perhaps to smash fireballs again if necessary.

He looked carefully around the archway, and then, with a reassuring glance at Shan, darted through it. When nothing happened, Shan followed. At first she could see only a vague green blur. Then she caught her breath at the unexpected beauty of the cave she had entered.

Light poured down from the ceiling, neither sunlight nor torchlight but werelight, a white light of enchantment that seemed to spring from the stone itself. Just below the ceiling, at the back of the cave, water broke through the stone and poured down in a silver stream, splashing into a pool that filled the centre of the cave. The area around the pool was green with trees and bushes.

Shan crept cautiously forward, following Fletcher, and found herself walking on grass. Although she stayed alert for the Arkan who must be nearby, she could not help but appreciate the beauty of the cave. She passed a pear tree and then an apple tree laden with fruit, and she saw blackberry bushes, raspberry canes, tall stalks of corn, and green tufts of carrot. The cave was carpeted with lush vegetation, and everything seemed to be in season at the same time. Even the inner walls were thick with ivy. Shan was amazed that Arkanan had created a place so beautiful.

The light of the torch seemed pale, unnecessary here. Twice Shan saw rabbits dart away into the bushes. She was sorry when she had to lead the way out of the cave, past a grove of nut trees and back into the dark.

"Didn't sense us, the Arkan, did he?" she whispered to Fletcher.

"Must have been asleep," said Fletcher.

Varian was not asleep. She had been sitting in her garden, almost unmoving and entirely hidden by trees, since Sevrin's death. Kron had given up trying to coax her away and decided to give her time to recover from her grief. Although she supposed she did feel a vague sort of grief for Sevrin, that was not what kept Varian immobile. It was more that Sevrin's death had shown her clearly what Arkanan had become, and she no longer wanted any part of it.

She heard the Wolves walk through her garden and for the first time in days felt a stirring of pleasurable emotion. She moved to where she could watch them. She knew they were marvelling at the trees and bushes she had planted, admiring the delicious fruit. Varian wished they would stay longer. Although she knew these Wolves must be on their way to destroy the Firedrake, it did not occur to her to try to stop them.

When they had left the cavern, she stood up slowly, stretching her tired body. She would go now far from the Plain, into her favourite place in the forest. When the Firedrake's destruction took her, took all of them, with it, she would be walking among the trees.

Shan felt desolate once she had left the garden behind. The torchlight that had seemed so strong before seemed pitifully inadequate now, and at first she stumbled a little on the uneven ground. She was also much colder. In the warm cave, the fine spray from the waterfall had been pleasant, but now her clothes and hair were damp and she found herself shivering. Miserably, she followed the writing into another cramped corridor.

The turns became more frequent, and Shan thought that the tunnels were becoming lower and narrower. The next time the tunnel forked she was certain of it, for Fletcher's head almost brushed the top.

"Maybe leading us the wrong way," she said.

"No. Going the right way, we are."

"How do you know?"

"Can feel the Firedrake," said Fletcher. "Very close now, the power of it and the wrongness. Can feel the piece of the Wheel."

A shudder ran down Shan's back. Not for the first time, she was glad she had not been born wizard.

The tunnel became so low that Fletcher had to stoop, and Shan was the first to become aware of a faint, reddish glow ahead. She stopped and pointed, and Fletcher said, quietly, "Yes. Almost there, we are."

The tunnel ended at a small cave and Fletcher stretched his back thankfully as he reached the relatively-open space. On the other side of the cave, red light poured from a low tunnel, so low that even Shan would have to stoop to enter it.

"The Firedrake," said Fletcher.

For an instant they looked steadily at each other, and then Fletcher ducked and entered the tunnel. Once past the entrance, Shan could stand upright, but her head brushed the ceiling and Fletcher had to walk in an awkward half-crouch. He reached another arched doorway and scrambled through it. Shan followed, emerging into a vast cavern. The red light came from the far end and Shan could not see its source, but Fletcher had stopped and was staring.

"The Firedrake, is that?" she asked, quietly.

Fletcher was silent. Shan looked at him and realized that he was standing rigid, staring straight ahead, not blinking. His teeth were clenched and the old lines of pain were clear in his set face.

"Fletcher. What is it?"

There was no response.

"Fletcher!"

Shan tugged at his hand, called his name, and finally, frantically, slapped his face, but there was no response. Tears began to leak out of her eyes again. She clung to Fletcher and pleaded with him futilely, begging him to wake up and come with her.

"Can't do it alone!" she sobbed. "Not alone, Fletcher!"

Suddenly she heard a sound from the end of the hall, the metallic rattle of a chain. She whirled in terror, and realized that Arkanan had come. She could see their black-robed figures, vaguely, against the red glow that must be the Firedrake.

For an instant she was terrified, expecting to die in flame, and she froze as completely as Fletcher. One of the Arkanan laughed, and spoke.

"Thou wast right, Hinton. The Firedrake has taken care of them for us."

Shan remembered, then, the tales Briar had told her of dragons, of how they could paralyze with their gaze. Fletcher had looked into the eyes of the Firedrake, and, if she had been able to see that far, the same thing would have happened to her. Her blindness had saved her.

"I told ye we had nothing to fear, now the madman is dead," said another of the Arkanan, and Shan realized slowly that they were not talking to her. They were talking to each other. They thought that Shan, as well as Fletcher, had been paralyzed by the Firedrake.

"We have now the renegade wizard. Perhaps we should try using him as Kron suggested."

If she were ever going to move again, Shan knew, she had only seconds to do it in. She dove for the tunnel.

A ball of flame sheared through the air above her and hit the stone wall. As she rolled, bruising her arms and back and shoulders, another fire-ball followed. She heard it hiss and sizzle over her head, and flames bloomed, up and down the wall. She ducked her head and rolled frantically away from the burst of heat, into the tunnel.

The world seemed full of fire. Flames shot in all directions, and Shan's eyes, dazzled, could see nothing of where she was. She rolled and dodged and avoided, as well as she could, the blasts of heat and the sparks that fell like terrible rain on her arms and hands. She was terrified of sparks landing in her hair, and kept brushing at it with desperate hands. At last she lunged to her feet and ran.

She ran in complete darkness, seeing nothing but fire images printed on her eyes, keeping one hand on the stone to her left, sometimes falling when the wall was no longer there, but always scrambling up, finding a wall somewhere, and running on. She ripped her knees and scraped her elbows. She ran in crazy blind zigzags through caverns and caves and tunnels.

When she could run no more, she dropped where she was, her whole body heaving as she panted. Her eyes were still full of fire. She squeezed them shut and opened them again, on darkness and silence.

For the first time since meeting Deakin and Fletcher, she was truly alone.

Chapter 30

Shan began to cry. Her sobs tore painfully at her insides. Tears spilled out of her eyes and ran down her face. The Arkanan had won. Deakin and Fletcher were gone. She was all alone in the dark, with no one to help her, no one to care, ever again. Since there was no one to hear her, either, she let herself cry, unrestrained.

Then she became suddenly, completely afraid, and she fell silent, stifling her sobs, swallowing tears, trying not even to breathe. For what if she were *not* alone? What if someone, or something, drawn by her crying, was creeping closer under cover of her noise? Rats, she thought with terror, what about rats? Must be rats in the Maze. What if they come and start gnawing at me?

She pushed herself to her feet with one hand on the wall. Bruised muscles screamed a protest, and all her cuts and small burns stung painfully.

Another sob burst from her: a low, hopeless sound of despair.

Would she die of thirst, she wondered, before she could find water in the dark? Or would she starve? Or would she simply freeze to death?

For she was very cold. Her clothes were damp from running, and while she had been lying still the cold had crept up on her, seeping through her thin tunic and into her body. She shivered constantly, and her teeth were beginning to chatter.

Slowly, she began to grope along the wall. She had no idea which way she was going, or which way she wanted to go. Phantom fires still haunted her vision. She strained her ears, listening fearfully for the scritch-scratch of little paws on stone.

Gradually walking warmed her, and as she stopped shivering she became calmer. She tried to push aside her misery and think. The Dancers had helped her once. Perhaps they could do so again. She licked her lips and tried to whistle the little tune they had taught her. After four attempts she succeeded in producing a thin, breathy whistle, but, although she waited hopefully for several minutes, there was no response.

Not in the woods now, am I? said Shan to herself. Can't expect them to come underground. But the thought of the Dancers and how they had once helped Fletcher lit a small spark of hope somewhere within her. It occurred to her that Fletcher might still be alive.

Frozen by the Firedrake, he was surely no threat to Arkanan. And, by the way they had spoken, they might have some use for him. Perhaps she could find some way to rouse him. In fact, perhaps all she needed to do was to get between him and the Firedrake.

But how would she find her way? For all she knew, she had stumbled into one of the dead-end, misleading corridors that honeycombed the Maze. She had no light, and no firelighter with which to make one. And she was all alone.

But after all, weren't you always alone, Shadow Eyes? she asked herself. Weren't you alone for years and years? Didn't you learn to do things by yourself?

She stopped crying and continued to grope along the wall, purposefully now. She had arrived here by keeping her left hand on the wall; if she kept her right hand on it, she might be retracing her steps. If she reached a dead end, she would simply go the other way. She would keep trying until she found Arkanan, or at least light. After all, how far could she have travelled in her blind rush? Surely not very far. She shuffled on, straining her ears for any sound, however distant, screwing up her eyes in a search for any light.

There was a jarring crash, and the rock seemed to shudder beneath her. Shan jumped. A moment later, the sound was repeated, a crack of thunder followed by diminishing echoes which rolled around the caves. The storm, she thought at first, and then remembered that she was under Cardy Plain. There was no weather here.

Another crash, and again the rock of the tunnel seemed to shift slightly beneath her feet. Must be Arkanan doing magic, Shan thought. Perhaps they were in their meeting room, and had left Fletcher unguarded, alone with the Firedrake. If she could find the meeting room again, she thought she might be able to find her way to the Firedrake's chamber. She moved as quickly as she dared. Whenever she found a choice of ways, she headed toward the thunder. After a time, she could also hear an occasional patter of falling stones.

The crashing sounds continued, at irregular intervals, louder and closer as Shan moved toward them. Eventually, faintly, from the same direction, she heard voices. Walking became unexpectedly easier, and she realized that she could see vague outlines. She closed her eyes and opened them again, and was sure. This tunnel was lit from ahead with a pale red light.

The light resembled the sullen red glow of the Firedrake, though Shan was certainly not in the cavern where she had left Fletcher. This was a long, fairly wide tunnel, with a cracked and uneven floor. She wondered if Arkanan had other magical creatures.

From below, making her jump, an Arkan voice shouted, "Help me! Concentrate! The ceiling will fall if we cannot stop this."

Another thud came from ahead, and this time Shan saw part of the floor ahead of her buckle, and a great chunk of rock sheared loose and crash down on its side. There was a hole in the tunnel floor, a hole which was being made larger as she watched.

More Arkan voices were shouting.

"What is wrong with it?"

"I know no more than thee."

"It is thy creature, Hinton."

Something shot up through the hole in the floor, something huge, glowing, red. Shan dove out of range before she realized what it must be:

the head and forequarters of the Firedrake. It struck like a snake, and for an instant she thought she was doomed. It could surely eat her in one mouthful. Then she heard a metallic clatter, and realized that the creature was chained. Its chain brought it up short before it could reach her.

Shan remembered that she must not look at it, and averted her eyes hastily.

"Hinton, take care of it." Another Arkan voice came up from below.

"We must all work together. Perhaps a chant will soothe it. Join with me, all of ye."

Arkanan began to chant, a slow, monotonous drone. Shan did not look, but she could tell by the sound when the Firedrake's great head began to weave from side to side in time with the chant. It took long sighing breaths, like the wind in a field of grain, and, as its mighty head swayed back and forth, its scales rubbed together, isinglass on isinglass. Abruptly it withdrew and dropped back down.

Shan crept closer. Large chunks of stone, heaved up from below, lay askew all around the jagged hole. She climbed over one and crouched between two more, putting one hand on each and leaning out over the hole to snatch a brief glimpse of the chamber below.

The Arkanan stopped chanting, and Shan jumped back, sure she had been seen. She had received only a confused impression of bright colours. Then one of the Arkanan spoke, in a normal tone.

"It is quiet now. We have nothing more to fear."

"But this proves what I have said." A woman's voice. "Even though the Three are no longer to us a threat, the Firedrake is no longer a safe way for us to maintain our lives."

"It proves nothing, Leban! The blind woman wanders still in the dark. Her presence disturbs it, that is all. She will not last long."

Shan leaned out and peered over the edge again, carefully. This time she could see that she was looking down on a mass of tumbled, sparkling gemstones. In the midst of them lay the Firedrake. It was a beautiful creature in spite of its great size — delicate, crystalline. The multi-coloured stones glowed softly in its reflected light.

"I want the wizard." The woman again. "All I ask is a chance."

"Thou knowest already it will fail, Leban," a man's voice said. "This wizard is a Wolf. He has killed. His body will be to thee of no use."

They were talking about Fletcher! Shan shifted around the hole, scrambling over a chunk of rock, trying to get a look at the Arkanan.

"Will ye allow me nevertheless to try?"

"Didst thou not see what happened to Kron? The new body made him vulnerable. He could have been killed with a sword. Didst thou not see? He lived in his new body only a few hours."

"Yes." The woman again. Shan had found a place where, by lying flat, putting her head down on the stone floor, and straining her eyes, she could see Arkanan. "But he put his hood back and walked in the sun."

The man replied, "Do what thou wilt then. I want nothing to do with it."

Shan had now seen all that she could, for she dared not look at the Firedrake, and the double images of the Arkanan were blurred by distance. Below her the creature lay quietly on its hoard of gems. Further away, near where Fletcher still stood frozen, Arkanan were standing talking. Something lay on the ground between the Firedrake and the Arkanan, and at first Shan thought it was a discarded robe.

Then one of the Arkanan said, "Let us feed to it first the madman, to sate its hunger before we begin," and Shan realized that they had brought Deakin's body to the Maze.

Her first reaction was fury. Deakin had died in the open air; they had no right to bring him here and sacrifice him to their creature. Then she realized that the chain of unmaking might still be around his neck.

From here she had no hope of making sure, and she did not waste time worrying about what she would do otherwise. It was a chance, and she meant to take it. If she could jump down, snatch the chain, and touch the Firedrake . . .

There was a long drop to the stone floor below. Shan circled the hole, calculating the best position for a jump. She decided that her best chance of surviving the fall was to land on Deakin's body. One of the chunks of rock was in the way of her takeoff; she would have to take a run, and leap over it. When she landed, she would almost certainly be within reach of the Firedrake, and she might have just enough time to touch it with the chain before it or Arkanan killed her. She realized that she had an advantage, for Arkanan must long since have trained themselves not to look in the direction of the Firedrake.

Shan backed away and readied her sore muscles for one last effort. She ran, launched herself into space, and twisted in the air to land on Deakin.

The landing was worse than she had anticipated, a solid jolt that slammed all the breath out of her body. Before she could stop herself she had rolled forward, one of her knees smashing hard against the stone. Tears of pain sprang into her eyes.

She did not try to stand. She did not try to look at Deakin. She grabbed for the chain, wondering for a second, even as she did so, if it would still work. If she broke it, would all the magic run out of it? Then she had seized it and it had snapped loose in her hands and she was scrambling toward the Firedrake.

Arkanan were shouting unfamiliar words, probably creating fireballs, and at least one of them was running toward her. Desperately Shan lunged forward, heart hammering, body slicked with sweat. She dared not look, but she could hear the Firedrake, just ahead of her, rustling as it moved. Its claws scrabbled on the stone floor. She reached out with the chain, and felt rough scales sliding beneath her fingers.

Then she found herself gazing up into the Firedrake's eyes. She was not sure whether she was paralyzed by its gaze, or whether she was just too weak and faint to move. In the depths of its great eyes she saw a man's eyes, looking at her with relief and gratitude, and she realized that the Firedrake had been reaching out to her as she had been reaching out to it.

The chain of unmaking was having an effect. As Shan gazed, the Firedrake grew brighter and hotter, and at its centre the red glow increased, as if a fire blazed in its heart. Shan could see its bones clearly through its isinglass scales, the wonderful, fragile artistry of it.

A moment later she found she could move, and she began to crawl away from the heat, dragging her injured leg. She crawled back as far as Deakin. One of the Arkanan was there as well, a woman, staring wide-eyed, frozen. As far as Shan could tell, none of the other Arkanan were moving either.

The Firedrake folded inward, the fragile skeleton collapsing silently into the fiery glow, flakes of isinglass falling and dissolving. In the heart of the fire Shan saw a salamander, the creature around which the construct had been built. It scampered across the floor and disappeared into a crack, leaving a trail of flame. At the same time the glow resolved itself into a wheel, a great wheel, a piece of the Great Wheel. It began to spin slowly, pulling all the fire into itself. Beside Shan, the Arkan fell into dust, her cloak folding in on nothingness. All the Arkanan were gone in the same instant.

When Shan looked back at the Wheel, she saw a man standing within it. He stretched out his hand. Shan turned to look where he pointed, and saw Deakin's body, rimmed with fire. The salamander tattoo on his arm seemed to be etched in gold.

Salamander, thought Shan. Protection from fire. Almost before she had formed the thought, she was tugging at Deakin, dragging him toward the Wheel. Her leg hurt so that she almost cried out, but she did not stop. The heat was like a wall and she panted as she forced her way through it. Sweat ran into her eyes. She staggered backward and gasped as she touched the Wheel, dropping Deakin, but the man had reached out from the fire and his hands rested on Deakin's chest for an instant.

The Wheel continued to revolve slowly, moving gradually upward, pulling the man away and leaving Deakin lying on the floor. Shan lost sight of the man, but she thought that he was smiling. The Wheel rose toward the roof of the cavern and dragged all the fire with it.

Deakin's chest rose and fell. He coughed.

"Deakin!" Shan screamed. He sat up and looked at her, dazedly, and she seized him in a fierce hug that hurt them both. Deakin pushed her away and coughed again.

"Did you see that?" Fletcher was suddenly beside them. He was still gazing at the Wheel. "Was Tarn, trapped in the Wheel! Helped Deakin as his last act, can you believe it? All that time. All that pain. And could still heal! If he could still do it, maybe I could learn it again, after all. Maybe could — "

"Maybe could stand there talking while the roof comes down on your head!" Deakin seized Shan's hand. "Fletch, move!"

The Wheel reached the roof and ground upward through the rock, and, as chips of stone began to fall, all three of them sprinted for the tunnel. Shan could barely run, but Deakin dragged her with him. Behind them, the cavern collapsed. They turned and saw stone piling up, filling one end of the cavern, burying the bright hoard of gems forever. The Wheel continued to grind through successive layers of rock on its way to the surface.

"Come on," said Deakin. "Aren't safe here."

"Wait," said Fletcher.

In a few seconds light began to glow in his cupped hands. It was strong, and did not flicker like ordinary torchlight. As soon as it was bright enough, Deakin grabbed Shan's hand again and they began to hurry through the Maze. Fletcher led, with the light. The sound of falling stone died away behind them.

"Should be safe enough here," said Deakin at last. He did not release Shan, but he helped her to sit down. "Hurt, are you? What's wrong?"

For the first time Shan saw that, although any serious injury had presumably been healed by Tarn, Deakin was a mess. The front of his shirt was covered in blood. One side of his face was swollen and bruised, and there was a cut high up on his cheekbone. Shan felt an impulse to giggle, and bit it back hard. She said, "Hit my knee on the floor when I jumped."

"When you . . . ? What . . . ?"

"Take us back to the village, shall I?" said Fletcher. "Can tell everyone our story then, can't we?"

"Don't remember anything after that fireball went off. Think you'll have to tell it, Fletch."

"Not me. Shan. Shan was the one unmade the Firedrake."

"Was she?" Deakin, after a long considering look, gave Shan his little smile. He discovered it was a mistake. He put a hand to his face and explored his bruised cheek gingerly.

"Did I get whoever did this?"

"Was probably a tree," said Fletcher. "Can hear the whole story when Shan tells it. Get away from here now, shall we?"

He and Deakin sat down, and Fletcher closed his eyes. Shan became aware of a distant trickling, dripping sound.

"Rain," she said, wonderingly. "Rain on Cardy Plain."

The rainwater continued to leak into the tunnel. Fletcher concentrated and Shan, with her eyes wide open this time, saw the world shimmer and twist as the magic worked. She felt a strong tug and saw the light change, saw the small bright flame in Fletcher's hand replaced by a dim misty haze all around. The sounds and smells of the world rushed in on her; splashes, a shout, the smell of wet stone, raindrops touching her face and wetting her hair. As her eyes came slowly into focus, she realized that they were sitting in drizzling rain, in the dawn, in front of Raven's house in Forix.

One of Gordin's men had shouted an alarm as they arrived, and others were running out of the houses. Marten reached Shan just as Deakin pulled her to her feet, and hugged her hard. This time she hugged back.

"All right, are you?"

"Mostly. Hurt my knee. Did it, we did! Unmade the Firedrake!"

Those close enough to hear her raised an excited cheer.

"And Arkanan are dead," said Deakin. "Gather everyone for the story. All should hear this."

The three of them waited while Gordin's men gathered. Some of them went out of the city to fetch the villagers. Marten stayed with Shan. He helped her to sit down on Raven's doorstep, and Fletcher examined her knee, which was starting to swell.

"Badly bruised, and likely twisted as well," he said. "Need a few days rest, you do. No walking."

"Bu . . . was planning . . . was hoping to go home." Shan glanced quickly at Marten, and explained to Deakin. "My brother, he is. Marten.

Knows where my family are living. Have a niece and nephew now, I do. A niece called Shan, like me."

Deakin looked consideringly at Marten, and Shan thought he approved. "One of Gordin's, are you? Can wait till her knee's better, can't you?"

Marten said, "Course. Waited a long time to take her home, I have."

"Think you've earned a few days off, Shan-Wolf." Deakin turned to Fletcher. "How about you, Fletch? Been thinking about where we go next?"

"Want to learn to heal again, magically. Think I can do it. Want to start by visiting the Queen again. Maybe if I learn the True Language, like she said. Wonder if she would teach me."

"Can't go to the Queen now. Can't let her know we don't have leaders. Don't want to all become Iluthians, do we?"

"Don't think the Queen could . . . "

"Think she could if she wanted to. Come back to the school with me," said Deakin. "Got to get things started, haven't we? Can't expect Redthorn to do it all. And have to get all the wizards together, don't we? Let them know they don't have to hide any more. Could be one or two know the True Language already."

"Not likely," said Fletcher, but Shan thought he looked hopeful.

"Besides, got good news for them, haven't we?" said Deakin. "About something else in Tarn's book."

Marten was mystified, but Shan knew he was talking about reversing the effects of the green wall. She wanted to be there, with Deakin, if that worked.

"Should come with you, shouldn't I?" she said.

"Can't walk yet," said Fletcher. "Besides, need you here. Need people everywhere, we will. People who know what's happened and can tell others. People to spread the word."

"Can join us soon," said Deakin. "When you're ready."

When everyone had gathered, Shan told the story. At first Deakin interrupted frequently with his own additions, but once she was finished with his part, he sat quiet and listened with as much attention as the others. Marten sat with Shan, protectively, and held her hand, sometimes squeezing it at the frightening parts.

"Would have liked to have been there," he said, at the end, when everyone was praising Shan. "Want to be fighting alongside you next time."

"Hope there won't be a next time." Shan thought it was nice to have a brother to protect her, even though she had just proved she could look after herself.

"Coming with you, I am," said Cat to Deakin. "Back to the school. All of us will come."

"Most of us," said Marten, smiling at Shan.

"Get our things, shall we?" Cat was eager to be off.

"Wait a few hours." Deakin had noticed that Fletcher was asleep. He nudged him gently. "Come on, Fletch. Let's get out of the rain."

Shan had had no sleep all night either, and was glad of Raven's comfortable beds. Marten offered to round up more people by evening and bring them to hear the story.

"And in a few days, take me home," said Shan.

"Of course. Be surprised to see me again so soon, they will. Was there about a month gone. Had to go see Dennen's daughter named."

"What about the boy?" said Shan. "How old? What's his name?"

"Three, he is now. Corben. Looks just like Dennen used to, all serious and freckled. See for yourself, you will, when we get home."

Home. It was not a word Shan had used in a long time. She thought about it as she stripped off her wet clothes, lay down comfortably, and pulled the blanket around herself. Beside her, Fletcher was fast asleep again. Deakin paced the single room, going over Shan's adventure, telling her what she should have done differently and what he would have done. He also seemed to think that she had done a lot of things right.

Almost smiling, Shan drifted off to sleep.